DATE			

Mirage

A Tom Doherty Associates Book • New York

Mirage

Soheir Khashoggi

MIRAGE

This book is printed on acid-free paper.

Book design by Liney Li

A Forge Book
Published by Tom Doherty Associates, Inc.
175 Fifth Avenue
New York, N.Y. 10010

Library of Congress Cataloging-in-Publication Data

Khashoggi, Soheir.
Mirage / by Soheir Khashoggi.
p. cm.
"A Tom Doherty Associates book."
ISBN 0-312-85835-3
1. Married women—Saudi Arabia—Fiction. 2. Arab Americans—Fiction. I. Title.
PS3561.H29M57 1996
813'.54—dc20 *95-45456*
CIP

First edition: February 1996

Printed in the United States of America

0 9 8 7 6 5 4 3 2 1

This is a work of fiction.
All the characters and events portrayed in this novel are either fictitious or are used fictitiously.

This book is dedicated to my darling daughters Samiha, Naela, Farida, and Hana. I couldn't have written this book without you. Thank you for being wonderful and loving, and most of all, for waiting so patiently. . . .

I would also like to dedicate it to the memories of my mother, Samiha, and my sister, Samira, who inspired me to write about the special bonds that exist between women in other places and other times—and about the kind of love that endures for a lifetime and beyond.

Acknowledgments

I want to express my deepest appreciation to Lillian Africano for her hard work in making this book possible. Her motivation and interest, and especially her knowledge of the Arab world, have added immeasurably to this book. Thank you, Lillian—it was really a pleasure working with you.

I'd also like to thank my wonderful family: Adnan, for being a marvelous big brother, protector, and friend; my brother, Adil, for his support and love; my brother, Essam, for his encouragement and enthusiasm; my brother, Amr, for his research and terrific sense of humor; my sister, Assia, for her loving care. I'm fortunate to have you all.

Thanks to all my friends.

My appreciation to Barry, for his encouragement and friendship.

To my agent, Sterling Lord, who helped make this dream come true, my gratitude. And to my editor, Natalia Aponte, my thanks for her support and guidance.

And, finally, to my dear sister-in-law, Layla Khashoggi, who proofread and wrote a lovely quotation, my love and gratitude.

Give me the old enthusiasms back,
Give me the ardent longings that I lack,—
The glorious dreams that fooled me in my youth,
The sweet mirage that lured me on its track,—
And take away the bitter, barren truth.

—FROM *GIROLAMO, DETTO IL FIORENTINO* BY WILLIAM WETMORE STORY

There is a seductive shimmer on the horizon of life. Within it lies the promise of love, the joy of fulfillment, and the tranquillity of peace. Approach it with great care, for it is as fragile as a mirage.

—LAYLA K.

PROLOGUE

Boston. The Present

The studio in which Barry Manning taped his radio show—a show that Jenna Sorrel disliked on principle but on which she was to be the guest in an hour—was in a renovated warehouse on Commercial Street overlooking the Boston Harbor. Jenna had not seen this block in years and was amazed at how gentrified it had become.

As she got out of the taxi she was so taken with the proudly refurbished loveliness of the old buildings that she hardly noticed the blue car slowly passing—or the red-haired man in it looking disinterestedly at her, then turning away.

She'd taken three steps up the sidewalk before she realized that she had seen the man before—that morning, near her favorite bookstore on Newbury Street—and that he had given her the same casual, businesslike glance then.

Her first instinct was to run. She turned back to the cab, opened the door, stopped.

"You forget somet'ing, lady?" The cabbie, a young Haitian, looked up from writing in his trip book.

"No. No. I thought I had." She sounded foolish even to herself. She *was* foolish, she decided. The blue car moved steadily down the street.

There had been a time when the fear of being followed was as much a part of Jenna's life as eating or sleeping. But the years had passed and nothing had happened, and now she could not remember the last time she had worried about the man who seemed always to be at the bus stop or the woman who seemed always to be walking her corgi or the car that seemed always to be in the rearview mirror.

Until just now.

She was sure it was the man she had seen near the bookstore. Almost sure. But what if he was? Boston wasn't such a large place. It was possible for a person to be on Newbury Street in the morning and on Commercial Street in the afternoon. But still . . .

Far down the street the blue car turned right and disappeared.

Jenna stood watching for a moment, then took a couple of deep breaths. *Forget it*, she told herself, *it's nothing. Nothing has happened in fifteen years, and nothing is happening now.*

She went into the building. A security guard sat at a mahogany desk. For a split second Jenna thought of asking him to look out for a red-haired man. *Forget it. Relax.*

She signed the in-out register. "I'm here for the Barry Manning show. Has a Mr. Pierce arrived?"

The guard scanned the page. "Pierce? No. Don't see him."

Damn. Jenna had hoped that Brad would be there to help her through her stage fright—the butterflies were already beginning to flutter their cold little wings—but apparently he was still angry. Or perhaps he wanted to remind her what it was like to be alone.

"He's not gonna be on the show, is he?" the guard asked.

"No. He's just . . . a friend. But if he does come, let him know where I am, will you? Wherever that might be?"

"Third floor. Right this way." The guard escorted her to the elevator and pressed the button.

The offices of the Manning organization were surprisingly small, and the few people all looked to be caught up in crises. Finally a woman with earphones dangling around her neck like a doctor's stethoscope noticed Jenna and introduced herself as Courteney Cornmeyer, the show's producer. "We're very happy to have you," she said sincerely, adding somewhat less convincingly, "I was reading your new book just the other night."

She propelled Jenna to the station "green room." "You can do your makeup here," she said, indicating a mirrored vanity table, "unless you want to change your mind and use Angela. She's awfully good."

"No! No, thank you," Jenna added hastily, realizing how inappropriately vehement she'd sounded. Professional makeup would be nice, but Jenna didn't want a stranger studying her face, noticing things she'd kept hidden for so many years.

"Suit yourself," Ms. Cornmeyer said agreeably. "Just make yourself comfortable, and I'll be back with Barry in a bit."

After closing the door behind her, Jenna sank into the upholstered makeup chair, took the cosmetic case from her oversize bag, and leaned towards the three-way mirror. First she brushed her thick chestnut hair. God, roots already? It seemed that she was having to go to the colorist every other week.

Pretending to be someone else was hard work, she thought for perhaps the thousandth time. A constant effort. The hair, the green contact lenses covering her own brown eyes. And the lies.

As she'd been instructed to do, Jenna laid on the foundation with a heavy hand—the Manning radio show had a studio audience and harsh studio lights. Unconsciously her fingers traced a delicate scar just above her left brow and another just at the hairline. The surgery to repair her face had been expert, but traces of it lingered, along with the memory of the man who had tried to destroy her beauty—and her life.

When she had given her olive complexion a flawless matte finish, she applied a cinnamon blusher and smudged her eyelids with charcoal shadow. She finished with black-brown mascara and paprika lipstick.

Jenna was lucky in her looks, she knew, and lucky in the way she had kept them—her next birthday would be her fortieth, but people always assumed that she was in her early thirties. Now, with just a few minutes of deft smoothing and contouring and highlighting, she looked a young thirty. And gorgeous.

She folded her hands, then unfolded them, drumming her fingers against her knees as she waited. Her throat was suddenly dry, her stomach clenched. Was it just stage fright that had her so jangled? The fight with Brad? The strange feeling of being followed?

Jenna got up, smoothed the wrinkles in her cream-colored cashmere suit, and wandered out into the hall. She almost collided with Courteney Cornmeyer, who had in tow a short, round-faced man with orangish skin. His coloring made Jenna wonder if perhaps he ate too many carrots, or used a defective sunlamp.

"Dr. Sorrel, I presume? Barry Manning." He extended a hand. As he did so, his pale gray eyes flicked over her—an inspection that from most men would have been straightforwardly sexual but from him seemed more neutral, perhaps simply professional. "What do you think, C. C.? Our distinguished guest is the world's leading authority on the abuse of women, the evil that lurks in the hearts of men, et cetera, yet here she stands, painted like a scarlet woman."

It was his voice, Jenna realized, that saved Barry from being a comic figure. With his moon-round face and orange skin, he resembled a jack-o'-lantern. He stood no more than five feet six—an inch or two shorter than she—but his voice was deep, resonant, commanding. At the same time it was almost a parody of itself. How can you be offended at anything I say, it asked, when I sound so absurdly authoritative?

"Don't the men on your show wear makeup, Mr. Manning?" she asked conversationally, a mischievous smile tugging at the corners of her lips.

"Sure they do. I do myself. In fact, we've never had a man refuse makeup. What was it, C. C., three weeks ago?—we had the president of the Hell's Angels. No complaint. As often as that crew bathes, he's probably still wearing the stuff."

"I'll bet you didn't suggest to the president of the Hell's Angels that he looked like a scarlet woman."

Manning laughed somewhat theatrically. "Touché! We've got a live one, C. C."

"Five minutes to air," said Courteney. "I'll be in the booth."

"So what happens now?" Jenna asked Manning. The butterflies were now in full flutter. "Is there anything I need to know? I've never been on the radio."

"TV?"

"No."

"Aha! A virgin. Sorry. Figure of speech. But seriously, there's nothing to it. C. C. will give us a countdown, the red light will come on, I'll introduce you, ask you about your book, you'll tell me about your book, we'll take some questions, you'll answer, I'll make some comments, and it'll all be over before you know it. Forty people in the audience. You've been at bigger cocktail parties. In fact, that's the best way to think of it: as if you're at a party where you meet people and they ask about what you do. It's just talk. No need to lecture."

Jenna breathed deeply. "All right. Let's go."

"Whoa! We've got four minutes—an eternity in this business, as you'd know if you'd ever had to fill up that much dead air. Let me ask you something. What's a nice girl like you doing in a place like this? I mean, why my show? Why not Donahue or one of those other sensitive types? Even Larry King." Manning smiled, no doubt aware of his reputation for skewering guests, especially those he deemed deserving of such treatment.

Yet for the first time in their conversation, Jenna felt that he was not playing a role, but seriously wanted an answer. "You know the saying 'preaching to the converted'?" she asked. "Lately I've begun to think that's what I've been doing in my work. I spoke at a symposium at Harvard yesterday—psychiatrists, psychologists, psychiatric social workers—and every one of them knew what I was going to say and agreed with it in advance, except maybe for a technical objection here or there. But your show, it's on a hundred stations—"

"A hundred and six and more every day. Move over, Rush Limbaugh."

"—most of them in very conservative markets. Many of your listeners haven't heard what I have to say, and many of them won't agree with me when they do hear it. I may or may not convert a single one, but at least I won't be preaching to the converted to start with. That's why I accepted the invitation to be on your show—although I admit I debated it for days."

Manning looked at her with unexpectedly quiet appraisal, but all he said was, "I love your voice. You could go into this business yourself. What's that little touch of an accent?"

"I was born in Egypt but grew up mostly in France. I married there and was widowed there very young." All lies, but repeated so often they had taken on their own kind of truth. "I came here fifteen years ago." Truth.

"One minute to air," Courteney warned from a wall speaker.

Suddenly Barry Manning was animated again, a boxer answering the bell. "Come on, Doc," he said, grabbing Jenna's hand and grinning his jack-o'-lantern grin. "Let's go change the world."

Barry Manning was right about one thing: It was over almost before

Jenna knew it. It reminded her of exams in college: unexpected questions, not enough time to say all she wanted, no chance to examine complexities.

The whole setup was disorienting. She did not know what she had expected—some sort of stage, perhaps—but instead there was a glass-enclosed booth in which she and Manning sat at a desk with three computer terminals. In a similar enclosure, separated from them only by a glass wall, Courteney and a sound engineer worked with equipment that looked to Jenna as if it belonged on the space shuttle.

The studio audience sat in plain metal folding chairs set in rows at an angle to the broadcast booth. Jenna looked for Brad. He wasn't there. Someone clipped a tiny microphone on her lapel. The funky blues instrumental that Barry Manning used as his theme welled up. The audience clapped fiercely as Manning bounced into the booth. After some brief opening remarks, he mentioned that his guest would be "Dr. Jenna Sorrel, the renowned psychologist and best-selling author" and cut to a series of taped commercials.

While they ran, he showed Jenna the computer terminals. Each displayed the name, city, and interest of a call-in questioner already waiting to talk with Barry Manning. "I have the best screener in the business working the phones," Barry said proudly. "Separates the wheat from the chaff. We tend to use the chaff."

Jenna, surprised at the note of cynicism, shot him a glance, but the pale eyes showed only concentration.

"OK. You ready?"

"Yes."

Courteney cued Barry and, holding up a copy of her latest book, *Prisons of the Heart: Women in Denial*, he reintroduced her as a best-selling author.

Jenna started to protest that although her books sold well for scholarly works, they were hardly blockbuster best-sellers, but Manning was already off and running. "So what is this book about, Dr. Sorrel? The domination of women by men? The abuse of women by men?"

"To some extent—and I certainly have written a number of papers on those subjects. But *Prisons of the Heart* explores questions I've heard so often, questions which seem to blame the victim: 'Why don't abused women leave the men who batter them?' 'Why don't they just run away to friends or family—or even to a shelter?' These are good questions, key questions, but what I've tried to show in my book is that there are no easy answers. What I often hear from battered women is denial. Some cling to that position for years, either out of shame or fear or a combination of reasons. The fear, I might add, is certainly not invalid, not when we consider the violence perpetrated against women who *have* left their abusers."

"Hmm. Let me ask you something, Doctor. You're obviously a very attractive woman—you don't mind my saying that?"

"Not at all." Some sort of trap being set, she thought.

"—Obviously very attractive, but I notice that there's no photo of you on your book. In fact, I went to the bookstore and found that none of your books have a photograph of you. Isn't that unusual for a well-known author?"

"A little unusual, yes." If she could help it, Jenna never allowed herself to be photographed or videotaped. But even if Barry Manning had somehow learned that, he couldn't possibly have learned why. Could he?

"Is that a feminist statement? That people shouldn't care what you look like?"

Of course he didn't know. He was only trying to make some obscure point.

"Actually, I'm one of those people who dislike having their picture taken. Call it a little phobia. Not exactly something a psychologist wants to admit having, of course." Jenna smiled as if relieved to confess this minor sin.

Manning laughed. "Psychologist, heal thyself, huh?"

"Evidently." Always deception.

When the call-in and audience questions began, Jenna knew what to expect—she had listened to Manning for a week to prepare herself—but still it all seemed to shoot by so quickly, so superficially, no time to look at deep issues, Barry trying to condense everything to sound bites.

And, of course, no one asked about the actual subject of her book. Everyone had his or her own agenda: abortion, gays, Madonna, and what the Bible had to say that might pertain to any or all of these. There was even an alarmed query about a girl place kicker on a high-school football team in New Jersey.

From a ruddy, gray-haired man in the audience, dressed as if he had stopped by on his way to the golf course: "I see we have another big brouhaha about so-called sexual harassment in the military, and at the same time some of these women are protesting about their right to go into combat. But if they go into combat and get captured, I guarantee you they're going to be sexually molested. So aren't they asking for the same thing they're complaining about back home?"

Jenna: "I know very little about the military, so I won't address the issue of women in combat. But let's look at your logic. All combat troops risk being killed. Does that mean they shouldn't complain if someone takes a shot at them back at the base, or in their hometown? And if they do object, does that mean they shouldn't be allowed in combat?"

Barry: "But you must admit that there's a certain incongruity in some of these feminist demands."

Jenna: "No, I must not."

From a disembodied telephone voice with a southie accent: "My uncle had this girlfriend, they lived together, you know, and she had a life insurance policy on him. And one night she stabbed him to death while he was asleep. When they arrested her, she said she was a battered woman. She had, like, these little bruises. And she ended up going scot-free. Does that seem right to you?"

Jenna: "I don't know the facts, so I can hardly second-guess a judge or jury. And while it would be hard for me to justify violence, even as a response to violence, I must point out that since we've ignored the epidemic of abuse against women so long, we may on occasion make mistakes in righting that wrong."

As the show drew toward an end, Jenna felt as if she had been in battle. It was all rush, back and forth, sound and fury. Yet, oddly, she felt as if she were winning—winning the studio audience, at least.

When Gary from Dubuque ("Or is it Dubuque in Gary?" Manning quipped) asked, "Are you an American?" the audience shifted uncomfortably.

"I wasn't born here," Jenna replied, "but I did become a naturalized citizen some years ago." By telling a number of convincing lies, she thought.

"And that gives you the right to tell Americans how to think, how to live their lives?" the caller demanded. The audience rumbled their disapproval.

"I wasn't aware I was telling anyone that."

"I mean, why don't you go to Russia, or what's left of it, and—"

Barry Manning hit the cutoff switch. "Go back to Gary, Dubuque." The studio audience cheered.

She worked hard for them, and they were with her, most of them so unlike the academic audience to which she was accustomed, who might hear the same appalling facts with polite applause and then discuss the work someone had done on a related topic back in '59.

There were thoughtful silences when Jenna pleaded her special causes: "Female children are still being mutilated in Africa, in the name of sexual purity. Millions of women still struggle against medieval constraints in fundamentalist nations. And here, here in America, the violence against women is escalating to horrifying proportions."

Even so, Jenna felt a familiar frustration. It was as if she couldn't bring her listeners quite far enough, couldn't make them feel what she felt: as if she had crossed a wild river and were beckoning them, calling for them to follow, but they couldn't hear her words or understand her gestures.

Then, just as the show was ending, there was a last question from an intense young woman, a college student, Jenna guessed: "Dr. Sorrel, have you ever been the victim—I mean yourself, personally—of the kinds of things you've talked about?"

It was a question she had anticipated, and for which she had rehearsed an answer. But coming so late, when she was weary and exhilarated and frustrated all at once, it took her by surprise. And for just a moment she saw the real possibility of shedding the long years' burden of pretending.

Why not? she thought. It would be so simple to speak the truth in front of all these witnesses, to tell who she was and how she had come to be here, so many thousands of miles from home.

It took only a moment for the fantasy of telling the truth to break through the clouds of long-standing fear, only a moment for the clouds to close over it again—just long enough to make it seem that Jenna had paused thoughtfully before giving what was in fact her prepared answer: "I'd rather not get into matters that concern my personal history. I'm a practicing psychologist with quite a few patients. A traditionalist when it comes to the client-therapist relationship. I believe the work goes better if the patient doesn't waste time and energy identifying with or rejecting what I have experienced in my own life."

She looked at the young woman who asked the question, looked at the audience who had followed her this far, and knew that it wasn't enough.

"I can tell you this much," she said slowly, quietly. "In some of the richest countries of the world, I've seen things, seen them with my own eyes, experienced things that . . ." She halted. What could she tell them? How it felt to be veiled in black, to forfeit one's identity while still a young girl? To lose a mother who could not go on as the lesser wife in her own home? To watch helplessly as a rain of stones snuffed out the sparkling life of a friend, a young woman whose only sin was to love outside the laws made by men? To—no, she couldn't tell them that. No. In fact, she couldn't tell them any of it.

To her astonishment, Jenna felt the hot-to-cold trace of tears down her cheeks. "Well," she said finally, "we've all seen things, terrible things, perhaps in our own lives, or in our neighbors', or certainly in the papers every day and the news every night. But if I have one thing to leave you, it's that to see with our eyes is one thing, and to see and know and feel and understand in our hearts is another.

"And I believe that only when we learn to understand in that way—in our hearts, if you'll pardon such an unscientific term from a psychologist—only then can we begin to learn the real work of healing, to do the real work of solving all these problems of which we've spoken, rather than fighting as a million private armies over every word, every thought, every belief that differs from our own."

A long moment of collective silence followed. Then, just as Barry Manning muttered, "Well said, Doctor," the audience broke into applause.

Jenna let their approval enfold her. She was exhausted. Now Manning was thanking the audience, plugging his next show, signing off. The theme music came up. The ON AIR light winked dark. It was over.

Jenna turned to find the host staring at her. "You lied," he said. Then his pumpkin face broke into a grin. "Easy, Doc! Don't look so shocked. I mean you lied about being a virgin. If you're new to this game, I'm Meryl freakin' Streep."

"I thought I messed up there at the end."

"Are you kidding? You had them crying along with you out there. You're a natural."

Outside the booth, what seemed like the whole audience waited to descend on Jenna and Barry. Several had bought Jenna's book on the spot—her agent had sent a dozen, just in case. The first to ask her to sign his copy was the man in golf clothes. The second was the college student.

As Jenna signed books and accepted compliments, she scanned the studio, still hoping. Still no Brad. But there, in a corner near the door, was a dark man, small of stature, lounging against the doorway. His posture was relaxed, casual, but something about him was oddly familiar, something that made Jenna tense.

As if in response to her scrutiny, the man straightened up, brushed his sleeve, and walked out. Had she imagined the way he looked at her, the intensity of his gaze?

You're losing it, she told herself. *The quarrel with Brad has thrown you off balance. If you go on like this, you'll be needing treatment yourself.*

When at last the crowd thinned, Barry approached Jenna.

"Can I buy you dinner, Doc? There's a terrific place on Commercial Street—"

"I wish I could," Jenna cut in, trying to sound regretful, though the last thing she wanted now was to deal with more of Barry's questions. "But I'm so tired . . . and I have a very early day tomorrow."

"Another time," he said, not seeming too disappointed.

They exchanged professional small talk—an invitation to return, promises to keep in touch—then Jenna was free. But to do what?

Up until a year ago she would have hurried home or to her office to lose herself in work. Then Brad had come into her life—and she had someone to share her triumphs, her defeats, someone to touch and hold and yearn for.

Stop it, she told herself, *you're thinking as if he were gone. And he isn't. He can't be. To be alone now, after a taste of warmth and intimacy . . . that would be unbearable.*

Once outside, she looked up and down the street but saw nothing suspicious, nothing out of the way. Just a bright sunny day and people going about their business. A cab pulling up almost directly in front of her. With a heartfelt sigh, she stepped inside.

• • •

Jenna's Marlborough Street apartment was considered luxurious by the few acquaintances who'd seen it: a spacious duplex in a century-old limestone mansion, two fireplaces, a skylight, a planted terrace, simple contemporary furniture mingled with a few Oriental antiques. But to her—or rather to the woman she had been, a woman who had lived literally in palaces—it was a quaint, cozy little pied-à-terre.

Not so cozy today, though. Not with the remnants of last night's intimacy reminding her of how wrong it had all gone. On the Chinese lacquer bar stood the nearly full bottle of Beaujolais Brad had brought. As he held her in his arms, the wine had tasted like sunlight. But after he'd renewed his proposal of marriage—and she had given the only answer she could give—the mood broke, and they had parted like strangers.

Now Jenna poured herself a glass of Brad's wine and drank a long swallow, but it no longer tasted of sunlight. She pushed the glass away. The apartment was astonishingly quiet. Oppressive rather than serene.

She wished her son, Karim, were home, even with his prickly eighteen-year-old's independence. But he was spending the summer with college friends, sailing the Greek islands—slipping away from her already, a grown man soon, out on his own.

Then she would be truly alone. Self-pity, the most ludricous of emotions. Some psychologist.

Why couldn't Brad be patient? she thought. Why couldn't he just trust her love? Suddenly she laughed aloud. It was a harsh, bitter sound. How could she expect absolute trust when she had none to give? There was a tap at the door.

With a rush of joy, she hurried to open it. "Oh, love, I—"

But the man looming in the doorway wasn't Brad. For a moment she didn't recognize him despite the red hair: he was bigger, beefier than he had seemed on Newbury Street or in the blue car on Commercial Street. Behind him stood a smaller, darker man.

The big man had ice-blue eyes, and he said two words that froze Jenna's soul.

"Amira Badir?"

"There . . . there must be some mistake." Her hand clutched at the hall table. Without its support, she might have fallen.

"I doubt it." The man flipped a badge and identification card. "INS. Immigration and Naturalization Service. We need to ask you some questions, Ms. Badir. We'll ask them at our office. Get your purse, your coat."

Moving like an automaton, her mouth dry with fear, Jenna obeyed. Feeling as if she were in a bad movie, she followed the INS men to their car, the blue car.

The big man opened the door to the back seat, but the gesture had nothing to do with courtesy. It was a command.

The two men sat in the front, the small man driving. The familiar streets of Jenna's neighborhood slipped away. There must be something she could do, she thought, but what? She had citizenship papers, a valid passport, but the name on them was Jenna Sorrel.

False documents. That was a crime, but how bad? Would she go to jail? Be deported? To al-Remal? Not that, please not that. It would be a death sentence. And what about Karim? What would happen to him?

Think, Jenna, think. Think, Amira. A lawyer. I need a lawyer. Brad's company has lawyers. The best. Dozens of them. Call Brad. They allow you a phone call, don't they? Maybe it can be worked out. Maybe they can at least keep it out of the papers. Because even in al-Remal, people read the New York Times. *My husband reads the* New York Times.

Oblivious to her desperation, the two men chatted in the front seat, workers doing their job. Jenna noticed a rental sticker on the windshield. Odd. *Do government agencies rent their cars? I suppose they must.* But green signs overhead. *We're on the Interstate. Logan Airport 1/4 Mile. We're turning.* Suddenly a terrible suspicion seized her. "Why are we going to the airport? Why?"

The red-haired man turned, a hint of amusement in the cold blue eyes. "We're Immigration, lady. We work at the airport."

Oh. Well, of course, it made sense. Only . . .

The car left the main approach to the terminal, took a service road, passed through a gate—there was some conversation between the small man and a guard—then rolled onto the tarmac and pulled up beside an idling Gulfstream with private markings.

"Everybody out," the big man shouted over the whine of the engines. "All aboard the pretty bird." He helped her out of the car and continued to hold her elbow.

The small man moved up on her other side. Jenna felt close to panic. "Wait a minute. I thought we were going to your office. What's this plane?"

"Going to New York," said the red-haired man. "Pay a call on the regional director. You're kind of a big deal, Ms. Badir."

Jenna didn't understand. Was this how the law worked in America? She'd been here fifteen years, had been involved in scores of cases in which the police had been called, complaints filed, arrests made. She should know these things.

She'd call Brad. Maybe they'd even let her call from the plane. But once inside the sleek jet, Jenna realized that there would be no call, not to anyone. Something was terribly wrong. It wasn't just that she was the only passenger. The pilot and copilot—she could see them through the open cockpit door—weren't Americans. Were they French? Or, no—it couldn't be.

An older man wearing a steward's uniform materialized beside her.

"Some coffee, madam? Or perhaps a soft drink?"

It was surreal. A nightmare. "Nothing. Nothing but an explanation," she demanded, mustering up a moment of bravado.

"Of course," the man said politely. "Someone will be along directly. But I'm only the steward. Won't you let me bring you some refreshment?"

"Yes, all right. A Perrier."

"Yes, madam."

When he brought the bottle, she drained it almost greedily. Stress. Thirst. *Should keep water handy in the office for my patients. Never thought of it before.*

The pitch of the engines changed, and she felt motion. *Fasten seat belt,* she thought, *must fasten seat belt.* Her head was very heavy, her eyes leaden. The steward was hovering, watching, concerned.

And now suddenly it was clear—so clear she almost laughed at herself for having ever imagined that she could run, that she could have freedom, life, love. As if in a dream, she could picture her husband, picture Ali, reaching out for her across the years. Ah, Ali, with his arms a billion dollars long, and now they'd caught her, and she was going home to die.

Just before sleep, two faces swam in the darkness before her eyes: Karim. And Brad.

Part One

AMIRA BADIR

Al-Remal ("The Sand"), late 1960s

Even against the molten noonday sun, al-Masagin prison loomed dark and forbidding, its massive iron gates reaching skyward. A second look would reveal a jagged dent in the right gate a few feet from the ground. It had been there for as long as most people could remember.

According to stories Amira had heard, it had been made by a young woman whose husband had been imprisoned for life. Maddened by grief, or so the old village women said, the wife got behind the wheel of her husband's car (an act forbidden by law), drove it to the prison—and crashed into the gates. The guards had opened fire, and the young woman was granted the speedy entrance to paradise she craved, there to await her husband.

It was a romantic story, a testament to the power of love, and thirteen-year-old Amira Badir believed every word. Love made people do strange and forbidden things.

Now she waited as Um Salih, the village midwife, rang the heavy brass bell in front of the prison. It made an oddly melodic sound for so somber a place.

A moment later, as if he had been waiting for the summons, a khaki-clad guard appeared. The gate swung open, revealing the dark maw of al-Masagin. The guard beckoned Um Salih to enter. Amira followed close behind her. The cheap flowered rayon dress peeping from beneath her black *abeyya* rubbed coarsely against her skin; the crude leather sandals chafed her feet.

She was accustomed to the finest of fabrics; the shoes she wore were made by an Italian boot maker who served only the most prominent of families. But today she was supposed to be someone else, not the daughter of Omar Badir, one of al-Remal's wealthiest men, but the niece of the village midwife.

Amira had played at masquerades before, gone into the souk wearing boy's clothes—white *thobe*, white *ghutra*, with sunglasses for added disguise. Dressed like that, she'd even driven her father's car, the first time with the help of her older brother, Malik. Malik did it for the sheer pleasure of breaking the rules; Amira did it to enjoy, if only for a few minutes, the freedom even the poorest male in al-Remal took for granted.

But this masquerade was no game. Life and death were the stakes here and, even more important, her family's honor. If Amira were to be discovered, she knew that even her father's wealth wouldn't protect her from the consequences—consequences she shuddered to imagine.

"Stop dragging your feet, laziness," snapped Um Salih. "There's nothing to be afraid of here."

The impertinence, thought Amira—then remembered she was supposed to be a poor girl assisting the midwife. Lowering her eyes, she murmured an apology.

The guard, a heavy man with a wheeze, coughed out a laugh. "Nothing to be afraid of in al-Masagin, Mother? Don't you fear being flogged as a liar?"

"If all liars are to be flogged," Um Salih replied, "who will do the flogging?"

The guard laughed again.

How could they talk and joke in this place? Amira wondered. As a young child, she'd tried to imagine what the prison might be like, but not even a nightmare could have prepared her for the cold, the dankness, and worst of all, the stench: sweat, blood, vomit, urine, shit. The smell of utter despair. The smell of impending death.

Ever since her best friend Laila—the daughter of her father's good friend—had been arrested, Amira had made this trip regularly, disguised as a male servant, bringing food and carrying messages between Laila and Malik. But this deception, this would be the hardest of all. The life of Malik's unborn child depended on it, and perhaps Malik's life as well.

The women's wing of the prison was quiet except for the crunching of the guard's heavy boots and the rustle of the two women's garments. A piercing scream bounced off the rough sandstone walls. Amira flinched, biting her lip to keep from crying out. She wanted to turn and run, to leave this terrible place and never return. But she had made a promise, and she would keep it no matter what.

"You see what I'm saddled with by my worthless sister?" Um Salih complained to the guard. "The girl wants to be a midwife, yet cringes at the cries of a woman in labor."

"It's not exactly music to my ears either, Mother," the man answered uncomfortably. Stopping in front of a barred wooden door, he turned a heavy key in the rusty lock, pushed the door open, then stepped well away to let the midwife enter.

Laila was half sitting, half lying on a mat of straw, her flowing robe stained with blood and birth fluids. For an instant Amira didn't recognize her. Barely nineteen, Laila looked twice that. Her eyes were glassy with pain, her breath a series of short, ragged gasps.

Um Salih set down her basket and rolled up the sleeves of her dress. Calling out to the waiting guard, she demanded boiling water. "Boiling, not just heated, do you hear? And hurry—this child will not wait while you drag your feet."

When the guard's footsteps could no longer be heard, Amira removed her veil and put a finger to her lips. "Don't say my name, Laila," she whispered. "I'm supposed to be Um Salih's niece."

"You're really here?" said Laila hoarsely. For the first time, something like hope lit her eyes. "Save my baby," she pleaded. "Don't let him be given away. Please. Please, you must make sure he has a good life. You must."

"I promise, I promise," Amira whispered, gently stroking her cousin's forehead. "It's all taken care of. Malik has seen to everything. But don't say his name, Laila, I beg you, don't say his name!"

From her basket, the midwife took a clean linen square. Upon it she placed the tools of her trade—a tube of antibiotic ointment, a tube of lubricant, packets of herbs, a needle and surgical thread, a pair of stainless-steel scissors.

Into a small drinking glass she emptied the contents of an herb packet, then added some pure drinking water from a large bottle she carried.

"Here," she said, handing the glass to Amira. "Give her a little at a time. Not too much, mind you, or she'll vomit it up."

In spite of the admonition, Laila gulped the herbal mixture greedily, desperate for relief from her suffering.

A moment later her back arched. From high inside her throat came a long, keening wail that raised the hairs on Amira's neck. It was the sound of pain and relief and unspeakable sorrow. She took her cousin's hand. "Squeeze it," she said. "When you feel pain, let me take some of it." With her free hand, she wiped Laila's face with a wet cloth, cooling her parched lips.

Amira had seen a baby born once before, when the Sudanese servant, Bahia, had her son. But that had seemed a joyous occasion, even with the cries of pain.

Laila's suffering seemed so much more intense, brute agony unalloyed with even the least atom of joy—as if there could be joy in a hellhole like this. "Can't you give her something, Um Salih?"

The midwife glanced toward the door. The guard, having fetched the water, had vanished again. Like all men, he considered all things female—birth, menstruation—unclean. "Yes, I could give her something. But with drugs women say things. They call out names. Of their husbands. Of others. Sometimes they call on them for help. More often they curse them for the pain. But they are always loud—loud enough to be heard all over this prison."

Laila's back arched again. She squeezed Amira's hand, the nails digging hard into soft flesh. She screamed. "God have mercy, God have mercy on me!"

"Hush, hush, everything will be all right," Amira crooned, understudying the soothing voice her mother used when she and Malik were ill. But her eyes pleaded with Um Salih: *Do something, please do something.*

"The herbs will help a little. But this one will have to endure what God meant for women to endure."

As the contractions grew stronger, Laila seemed to weaken. Her skin turned the color of ivory.

"Is she going to die, Um Salih?"

"Not tonight, child, not tonight."

No. Not tonight, Amira thought. Tomorrow. Laila would die tomorrow, die by stoning in the dirty little square in front of the prison. All that was keeping her alive was the tiny other life within her body. Once that was taken from her, so would her own life be. And for what? For loving Malik? For not loving the cruel and crippled old man who happened to be her husband through no wish of hers? Why?

"Don't cry, child. You must not cry now. We have hard work and a long night ahead."

And still the labor went on, Laila's torment worse than anything Amira had ever seen or imagined. With the cell's single bare bulb dimming and glaring as a generator somewhere outside sputtered, then throbbed to life again, Amira more than once felt that she was caught in a nightmare, that soon she would waken and everything would be the way it was.

• • •

For as long as Amira could remember, Laila was her heroine, more like an admired older sister than a friend. And Amira was Laila's favorite despite the difference in their ages. They spent more time with each other than with anyone else. Malik was there, too, more often than not.

Were Malik and Laila in love even then—not like a grown man and woman, of course, but in the way the poets describe it, love written on souls and in the stars? Certainly it never seemed to matter to Laila that Malik, too, was younger than she, nearly two years younger. But even as a boy, Malik had always seemed old beyond his years.

None of it counted for anything beyond the childhood gardens where the three of them played and laughed and made secrets and dreamed. When Laila was fifteen—with little time left to waste, in her parents' view—her father arranged her marriage to one of his close business associates. The man was fifty-two and noted for his devotion to the Koran, hunting, and money—although not necessarily in that order.

For a time after the wedding, Laila contrived ways for her and Amira to be together. The first time she showed up unexpectedly at Amira's house, she announced with a mischievous grin: "My husband thinks I'm at my mother's today."

"But won't he be angry if he finds out you've lied?" Amira asked, aware as always of the many rules that governed a woman's existence.

"Probably." Laila yawned, as if her husband's anger were of little concern.

Amira marveled at her indifference. "But why couldn't you just say you were coming here? Our parents are good friends, after all, and surely your husband—"

"Amira, Amira," Laila sighed impatiently, "don't be such a child. A wife soon learns when a lie will please her husband far more than the truth. For example, why should I tell Mahmoud I'm here—or somewhere else—when it makes him happy to believe I visit my mother dutifully and often?"

As Amira frowned thoughtfully, her friend smiled sadly. "After all," she continued, "when he comes to my bed at night, when he pokes and pinches and grunts and groans, shall I tell him he sounds like an old donkey—and smells like one, too? Or"—she paused for effect—"do I pretend that he honors me with his attentions, no matter how vile and disgusting they are?"

Amira had no answer.

Despite the veiling and the walls that separated men from women, sex was no secret in al-Remal, not even to children. But Laila's talk of married life made it seem unnatural, even sinister. Still more unpleasant was the assumption that in this matter, as in all others, a wife owed obedience to her husband.

Two years into their marriage Laila's husband was thrown from his horse while hunting. The accident crushed a bone in his spine and left him paralyzed from the waist down. Though Laila publicly wept and wailed as a good wife should, privately she seemed almost to welcome his disability—shocking Amira again—because it would mean the end of some of his husbandly demands. But where previously he at least had been a vibrant figure, now Laila's husband was merely an ill-tempered, whining old man who demanded her constant attendance as nurse and body servant.

The following spring, when Malik came home on holiday from Victoria College, the exclusive British-style boarding school in Cairo to which he had been sent, Laila used Amira as a go-between to arrange a secret meeting with him. Amira knew that this was forbidden; despite their childhood together, the two should not now be alone without the knowledge and approval of Laila's husband. But how could such a thing be truly wrong? It was the first of many such meetings, and though Malik was two short months from graduation, he found one reason after another to make weekend visits to his family.

Then, for no reason that Amira could fathom, there came a time when Laila grew more subdued than ever before. And one morning when Amira went to visit in hopes of cheering her cousin up, the servant who answered the door turned her away with the icy announcement that Laila's name was never to be spoken in that house again. Unable to learn anything further, Amira had no choice but to raise the subject that night at dinner.

"Has she died?" she asked timidly.

Her father's ruddy complexion flushed crimson. "She is worse than dead!" he thundered, "although she will certainly die, too. That woman"—he would not use

Laila's name—"is with child. Not her husband's! She has shamed herself and dishonored her family! There is only one rightful end for such a woman!"

The punishment for the act Laila had committed was death.

• • •

"Push," the midwife commanded, reaching a gloved hand inside Laila, her fingers probing the birth canal. "I feel the head. A little longer, and it will be over."

"I pray it's a boy," Laila gasped out. "I pray he never suffers like this, that he never endures what a woman must endure."

Amira searched her mind for words of comfort. What could she say to Laila that would drive the specter of death away, if only for a moment? "Courage," she murmured, "courage, Laila dear." But would *she* have the courage to endure this—a filthy jail cell, cast out by her family, abandoned by family and friends? Knowing the child she gave her life for would never even know her?

Amira blinked back tears; she had no right to cry. She wasn't the one whose life was over.

"Another push," the midwife commanded, her hands pressing on Laila's abdomen. Moments later a head appeared, then shoulders, expertly guided by Um Salih. It was over. A tiny baby girl, wet and slippery, with a thatch of black hair and dark, almond-shaped eyes.

Just like Mama's, Amira thought, caught up in the wonder of this new life, forgetting for just an instant the circumstances, wishing her mother could see the child. But that could not happen. The secret was too dangerous. Outside of this room, no one but Malik would ever know whose child this was.

Um Salih cupped her hand over the baby's mouth to keep her from crying, then handed her to Amira. As she'd been instructed to do, Amira slipped a ball of cotton into the tiny mouth, praying this precaution would cause no harm. She wrapped the infant in a blanket and placed her in Laila's arms.

Laila held her child, fingers tracing the features of her face—the forehead, the tiny nose, the cleft chin and delicate ears—as if to imprint the image of the baby she would never know. It was only a moment; it was all there could be.

At a signal from Um Salih, Amira gently took the baby back. She removed a small bundle from the midwife's basket, and put the newborn in its place.

Quickly and skillfully Um Salih delivered the afterbirth and cleaned the young mother.

"Save her, Amira. No matter what happens, you must save her." Laila's eyes were feverishly bright, her voice almost inaudible.

"I will," Amira promised. "I will." She held her friend in her arms, knowing that it would be for the last time. "Good-bye, Laila. Good-bye. God be with you."

"Good-bye, Amira. Don't forget."

"I'll never forget you."

Closing her eyes, Laila sank back on the straw, exhausted.

Um Salih unwrapped the bundle from her basket. It contained an infant, its skin purple-blue, dead since late that morning. Among the poor of wealthy al-Remal, death often followed closely on birth. For Um Salih, it was not difficult to find this lifeless baby boy. It had been born to her niece, and it took only a few small coins and a little persuasion to buy its body.

The old woman wet the tiny corpse with water, then smeared it with blood from the afterbirth. Placing the baby beside Laila, she covered it with a white linen square. "Guard!" she called. Footsteps were heard approaching from far down the corridor. "My work is finished," Um Salih told him. "The child is dead. Allah took him early." She drew away the handkerchief.

The guard looked for only a moment. "Just as well," he said, not unkindly.

Um Salih signaled Amira brusquely. "Bring my things, worthless."

"Yes, Aunt."

Leaving the prison, praying that the baby would be able to breathe but would not cry, Amira wanted to run. But Um Salih moved slowly, the picture of an old woman whose hard task was completed and who had no need to hurry. Of course, as long as they did nothing to attract attention, no guard would want to look in the basket: unclean things in it, female things. Amira matched the midwife's pace, and the gate clanged shut behind them.

SORROW

The hour's walk to Um Salih's village felt like a march of a thousand miles. Night had fallen, and the air was cold. Amira had never been so tired in her life. As if to make up for the enforced silence of its first moments of life, Laila's baby began to cry lustily as soon as the cotton was removed from her mouth.

Amira wanted to stop, to hold the infant and rest a while, but Um Salih insisted they move on. "She needs mother's milk. Someone is waiting to give it."

"We can't just let the baby cry," Amira persisted. "Surely you can do something to make her feel better."

Perhaps remembering that Amira was the daughter of Omar Badir, Um Salih relented. Wetting a cloth, she dabbed it with sugar and offered it to the infant to suck. The sweetness—or perhaps simply the touch of a human hand—seemed to soothe and comfort the child. A few minutes later, she was back in her basket, fast asleep.

Just outside the village a silver Porsche shimmered in the moonlight. As the women approached, Malik stepped from beside it. Usually fastidious—Amira often teased him for being vain—he was unshaven and unkempt. His creamy white *thobe*, woven of the finest Egyptian cotton, looked as if he'd slept in it. He embraced Amira, held her close for a long moment.

"I was so worried," he said without preamble. "I was afraid you'd been found out. I thought they'd taken you . . . I didn't know what to think. I never would have forgiven myself if anything happened to you. But you're here now. How is Laila? And the baby, what of the baby? Tell me quickly, for God's sake!"

Ignoring the question about Laila—for how could she be in such circumstances?—Um Salih lifted the cover of her basket. "A healthy baby girl, sir. She'll be a great beauty, I promise you."

Malik reached for his daughter, touching her face as her mother had. "I'll call her Laila," he said, more to himself than to the two women. "I'll do everything for her. Everything and more. Everything I would have done—should have done—for Laila."

"Don't think of it now, brother," said Amira. "There's nothing you could have done." It was true.

• • •

When Laila's crime came to light, Malik had wanted to step forward. "The sin is mine, too," he said. "Why should I escape when her life is lost? We loved together; it's just that we die together."

But through Amira, Laila had forbade him to do so. "Giving up your life won't save mine. It would be a useless sacrifice. Worse, it would make our child an orphan. I won't allow it."

All those terrible weeks Laila languished in al-Masagin, Malik paced and roared, like a caged animal. "I can't let this happen, Amira. What kind of man just stands by when the woman he loves is in danger?"

"A wise man, in this case," Amira said, trying to persuade her brother that self-preservation did not equal cowardice. "How would it help Laila if you committed suicide?"

And still Malik refused to accept what seemed inevitable, hatching one wild scheme after another and trying them out on his cousin and best friend, Farid. Could the judges be bribed?

"Not for the sums you could raise," Farid replied. "And while no one would be insulted by the offer of a truly princely sum, the risks in proposing an inadequate bribe would be grave, cousin."

Malik yielded to his cousin's judgment. Within the Badir family, it was generally assumed that Farid, in spite of his fondness for jokes and play, had inherited the intellectual gifts of his father, Tarik, an eminent mathematician. So it was Farid who kept Malik firmly anchored in reality after the trial and the foregone verdict, when all he could think of was an assault on the prison, a rush for the airport, escape in a commandeered private jet.

Though he had a few friends loyal enough—or crazy enough—to join him in such a venture, Farid pointed out that none of them was a pilot. And though pilots could be found who would do many dangerous things for money, none would risk being shot down by the Royal Remali Air Force for protecting an adulteress.

In the end, it had all come down to this moment in the desert moonlight, gold tinkling palely yellow from Malik's hand into Um Salih's.

"Thank you, sir. A thousand blessings." The old midwife touched her forehead in a gesture of respect.

Amira stifled a smile as she recalled how the old woman had badgered and insulted her in the prison. Now that there was no need to play a part for the guards, Um Salih was once again a humble peasant, in the presence of wealth and power.

Malik responded with equal courtesy as he went over the arrangements he'd made for his child. "The wet nurse you've chosen. She's healthy?"

"Oh, yes, sir, indeed she is. My niece, Salima."

"A true niece or an invented one?" Amira asked mischievously, recalling the part she had just played.

"Hush, Amira. Shame on you!" Turning to the old woman, Malik apologized. "I beg your pardon, Um Salih. Sometimes my little sister forgets her manners."

The midwife inclined her head slightly, a gesture worthy of a royal princess. "As I was saying, sir, my niece gave birth only yesterday, but alas, her child—the baby boy we left at the prison—did not survive. A sadness of long standing . . . she and her husband have tried for many years to have a child. But let me assure you my niece is otherwise strong and healthy. This baby will have the best of milk and the best of care, I assure you."

"I'll come for her as soon as I can. It may be a few months, it may be a year. But don't worry, you'll be taken care of, you and your family, for as long as I live."

"Everything will be as you wish, sir. You have nothing to fear from your poor servant."

Amira knew that was true. Malik would keep his word, she was sure of that. But even if something happened, if his gold stopped coming, Um Salih could never tell the story of what had just taken place in al-Masagin prison. If she did, the first word would be worth her life.

It was time to leave, but Malik's gaze lingered lovingly on his sleeping daughter.

"Would you care to hold her, sir?" The midwife reached into the basket, picked up the baby, and placed her in the crook of Malik's arm.

He held her in silence, his dark eyes glistening.

Amira and the midwife were quiet, too, as if by mutual agreement, while father and daughter shared their first communion under a sheltering desert sky.

Later, as Malik and Amira drove away, he said, "I mean it, you know. She'll be my sun and moon and stars." Amira studied her brother's face. It seemed older, more rugged, than it had a few short months ago. The tears in his eyes had spilled onto his cheeks. But Malik never cried, she thought, not even when they were little.

After another silence, he said, "It can't be in al-Remal, of course. I'll be in exile, an expatriate. I don't know if I'll ever come back." He looked at her penetratingly. "Someday you may have to make the same decision."

As they approached the gate to their home, Malik cut the motor. "Go around to the back. The door will be open. I've arranged it with Bahia. She loves you, Amira . . . she wouldn't even take the money I offered. Go to her room downstairs. That way no one will hear you. She'll have a nightgown waiting. Change there and then go to your room. If someone wakes up, say you couldn't sleep. Bahia will back your story."

It sounded so easy. Deceiving their parents. And though Amira had never before told them a really big lie, she found she was ready to begin. "What about you? Are you coming with me?"

Malik shook his head. "Too suspicious. I'll stay out for another hour or so. I can always say I was with my friends." He smiled, though his face was still sad. "It's different for me, you know that."

Amira knew. Malik was supposed to be enjoying his summer holiday, and even if he stayed out all night, Father wouldn't really mind. As she opened the car door, Malik reached over and took her hand. "I've made a promise, little sister. To myself and to Allah. Now I make it to you: Never again will I be powerless. Never will I be too weak to save someone I love. Remember that."

A short time later, Amira was in her own bed. Though the grime of the prison lingered on her skin—she didn't dare risk a shower—her nightgown was clean and crisp, her sheets fragrant with lavender. *I'll never be able to sleep*, she thought. *If I close my eyes, I'll see Laila's face—and that terrible prison cell.*

Yet Amira did sleep, deeply, dreamlessly, not to open her eyes till the Sudanese servant, Bahia, shook her awake. "I brought you a tray," she said with a conspiratorial smile that glinted with gold. On the tray was a steaming pot of tea, some toasted bread, a dish of olives, and a round of white cheese.

"Thank you, Bahia. And thank you for—"

"Hush, child. The less you say, the less I'll know, the less I'll have to answer for."

"And Malik—is he still asleep, too?"

"Oh, no, your brother was in the kitchen when I woke. From the look of him, he didn't sleep at all. But what do I know?" Again the conspiratorial smile. "He's with your father now, in the big study. With the door closed."

Amira bolted up in bed. Something important was going on. It had to do with the baby, she was sure of that. But what on earth could Malik be discussing with Father? Ignoring her breakfast, she gave herself a perfunctory wash. After running a comb hastily through her thick raven hair, she dressed quickly and ran downstairs.

The study door was indeed closed. Amira put her ear to it, but all she could hear was the rumble of male voices. Did she dare? She did.

Holding her breath, she turned the knob, gently, gently, then pushed, just a little. There was a creak. Amira froze. But the conversation continued.

"I'm not a boy," Malik was saying. "I'm a man, and I'm old enough to know what I want in life. I have no interest in studying international law—or business. So why should I waste your money—and my time—at the Sorbonne? I want to make my way in the real world, as you did."

Amira held her breath, waiting for an explosion. It didn't come. But how could Malik turn his back on the wonders of a European college—when she would give anything to be in his place?

"An admirable goal, my son."

Was Father being sarcastic?

"And exactly what business—as the man you are—have you decided to enter?"

"Shipping," Malik replied, as if he had given the matter a great deal of thought. "But I'm no fool, Father. I know I can't do much without your help. And so I'm asking a favor, one that I'll never forget. Will you put in a word with your friend Onassis? Will you ask if he can fit me in someplace? Anything at all. I'm willing to work and learn. As you did."

"Ah." Amira was sure her father was smiling. How many times had he told the tale of how he had started trading in silk at seventeen, without any formal schooling worthy of the name? Of his success, the whole kingdom knew.

"But that was another time, my son," Omar said, his tone mild rather than compelling. "Nowadays, a college education can be extremely useful for a man . . . some even say necessary."

"You know I'm not a great student, Father. You've said so yourself, and more than once. I have my diploma from Victoria. Whatever else I need, I will learn, I promise you." There was a pause. Amira could imagine Malik flashing the grin that few could resist. "Besides," he continued, "aren't you always criticizing so many of your friends' sons who go to European colleges? I've heard you say the only degrees they earn are from the casinos and whorehouses. Surely you can appreciate my wish to do better than that?"

Omar laughed. There was the sound of a telephone being dialed, then a conversation in English. When it was over, Omar said, "Onassis has a position for which you can be trained. Not in Paris . . ." He paused. Was he inviting Malik to protest? "Not even in Athens. In Marseilles."

"Whatever it is, I'll take it. Thank you, Father."

"Mind you, he'll give you a chance, but that's all. You'll have to earn your own success."

"I will."

"Good."

Hearing the scraping of chairs against the floor, Amira scampered away. But as soon as Omar left for his office, she waylaid her brother. Bahia was right, Amira thought; Malik hadn't slept. Though he had shaved and dressed in a fresh robe, his eyes were bloodshot and weary. "I heard you talking to Father. Why did you tell him you didn't want to go to the Sorbonne? That isn't true, you know it isn't."

"It is now, little sister," he said, ruffling her hair. "I have responsibilities, remember? It's a small enough sacrifice . . ." His voice trailed off, his sentiment a reminder of what was soon to happen.

The morning stretched before them. What was there to do on such a day? What was there to say?

Amira wanted to be with her brother, but he chose solitude, shutting himself in his room. She tried to do the usual things, but when she tried to read her books, the words made no sense. When she tried to help Bahia in the kitchen, she felt as if she might burst out of her skin.

And still the hours had to be endured.

At one o'clock, after the noon prayers, Laila would die.

Just before eleven, Malik burst into Amira's room. "I can't help it, I'm going down there. To be near her."

"No, Malik, don't. Someone might suspect—"

"No one will suspect anything. I'll just be a rich kid looking for a nasty little thrill." Bitterness was hard in his voice.

"Then I'm going with you."

"Absolutely not. This isn't going to be something a girl—a kid—should see."

"I wasn't too much of a kid to see the inside of al-Masagin prison last night. Have you forgotten already?" *Malik needs me*, she thought. *The way he is now, who knows what he might say or do?*

They argued. Malik forbade her to go, and she defied him. "If you don't take me with you, I'll go on my own."

Malik said nothing. Amira took that as consent.

Long before the sun reached its midday position, she stole out of the house, with her boy disguise in a bag. Retracing her steps of last night, she ran to Malik's car, where she slipped on the white *thobe* and *ghutra*, the sunglasses.

• • •

The barren square was baking with the strongest heat of the day, a thick wooden post planted at its center. Someone—who? Amira wondered—had dumped a pile of large, smooth, white river stones a few paces from the post.

At first Amira thought there must be some mistake, some reprieve. Except for a policeman or two, the square was empty of people.

Then she saw them, dozens, hundreds, crowding in the shade of doorways and prison walls. She recognized a few friends of her father's or of Malik's, but most of the people seemed to be the poor. And a great many were women.

As the midday sun burned the sandstone walls of al-Masagin, Laila, blindfolded, was led out and tied to the stake. Scarcely a dozen yards away, Laila's family were lined up, as stiff and rigid as statues. By law they were compelled to be here, the men to share Laila's shame and dishonor, the women to witness what could easily happen to them if they strayed from the rightful path.

Amira felt as if she might faint, but when she looked at Malik and saw how terrible he looked—his skin pasty, his face contorted with anticipated pain—she found her courage.

Slipping her hand into his, she held it tight. He was whispering something, and as she strained to hear, she realized it was a prayer. An official read a declaration of the crime and sentence. Then, at some signal Amira missed, Laila's eldest brother stepped forward, a fist-sized stone in his hand. Only a few feet from his sister, he suddenly hurled the rock with all his might straight at her forehead.

This image burned itself into Amira's brain. Did he throw with such strength out of hatred, for the shame Laila had brought her family—or out of love, to kill her instantly and spare her what was to follow?

Whatever his intention, he failed in it: at the last split second, Laila turned her head as if searching for someone—Amira could swear she looked directly at Malik—and the stone struck a glancing blow.

Blood gushed. Laila sagged, straightened, shaking her head as if to clear it. And then came a sound like the snarl of a vicious dog unchained.

The crowd surged forward, almost fighting one another to get at the rock pile. Suddenly the stones were flying as thickly as a flock of frightened white birds in the square. To Amira's horror, the women were the fiercest executioners, screaming curses as they threw, then scurrying to grab another stone.

For a few seconds Laila twisted, first to one side, then the other, as if trying to avoid her unseen attackers; then she collapsed in her bindings, the rocks thudding into her body, knocking her head loosely, sickeningly, from side to side. It ended as abruptly as a desert thunderstorm, a last stray stone rattling across the baked earth.

A man came out of the prison. He applied a stethoscope to Laila's battered chest and nodded to a group of guards. Quickly they carried the body back into the prison, without even wrapping it. Somehow that final indignity tore at Amira's heart. Was Laila not to have a decent burial?

The crowd melted away, the angry roar muted now. Still holding Malik's hand, as young men often did, Amira led him away from the square. His eyes were blank, unseeing; he moved like an automaton. When they reached the car, she released him. Pressing her hands against her cold, clammy skin, she doubled over, vomiting into the dust.

Malik seemed not to notice. Staring straight ahead, he turned the key in the ignition; the car lurched forward, then careened into the road as Malik floored the accelerator. On the drive home, he spoke only once, his face sculpted in cold fury.

"Never again. I swear it."

MALIK

1970

The plane banked, one wing pointing to pure blue sky, the other to khaki desert. Sky and desert. Al-Remal.

One night in Marseilles—in a smoky café crowded with seamen and the occasional tourist in search of "atmosphere"—a business acquaintance of Malik's, a middle-aged American well advanced in drink, had become sentimental and sententious. "I'm gonna tell you young fellas something," he informed the group around the table. "You're all away from home and think you're going to make a pile of money and go back in style. But you can't. You can't go home again. A famous writer said that. I forget who, but truer words were never spoken."

"What does it mean?" Malik asked. In all honesty the remark made no sense to him.

"It means you can't go home again, damn it, no matter how much you might want to." The drinker reiterated that the quotation was from a famous writer, also an American apparently, and attempted to explain its meaning for himself, personally. It still made no sense.

One of the party, a multilingual young Lebanese, tried to translate the thought into Arabic. Malik tried, too. They found that it could not be done. Maybe the saying was true in America, but not in al-Remal. Not anywhere in the Arab world. An Arab could always go home, and almost always did, no matter where he had gone, no matter for how long.

Yet afterward Malik often thought about what the man had said, and came to see that, in a way, the words applied to him. It was not that he could ever come home a foreigner—another concept that made no sense—but that al-Remal could be all too familiar, like an ill-fitting *thobe* or bedclothes that tangled and bound.

He felt that way now. He had felt that way ever since the day they killed Laila. Never again. He could not think of Laila without thinking those words, his oath to himself and to God. And he could not think of the Laila he had loved without seeing in his mind the Laila he loved now. An infant when last he beheld her, would she be walking now? Would she know words? Would she know him? It had been a year, a little more than a year.

If all went as planned, he told himself, he would never be without her again. The steward had to remind him to fasten his seat belt for the landing.

Farid was waiting at the gate. Growing up, Malik had never seen a full-length mirror—large mirrors being frowned upon in al-Remal as irreligious, idolatrous—but France was full of them, including one at a circus that had reflected him shorter and broader than he was. Looking at his cousin, who resembled him greatly but in a shorter, wider way, was a bit like that.

Farid kissed him in greeting. "God's peace be with you, my cousin."

"And with you, cousin. Your father is well?"

"Yes, by the will of God, and your father, too." The formalities satisfied, Farid held Malik at arm's length, squinting at him as if examining a bolt of cloth in the souk. "I see you've become an infidel, cousin, or at least a diplomat."

Malik turned his palms up, pretending not to understand.

"Your *complet*, your suit," shouted Farid, using the French and English because there was no Arabic term for it. "Whatever you call these astonishing rags."

Malik had put on his *ghutra* aboard the plane, but had decided not to change his business suit for a *thobe*. The combination of *ghutra* and European garments had, in fact, recently come into vogue among Arab diplomats in the West.

"These rags cost me a month's pay, cousin," Malik exaggerated.

Farid fingered the material and nodded sadly. "Alas, the Christians have robbed you, cousin."

But Malik could tell that he admired the exotic clothing.

Farid signaled a Palestinian porter for Malik's luggage. The airport seemed busier than Malik remembered it. As his cousin escorted him past the customs desk with a wave to the official in charge, he could feel pity for the foreign businessmen turning out the contents of their suitcases. Heaven help them, he thought, if they had been so foolhardy—or so ignorant—as to bring in such forbidden items as liquor or *Playboy* magazines.

Here and there, king's guards, armed with automatic weapons and wearing *ghutras* checked with green—the color of Islam—stood watch over the milling civilians. He realized that he had never really noticed the guards before. They had been part of the scenery. They would be the ones to intervene, he supposed, if something went wrong, if someone sounded the alarm.

Farid's car was a Buick, two or three years old—a dream for most Remalis, but not a token of great success for a man of Farid's family. "I'm on the waiting list for a new Lincoln Continental," he explained, adding ruefully, "I hope I can pay for it when it arrives."

He swung onto Airport Road with scarcely a glance, ignoring the blaring horn of a truck that swerved past the Buick with inches to spare. "Your flight was good?" he asked Malik. "These jets are very safe, I hear."

The flight had been very good, Malik allowed, and by all accounts the new aircraft were very reliable.

"Tell me about France," said Farid.

Malik settled back in his seat. This was not Europe, he reminded himself. It would be unthinkably ill-mannered to broach directly the topic that was on both their minds.

He patiently answered Farid's questions about French weather, French food, and especially French women. The first two subjects were easy enough to discuss. The third was more personal; Malik made vague remarks that his cousin could interpret to his satisfaction, then changed the subject. "What is all this traffic, Farid? It looks like the Champs Élysées."

Airport Road did seem busy, at least a dozen vehicles in view at any given moment; not long ago, to meet three in a mile would have been an event.

"It's the oil, cousin. The thing just keeps getting bigger, as you well know, pouring money like the fountain in the royal palace spills water. We're all going to be rich, God willing."

"God willing. And may a little of it splash my way in France."

"And how is your business there, cousin?" asked Farid, edging closer to the important matter. "Do you do well working for the old Greek pirate?"

"Well enough." Malik laughed; it was not the first time he had heard his employer described in those words. "Well enough, and, God willing, even better someday—but perhaps not working for Onassis."

Farid raised an eyebrow. "Better than Onassis, cousin?"

"That's not exactly what I said." Without going into detail Malik explained that, working in shipping in a place like Marseilles, he sometimes met prospective clients who had special needs. "Sensitive cargoes—you understand, cousin?—that Onassis would never handle because it would be politically dangerous for him if the cargoes were . . . intercepted. When you're as big as he is, you depend not only on your customers but on the goodwill of governments all around the world. That goodwill is worth many millions."

Farid turned his hands on the wheel to indicate that this was all so obvious that any child would grasp it.

Malik smiled inwardly. "As you will understand, cousin, what such a client needs is not an Onassis tanker. What he needs is a tramp steamer, a nondescript old workhorse registered in, say, Panama—"

"Onassis allows this?" Farid asked.

It was a good question, reminding Malik of the intelligence his cousin often masked with good-natured clowning.

Only three weeks earlier, Malik had finally summoned the courage to ask the old man's permission to conduct certain outside projects on a free-lance basis. Onassis had glared at him for a long moment before clapping an arm across his shoulder. "I should have known that Omar Badir's son wouldn't be content to work for anyone else, even me. But I haven't forgotten what it's like to be young. Someday you'll go. Meanwhile, stay with Onassis. Who knows, you may even learn something. As for these special projects, you have my blessing on three conditions. First, you work on your own, on your own time. Second, my name is never mentioned. Third, ship nothing of which your conscience disapproves."

"I spoke with him," Malik now told Farid. "I owed him that. He has no objection."

"Ah, good. God wills it, then." Farid leaned forward, squinting up through the windshield as if trying to discern some imminent change in the desert weather. "So you are doing well?"

"As I said, well enough." At last they were getting to the point.

"I wonder," Farid said, "if you've had much time to consider the matter of the child."

Only every waking hour, thought Malik. It was why he was in al-Remal at this moment, after all. "I have," he said. Suddenly a panicky thought seized him. "You got my letter, didn't you?"

"Yes, of course. And destroyed it, as you asked, and pretended to have lost it."

"Good." Malik relaxed. "Well, what do you think? Will it work?"

Farid pulled the car over, stopped, and turned to look Malik full in the face.

Malik understood. It was all but impossible for a Remali to discuss serious matters when he could not look the person in the eye.

"Perhaps you've lost touch, just a little, with Remali ways. Also, it seems to me that in this matter you may be letting your heart rule your head. You suggested two plans." Farid raised two fingers, a glimpse of his professor father in the gesture. "First was the idea of pretending that the girl had been sold for adoption to a French man and wife. I think even you can see the flaws in this approach. Children are sometimes sold, true, but Mahir Najjar isn't of the class who would do such a thing, but even if he were, he would never do it outside the faith. Even knowing the truth, he would also know what people were saying, and the shame would make him resentful, and no matter what you paid him, sooner or later he would turn against you."

Malik sighed. "You're right, of course. The more I thought about it, the more I came to the same conclusion. That's why I said that the other plan might be better."

"And it is. But let's look at it more closely. As I understand it, the idea is that the child has some rare illness. Nothing can be done here in al-Remal, obviously—there's not a real hospital in the country. But an anonymous benefactor arranges for the child to be treated in France. We could even let people assume that the benefactor was Onassis, acting on your plea on behalf of a poor family of whose plight you happened to learn."

"Well, let's leave Onassis out of it. Just an anonymous benefactor."

"All right. But do you see how convoluted this is? For one thing, the child eventually must either be cured or die."

"But that's the whole point. After a few months, or a year, or two, word comes back that the treatment has failed. The parents grieve for a time, and then the whole thing is forgotten."

Farid grimaced. "In that case, we would be very close to telling a direct lie, which I would rather not do. And do you want to send a child into life under the word of death—yet a second time?" Quickly he opened the car door and spit on the ground—a sign against the evil eye.

Almost involuntarily, Malik did the same. "No," he said softly.

"No," agreed his cousin. "And there's another complication. You know better than I, but isn't this business about the unknown donor and the sick child exactly the kind of sentimental tale the Western newspapers love to wipe their tears on? What if it came to their attention somehow?"

"You see only the dangers, Farid," Malik said, more sharply than he would have wished. "It's true that the dangers are real," he added placatingly. "But the point is that something must be done—and soon. My daughter is more than a year old and wouldn't know me from Mahir. After a certain point, she'll always be the Najjars' child, never quite mine."

"You're absolutely right, no question," Farid said, placating in his turn. "That's why I asked if you had given more thought to the matter. Because it seems to me there's a solution that dodges all the swords and arrows."

"Forgive my bluntness, cousin, but I have only these two days before returning to Marseilles. What do you have in mind?"

Farid stroked his mustache thoughtfully. It was a gesture Malik would never have noticed a year ago, but living in France, where clean-shaven men were not uncommon, he had come to see how much masculine pride his own countrymen took in the hair on their upper lips. In al-Remal, except for oil-company foreigners, men without mustaches were as rare as comets, and he who had only a thin or scraggly growth suffered a certain diminution of status regardless of his other accomplishments.

"It seems to me," said Farid, "that our plans so far have held to one star, that of bringing the girl out alone. But wouldn't it be simpler to bring them all?"

"All? Who is all?"

"Mahir Najjar and his wife, along with the child. Surely a man in your position needs servants, or will need them, and who could serve you better than a good Muslim couple from your own land?"

Of course. Malik could only wonder why he hadn't thought of it himself. Obviously he was too close to the problem, heart over head, as Farid had said.

"Mahir Najjar can drive, I'm told, although of course he doesn't own a car," Farid continued. "Couldn't a rising businessman like you use a driver?"

At the moment, Malik owned a little Peugeot that he had bought secondhand and that he drove himself. But certainly, if things worked out, he would soon possess more impressive transportation, and having a chauffeur was not a bad idea at all. It would enhance his prestige, be good for business.

"Besides everything else," said Farid, "the wife has a certain reputation as a cook. I know the French boast endlessly about their cuisine, but when was the last time you had a good *kabsa?*"

Malik raised a hand. "Enough, cousin. The stars do not need painting. Your idea is perfect. You've taken the world off my back." Indeed he felt almost light-headed with relief.

To Malik's surprise, Farid pulled a long face. "It's a serviceable idea, if I say so myself, but not perfect. It has one flaw: Mahir Najjar may not agree to it."

"What? Why not? Have you spoken with him?"

"Only casually, of course."

"And what's the difficulty? Surely he knows I'll treat him fairly—more than fairly."

"Part of the difficulty is that he's from Oman, and you know how Omanis are—as soft-spoken as doves but as stubborn as camels. And as proud as hawks—in a dovelike way, that is."

"Well, what does he want?"

"For one thing, he wants to talk directly with you, not me. Pride, as I said. But the real problem is not with him but with his wife, Salima." Farid consulted his watch, then looked to the sun to confirm the timepiece's accuracy. "We'd best move along, or we'll have to stop for prayer."

Malik appreciated his cousin's need to put the conversation on a less formal level. One of the first things that had struck him in France was the readiness—and the crudeness—with which men spoke about their women. In al-Remal, men never mentioned their wives in ordinary talk with other men, and to speak even of a third party's wife, Mahir's in this case, was discomfiting.

"Now and then," said Farid, "you see a man who is a slave to his wife. I don't say that about Mahir, but his concern for her wishes does seem extreme. It's interesting that he hasn't divorced her though she's borne him no children. It's also interesting that he hasn't asked you for the money to take a second wife. Perhaps that is why he wants to speak to you, but I doubt it. I think Salima influences him against the idea."

Malik shifted impatiently. "All this is interesting, as you say, cousin, but what does it have to do with whether they come with me to France?"

"Well, I gather that Salima simply doesn't want to go there or anywhere else. She's happy here, among her kin and friends."

"But the move wouldn't be permanent. A year or two, no more."

"Mahir knows that. But apparently she's adamant, and he bends to her."

"If it's a question of more money, I can come up with it—up to a point."

"Perhaps that will do the trick after all. But to tell you the truth, I think only one thing would convince them both."

"Well, what is it?"

"The possibility of having children of their own—a son, of course, especially."

Malik threw up his hands. "Unfortunately, cousin, there's not much I can do to help them with that."

"Ah, but perhaps you can. Mahir and his wife are still young. Perhaps their problem is a medical one. Aren't there doctors in France who specialize in this sort of thing?"

"Yes. I'm no expert, of course, but I hear that they're making new discoveries practically every day."

"There's your lever, then, for moving the immovable Salima and her husband."

"I can't promise them anything, Farid."

"Of course you can. You can promise them hope."

On their left the town loomed up. For a moment Malik hardly recognized it. New concrete buildings lined the highway like so many gray elephants. Between them, though, he caught glimpses of the old quarter, the upper floors of the buildings wreathed with *mashribaya*, the latticework screens from behind which the women could look out on the streets without themselves being seen. *Even the buildings*, thought Malik, *are veiled.*

As if echoing the thought, Farid said, "Your main problem will be overcoming the old way of thinking. You know: *Maktub.* It is written. It's God's will." He shook his head to indicate that he would say no more on the subject. "Well, we are almost there, gossiping like women as we have been."

"Cousin, you say that I can give Mahir hope, but it's you who have given me hope. I cannot thank you enough. I wonder if one day—soon, God willing—you will come to work with me in Marseilles. We would make a team."

Farid smiled. "I may well do it, cousin. God knows I lack the head to go into the family business." With that, they were at Omar Badir's house.

• • •

The home he had grown up in, large as it was, felt somehow smaller than Malik remembered. Even his father seemed a millimeter shorter, a fraction frailer. But the old man still had the look of a falcon, and when the ritual of greeting had been accomplished, the falcon's eyes fastened on Malik's suit.

"Malik was just telling me, Uncle," Farid said mischievously, "that he's the best-dressed man in Marseilles." Farid, for no reason anyone could fathom, was the favorite nephew, allowed to dance where Malik himself feared to tread.

"Are we in Marseilles?" Omar smiled, but the smile had a knife's edge to it.

"My apologies, Father," Malik hastened to say. "I fell asleep on the plane"—it wasn't quite a lie; he had dozed—"and didn't find time to change. I'll do it now, if you'll excuse me."

"No, no," said Omar, mollified. "Stay as you are for the time being—until prayer, that is. Meanwhile, there is a man I want you to meet." He called for Bahia. The servant appeared with a dark-eyed baby in her arms. The infant's swaddling clothes had been pinned with amulets, each with a Koranic inscription to ward off jinn—the supernatural beings who took shape in order to commit all manner of evil deeds. "Your brother, Yusef," Omar said proudly to Malik.

When Malik had learned in France that he had a half brother, his reaction had been strangely detached, as if he had merely found an interesting story in the newspaper. Now, with the child gurgling and smiling before his eyes, a dangerous undertow of emotions pulled at him.

Growing up, he had longed for a brother; nearly all his friends had them, often three or four. But this little creature was young enough to be his own child. Suddenly he had to resist physically the urge to tell Omar that he was not only a father again but also a grandfather. He felt relief when the old man signaled Bahia to take the baby away. It was nearing prayer again.

After a little conversation about Onassis—Malik found his father's comments insightful, if perhaps slightly tinged with envy—Omar indicated that the conversation could resume at dinner. "Make yourself at ease," he told Malik—meaning change into proper garments. "After you've paid your respects to your mother, take a moment to do the same with Um Yusef. And don't neglect your sister. She's been sticking her head out of the women's country"—the words referred to the women's section of the house—"every time the wind blows, thinking it's you arriving."

Malik longed to see his mother and sister, but feared that "paying his respects" to his father's second wife would be awkward. She was only a matter of months older than he was, and had never appeared to like him. But as it turned out, his stepmother was still so overjoyed at having a son of her own—an accomplishment that earned her the right to be called "Um" or "Mother" of Yusef—that she was positively cordial.

With a son, Malik reflected with a taste of bitterness, she had a security she had not enjoyed before. A security gained at his own mother's expense.

"But you'll want to say hello to Amira," she finally burbled. "I think she's up in her room. Do you know the way? Oh, how stupid of me—of course you do."

Malik climbed the familiar stairs and, in the Western fashion, knocked at the door. For a moment he didn't recognize the woman who answered. Then he did.

Clearly, Amira was the desert flower that waits for the rain to bloom. When he'd last seen her she'd shown only a hint of ever becoming anything more than a tomboyish adolescent, but before him now stood a beauty. "Little sister?" he heard himself ask.

"Who else, big brother idiot," she said and threw herself into his arms. How was he, how was Marseilles, how did he like being in al-Remal—as always, she was full of questions.

"Has Farid spoken with you?" Malik managed to interject. "About his idea for Laila?" The rudeness was forgivable. Time was short: the radio was cautioning that prayer time was near.

"Yes. Meet me in the garden after dinner. Then we can talk."

"All right. Oh! I met our new brother."

"He's a sweetness. But did you notice the charms?"

"Yes." The custom of covering an infant with protective amulets was widespread, but among educated people it was only a custom. To take it seriously carried a certain aura of peasant superstition. Commenting on it at all was a small, delicious act of brother-sister conspiracy against their father's second wife.

"You see what I must live with," said Amira, "although certainly she's more pleasant than she once was. Go. We'll talk later."

Malik hurried to his room to find a *thobe* and sandals to replace his suit and shoes. Already the radio was sounding the muezzin's call, every line but the final one repeated:

"God is more great.
I testify that there is no god but God.
I testify that Mohammed is the Prophet of God.
Come to prayer. Come to salvation.
Prayer is better than sleep.
There is no god but God."

In the darkening garden Malik wandered among the oleander and bougainvillea, savoring the fragrance, smiling at the sound of the little fountain whose tiny trickle proclaimed his father's wealth. He remembered the story, famously known, that when the Americans and British had first come to search for oil, the king of al-Remal had prayed that their drills would strike water instead.

It was the beautiful hour, as Malik had always thought of it, the interval just before night, when day's heat had broken and was radiating back to the sky, making the bright early stars shimmer against a background of deepest cerulean. France had many wonders, but none to match the desert stars of al-Remal.

"Brother?"

"Who else, little sister idiot."

Laughing, Amira stepped from the shadows to take his hand. "I've missed you," she said simply.

"And I you."

"I doubt that you've had time to miss anyone. Your days must be very busy. Not to mention your nights."

"My days certainly. My nights, I'm afraid, are rather lonely."

"I'm sorry, brother. I wasn't thinking. I suppose I was just being jealous."

"Jealous?"

"Envious." Amira looked up at the sky, but there was no longer enough light to read her expression. "Sometimes I think I'd give anything to do what you're doing."

"To work like a slave for Onassis?"

"I don't know. To be in France. To do as I wished."

"And what would that be?"

"I don't know that, either. To go to school, I think. A real school."

It was what she had always wanted, but to hear it from this new Amira, this stunning young woman, made it different—more serious, yet also more disconcerting. His sister had always been unusual. He remembered her courage that day in the square, when his own courage had nearly failed. "I said once that you might have to leave al-Remal," he told her. "Do you remember?"

She made a gesture of impatience. "A dream," she said. The moon, nearly full, peeked over the garden wall, throwing date palms into silhouette. "I still have Nanny Karin. We study together now. She orders books from London. I pay half, sometimes more. And Farid brings us little lessons in mathematics."

"What does Father say about all this?"

"You know Father. He's a dinosaur, certainly, but he can surprise you by taking an enlightened view now and then—especially if there's gain in it. I've convinced him that times are changing and that an education will make me a more valuable wife."

It took Malik a moment to realize what she was saying. "Surely he's not thinking of marriage for you just yet."

"Of course he is. Why wouldn't he be?"

"He's spoken of it?"

"No. But he's thinking of it."

"Does he have anyone in mind?" The whole topic had caught Malik by surprise.

"I think he's considered several candidates. He drops little hints now and then—praise of this one, criticism of that one, to see how I'll react, I suppose. But he's said nothing outright."

Malik had the odd sensation that time had slipped. It was impossible that he should be talking with Amira about her marriage. Only yesterday she'd been the vexatious little sister rushing in to kick the soccer ball he and his cousins were passing—right over there, two date palms for goalposts.

"Well, it's early yet," he muttered, trying to remember what a brother's role was supposed to be in all this. "You're still very young." But that was his year in France talking, he knew. Here in al-Remal, their father might choose a husband for Amira tomorrow.

"I don't want to marry," said Amira, "but I must. I don't want to leave this house, but I do. I want to go to school in Europe, but I can't." In her voice Malik heard the rebellious girl who had disguised herself in order to drive a car, but in the moonlight, silver-bright now, tears glinted on her cheeks. "I won't marry someone I don't want," she said. "I won't be like Mother. I won't be like Laila. I won't!"

"Of course not, little sister," he comforted her, though the mention of Laila cut deep. "Good willing, when the time comes, there'll be someone wonderful, and you'll have a wonderful life together." He felt like a fool saying it, but what else was there to say?

Amira was silent for a moment. Then, as if they had been chatting about old times all along, she said, "Did I tell you that I see Um Salih often these days? She helped with Yusef's birth. Of course, that was my doing. But now Um Yusef worships her. She'll be on the list for Ramadan money from now on."

"In other words," said Malik, glad that the subject had changed, "Father's paying her and I'm paying her. That old woman will own al-Remal before she's through."

"It's possible. I've never known anyone like her. She's a force of nature." Now she was smiling.

The quickness with which a woman's mood could change, Malik told himself, was a thing he would never understand.

"Listen," Amira went on. "Farid's plan is a good one. Are you going to do it?"

"I'm going to talk with Mahir Najjar, but Farid says the man won't agree to it."

"I think he will. Um Salih says they both want children more than anything. She also thinks that whatever the problem is, it can be fixed. 'A cracked pitcher, not a broken one,' as she puts it. Of course, that's pure intuition, not a shred of medical science in it. But she has a way of being right in these matters."

"As I said, I'll talk with Mahir. If he does agree, it shouldn't take me more than a few days to arrange the papers. We employ hundreds of foreign workers, and Onassis makes sure that the bureaucrats are well oiled."

Amira said quietly, "So little Laila will grow up in France, *Inshallah*."

"*Inshallah*."

"I wonder, brother—it's something I've meant to ask: Do you plan to raise her in the faith?"

It was a question Malik had thought about often, but had never tried to put into words. "If all goes well, Salima Najjar will be doing most of the raising for a while, so there's that to consider. But later . . . it's hard to explain. I still believe in God. How else explain all this?"—he swept a hand toward the diamond heavens—"and I still believe that Mohammed is his prophet. But I can't believe in—can't accept—some of the things that are done in God's name or Mohammed's."

Amira nodded. "Those are my feelings as well." They had lowered their voices even though there was no one to hear. The words they were speaking were forbidden.

"Of course," said Malik, "when she's of an age, I'll force her to take the veil, make sure she never sees the inside of a book, and—"

"You can't be serious!"

"No, but I wanted to see the look on your face."

"Idiot."

"What I really think," Malik said contemplatively, "is that when Laila is your age, it will be very hard to tell her from any other little *Française*."

"I like that picture. I don't know how it will sit with Father, though." She came close and hugged him tight. "I've missed you, brother."

"And I you."

They talked in the garden long into the night; there was no certainty when, if ever, they would have an hour alone together again.

• • •

With Farid as the go-between, Malik arranged a meeting with Mahir Najjar. His home was no place to talk business, Mahir insisted; he was beset there by relatives and in-laws, he claimed.

Suspecting that the man wanted mainly to be out of the hearing of his wife, Malik agreed to meet on neutral ground: a coffeehouse in a poor section of town, where neither man was likely to encounter close acquaintances. "I will want to see my daughter," Malik added, "whether or not we come to some agreement."

In order not to be conspicuous in the neighborhood, he borrowed a *thobe* of Farid's that had seen better days. He went early, just after dark, and sipped coffee and sweetened tea while a storyteller related an adventure of the hero Antar, known all across the Middle East.

The son of a desert sheik and a black slave from Africa, Antar had gained his freedom through acts of bravery, and though he was ruthless against his enemies, he was always a friend to those who suffered injustice at the hands of the powerful. In this particular story, Antar was in danger because of his love for the daughter of a prince.

Malik had heard it before, but the storyteller was not unskilled, and it was pleasant to sit in the crowded coffeehouse, a man among his countrymen, needing no explanation except that he was there.

Mahir arrived and stood against the wall while the inevitable tragic death of the girl and Antar's fierce retribution against her evil father were recounted. With the tale's end, the crowd thinned, and Malik and Mahir took a table that offered a reasonable degree of privacy.

Mahir Najjar was a small, rather dark-skinned man several years older than Malik. He had perpetually sad eyes, so that a nervous tic that occasionally twitched his nose and mustache caused him to resemble a melancholy rabbit.

One thing Malik had learned was the worth of appearances. With the possible exception of Farid, he trusted Mahir as much as any man he knew. After the necessary courtesies, Malik decided on a direct approach. "A man in my position needs a driver," he stated flatly, "and I thought of your honorable self before anyone else."

Without mentioning Salima, he added that he would be needing a cook and someone to look after his child, making it clear that Laila would be going to France one way or the other. He would pay well for these services, he said. He named a figure.

On hearing it, Mahir's eyes became sadder and his tic more noticeable. "As always, sir, you are most generous. But I already have an excellent position driving a water truck for the oil Americans."

"Ah. Well, then, you are to be congratulated for your industry and initiative. I'm sure you've heard, as I have, that many who work for the Americans find many opportunities to better themselves. Why, one fellow even went on to become a millionaire."

Mahir nodded tentatively, as if he were not sure where Malik was going.

"Naturally, I would not want you to pass up an opportunity for such wealth. Nevertheless, I still need a driver and a cook." Malik named a higher figure.

Mahir thanked him. "But France is far away," he pointed out, "and a man has responsibilities to his kin as well as to himself."

"Quite right," Malik agreed—and then named a still higher figure, insisting that it was final. "And the move to France need not be permanent," he noted.

Mahir's eyes became sadder than ever. "If I were only younger, sir," he lamented, "if it were not for my relatives . . ."

"Well," said Malik, with a hint of exasperation, "this is either written—*maktub*—or it is not."

Mahir agreed that this was certainly true.

For a moment Malik feared that they were genuinely at an impasse. Yet Mahir made no sign of breaking off the discussion. Instead, after a suitable interval, he said deferentially, "Tell me, Malik, son of Omar, will you be coming home soon to claim a bride of your own?"

Malik smiled inwardly; Farid had prepared the ground well. "I doubt it," he said casually. "What's the hurry?"

"Very wise, very wise. Sometimes I wish I had waited myself. But don't you feel the need to start a family, while you are still young?"

"Oh, I suppose every man feels that way, but as I said, what's the rush?"

"Indeed, indeed, plenty of time." The eyes were no longer sad, and the tic was much diminished.

"Possibly I've been in France too long, Mahir, and I have become infected with French ways." Malik explained that the French were late marriers, not only the men, but the women. French females not uncommonly married as late as twenty-five. Even thirty. "No, don't look at me like that, Mahir. It's the truth."

"But who would marry a woman of that age, unless he were very old himself, or she were rich?"

"Well, why not? Frenchwomen keep their looks very well—much better than ours do, I'm ashamed to say. Besides, even at thirty, they can have as many children as they want."

"Now how can that be?" The eyes were those of a man with fever, and the tic had vanished entirely.

Malik shrugged. "It's simply a question of medical science. Unfortunately, we have nothing like it here." He paused for effect. "There have even been cases where women of advanced age had other difficulties. Yet the French doctors can remedy these as well."

The fevered eyes blinked rapidly as Mahir struggled to take in the wonders Malik described.

"Miracles," Malik continued. "Nothing short of miracles are performed in France. With the grace of God, the doctors assisted an acquaintance of mine. His seed, alas, was weak, but the doctors strengthened it. Now he and his wife have a son." Malik smiled at this happy conclusion to his narrative: a true story, albeit a rather simplistic explanation of artificial insemination.

"Is this true, Malik ibn Omar? Is this really true?"

"What I have said happens, happens."

For perhaps five seconds, Mahir could have posed as Antar's smaller brother. Then he slowly sagged. "They must all be millionaires in France," he said, "to be able to afford these doctors."

It was the moment Malik had been waiting for. "Well, that's the thing, you see," he said, signaling for more coffee. "In France, the employer customarily pays the medical bills of those who work for him." It was not strictly untrue, he told himself; it would be the custom of at least one employer.

Not long after that, Mahir declared that relatives or no, water truck be cursed, he had always wanted to see the world, and named a figure of his own.

When the pleasure of bargaining was finally done, Mahir invited Malik to his house—"to taste some of the cooking you'll be enjoying, and of course to see the little one."

"You're too kind. I wouldn't want to disturb your relatives."

"You are my employer. If you do me the honor to visit my home, what should they have to say about it?"

There were no relatives, as it turned out, in Mahir's small and hot but immaculately clean house. There was only Salima coming to her husband's call, glancing in question to his face and finding the answer.

But Malik scarcely noticed this, for in Salima's arms was Laila, her dark clear eyes gazing into his with what, forever after, he would swear was a look of eternal recognition.

Part Two

CHILDHOOD

1961

The soccer ball that Malik remembered, Amira remembered, too. She had been no more than five or six when it came bounding out of the cacophony of the boys' game, stopping an inch from her white sandals. It seemed as big as a planet, but the temptation to kick it was irresistible.

The first try failed. Her favorite dress—white with a bow that tied in the back—betrayed her; it was ankle-length, of course, with long pants under it, and when she drew back her foot, she stepped on the hem, got tangled, and missed the ball completely. The boys hooted.

She lifted the dress just enough to gain free movement and kicked with all her might. The heavy ball stung her toes but sailed like something in a dream—into the fountain. For a moment there was chaos, even Malik shouting at her, until her aunt Najla appeared and towed her back to the group of women and younger children.

It was a small memory among countless others that, years later, Amira retrieved with bittersweet nostalgia, turning them over in her mind as another woman might leaf through a photo album. Often, while rain fell on chilly Boston or snow piled in its streets, she would think of her father's house with its sunlit garden.

Although shielded by high walls on two sides and by the wings of the house on the other two, the garden was far from being the shadowy, secret keep that many Americans seemed to imagine an Arab home enclosed. It was more like a playground, a bright space always alive with children—cousins, of course, almost every day, but also the children of neighbor women and of other visitors, as well as those of the servants; sometimes there were special guests, little royal princes and princesses not so very different from Malik and herself; less often, the inexpressibly exotic offspring of American oil-company executives or European businessmen.

The garden was a place of play and openness and green growing things—jasmine and oleander and jacaranda, lovingly tended and nurtured with water more precious than oil. It was the garden Amira thought of when she thought of happiness. In memory and in fact, it blended with the house itself, a rambling Mediterranean-style stucco villa with tall arched windows that could be shuttered against the midday heat. Women and children alike shifted perpetually between the outdoors and the rooms of the women's country within.

In the fiercest heat of the day everyone settled in the shade of the arcade that ran along the ground floor of the main wing and formed a kind of middle ground between outdoors and in. The women worked at small chores and talked, sometimes even sang; both the talk and the singing were done softly if there were men at home, since women's voices heard unrequested in the men's part of the house represented gross misbehavior.

In the direct presence of adults, the children were expected to listen respectfully, speaking only when spoken to. Boys had a bit more latitude than girls in this respect, but even they were never allowed to become loud or unruly.

Amira could remember it exactly: the heat made only just bearable by the shade, the kitchen fragrance of cardamom or cloves or rosemary spicing the scent of stewing lamb, the soft voices and laughter of the women. Sitting politely while the grown-ups conversed was never the intolerable burden that it would have seemed to an American or European child. For one thing, that was simply the way things were done; for another, the conversation could be fascinating. Amira's mother, aunts, and their friends talked of matters that concerned them deeply—money, sickness, marriage, childbirth, the ways of husband and wife—and little or nothing was censored or softened because children were present; after all, they would need to understand these things for themselves before many more years had passed.

One day, for instance, the topic was a new marriage that had met trouble. "Not a drop of blood on the sheets," said Aunt Najla, who had heard the story from one of her friends. "As there would have been if her husband had penetrated a virgin," she added, for the benefit of the younger children.

There were sad noddings; it was every decent woman's nightmare. "Did her husband divorce her immediately?" asked Amira's cousin, Fatima. "Did he send her back to her family?" A bride proved unvirgin could expect nothing more.

"Did her brothers kill her?" asked Halla, a neighbor.

"No," Najla replied. "She was neither divorced nor killed. Naturally, questions arose. It wasn't a matter of money: the groom is rich and not at all miserly." She was referring to the fact that even if the bride were not pure, her husband would still owe half of the bride-price—a large sum—to her father, but would have no wife for the expense.

The women nodded again, this time with understanding, and someone said, "I see."

"Yes," said Najla. "Obviously the fault was his. Either his male member was not up to the task, or for some other reason he would not do his husbandly duty."

That changed everything. Now it was the woman's right to divorce the man. Islamic law said so. Yet this course of action presented its own problems, and was rarely taken. For one thing, divorce, regardless of the reason for it, greatly diminished a woman's prospects of making another marriage.

"But what's wrong with him?" asked Fatima.

The others groaned at her naïveté. Certainly everyone knew that normal men could not contain their lust if it were provoked; it was the whole reason women hid their faces, their hair, even their arms. "Have you never heard that there are certain men who cannot perform?" Halla demanded. "For example, some prefer boys—or even men—to women."

"I hardly think that this is such a case," said Najla authoritatively. "But it's well known that otherwise normal men can sometimes become disabled, from illness perhaps, or injury—"

"Not my husband," Halla cut in. "When he broke his leg, he was like a goat the whole time it was mending."

"—or for other reasons that only God understands. It's said that the excitement of the occasion itself undermines some men's powers. But the point is that the affliction, through God's grace, is often only temporary."

That set off a discussion of how long a man should have in which to overcome such a condition before it was considered permanent and therefore actionable. The consensus was that a month, perhaps two, was proper, although someone said that in the Trucial States, as much as a year was customary. In the end, one of the older women, by stating the undeniable truth that whatever happened was by God's design, for all power was his, signaled that the subject was exhausted.

Amira had listened intently—not out of titillation, for nothing could be more ordinary than talk about sex (one of the first things to perplex her about America was the existence of a debate about something called "sex education"). Nor was it a matter of learning a potentially important lesson—for, like any young girl, she was certain that her husband would never suffer from a lack of passion.

Looking back across a gulf of lonely time, Amira-in-exile could see that what counted was simply being part of it all, of the circle of relatives and friends in the women's country. Never since those childhood days had she known such a sense of belonging and acceptance.

• • •

The first cloud over Amira's young life came from the other world, an entirely different world that occupied the same house, the men's world, a place she rarely saw and in which things happened that were as beyond her control and understanding as the ways of God himself. The cloud came when Malik, who had been in conference with their father—an event in itself—burst into the kitchen with astonishing news: "Little sister! I'm going to Egypt, God willing! To Cairo!"

"Is Mama going with you?" It was all she could think of to say. She was six. The only thing she knew about Cairo was that her mother came from there.

"No, idiot. I'm going to Victoria College."

"What's that?"

Malik spread some brochures on a table. "Here. Look."

There were large stone buildings and green lawns, and among them boys in strange clothes—jackets and ties like the oil-company foreigners sometimes wore.

"Who are all these boys?" Amira asked.

"Students, just like I'll be. People who go to school to learn things. Look, that's the British flag. It's a British school."

"These are British boys?"

"No, they're Arabs, just like me. And Egyptians, of course. And some Persians. It's a British school in Egypt."

Amira contemplated this information. "When I'm as old as you, can I go there?"

"Don't be stupid."

"I'm not stupid. Why can't I go?"

"Because you're a girl, silly."

She could see that it was true—there were no girls in the pictures, no women even—and she knew it in her heart as well. "I want to go," she said. "When I'm eight, I'm going to go."

Malik tousled her hair. "You can't, little sister."

"Yes, I can!"

Just at that moment, Jihan, their mother, walked in.

"What's the fuss?"

"Mama, Malik says I can't go to Victoria. Make him stop saying that."

"Aren't you happy your brother's going to such a fine school?"

"Yes. But can't I go too, when I'm old enough?"

"Well, we'll see, little princess. It's not something you should be worrying about. It's a long time away, and all things are arranged by God."

Amira knew when "we'll see" meant maybe and when it meant no. This "we'll see" was like a door closing, but she stubbornly chose to interpret it otherwise. When Malik went to Cairo, she clung to the dream that someday she would join him there. She begged Jihan to read his letters over and over so that she could absorb every word.

Many famous men had gone to Victoria, Malik boasted, even royalty—for example, young King Hussein of Jordan. The professors all dressed like Oxford dons, whatever that was; apparently they wore long black *thobes*—Amira pictured them as Bedouins. The schoolwork was very difficult, one letter said with a hint of despair. The history courses endlessly detailed European kings and conflicts that made no sense in Remali terms.

The language courses apparently were even worse. When Malik came home for Ramadan, he showed Amira some of his textbooks, the incomprehensible English and French letters bearing no resemblance to the flowing characters of Arabic. Proudly, if haltingly, he read her a quotation from a renowned British poet whose name translated as "brandish a lance." The English words were only noise, but she made him point to each one as he read it.

Despite the difference of over two years in their ages—just right for engendering incessant squabbles—Amira and Malik had always been close. Even adults commented on it, not always approvingly; an aunt had once said sadly that it was because there were only the two of them—two children, one of them a girl, not being considered much of a family in al-Remal.

Now, with his veneer of cosmopolitanism and education, Malik was a hero to his little sister. She counted the weeks till his return on holiday or for the long summer break when the British professors fled the Cairene heat, and when at last he did arrive, she pestered him mercilessly to tell her all about Victoria College and all the things he had learned.

One incident that first summer both terrified Amira and, if it were possible, magnified her admiration for her brother.

• • •

It was an unusually quiet afternoon in the garden. The women and most of the children had gone inside to nap. Malik and a visitor, Prince Ali of the royal house of al-Rashad, sat at a table playing chess. Nearby, perched on a marble bench, Amira watched the game. Girls did not play chess, but Malik loved the game, and Amira had learned most of the moves by observing him.

Malik moved his knight to king five. "Watch your queen," he said in a friendly manner.

Amira shook her head imperceptibly. Even she could see that this was not the real threat.

"Don't worry about my queen," the prince said, shifting it across the board and out of danger.

As soon as he removed his fingers from the piece, Malik pushed his own queen forward, capturing the pawn next to the black king. "Checkmate," he said with a smile.

"Cheap trick!" the prince shouted, his face mottled with anger. With one sweep of his arm, he flipped the board from the table, sending pieces flying.

One hit Amira in the eye. "You hurt me," she moaned and began to cry.

The prince froze for a moment. "Bitch," he muttered, as if to cover his inexcusable display of temper.

Malik moved so quickly that Prince Ali was on his back before Amira realized that her brother had hit him.

The shock was so great that she quit sobbing and held her breath. For one man to lay hands on another was a terrible insult; to strike royalty was unthinkable. Had anyone seen? Across the garden, Bahia seemed to be studying the tops of the date palms.

The prince staggered to his feet. "You'll pay for this," he said—although he kept his distance.

Amira could see that Malik was afraid, but his voice revealed only contempt. "Oh, really? Who will you tell? Your father? Your brothers? Will you tell them what you said to my sister?"

The boy glared daggers, then stalked off without another word.

That night Amira and Malik discussed the episode in thrilled whispers. She was certain that royal guards would arrive at any moment to arrest him; what he had done was against all the rules. With somewhat less confidence, he assured her that no such thing would happen. The other boy was too much of a coward, prince or no. Malik worked himself up to a bit of bravado. "The thing about rules, little sister, is that sometimes they have to be broken. What is important is to know when."

Amira had never heard such a statement, not even from an adult, but somehow it fitted her brother. Besides being a scholar and a man of the world, Malik now appeared to her in the swashbuckling role of a desert bandit sheik.

• • •

"Mama, am I going to Victoria this fall?"

The second summer both dragged and rushed toward an end. Amira was nearly eight now, and if she were going to Victoria, this was the time.

Jihan sighed. "No, beauty, you're not." The sadness in her voice left no room for doubt.

"But I want to."

"I know. But I've told you—anyone can tell you—girls don't go to schools like Victoria."

"Why not? I've learned things from Malik. He gives me his old books. I can do the lessons he did when he first went, almost as well as he could."

Jihan looked at her in wonder. "Are you serious, darling? I knew you looked at his books, but I didn't know that you were actually studying them." Then her mouth tightened. "I'm proud of you, Amira. You're a very intelligent girl. But get Victoria College out of your head. You simply can't go."

"But I want to! I *want* to!"

It ended in the nearest thing to a temper tantrum that Amira had ever had—enough, eventually, to bring Omar storming into the women's country.

"What's all this uproar?" he demanded of Jihan. "We can hear you out there! Does the peace of this house mean nothing?"

"My apologies, husband. It's my fault."

"What troubles the little one?"

"A girlish fantasy, nothing more," Jihan explained briefly, passing so lightly over Amira's dream as to make it seem a joke.

Omar softened. "Listen, little princess, you don't want to go off to dirty, ugly old Cairo and leave all your cousins and friends. Think of all the fun you'll have here. Don't you have a birthday coming up? It seems to me that we'll have to plan something special for you."

"But Malik doesn't mind Cairo, Father, and I'd be with him."

Her father frowned. Amira was not exactly contradicting him, but close enough. "Listen, daughter, and listen well. Your brother will be a man and needs education for a man's tasks. You are a girl, and the only thing you need to learn is to be a modest and obedient wife for the husband you will have someday, God willing. Now let there be no more of this."

He turned on his heel and walked out. Amira knew better than to say another word. That night, she cried herself to sleep in Jihan's comforting arms, all her hopes come to nothing.

An evening or two later she overheard her mother and father talking. "As always I bow to your wisdom and judgment," Jihan said, her tone that peculiar combination of wheedling, flattery, and insistence she used when she wanted something from Omar. "But while I agree with you that Bahia is an excellent servant, she is, after all, only a servant. I only bring this matter up because I know that a man of your position and stature would want his children—both his children—to be well prepared for the future.

"I know you are aware that times are changing. Girls are to be educated now, at least to some extent. You yourself told me that the government plans to open a school for them—in less than two years, I believe you said. I know that if you were not so busy, you would have considered the matter of a proper nanny yourself. So I hope you will not take it amiss if I urge you to do so now."

A moment later, Amira heard her father's rumble: "I have made a good living all these years, thanks be to God, by being aware of changing times, although I haven't always liked them. I dislike what you tell me, too, but there is something in it. Let it be done."

That was how Miss Vanderbeek, Nanny Karin, came into Amira's life.

NANNY KARIN

"What's she like, your blond nanny?"

Amira had heard the question a hundred times in the years since Miss Vanderbeek had joined the Badir household. Nannies were a staple of talk among her peers, all of whom had one. But no one else had a nanny like Miss Vanderbeek. Amira always tried to find a complaint to make about her—she was too strict, too serious, too foreign—because as everyone knew, it was bad luck to praise those you loved.

"Oh, she's all right, I suppose." She shrugged now, making a small concession to approval because the person asking was Laila, and it was hard to hide the truth from the girl—the young woman, really—who had become Amira's closest friend, now that Malik was so far away.

"Come on, now. Do you think she's pretty?"

Amira thought that Miss Vanderbeek, with her milky skin and eyes the color of the clear noon sky, was beautiful. "I don't know," she said. "*She* doesn't think so. And she *is* awfully thin." That was true. By Remali standards, Nanny Karin was almost emaciated. Everyone said that she would never find a man. But she had found one once.

"European women are thin. Look at Brigitte Bardot."

"Who?"

"The French movie star." It was the kind of worldly information Laila always seemed to have at her fingertips. Amira had never heard of Brigitte Bardot.

"Skinny as a snake," Laila continued. "But European men think it's sexy. Is Miss Vanderbeek sexy?"

"Laila!" Amira had heard about the conjugal relations of men and women for as long as she could remember, but the suggestion that some particular women—especially Nanny Karin—might be "sexy" was shocking.

"Relax, little sparrow. I'm only joking. I know she's had a tragic life."

That was true, too. Both of them were silent for a moment, contemplating the delicious sadness of it.

• • •

"I came to al-Remal when I was just twenty-two," Miss Vanderbeek had told Amira, "to work as a secretary and translator for a Dutch construction company. We were building a plant to take the salt from seawater and make it fit to drink." She sighed deeply, as if the memory were still too painful to contemplate.

"And then you fell in love," Amira prodded, for she cherished the tale of her nanny's romance and never tired of hearing it.

"Yes." Miss Vanderbeek smiled. "I fell in love."

"With a Saudi. A pilot."

"Yes. Actually, he owned his own plane and carried passengers between the main cities and the small coastal towns of Saudi Arabia. It was on one of his flights that we met. We exchanged a glance," Miss Vanderbeek continued, "nothing more, but that was enough."

Amira sighed. To meet one's love floating above the clouds, to recognize one's qismah, *one's destiny. Could anything be more romantic?*

"Lutfi wasn't like the other men I've met here," Miss Vanderbeek explained. "Just because I was a Western woman, he didn't try to take advantage of me . . ."

Amira nodded vigorously. She knew her nanny could never have passed Omar Badir's door if her reputation had been clouded with even a hint of impropriety.

"No, he behaved honorably from the start. He wanted to call on my family, but my parents are dead, and I am alone in the world. And so he came to the man who seemed to be most responsible for me—my supervisor, Mr. Haas."

Amira smiled. She liked this part of the story, which seemed a testimony to the perseverance of true love.

"But Mr. Haas was an engineer with a rather scientific and unsentimental nature. He simply could not understand why this pilot— 'a pleasant enough fellow,' he said—began calling at the office once a week, bringing gifts, making pleasant small talk, mentioning my name as if in passing. Of course, Lutfi was hoping for an appropriate response so he could take the next step and begin discussing his qualifications as a husband. But Mr. Haas never said a word. Poor Lutfi." For a moment, Miss Vanderbeek seemed to be lost in bittersweet memory.

"When he told me later how desperate he was to make himself understood—without, of course, coming right out saying it was me he wanted—I didn't know whether to laugh or cry. Finally, on the sixth visit, when he was ready to state his purpose openly, regardless of the consequence, Mr. Haas mentioned that I was planning to convert to Islam. It had nothing to do with Lutfi, my decision to convert. Al-Remal was the home I had been searching for since my parents died—and Islam was its religion. But Lutfi, that dear man, he was struck speechless by what he thought was a sign from heaven: that his greatest wish was in harmony with God's will. He set his gifts on Mr. Haas's desk, went to his plane, and flew away.

"Finally my supervisor understood that he had been a bit blind. That afternoon when he told me that I seemed to have an admirer, when he saw my face, he said,

'I've been blind and a fool.' After that he was more than ready to play matchmaker—or whatever else it took to help us get married."

Miss Vanderbeek paused. Her shoulders slumped; her eyelids seemed to droop in an attitude of dejection. This part Amira did not like, for she much preferred stories that ended with "happily ever after."

"But Lutfi's family did not want him to marry me. They didn't care whether or not I converted. To them I was still a foreigner. A woman without a male relative to uphold my honor. A woman who worked among men." Miss Vanderbeek spoke the words as if they were curses, and Amira flinched at the harshness of her tone.

"They could not stop him from marrying me, or so they said. But they told him that if he acted against their wishes, he would no longer be welcome under his father's roof. It would be as if he were dead.

"Poor Lutfi! How he despaired. He said he could not live without me—yet he could not desert his family."

"But you urged him to be patient. You said you would wait for him until his family relented," Amira filled in. "Forever, if necessary."

"Yes." Miss Vanderbeek's voice was almost a whisper. "Forever. But we did not have forever. Two years later, Lutfi's plane crashed in the Red Sea near Jeddah. There were no passengers. And Lutfi's body was never found."

Amira reached out and touched her nanny's hand. "But you stayed here in al-Remal."

"Yes, Amira, I stayed. I remained with the Dutch company until the project was finished. Then I worked for an American corporation, teaching languages to its employees and their children. But . . ."

"But you weren't really happy with the Americans."

"No, no, I wasn't. It felt as if I were living in Texas rather than al-Remal. So, when I heard the Badir family was looking for a nanny who could also be a tutor . . ."

"You came here. And you'll stay here forever—and we'll all live happily ever after."

Nanny Karin did not answer. She simply stroked Amira's hair and smiled her sad smile.

• • •

"That's why I wonder what she's really like," said Laila now. "Tell me."

"Well, she's not like the other nannies."

"Wait! Do I see a pillar of flame? A message from God?"

Amira laughed. "You know what I mean." She wasn't talking about Nanny Karin's blond hair. Miss Vanderbeek was different in more important ways. Most of the nannies were poor women from countries like Yemen or Ethiopia; Bahia was from the Sudan. Most, like Bahia, had been slaves until, barely a year ago, the king had finally abolished slavery, at least technically. And most, again like Bahia—and like the great majority of women in al-Remal—were illiterate.

"Sometimes I don't understand why she stays here," Amira said. "She could be teaching in a university somewhere. The things she teaches me . . ." Amira reached for the words, trying to explain how Nanny Karin painted word pictures of the world outside of al-Remal, how she brought to life its colors and textures and smells. But seeing the impatience in Laila's face, she settled for: "Do you know I read English almost as well as Malik?"

"Really?"

"Don't tell anyone. Father wouldn't like it if he knew."

"Ha! And Malik would be jealous."

"And she's teaching me arithmetic." Saying this, Amira lowered her voice.

"What do you mean? Two and two are four?"

"We did that when she first came. I'm learning percentages now."

"What on earth for?" Laila looked genuinely surprised.

"Nanny says you never can tell when something will come in handy. She says that the schools they're starting for girls are just a beginning. All they teach now is the Koran, but someday girls will learn just like boys."

"Amira! Isn't that against the Koran itself?"

"Nanny says it isn't. She says that nothing in the Koran says girls should be ignorant. It's like the *gutwah*, the veil. That's not the Koran either. Some rich women started wearing it a long time ago to be fashionable, Now everyone does it. But it's not in the Koran."

"Miss Vanderbeek told you all this?"

"Yes. But please don't ever mention it, Laila. I know it sounds awful, but it really isn't."

"Don't worry. Your and Miss Vanderbeek's secrets are safe with me," Laila said a bit petulantly. "But she's not the only one who knows things. Did you hear about the village girl who drowned in the well?"

"Of course." How could she not have heard of it? It had been on everyone's lips for two days.

"Well, it wasn't an accident. And it wasn't suicide, either."

"What do you mean?"

Now it was Laila's turn to lower her voice. "Someone saw her going into a man's house in town. Her brothers found out. They threw her down that well. Everyone in the village heard her screams."

"Laila! How do you know all this?"

"I told you Miss Vanderbeek wasn't the only one who knows things. Would you like to hear more, little sparrow?"

Amira settled back to listen. Learning from Miss Vanderbeek was fun, but hard. It was nice to have a friend like Laila to talk with about real things in the real world. Someday soon she would tell Laila about her secret wish—that Laila and Malik would marry, and they would all live together.

FRIENDSHIP

It wasn't just a fantasy. It could easily happen. In many ways, Laila Sibai was an ideal choice to be Malik's wife. Her father, Abdullah, was Omar Badir's lifelong friend and his business partner, so the alliance would make sense economically, uniting the two friends' fortunes.

True, Laila and Malik were not cousins, but the preference for marriage between cousins was less pronounced in al-Remal than in many Arab countries, and in any case Laila was virtually the same as a cousin, known to everyone, spending almost as much time at the Badir house as at her own. Her mother, Rajiyah, was Jihan's close friend.

Besides—not that it counted for much in arranging marriages—Laila and Malik liked each other. Amira remembered Rajiyah scolding Laila more than once for playing and talking with Malik more than was seemly with a boy who was not *mahram*—that is, a male relative she could not marry.

Even after Laila had reached puberty and took the veil, Amira came upon her and Malik laughing in a secluded corner of the Badir garden. Amira must have looked shocked, because Laila smiled and said, "What's the matter, sparrow? Should your brother and I become strangers just because I'm wrapped in cloth?"

That was just like Laila, who seemed to share Malik's philosophy about knowing when to break the rules. Even if Amira disapproved—and she was not sure she did—she would never have said so. She idolized Laila. Obviously one reason the older girl gave her such attention was because of Malik, but what did that matter? Amira idolized Malik, too. From her point of view, the perfect thing would be for her brother and her friend to marry.

It probably wouldn't happen, though. The problem wasn't so much that Malik was younger than Laila—it was only a matter of a year or so, and the Prophet himself had married a woman nearly old enough to be his mother—but that Malik was still a schoolboy, and Laila was a marriageable young woman. Her father could hardly be expected to wait for his old friend's son to grow up; he would be looking for a mature and substantial husband for her—and soon.

• • •

"Listen! It's them."

A summer had passed, and another was not far away. Laila and Amira were huddled in Laila's father's library, forbidden territory for females, but Abdullah Sibai was in India buying silk, and there were no other men around. Under such circumstances, Laila's mother often became inattentive, and Laila and Amira slipped into the library to listen to Abdullah's elaborate and hugely expensive radio. Amira's father had one just like it—he and Abdullah had gifted each other with the sets, on which they monitored news and financial developments all over the Middle East.

Laila and Amira put the radio to a different but equally international use: they listened to music from as far away as Istanbul and Cairo. Cairo was their favorite because of the greatness of the Egyptian singers: Abdul Wahab, Farid al-Atrash, and the incomparable Um Kalthoum. Sometimes, too, they could pick up a Cairo station that played Western music; it was there that they heard a group of musicians that Malik, with British-school snobbery, had mentioned to them as being all the rage in Europe. They were called the Beatles.

"Turn it up," Amira begged.

"No. Mother will hear. Let's dance."

Laila had shown Amira how Western teenagers danced (where she gained such esoteric knowledge Amira still had no idea). It was as different from the dancing Amira knew—*beledi* dancing, which Miss Vanderbeek said Westerners called "belly dancing"—as the music was from anything she had ever heard. It was all wild and free, almost madness—but fun. As she danced she tried to catch the English lyrics, but words in a song didn't sound like words read from a book. She could make out "baby" over and over again—though what a baby had to do with it she couldn't tell—and the phrase "twist and shout"; she would have to look up "twist" in Miss Vanderbeek's dictionary. Malik had told them that the song was already passé, Cairo being years behind the times when it came to rock and roll, as the music apparently was called.

The song ended on a series of pounding notes on instruments Amira did not recognize, and almost immediately the station began to fade.

"Just as well," said Laila. "We're tempting fate as it is. Let's go to my room."

The Sibai home was virtually a replica of the Badirs', only the furnishings different. Laila's room overlooked the garden from the second floor, just as Amira's did—she at last had her own room, a sign that she was approaching womanhood. Flushed from dancing, they collapsed on the bed.

"Well, little sparrow, I hope you enjoyed that," said Laila, "because I'm sorry to tell you we probably won't be listening to the radio much anymore."

"Why not?"

"I think my father has chosen a husband for me. I think he'll make his decision known when, God willing, he returns from India."

Amira tried to sound enthusiastic. "Laila! This is wonderful news. Congratulations. Who is it?"

"I don't know. I only hope he's not too old and ugly."

"Oh, he won't be. I know he won't."

"God willing."

"But this is so exciting!"

"Yes," Laila agreed. "Yes, it is. To tell you the truth, I'm thrilled. Isn't it what we all dream of? But at the same time, it'll change things between you and me."

Amira felt her heart sink. "Are you saying we won't be seeing each other anymore?"

"No, no! Of course not. We'll see lots of each other, God willing, even if I live far away. It'll just be different."

"Well, of course. With a husband—and children, may God give you many."

"Yes. It's like entering a new life. I'll be a real grown-up, and I'll have to act like one. My duty will be to my husband, whoever he might be." Laila was silent for a moment, then said, "I wish that . . . well, never mind what I wish. It's unimportant." Suddenly she brightened. "Did you know that I've driven a car?"

"What? When?" It was illegal for women to drive in al-Remal. The sight alone would have drawn the religious police, the regular police, and a crowd of angry citizens.

"With Malik, last summer. I disguised myself as a boy. Sneaked some clothes from my brother Salim's room, wore them under my *abeyya*, which I then took off. It was an adventure. We went out into the country, out where they're building the new airport, and Malik showed me what to do."

"But Laila, what could have possessed you?"

"You're right, it was crazy. Anything might have happened—what if the car had broken? But I'll never forget." Again Laila paused, reaching out to stroke Amira's hair. "You should do it, little sparrow. Get Malik to take you. He's your brother, *mahram*. You won't even have to make up a story to get out of the house with him. I do recommend the disguise, though, in case someone sees you driving, Besides, it's fun to masquerade as a boy."

"Oh, I couldn't. Never."

Laila smiled and hugged her. "Why not? Do it, sparrow. You'll be married too, before you know it, and then it'll be too late."

• • •

Malik came home early that year. Israel and Syria had been trading artillery shells and bombs for months, and the universal belief was that the Israelis would attack Egypt next—or that Egypt would strike first, in self-defense.

In mid-May, President Nasser mobilized his nation's armed forces. Malik got out on one of the last flights from Cairo and barely had time to unpack his bags before the Six Day War was over.

Sabers rattled mightily during those few days, but there was never the possibility that al-Remal would join the fight. The Remal king fulminated bitterly against the Israeli aggressors yet made it clear that their great allies, the Americans, were welcome and honored guests in the country and should be treated accordingly. At the same time, he canceled all official appointments with Americans—and, of course, anyone who had invited an American to a private party followed suit.

It was a difficult time for everyone. The precipitous defeat of the nation that all the Arab world looked to for leadership was depressing. Even Malik was moody and irritable, a state in which Amira had rarely seen him. She thought at first that it was only part of the general gloom; then too, he was at an age when boys seemed to become moody. At last it came to her that his discontent might have to do with Laila's upcoming marriage.

• • •

"My friend, Abdullah Sibai, has chosen wisely for his daughter," said Amira's father, as the Badir family sipped their coffee after the evening meal. "General Mahmoud Sadek is renowned for his piety. And he is a formidable horseman and hunter."

"He has a good appearance," said Jihan agreeably. "And I'm told the king regards him as a good friend. But I wonder if he might not be a bit old for Laila. She is so high-spirited, and he is, after all, in his fifties."

An old man, Amira thought. Her friend was going to marry an old man! What must she be feeling?

• • •

But when Amira questioned her friend, Laila's enthusiasm for her upcoming marriage was unbounded. "He's very rich. And very generous. You should see the gifts he's been sending to the house. A jeweled belt from Beirut. A gold mesh handbag from Tiffany in New York! A magnificent silver tea set from London. Something new every day!"

"That's wonderful, Laila, but—"

"And he's had the most tragic life," Laila continued. "He's lost two wives in childbirth, can you imagine? My mother assures me that if I give Mahmoud a son—or even a daughter—he'll treasure me until the day he dies. Isn't that romantic?"

Amira nodded, still not certain in her own mind that this marriage could be described as romantic. "I had a letter from Malik today. He'll be home on Thursday, for a week. Will you come to visit?"

Laila was silent for a long moment. "I don't think so," she said softly, a hint of sadness in her voice. "I don't think that would be proper . . . now that I'm betrothed to Mahmoud."

"Oh."

"Never mind, little sparrow. There's so much to be happy about. Tomorrow I'll begin choosing clothes. Mahmoud has sent sketches from Paris. And we're going to Istanbul—for at least four weeks, isn't that glorious? And after that, I'll be redecorating Mahmoud's house. He says I can have carte blanche, no matter what it costs. There's so much to do, Amira, I don't know how I'll find the time . . ."

• • •

Malik was as spiritless as Laila was bubbly. One morning he sat in on Amira's lessons with Miss Vanderbeek. He complimented them both on Amira's English and French, but soon grew restless and excused himself. Amira asked to be excused as well. She found him in the garden, tossing pebbles into the fountain.

"What's the matter, brother?" She gathered her courage. "Is it Laila?"

"Laila? What gives you that idea? It's life, little sister. It's passing me by. I have no control over anything. A war has come and gone while I blinked. I spend most of the year in a different world, then come home to the same old one. It goes on endlessly and nothing changes—not for the good, anyway."

"It's all in God's control, my brother," she said, feeling the words' ineffectualness as she spoke them. Malik merely grunted.

"Will you teach me to drive, brother?"

His eyes snapped angrily towards hers. Then, just as suddenly, his old smile replaced the glare.

"She told you about that, did she? Trust a woman with a secret. Well, why not? Will this afternoon be soon enough?"

"Well, there's no rush. God willing, I—"

"None of that, little sister. She who hesitates is lost. It's now or never."

That was how Amira found herself behind the wheel of a Mercedes sedan in the wasteland beyond the new airport, where the road was little more than a track in the desert. She was wearing an old *thobe* of Malik's and had covered her hair with a boy's white *ghutra* that he hadn't worn in years.

There were no driver's licenses in al-Remal, partly because there were so few cars, partly because the few that existed tended to be regarded in the same light as horses. Any boy who had an adult male's permission could drive, even if he could barely see over the dashboard.

"All right, put it in first gear. Now let out the clutch and press the accelerator . . . *easy* I said!"

The car jerked and stalled. Amira's legs were just long enough to reach the pedals.

"Try it again. And don't worry about going off the road; it's hard pan here."

She tried again and stalled again. And again. Then she managed first gear but stalled when she shifted to second. Each time, Amira remembered Laila's fear of a breakdown.

Then, suddenly, she got it. She took the Mercedes through first to second—with only a little grinding noise—and then to third. The landscape was rushing by faster than it ever seemed to do when Malik was driving, and she was grateful for his steadying hand on the wheel. Then she pushed it away. She had been oversteering, she realized. All that was needed was an easy turn of the wheel, a light touch on the pedal.

The feeling of having the powerful machine in *her* power was magical. She drove in circles and figure eights. She learned to use the brakes and, at Malik's instruction, switched on the headlights, blinked the turn signals, even ran the windshield wipers; the fact that German engineers had provided for such an unlikely event as rain impressed her.

"All right, little sister, we'll run out of gas at this rate. Slow it down. Now stop."

She braked to a halt that was only slightly too abrupt. "Can't I drive back to town?"

"No. That's enough." Malik shut off the ignition, got out, and came around to take the driver's seat. "You liked that, did you?"

"I loved it!"

"Well, now you know how to drive. It's something you never forget."

Was that what Laila had meant? Or was it all of this, the whole experience, the feeling of power, all the while dressed like a male, doing something only males were permitted?

Malik started the engine and turned toward home.

"Thank you, brother. Can we do it again sometime?"

"Who knows? But there's the airport. Maybe you'd better put your girl's clothes on and hide the *ghutra* before we get any closer in."

"Oh, all right."

She reached under the seat for her dress.

"No!" Malik said suddenly. "Don't do it now. There's an army Jeep coming up behind us." He glanced worriedly at the rearview mirror. "Damn it! I think he wants us to stop. All right, don't worry. Just remember you're a boy, and don't say anything unless you're asked."

He pulled over. The Jeep swung around the Mercedes and stopped in a cloud of dust. A small, wiry man wearing a pistol and a larger man with an automatic weapon got out and approached the car. In the heat of the desert, Amira felt as if she were freezing.

The man with the pistol peered in the window and smiled. "It's you, Malik son of Omar. Just when I was sure I'd caught an Israeli spy. The peace of God be with you."

"The peace of God and his compassion with you, Salim son of Hamid. I started to say 'Lieutenant,' but I see that you're a captain now."

"The spoils of war, young sir. Not that we got within a thousand miles of the shooting—which was over soon enough, God knows. But the airport, which is my duty to guard, is still in Remali hands, by God's will." Despite his friendly words, the man had an intense expression, which he now focused on Amira.

"But who's this?"

"The offspring of an acquaintance," said Malik casually. "In a moment of weakness I agreed to be a driving instructor."

The man was staring so hard at Amira that she instinctively lowered her eyes and turned her face away. *Caught.* She was sure of it.

"Modest," the captain said. "As modest as a girl. A good thing to be modest, with such an ill-featured face as that."

Amira's cheeks burned. How dare this stranger stare at her and insult her? Then she realized that he was only being polite, substituting an insult for a compliment to avoid bringing her bad luck.

"It's good to see you, Salim. May we meet again soon. But unless you'd like to interrogate us, I hope to join my family for prayers, God willing."

The wiry man laughed. "Even if I liked it, Malik son of Omar, you and your young friend might not. Go in peace. Your father is well?"

"Alive and cantankerous as ever, thank God. And yours?"

"Hanging on, praise God."

"The peace of God go with you."

"And with you."

Half a mile down the road, Malik finally let out a long breath. "You can change now, little sister. You did well. Were you afraid?"

"A little. He stared at me so."

Malik laughed. "Yes, he did."

"Do you think he knew I was a girl?"

Malik laughed harder. "Salim ibn Hamid is a good enough man, I suppose, if a little dense. I know him only slightly. But it's said that he's one of those who finds pleasure in boys—boys too young to shave."

"Oh, my God!"

"Yes, it appears you've made a conquest, little sister. I can hear the poet now: 'The Star-Crossed Love of Salim and Amira.' The Egyptians will make a movie of it."

"Malik!"

"By God, I want to thank you for asking me to do this, little sister. It's reminded me that God in all his greatness also has a sense of humor. The Arabs fight the Israelis, who are nothing but their cousins. Laila is betrothed to a man older than her father. And tonight Salim ibn Hamid will bay the moon for my sister, dreaming that she is a boy."

Malik could not seem to stop laughing, and then Amira was laughing too—with relief, with joy, with youth, with her taste of forbidden freedom. All the way home, every little thing they said or saw set off another round of laughter.

BLACK DREAM

The desert was bright all around, the wide sky flawlessly blue. Jihan was standing in a shallow pit in the sand. It only came up to her waist, but when she tried to step out, she couldn't. The sand slid beneath her feet, and somehow the pit grew deeper. The harder she climbed, the deeper she sank. Soon the rim was over her head. She used her hands, but the hot sand crumbled as she clawed at it. The hole deepened, and the sand choked her. She screamed for help. People appeared above her against the shrinking sky. Shouting something she could not understand, sand cascading down under his feet, Malik leaned in, smiled encouragement, and turned away; Amira knelt on the rim in tears before fading like a mirage; Jihan's parents shook their heads sadly before walking on. The pit was as black, the hissing sand as suffocating as smoke. Now only a small, faceless figure perched on the rim, high against the last of the light, calling her name.

Jihan woke up, heart pounding, shivering in sweat.

Like most Remalis, she took great stock in dreams, and she knew exactly when she had first had this one. It was noted in a small diary she kept. *Black Dream*, the entry said. She did not bother to elaborate or—as she sometimes did when a dream was portentous but mystifying—to hire an interpreter. She needed no professional to tell her that this was a dream of her own death.

Black Dream, and then, a few weeks later, the same notation, followed after another two weeks by *dream again*. Soon the dream took on a presence almost as real as the people around her, and Jihan knew with a certainty that terrified her that it would never go away.

She looked through the pages of her diary to confirm the timing of the first dream. Yes, it had come exactly three days after the entry: *Omar tells me he is taking another wife.*

THE END OF CHILDHOOD

Laila was married in early fall. Malik had already left for Cairo. The wedding was the most elegant Amira had ever seen or could imagine. Laila, decked in silk and dripping with gold, everything about her done to perfection, looked as beautiful as one of the virgins promised to the faithful in paradise.

Her groom was far from the elderly gentleman Amira had made him in her mind. Mahmoud Sadek was as handsome as everyone said, and though not a large man, had something about him that made him seem so. Even Omar Badir and Abdullah Sibai had the aspect of younger brothers in his presence.

Then it was over, and Laila was gone. The couple would honeymoon in Istanbul. For a few days Amira lived on the remembered glory of the wedding. Then a gray despondency descended on her. She was lonely.

She tried to spend time with her mother, but Jihan seemed to be in her own world these days. Even Miss Vanderbeek was gone, taking her annual vacation somewhere in the south of France. On top of it all, Amira's body was changing; she had not bled yet, but things were happening within her that sometimes seemed like torment.

It helped when Laila's letters began to arrive, a new one every day. She raved about the luxuriousness of her honeymoon hotel, the beauty of the Bosporus, the treasures of the Topkapi museum.

> *You should see the jewels, Amira, the fabulous diamonds and rubies and sapphires that the sultans gave to their wives. They must have loved them very much indeed. I miss you very much and wish you were here to share all these wonders with me. But I don't think Mahmoud would like that. Never mind, I will soon be home—and I will be your friend always and forever.*

Amira read and reread these sentiments, silently affirming her friendship "always and forever."

In the third week of Laila's honeymoon came a note in her exuberant hand warning, "*State secret! Hide this away! Aren't they cute?*" and a postcard-sized photograph of the Beatles. Amira was vaguely disappointed. The musicians looked rather like oil-company foreigners wearing strange wigs. But in tribute to the shared memories the picture represented, she slipped it between the pages of one of the textbooks Malik had left her. Every night she took it out and wondered what Istanbul was like, and Cairo, and London, and all the other places she might never see.

One midmorning, at an hour when Omar was always in town on business, Amira's loneliness and the urgings of her body made her do a crazy thing. She went into her father's study and turned on the radio. It took her a while to find the Cairo station, but at last there it was, a Western song playing, rock and roll; it wasn't the Beatles, but the music was similar. She lifted her skirt and danced, watching her own long legs as she twirled, trying to regain that feeling almost forgotten, that brief sunburst of freedom.

It wouldn't come. The music wasn't the same, there was no Laila, nothing was right. She should work on the lessons Miss Vanderbeek had left her, or maybe experiment with makeup. Or do something else. But she was still dancing, mechanically and aimlessly, when her father's voice thundered from the door.

"What are you doing! By God, that I should see this! Are you my daughter?" His face bloodless with anger, Omar reached her in one stride and dragged her from the room by her hair.

In the women's country there were gasps when he burst in. "Where is my wife! Where!"

Jihan materialized as the other women vanished in a whisper of cloth and a clatter of sandals.

"What is it? What's wrong, my husband?"

"I told you. I warned you. It's time and past time. It will be done now!"

Jihan shook her head. "But, husband, she's not yet reached her time. She's still a child."

"A child I've just seen flaunting herself like a Cairo whore, in my study, to my radio. Go! It's still on. Go hear the godless music for yourself."

"I believe you, Omar. Punish her as you wish. It's just that she hasn't started yet and—"

"Silence!" Omar spotted Bahia hovering in a corner. "You! You know what's to be done. Go fetch what's needed."

Amira had never known such terror. She had sinned greatly. Not just the sin of her shameless dancing, but the far worse sin of arousing *ghadab*, rage, in a parent. Children who did that endangered their very souls. She cried helplessly while Jihan made feeble protests that Omar, now stonily silent, ignored. Bahia reappeared carrying the *abeyya*.

"This is not her punishment," Omar told Jihan. "I will decide that later. This is what God ordains. See that you do it." He turned and left.

They took her to Jihan's room. Amira still wept. Veiling was supposed to be a happy and proud occasion, a passage into womanhood, but she had ruined it beyond hope. "It's too soon," she murmured. It was all she could think of to say in her defense.

But now it was her mother who was stern: "It's soon enough. Do you dare dispute your father?"

The long black veiling robe came down, covering her face, dulling the colors of the room, the colors of her childhood, shrouding her face from all who might take joy in seeing it—but also, thank God, hiding her tears.

Part Three

JIHAN

"Mother, don't you want to join us outside? Auntie Najla's in rare form. Mother?"

"I'd rather sit here, child. I'm tired."

"You can sit outside. Come have some tea. It's a beautiful day."

In the end Jihan let Amira coax her out to the shaded arcade, but the other women's faces, their eyes, their sudden silence breaking into oversolicitude, told that they all saw the dream on her.

She no longer kept the diary, for the dream came nearly every night now, so that she dreaded sleep. Worse, it haunted her waking hours as well. It was as if the whole familiar world—the house, the garden, the faces of everyone she knew—were only a shimmering, gossamer veil that might lift at any moment to reveal the sand pit snarling like a black jackal beyond.

She knew that something was wrong—wrong with her, wrong with the way she was acting. It was sinful. First and second wives did not always get along—although quite often they did—but both women were expected to keep any dissonance between them from intruding on their husband's happiness. Jihan had failed in this, even denying Omar her body for many months now. Certainly that was a sin, and she dreaded having to account for it in the time to come.

But weren't there reasons?

You'll be the only one, always, the only star in my sky. It was another diary entry, from another time. She had been fourteen when she wrote it, on the morning after her wedding night. Omar, who was eighteen years older, had said it to her. In those days he often spoke to her in words that sounded like poetry—in those days and for months and years afterward. And it was more than words. They had had an understanding. They had had a happy marriage. Perhaps that was why he did not divorce her despite the thing, all the things, wrong with her now.

The only one. She shook her head and in her mind gave a bitter little laugh. Instantly, from the women's eyes, she knew that she had made the sound aloud.

"Your throat is dry, Um Malik," said Um Yusef, gracefully covering the moment. "Let me bring you some tea." She hurried to the task as a good second wife should. Jihan watched her narrowly. It was well enough, she was thinking, for Um Yusef to make a show for the others, but the truth was that this pretty, pretty, young, young, young woman not only occupied the place of second wife but had usurped that of first wife as well. Ever since Yusef's birth, all of Omar's attentions had centered on the baby and its mother. Where was the respect, the veneration, that was due to the first wife, the mother of the firstborn son?

But it was her own fault, Jihan knew, only hers.

• • •

Is it my fault? Amira wondered, watching her mother nod as if she were having a conversation with herself. *Is it something I did? Is it because I was a bad daughter, that one night, that my mother and father have become strangers? Is that why my mother has changed so much, so quickly?*

She hardly recognized Jihan these days—the dull eyes, clouded as if with frost, that once had sparkled; the tight, pursed mouth that had charmed with its smile, its laugh, its quick jokes and compliments and kisses; the sunken, defeated body that had never been able to sit still for five minutes, so full of life it was, yet now lay motionless for hours in a darkened room. Her mother was an Egyptian, a Cairene, a sophisticate from the capital of the Arab world, exciting and even deliciously scandalizing to the conservative Remali women around her: "Movies? Well, of course, they're against the law here, but in Cairo we saw them every week. Yes, women too. Even American movies. Do you know the story of Scarlett O'Hara, who fell in love with a rich sheik and then with a handsome smuggler? Be serious, you've never heard of her? Well, let me tell you . . ."

Now that same woman hunched in a chair in the corner, looking like someone's crazy great-aunt who might at any moment start muttering darkly about how things were better under the old king.

• • •

"The king was very handsome, very elegant, wasn't he, Mother?"

"What? The king? Farouk, do you mean?"

They were in Jihan's room, the curtains drawn, twilight in the middle of the day. Jihan lay with a cooling damp cloth on her forehead.

"Yes. Farouk."

Jihan sighed. The Cairo Horseback Riding Club. A day in spring. Herself as a girl. The king passing by with his entourage, a glance at her, a greeting to her father. "When he was young, there was no man more handsome than Farouk," she said. "People forget, because of the grotesquerie he became."

"When he asked about you," Amira prompted, "your father said you were already promised, didn't he?" It was a story her mother cherished, she knew.

Jihan only nodded. Who knew what was true? Her father might have made it all up to please her.

"What if you'd married the king? What then?" Anything to keep Jihan talking, to break the shell she had grown that was slowly crushing her.

"Only God could tell you that." Jihan smiled thinly. "But if it had happened, where would you and Malik be? Let me rest a little, my heart. I'm tired." Suddenly, for no reason at all, she thought of the Muntaza, the royal palace at Alexandria. On the grounds was a pool with water lilies. It was said that Farouk liked to watch very young women, as many as a dozen at a time, swim naked among the lilies. Thinking of that, she drifted to sleep, and before her dreaming eyes the lily pond was replaced by the shining desert . . .

• • •

"I know you have responsibilities there, and that it may be difficult, but if you can possibly come home, even for a few days, please, brother, come soon." Amira signed the letter and gave it to Bahia to mail. She hoped she had conveyed the urgency of the situation without sounding hysterical. It was as if their mother was slipping away a piece at a time. In the last few days Jihan's mind had begun to wander, like that of an old woman on her deathbed. Just yesterday she had stared into empty space and said, "Why, Malik! Where have you been? How did you get so dirty?"

Amira was frightened. "Malik's not here, Mother. You know he's in France."

Jihan's smile faded. "Of course. I must have been daydreaming. But I saw him so clearly, just as he used to be."

Perhaps Malik could help. Nothing else seemed to.

When had it all started? How? Was it that night when Amira had shamed her parents? Was she to blame?

It was two years ago, just after Omar had announced his intention to take another wife, a few months before the horror of Laila's execution. Amira had just moved into a room of her own, and she was awake late, trying to finish one more chapter in a history book Malik had sent her. From her mother's room came muffled sounds—she recognized her father's deep rumble, but could not make out his words. Then Jihan's voice was raised in a pleading tone Amira had never heard her use: "Please, Omar, you know how I feel. Please just leave me alone!"

Amira did not know why she did it, she knew it was wrong, but she slipped from her bed and went down the hall. Jihan's door stood slightly ajar.

"You know that this is sinful," Omar was saying. He sounded half bewildered, half angry. "You live under my roof. You accept my protection. You are my wife, and you will be my wife."

"No! Please!"

As if she were someone else watching from a distance, Amira saw herself open the door.

Jihan was huddled on the bed, Omar leaning over her. Amira had never entered on such a scene. She knew immediately that she had made a terrible mistake. Yet she could not turn away.

Jihan saw her first, then Omar turned. Both of them had horror and guilt on their faces, but her father's expression quickly turned fierce.

"What are you doing here?"

Amira wanted to sink into the stones of the floor, but she had to say something. What came out was, "Why don't you just . . . leave her alone." She had never been so terrified.

For a moment she thought that Omar would strike her—he raised his arm. But then he pointed to the door and, his voice trembling, commanded, "To your room! Never dare again!"

She ran like an animal freed from a trap. Seconds after she had burrowed into her bed, she heard his heavy footsteps passing in the hall.

For days she did not see her father and hardly dared to look at her mother. Yet Jihan acted as if nothing had happened, or as if she had more important matters on her mind. Amira had the heady feeling of reprieve that children experience when, caught in some misbehavior, they find that their parents are too distracted by the adult world to exact punishment.

Then one morning she woke to another sound from her mother's room—a blood-chilling wail, hardly human. She rushed into the hall but, frozen by what had happened a few nights before, could not bring herself to open the door. Bahia, appearing out of nowhere, pushed past her and into the room. Jihan was standing by the bed, staring at it. It was covered with blood. So was the lower half of her nightgown.

"Allah! What is it? Is she cut?"

"No, little miss. Nothing like that. But go and have someone send for the midwife." Bahia had her arms around Jihan, comforting her as if she were a child.

"But what's the matter?" Amira had never seen such despair as on her mother's face.

"She has miscarried. Undoubtedly something was wrong with the fetus. It is God's will."

• • •

For Jihan, the pregnancy had been a miracle and a desperate hope. The conception must have occurred on the last night she and Omar made love. After their years together he did not come to her bed often, and when he did, the act lacked ardor. She enjoyed it in a mechanical way—Omar had always been a proficient and unselfish lover—but that was all.

This night was different. He did not press his desire directly or soon but sat beside her, stroked her hand for a moment, and said, "Let us talk for a while, Beauty. It seems we never have a moment alone together these days."

"Is something wrong, Omar?" His words were so unexpected.

"Wrong? Nothing at all. I was just . . . thinking. And remembering."

"Thinking and remembering what?"

He smiled, a small, shy smile that she had not seen in years that made him look youthful, almost boyish, behind his graying beard. "Remembering the time when your voice was to me like the sound of splashing water to a man burning with thirst. And thinking that it is still that way."

"Why, I hardly know what to say," she laughed, flushing with pleasure even as she wondered what brought all this on. "You've found a trick that will make you a hero to every husband in al-Remal—how to strike a wife speechless."

Omar laughed, too. Then an awkward little silence followed.

"Did I mention that I had a letter from Malik yesterday?" Jihan finally ventured.

"Yes."

"He sends you his deepest respect and regards."

"Yes, you told me. And he is well, you said?"

"Yes, thank God. And doing better in his studies."

"Mmm. That's interesting, because I received a letter from his headmaster today. It seems Malik held a rather expensive party for the other boys in his dormitory—all of the other boys."

"Is that against the rules?"

"Apparently. God and the English know why."

Omar had never expressed anything but sternness at Malik's lapses. It amazed Jihan that he now seemed to be taking the boy's side against the school authorities.

"He's missed some classes, too," Omar said, "but I already knew about that. Do you know what he was doing? Calling on merchants. I have two new clients in Cairo thanks to him—good clients. Still just a boy! Naturally I gave him a commission, just as I would anyone. I imagine that's where the money for the party came from. Still, I'll give him a serious talking-to the next time he's home. Generosity is blessed by God, but there's a line between generosity and waste."

Jihan couldn't help smiling at her husband's attempt to disguise pride with gruffness. "His father's son," she said.

"Well . . . I'm sorry to bother you with business matters, my dear. Besides, it was your voice I wanted to hear, not mine."

He was in an exceptionally good mood, Jihan decided. After waiting to be sure he had finished speaking, she said, "God has blessed us in both our children."

"Hm? Amira? Yes, she's growing fast. It won't be long before we'll have to find someone for her."

"Did you know that she speaks French like a little Parisienne?" Jihan asked, turning from a subject she did not want to discuss.

"French? The foreign woman teaches her French?"

"Yes. She's a good teacher, apparently. And very devout. We're lucky to have her, God be thanked."

"French." For a moment Omar's expression darkened. Then he waved a palm dismissively. "So be it. Who knows, she may marry a diplomat. Yet certainly times are changing."

"When I was a girl, I knew a little French."

"Yes," Omar chuckled, "and it's well you've forgotten it, you were so prideful of it, my little Cairene." Again he smiled the shy smile. "Listen, my beauty, I know it's no special occasion, but it occurs to me that I don't often tell you what you've meant to me—as a wife, as the mother of my children. Perhaps this will help make up for the poverty of my words." He held out a small box of kid leather with gilt trim.

"For me? But, my husband, I've done nothing to deserve a gift—"

"Open it."

She did and gasped. It was an emerald necklace, the flawless, flashing green gems set in gold with clusters of small diamonds around them. Even for Omar, it was an extravagance.

"It's too much. Oh, Omar!"

"Not enough, not nearly enough. I love you, Jihan. You will always be my wife."

"But . . . thank you." She kissed him. "May I put it on?"

"By all means. I know how women are. Try it with whatever clothes you wish, to your heart's content. Then leave it on and come to me wearing nothing else."

That night Omar was like a young bridegroom, rising to his desire for her three times. Some women would have let it be known to the others the very next day, but Jihan, for all her liveliness, was too demure for bawdy bragging. Besides, showing off the necklace was more than enough.

Three weeks later, her husband informed her that he had decided to take a second wife, the daughter of one of his cousins.

She should have known, Jihan told herself. She should have suspected the shy smile, the sweet words, the ridiculous gift. After a day of tears and hate, she had a shrieking confrontation with Omar in the hall, demanding a divorce, throwing the necklace in his face. Most men would have summoned a witness and divorced her on the spot, but Omar said with dignity, "I told you that you would always be my wife," and walked away. Only then did she realize the bitter ambiguity of his promise: always his wife, but not his only wife. She ran screaming back to her room.

Bahia retrieved the necklace. "When she is calmer," she told the other women, so that there should be no misunderstanding, "I will return it to her jewelry box. The day will come, God willing, when she will wear it proudly."

She replaced the necklace the day her mistress told her she was pregnant.

Jihan locked on to the idea that her pregnancy would change everything. If she could give Omar another child, certainly another son, he would forget his fantasy of taking another wife. Surely that was his only motivation—to have a woman by whom he could father more children.

She did not know why she had failed to conceive after Amira. Clearly it was God's will, but as for other reasons, she had none. Now, after thirteen futile years, she was again with child. It was a miracle. She staked all her hopes on it. At the same time, she could not forgive Omar for his betrayal. She turned him away, that dreadful night when their daughter walked in on them. Yet even then she was only waiting for the right moment to tell him the wonderful news.

Then, at the end of the third month, came the morning of blood. The midwife had nothing more to say than the obvious; it was a miscarriage. But the bleeding continued, and a doctor was summoned. There were only five in the kingdom, three attending on the royal family. This man, a short, balding Turk, was one of the three. Like all Remali women who needed a full physical examination, she wore a veil while the physician probed her nakedness.

"Madam," he said when it was over, "your last delivery must have been very difficult."

"It was," she answered. "I'm told I could have died."

"I was sure of it. Internally, there is a great deal of damage. Scars. Adhesions. Have you had pain?"

"Some."

"The surprising thing is that you conceived at all. I'm very sorry to say, madam, that you will have no more children. I would even recommend, for your health, that you consult a specialist in Europe, a surgeon. I'll tell your husband this and give him the names of two or three men on whom you can rely absolutely."

"It's kind of you, sir, but I doubt that it will come to that."

"Probably not," the doctor said with a trace of anger. "In al-Remal we are certain that everything follows the will of God, and that is certainly true. But what makes us think that the will of God is not expressed in the healing hand of modern medicine?"

"I don't know, Doctor," Jihan replied. "I'm only a woman."

• • •

That was the beginning. Until then, the dream had been only a coincidence, a diary entry. Now it came more and more often, until it was a constant torment, like the presence of the new wife herself.

Then out of nowhere came the real-life nightmare of Laila Sibai, a girl she regarded almost as a daughter. She dared not protest, dared not say a word against the sentence and execution, not only because her whole world demanded acquiescence but because she was terrified by a mother's intuition that Malik was involved. She thanked God when he left for Europe. Yet now he was truly lost to her, not merely a boy gone off to school, but a man gone out into the world. And soon Amira would be lost as well, lost to a husband who would take her away like a camel bought in the market.

Omar married his cousin's daughter, and then she was pregnant, and then she was Um Yusef.

The Koran said that a man must not have more than one wife unless he could treat them equally. Omar tried to give as much attention to Jihan as to his bride. She disdained him. If she could not be the only one, she would not be anyone.

The concept of depression as a clinical illness did not exist in al-Remal. There was not a single psychiatrist or psychologist in the country. When Jihan's affliction became unbearable, she tried folk remedies, including hashish. Although illegal, the drug was widely available and sometimes used medically; Jihan had seen women take it as an anesthetic and relaxant in childbirth. It did not help her. The initial pleasant dreaminess evaporated when she glanced in the little mirror on her dressing table. Look at the lines! At thirty-two she was old and ugly. She left the room and immediately ran into Um Yusef, who seemed as youthful and beautiful as an angel. Jihan never tried hashish again.

In the end, at the urging of Najla, Amira, and even Um Yusef, she sent for the same doctor who had examined her after the miscarriage. He assured her that this time there was no need for her to disrobe. All she needed was something to help her sleep. He gave her a large bottle of pills, instructing her to take one just before bed, but never more than two in a given day.

Jihan used the pills for three nights and slept like the dead. That was just the trouble: she woke feeling as if she were dead. She knew why: although she could remember nothing from her deep sleep, she was certain that she had had the dream and had dreamed it all the way through, without the escape of waking up. She was dying every night. She put the pills away. From then on, nothing was better, everything was worse. There was no help for her, none on earth.

• • •

"You called me, Mother?" Even though she had watched Jihan decline for months, the way her mother looked still shocked her: unhealthy complexion with no makeup, hair disheveled, clothes smelling of too-long wear.

"Called? Yes, I suppose. Sit, child."

Amira obeyed. For a long time Jihan said nothing, merely stared into space. Then suddenly she blurted, "To fight with a man brings only pain and suffering. Obey your husband and bend to his will. Remember that and you'll be happier than I have been."

"Yes, Mother. Of course."

Another long silence, then: "Times change, as Omar says. The world changes. People say they wish they could turn back the clock. I wish I could turn it forward. I wish I were your age. I wish . . . ah, well."

Her mind wanders so, thought Amira. It was getting worse and worse. Yet what was to be done? No one knew. Bahia was sure that her mistress was beset by jinn, and sometimes Amira herself wondered if there weren't something to the ancient superstitions about these malevolent spirits.

Miss Vanderbeek, as worried as anyone, took a far different tack. There were doctors in Europe who treated illnesses of the mind, which was what this was. One of these specialists should be summoned regardless of the cost. Her explanation of the field of psychology sounded almost as fantastic to Amira as Bahia's pronouncements about jinn, but anything was better than doing nothing. Just yesterday Amira had taken the unprecedented step of bringing the suggestion to her father.

At first Omar had bridled at the idea—or perhaps at his daughter's presuming to advise him. "I've heard of this sort of thing," he grumbled, drawing himself up. "Doesn't it seem to you to go against God, who holds all our fates in his hands?" Then he slumped. "I don't know. I've racked my brain and thought of a thousand things, none of them worth a grain of sand. Perhaps there is no harm in trying what you say. I'll make inquiries."

• • •

"Let me brush your hair, Mother," Amira said now, noticing that Jihan was tugging at the tangled strands.

"What? Yes, that would be nice. Thank you, Najla. I mean Amira."

Amira brushed out the knots, then neatly braided her mother's hair. "There! Much better. Do you want the mirror?"

"No. I know you did well. Look." Jihan opened her hand. "My father gave it to my mother. I don't know why I've never shown it to you."

"Mother! It's beautiful!"

It was a ring, a sapphire, almost midnight blue, set in gold.

"It's like the night sky, isn't it, little princess? Dark and deep. And see, there's the star. Only one. Do you see?"

"Yes, it's beautiful."

"It's for you. You'd have it anyway, of course."

"Mother, what are you talking about? It's yours. You keep it. Many years from now—"

"No. I'm setting the clock forward. It's for you."

Once Amira finally accepted the ring, albeit under protest, Jihan became almost cheerful. She bathed, put on fresh clothes, and allowed Amira to do her makeup. "Make me beautiful again," she said with a little laugh.

"You are beautiful, Mother."

That night, waiting for sleep, Amira had hope for the first time in months that her mother had turned a corner. Still, she wished that Malik were here. She wondered if he had received her letter yet. She pictured him pacing, sleepless with worry, in an apartment in France. Had she been too alarmist? She would write him again tomorrow.

She woke in the night to find Jihan standing by the bed.

"Mother? Is something wrong?"

"No, dearest. I went to refill my water pitcher—there was no sense in troubling Bahia—and looked in on you to say good night. But you were asleep."

"Asleep? Yes. It's late, isn't it?"

"Is it? I suppose it is. Good night, little princess."

"Do you want me to sit with you?"

"No. No, darling. Good night."

"Good night, Mother."

• • •

When she woke again it was still not light, and she thought for a moment that the woman standing over her was Jihan again. But it was Aunt Najla.

"You're awake, child? Oh, my child, a terrible thing has happened. Amira, your mother is dead."

By dawn women were everywhere in the house—aunts, cousins, in-laws, all in black. No one would tell Amira exactly what had happened, but once she heard a voice from the men's section loudly cursing the doctor and his pills, and then she walked into the kitchen to hear Najla saying, "She was wrong to leave her daughter."

"No!" Amira shouted. "She never did anything wrong! What did she do wrong? Tell me!"

The women in black shook their heads and clucked. "A terrible thing for the child," someone muttered, but Amira could tell that they were shocked at the disrespect she had shown her aunt.

"Forgive me," she said, and soothing hands comforted her.

• • •

The women prepared Jihan for burial, which would come that same day, according to custom. They washed the body, wrapped it in white linen. As the cloth was wound, Amira took a last look at her mother's face. In death the sadness and weariness had vanished, and Jihan looked even younger than the young woman she still had been—as beautiful, perhaps, as on that long-ago day at the riding club in Cairo, when a king had desired her.

Suddenly Amira could not hold back the tears. "Wake up, Mama! You can't leave me alone. Please don't leave me alone!"

"Stop it! Stop it, shameless girl!" It was Najla again, pulling on Amira's shoulder, dragging her away. "Don't you know that your mother is in paradise? Do you want your tears to torment her there?"

Amira knew that it was wrong to cry for the dead, but she couldn't seem to stop.

In the hallway there was a hubbub, and Bahia scurried up. "Little miss, your brother . . ."

Behind her was Malik, shock written on his features. "I got your letter," he said. "I took the first plane. I . . ."

He stopped. They both knew that there was nothing to say.

GOOD-BYES

"I should have been here," Malik said, his voice hoarse with sorrow, his eyes brimming with unshed tears. "I could have done something . . . surely there was something . . ."

Amira reached out, laying a gentle hand on his shoulder. "It was my fault, brother, not yours. I was here and you were not. I was the one who saw that she wasn't well. I should have watched over her more carefully. I should have spoken to Father sooner. If she'd seen one of those specialists, one of those doctors who heal the mind . . . If we'd—"

"If, maybe, perhaps . . . what does it matter now? I failed her. It's a son's duty to protect his mother, and I failed." Staring into the velvet darkness of the garden, he drifted into a misery too private to share.

Amira wanted to comfort her brother, but how could she when she was without comfort herself? At least Malik had been able to say good-bye to their mother, for it was he who had led the procession of men who buried her. It was he who uncovered Jihan's face before her body was laid to rest; it was he who would cherish that last precious glimpse of the woman who had given them life. Jihan Badir had loved both her children, Amira knew that, but to the world, she was first and foremost Um Malik.

Amira sighed heavily.

As if he heard what was in her heart, Malik squeezed her hand. "I marked the place," he said softly. "I marked Mother's grave with a stone . . . so you would know it."

Amira was touched, yet also faintly shocked by her brother's gesture. The grave of a good Muslim was always unmarked. "What a strange thing to do. What kind of stone?"

"Just a rock I picked up on the beach at Saint-Tropez." He shrugged. "I'm an idiot, you know. When I saw it in the water I thought for just a heartbeat that it was a ruby. It was that red. I picked it up and saw that it was just a stone, but still, it was pretty. When it dried, of course, it was nothing, but by then I had decided it was lucky. So I kept it."

"You left it there for luck . . . for Mama?" Amira found this paganistic idea disconcerting.

"I don't know. Maybe. Mama didn't have the luck she deserved. Who knows? Anyway, as long as it's there, you'll know where she is. Maybe then you'll forgive me for being a man," he said with a gentle smile.

Startled by his half-serious observation, Amira protested: "But there's nothing to forgive, not with you." She flushed with guilt, remembering just how recently she'd resented Malik for having privileges denied to her. "Anyway, it isn't you I get angry with. It's just the way things are."

Malik nodded gravely, as if her thoughts and feelings were as important as his.

"So now you're without your lucky piece."

He smiled again. "I've decided that I've got more luck than anyone needs. Either that or I don't need luck. Things are going well for me, little sister. I wrote you that I'd moved up in the organization. I've moved up again since then. But I've made some deals on my own, too. Complicated stuff, no need to go into the details. I try not to conflict with my duty to dear old Onassis—not too flagrantly, at least. But I don't think I'll need to be with him much longer." He paused. "Remember what I told you, Amira? If you ever need my help, I'll be there."

Amira nodded. She knew Malik meant what he said, but what kind of help would she need, living as she did, having so little to do with the outside world? "And you, brother, will you be choosing a wife soon, someone to help you with Laila?"

"Not likely," Malik said ruefully. "When it's time to send Salima home, I'll hire the best nanny money can buy for my daughter. But as for me, well, there's no one woman in my life just now. Many more than one, to put it another way."

Amira averted her eyes. It was one thing to know that Malik had loved Laila in that intimate way; it was quite another to imagine her brother with legions of faceless foreign women.

"Don't worry about me, little sister. Life is good in France. It's not like here. Oh, people are much alike everywhere. All the same, it's freer there. Easier. You don't have to worry every time you turn around whether you're committing a sin in someone's eyes." His mouth took a bitter little twist. "I think I've seen real sin. You have, too. You were there." A long pause. "It's a different thing to be a woman in France. Girls there can go to university, become whatever they want. Professors. Lawyers. Doctors. Maybe . . . maybe you should come over sometime. If you stay here . . . well, look at Mother's life."

Amira had thought about it, daydreamed about it in a what-if sort of way. But to actually leave al-Remal . . . her imagination had not yet made that leap.

* * *

Sleep was fitful as Amira awaited the sun. When at last it came, she dressed quickly and slipped out of the house. If her father knew what she was doing, he would be furious. But in her desolation Amira didn't weigh the risk. Everyone she cared for was gone, everyone except Malik, who would soon be leaving.

Wrapping her veil tightly around her, she walked the three miles to the mosque. Eyes cast downward, she searched.

Where was it, the marker her brother had left? Perhaps someone had picked it up . . . perhaps the sand had covered it over during the night. Frantically she searched, pacing forward and back. There, at last, the oxblood-colored stone Malik had described, a solitary jewel against a bed of sand.

Amira dropped to her knees, her lips moving in silent prayer. Surrounded by silence and stillness, Amira knew she was not alone. She felt her mother's love, sensed her mother's heart reaching out to her, from beyond the grave.

She looked to the sky—for so strong a feeling there should be a sign, a fire in the heavens. But there was only the blinding sun. She whispered good-bye, drew her veil, and began the long walk home.

ALONE

"Wake up, laziness, wake up. Are you a queen in a palace that you sleep until noon?"

Amira rubbed her eyes and stretched, glancing at her bedside clock. "But Auntie Najla, it's only half past eight, and I was up very late studying for my examination . . ."

"Only half past eight? Only? Allah, Amira, a good wife could prepare food for an army before nine o'clock—and see to her husband and children as well. Examination indeed! When I suggested to your father that some education would make you a better wife, I didn't expect you to neglect the really important elements of a woman's life. Or do you think, my high-and-mighty miss, that the diploma you crave will make you better than the good wives of al-Remal? More important than the other women of this house?"

Amira bit back a sharp retort. No, she didn't think she was better than the other women of the house. But she was different; she felt that every day of her life—and never more so than since Jihan had died. The books she devoured, the home study courses she took, the secret yearnings she harbored, all these set her apart. Yet what was the point of trying to explain herself? Anything she said would be taken as disrespect and reported to her father. All in the name of teaching her to be a good and modest woman, of course.

"Well, then," Najla went on, apparently appeased by Amira's silence, "hurry up and get dressed. Your father mentioned he would enjoy a good *saleeq*—yes, that's what he specified—and if we don't hurry, Allah only knows what will be left in the market."

Only half listening, Amira pulled out of bed, slipping a cotton robe over her nightgown as she moved towards the bathroom. She didn't feel comfortable showing herself to either Aunt Najla or Aunt Shams. Maybe it was because they were so shapeless and—in spite of their preoccupation with other people's sexuality—sexless.

To Amira, in their dark, cheerless clothes, they resembled the witches in the illustrated *Macbeth* she had stayed up most of the night to finish. Sometimes she felt sorry for her aunts—living here, in her father's house, this was all they would ever have or hope to have. But did they have to make her life so uncomfortable—spying, prying, telling tales on her just to curry favor with him?

Bending over the marble bathroom sink, she brushed her teeth and scrubbed her face vigorously with the perfumed French soap Malik had sent—a fragrant reminder of the wonderful world that existed outside al-Remal.

"*Yallah*, *yallah*, hurry, hurry, Amira," Aunt Najla called out. "All the best cuts of meat will be sold by the time you rouse yourself—and we'll have nothing left but gristle."

Amira hurried. If she did everything her aunt asked now, perhaps she would be left in peace later, so she might study with Miss Vanderbeek, who now acted as her personal tutor. The time they shared was like a magic carpet that transported Amira to other places and other times. To eighteenth-century Russia, where a great queen named Catherine ruled with as much power and ferocity as any man. To nineteenth-century France, where a woman took the name of George Sand, wrote provocative novels, and lived openly with the composer Chopin—a man who was not her husband. To England, where Jane Austen, who had been almost as cloistered as Amira, exquisitely dissected the society she lived in.

"Never have I had a more eager student," Miss Vanderbeek said approvingly.

Yet now that the coveted diploma was within reach, Amira felt a growing sadness. What meaning would a piece of paper have to someone like her? She could dream about Paris, but the only journeys she could make were to the souk. Or to the homes of other cloistered women.

These were the boundaries of her life. She thought of Malik, wondering what his day would be like, trying to imagine a life as rich and varied as hers was limited.

She slipped on a favorite cream-colored linen dress, then tried on her new gold earrings, a gift from Um Yusef on Amira's sixteenth birthday. But who of any consequence would see—or care—whether she looked pretty or not? With everyone she loved dead or far away, it seemed as if all the warmth and pleasure had gone from this house. Now there was just fussy Aunt Najla and picky Aunt Shams.

A few minutes later, wrapped in identical black *abeyya* and veils, Amira and her aunt climbed into Omar's black Bentley, one of a collection of expensive foreign cars that afforded him both pleasure and prestige.

In spite of the heat, Aunt Najla settled into the fine leather upholstery with a sigh of contentment. Shopping was a highlight of her aunt's day, Amira knew, for she could remember when only men and servants ventured into the market. But in keeping with his concessions to modernization,

Omar allowed the women under his protection to shop outside the home—as long as they were driven by a man, according to law.

Along the single-lane road, the powerful car moved slowly, its progress retarded by an old man atop an aged donkey. The driver honked. When both his vehicle and his impatience were ignored, he sighed deeply, lit a cigarette, and resigned himself to the will of the Almighty.

In time, car and passengers reached the open market, which consisted of a dozen rickety wooden stalls wreathed in a cloud of dust.

The aroma of fresh fruit intermingled with the metallic odor of fresh-killed lamb. "Buy my melons, as sweet as sugar," called the fruit seller. "Pistachios fit for a king," beckoned the nut vendor. "Not a piaster more if my life depended on it," shouted a customer in the last throes of bargaining.

Aunt Najla led the way to the butcher, Abu Taif, a lean, stringy fellow wearing a bloodstained apron over his *thobe*. Standing beside the dozen or so lamb carcasses that hung in front of his stall, he bowed and smiled, showing the two gold teeth that reflected his prosperity.

Wordlessly nodding a greeting, Aunt Najla went to work, poking and probing and sniffing one leg of lamb after another.

"Madam, I implore you," Abu Taif pleaded, "all the meat is excellent and fresh, tender and without blemish. Choose any piece, without looking, and I swear on my honor it will please you."

Aunt Najla ignored both pleas and promises, continuing her inspection for another moment or two. Then she pointed to her choice: "Three kilos. For *saleeq*, so leave the meat on the bone."

"At your service, madam." The butcher bowed again, quickly producing a cleaver and two saber-sharp knives. Wiping them ceremoniously on his apron, he went to work, first hacking away the choice leg portion from the lamb, then weighing it. After trimming the fat, Abu Taif cut the meat into fist-sized chunks and wrapped it in coarse brown paper. He noted the purchase in his smudged and stained ledger (Omar would pay the account at the end of the month) and handed the package to Aunt Najla with a flourish.

Next door, at the greengrocer's stall, she quickly selected a dozen tomatoes bursting with juice, a large bunch of parsley, potatoes, onions, and three heads of lettuce.

The two women hurried past the coffeehouse, where old men lounged, sipping dark, thick coffee flavored with cardamom, listening to the plaintive melodies of Um Kalthoum. Here and there, dark shapes much like Amira and her aunt darted in and out of stalls, hurrying about their business lest they be thought immodest.

The next stop was the spice shop in the covered arcade. As Amira inhaled the heady bouquet of cumin and cinnamon and allspice and nutmeg and coriander, her aunt fired off her order: "Two hundred grams of allspice. Some *hab hilu* and some dried mint. Make sure it's good, mind you. None of that flavorless stuff with the bugs in it that you gave me last time."

"I humbly beg your pardon, madam," said the shopkeeper, Abu Tarek, with elaborate courtesy. "I assure you that will never happen again." He turned and smiled at Amira, whom he'd known since she was a little girl, taking a liberty he would soon take no more.

Once served, the women moved on to Hafiz's perfumery in the covered arcade. The air here was rich with essences and oils from Damascus and Teheran and Baghdad—ingredients old Hafiz could blend in a thousand and one combinations. His wife, Fadila, known for her skills in casting horoscopes and reading the stars (a talent that was strictly forbidden yet eagerly sought), often acted as adviser to the shop's clientele; discreetly, she would suggest jasmine oil to please a beloved, or perhaps a rose fragrance to revive a husband's waning ardor.

Aunt Najla ordered her usual gardenia and heliotrope blend. Though there was no beloved to savor it, the powerful fragrance did serve to signal her impending arrival in a room.

The last stop was the fabric store, where bolts of Damascene silk and Belgian lace were displayed in every color and hue. Here, too, Aunt Najla would be faithful to what she always wore: dark blue with occasional accents of white lace. No sooner had they entered the shop than the proprietor snapped his fingers, summoning one of the legion of small boys who ran errands for a piaster or two. Coffee was ordered, sweetened tea for Amira. As Aunt Najla settled into a deeply cushioned chair, the proprietor began, without being told, to unfurl bolt after bolt of navy blue fabric: silk, chiffon, crepe de chine, and taffeta, for linings that rustled.

Suddenly Amira felt as if all the air had left the room. She tried to breathe deeply, but the feeling grew stronger, till she was forced to flee the tiny shop. Closing her eyes, she leaned against the stall, trying to imagine the dark, cool vastness of the desert at night. She stood there for a long time until Aunt Najla came outside and shook her shoulder. "What's wrong, niece? Is it your time of the month? That's no excuse for acting peculiar, you know. A loving family will forgive you such nonsense, but a husband, well, a husband expects his home to be run in an orderly and normal fashion. Do you understand?"

Amira nodded. She understood very well what a husband expected. Hadn't she seen the example of her own father after her mother's death? After a mere few weeks of mournful demeanor, his life went on as usual. To Amira, the heart had gone out of their home. Yet Omar seemed scarcely to notice, inspecting his freshly trimmed beard each morning in the same self-satisfied way, enjoying his evening meal to the fullest, rolling the last bit of pita to mop his plate, just as he always did.

"Are we going home now?" Amira asked, hoping perhaps to salvage some of this day.

"Certainly not," Aunt Najla replied brusquely. "I promised Shaikha Nazli I would stop by. She hasn't been feeling well—this last pregnancy, you know—and I promised I would give her some of the salts my mother used to make, to reduce swelling in the legs."

Amira groaned inwardly. She had nothing against Shaikha Nazli, a statuesque redhead born in Lebanon and married now to al-Remal's oil minister. But a visit to her large and elaborate palace was never brief. Today would be no exception.

"*Ahlan wa sahlan,*" the Shaikha enthused as the two women were escorted into her marble drawing room by a Pakistani servant. "Please, make yourselves comfortable. My home is yours."

Comfort was out of the question, Amira reflected, for the room, like the Shaikha herself, was clad entirely in ornate French reproductions, heavily gilded and designed more to impress than to enjoy. Still, Amira smiled politely and perched dutifully at the edge of a Louis something-or-other chair.

Minutes later a pair of servants in livery—the only servants in al-Remal so clad—entered the room. They offered coffee, tea, cold fruit drinks, and pastry, followed by a smoking brazier that burned sandalwood. Amira took a fruit juice because to refuse would have been impolite. And when the brazier was passed to her, she wafted the scented smoke under her arms and around her body, to refresh and deodorize, as was the custom of the desert.

"I brought the salts for your legs, dear Nazli," Aunt Najla said, proffering a large glass jar. "But I do hope you're feeling better."

"I am indeed, Allah be praised. And my dear husband has been so kind, so thoughtful. When he was in London last week—an important conference, you know—he brought back such beautiful gifts, I actually wept. And do you know what he said? He said that all his wealth could not begin to provide the gifts I deserved."

"Thanks be to Allah for such devotion," Aunt Najla intoned.

"Would you like to see my gifts?" the Shaikha asked hopefully, much as a child would.

"Certainly, dear. We rejoice in your pleasure—don't we, Amira?"

"Yes, yes, of course." Amira sat up at attention, knowing she would pay later for any lapse in manners.

As soon as the Shaikha swept out of the room in a swirl of silk and gold, Aunt Najla began to cluck sympathetically. "Poor woman. She's walking at the edge of a precipice, and everyone knows it."

"But why, Auntie? She seems happy enough."

"Happy? Don't be ridiculous. She's trying to put a good face on her situation—as any decent woman would—but if Allah in his wisdom sends a daughter instead of a son, well, then it's certain there will be a third wife, as everyone knows."

Of course. Though the Shaikha's fair complexion and flaming hair were considered uncommonly beautiful here, she had produced, in quick succession, four daughters—much to the delight of the oil minister's first wife, who had borne him three sons. If there were to be yet a third wife, poor Nazli would certainly lose face and social standing.

As the Shaikha swept into the room once more, she held out her arm, displaying a gold Patek-Philippe watch studded with diamonds and emeralds. "Isn't it lovely?"

"Breathtaking," Najla agreed. "And it suits you so well."

"It's beautiful," Amira chimed in.

"And see what else my dear husband brought home," Nazli said, indicating a stack of dinner plates being carried by a servant. "Limoges, service for fifty. In the pattern I had admired when we visited France on our honeymoon. He remembered . . . seven years and he remembered," she said, her voice wistful and tender.

Najla shot her niece a meaningful look, even as she went on to compliment the oil minister's taste and his thoughtfulness. "May Allah grant you a son," she murmured under her breath.

• • •

Since Omar had announced his intention to lunch with a business acquaintance, the women of the house dined lightly: *hummus* with pita bread, a selection of cheeses and olives, a salad garnished with mint and lemon and olive oil, a bit of leftover *kibbe.*

As soon as the meal was finished, preparations for the next began. With her aunt standing by to supervise and instruct, Amira rinsed the lamb chunks. "Put them in the bottom of the pot," Aunt Najla instructed. "No, not that one, the big one. Good. Now get the rosemary leaves and two cinnamon sticks."

"I know," Amira said, as she quickly added some of the sweet spice called *hab hilu*, pepper, a piece of *mistika*, and a piece of the lichen called *shaiba*. All this was covered with cold water and set on the big English stove to simmer.

Two hours later, after her afternoon nap, Amira removed the lamb from the pot, strained the stock, and added water, to make eight cups. She measured two cups of rice into the stock and set the pot back on the stove.

"Cook it slowly now," Aunt Najla admonished. "About forty-five minutes or so. You don't want the rice to stick."

"Yes, Auntie." Amira had seen her mother prepare the dish dozens of times, but it was best to humor her aunt. When the stock was all absorbed, she added two cups of milk and continued the cooking until the rice was soggy. When Amira heard Omar enter the house, she added some salt and let the mixture cook for a few more minutes. Finally she turned the mixture out onto a large platter, dotted it with pats of butter and arranged the cooked meat on top.

• • •

"Good," Omar said with a contented sigh, "very good indeed."

Najla sighed, too, as if a verdict of utmost importance had been rendered. Never mind that it was part of a daily ritual; the man of the house must be satisfied in every way, and no woman could afford to be complacent when it came to his care and feeding.

"And you, my daughter, did your hand sweeten this delectable dinner?" Omar asked, turning to Amira.

Now this was a surprise, for since her mother's death Amira's relationship with her father had become distant at best. "Yes, Father," she replied, casting her eyes downward onto her plate, not sure whether her heart should resent or accept the compliment.

"Excellent, excellent." Omar smiled benevolently. But when he patted the hand of his young wife, Amira's feelings hardened against him.

"Well, then," he said, clearing his throat to indicate the importance of what would soon pass his lips. "It's time to share my good news. Today I have spoken with no less a personage than His Royal Majesty, our beloved king."

There were murmurs of appreciation at this news, though in fact every subject in the kingdom—not just influential ones like Omar—had access to the ruler at the weekly *majlis*, where grievances and requests were heard all day long.

"And," Omar continued, "His Royal Majesty has honored my house. It has been decided that his son, Prince Ali al-Rashad, will be married to Amira."

The women began ululating, a sound of joy and celebration. Omar smiled. "Though I refrained from boasting, His Majesty was favorably impressed with Amira's education. He graciously said that my daughter would be a great asset to his house and to the kingdom."

Amira said nothing. She had known, ever since she was a little girl, that this day was coming. But now that it was here, she didn't know how she felt. To leave her father's house—hadn't she dreamed of that? To become a princess, a member of al-Remal's ruling house—wasn't that every young woman's dream? How Laila would have loved this, she thought with a twinge of sadness.

"Well, daughter," said Omar, "to be modest and quiet is admirable. But at a moment like this, a smile of happiness would be more than appropriate. And perhaps a prayer of thanks that Allah has provided so well for your future?"

"Yes, Father, I do give thanks to Allah. And to you," she added with sincerity, knowing that it was in Omar's power to marry her to anyone. Yet he had chosen for her a prince, well known and well loved. Everyone knew of Prince Ali. He was a pilot, a hero of al-Remal. He flew the kingdom's newest planes, he soared in the skies like a falcon. Life with him would have to be better than life at home—wouldn't it?

Part Four

ALI

"The foreign dressmakers are here," Bahia announced stolidly—as if a visit from the French couturiere Madame Grès were an everyday occurrence. "Your aunts wish you to come down at once."

Amira snapped shut her copy of *Madame Bovary* and looked imploringly at Miss Vanderbeek. "We'll have to stop now. I don't really want to, but . . . well, you know . . ."

"I do know," the Dutch woman said with a smile. "Now that you have your diploma, French literature just can't compete with French couture."

"But that's not so," Amira protested. "I want to read everything, to understand about people who are different from people here in al-Remal. I want to know what they think and how they feel. But there's been so little time, what with shopping and visits and getting ready for the wedding." Then, realizing she was being teased, she smiled, too. "You do understand."

Miss Vanderbeek nodded. "In truth, you don't really need me anymore, Amira. You're as fluent in French as I am, and your English is quite good, too. You have your reading lists—and the intelligence you were born with, *ma shallah*. There's not much more I can teach you. If you were going on to university . . ." She trailed off, for she had broached this subject before, urging her pupil to continue her studies, if only by correspondence.

"I want to, I truly do, but I can't make that decision without my husband's consent."

"I know," Miss Vanderbeek sighed. "I know."

There was a long moment of silence.

"I suppose we must be saying good-bye, if not today, then very soon . . ."

Amira's eyes filled with tears. For so long the beautiful blond nanny had been her window into the world outside al-Remal, the one who described its colors and textures and smells. She was the one who pushed Amira to read beyond the printed words, to ask questions and not always be satisfied with easy answers. "I don't want to say good-bye," Amira said, her voice catching in her throat.

"I know."

"I wish . . . oh, I wish you could come to live with me in the palace."

"Perhaps one day I'll come to teach your children."

Amira was not cheered. Miss Vanderbeek was one of the best parts of her own childhood, and somehow she did not want to give her up, not even to a child that she might bear. Tears slipped from her eyes and onto her dress.

The Dutch woman held out her arms, and as Amira shared her embrace, she thought once again that everyone she loved seemed to go away.

• • •

Downstairs, in the main salon, Amira's aunts were whirling like dervishes, trying with a flurry of activity to hide the fact that they didn't quite know how to entertain the foreigners. At their bidding, a rapid parade of refreshments appeared. In lieu of Coca-Cola, which, along with many other American products, was on the Arab boycott list, they offered pomegranate juice mixed with water, followed by roasted chick peas, candied almonds, salted pistachios, and chewy Turkish delight.

As soon as Amira appeared, she was thrust at the French contingent—headed by no less a personage than Madame Grès herself. "You honor our house, madame," Amira said. "I hope your trip here was a pleasant one?"

"Most pleasant, ma'mselle," the designer replied.

"And your accommodations, are they comfortable?"

"Very comfortable. Thankfully, the Intercontinental has strong air-conditioning and a large swimming pool. My staff made good use of both as soon as we arrived last night."

"I'm sorry we have no air-conditioning here, Madame Grès, but my father believes it to be unhealthy."

"*Ça va*, ma'mselle. Please don't concern yourself. Now if you are ready, I would like to present the group of wedding dresses I have selected for your consideration."

The large high-ceilinged room had been cleared, except for a row of chairs and some small marble tables. Amira seated herself on an upholstered armchair; her aunts positioned themselves on either side. Flanked by her personal assistant and two female fitters, Madame Grès stood at the doorway to the dining room, which, for the moment, was serving as an informal changing room for the three models who'd accompanied her.

At a signal from her, the assistant turned on a cassette player, and the strains of Mozart's chamber music filled the room. A moment later, the models appeared, wearing fairy-tale gowns of silk and satin and lace.

Strange, Amira thought, as she watched the fashion show that had been created for her alone. Grès was a name she had often read in magazines, a world apart from al-Remal. Now that world had come here, to her, and all because she was marrying Ali al-Rashad. And this was just the beginning. Perhaps marriage would be more than just an escape from her father's house. Perhaps it could be wonderful, after all, just as poor Laila had once imagined.

Amira studied the gowns thoughtfully, nodding dutifully as her aunts made comments on this one and that. When she pointed to the simplest of all—a princess style in creamy white silk, its bodice delicately embroidered with seed pearls—the designer murmured her approval. "A fine choice, ma'mselle—my personal favorite."

Next the models began showing selections for Amira's trousseau: fashionable suits, stylish dresses, and chic, daring evening gowns. Though she expected to be veiled and covered for the rest of her life, Amira would wear these beautiful things for her husband. Her prince.

"The white linen suit," she murmured, as a tall, willowy model paraded before her. The designer's assistant noted her choice.

"That dress," Amira said, indicating a flame-colored silk, "and the emerald green gown."

"The Empire style will suit you, ma'mselle," the designer said. "I think you might also like the white strapless gown that's coming out next."

"I'm sure it's lovely," Amira said, "but I don't think I need any more gowns."

The designer laughed. "Your fiancé disagrees, ma'mselle. He feels you should choose at least a dozen gowns. And suits and dresses as well."

I already have so much, Amira thought, but not wanting to offend either Madame Grès or Prince Ali, she complied.

When the fashion show was over, she thanked the designer for bringing such lovely things and then adjourned to her bedroom with two fitters. As an accommodation to the royal house of al-Remal, the fitting process, which was normally complicated and time-consuming, would be accelerated.

As the women took her measurements, Amira gazed at the ever-growing trousseau that spilled out of her closet and filled every available surface: handmade Italian shoes in a rainbow of colors; silk lingerie from Hong Kong, most pieces in virginal white but a few nightgowns in soft shades of apricot and peach; richly embroidered sheets and pillowcases of Egyptian cotton, ordered by her aunts so Amira would not go to her husband's house empty-handed. Small chance of that, she thought, not with the abundance of lavish wedding gifts accumulating in the library—all destined to be part of her new life as a married woman.

How curious a woman's life was, Amira reflected. Ever since Jihan died, she might as well have been invisible in this house; now it was as if the world revolved around her. It was a feeling she didn't fully trust. Laila had had such a moment—and Jihan, too. Perhaps most of the women of al-Remal had felt like this when they were wed. And then they had become invisible once again.

Perhaps that wouldn't happen to her, Amira thought hopefully. Her prince had been educated in Switzerland and England. He couldn't be like her father or the man Laila had married. Perhaps he would be like the men in the novels she read, men who adored their wives—and treasured them in ways she'd not yet seen in al-Remal.

• • •

By the time the Grès entourage left, it was time to dress for tea. Not just any tea—for today Amira's aunts would receive Prince Ali's mother and sisters. Today Amira would meet her in-laws for the first time.

She showered hastily, then scrubbed her face with a rough washcloth, bringing a smudge of color to her cheeks. Carefully she brushed her thick, dark hair to a glossy sheen. Should she wear it loose, in a flattering cascade of waves that reached her shoulders? Or pulled back in a more modest but less flattering chignon?

She could almost hear one of Aunt Najla's favorite sayings: "Eat what you please but wear what pleases others." Amira pinned her hair back and chose a dress that would surely please her aunts: a demure navy blue silk with a crisp white collar. *I look like a schoolgirl*, she thought. *That should please my family—and perhaps Ali's, too.*

• • •

Faiza al-Rashad, known as Um Ahmad in the royal court, swept into the Badir house as if she owned it. Amira's aunts fluttered around the great lady, murmuring politenesses as they bowed respectfully before her.

With great deference, the king's ranking wife, followed by her two daughters, Munira and Zeinab, was shown into the large salon. A servant stood by as she shed her veil and robe, revealing a gray silk Lanvin suit. She was seated in the largest, most comfortable armchair, a footstool placed beneath her Ferragamo-shod feet.

A moment later, Amira presented herself to Faiza. "God's peace be with you, honored Mother," she said, lowering her eyes decorously as she kissed the older woman's hand.

"And with you, my child." Faiza tilted Amira's face upward and studied it for a long moment. She nodded, as if satisfied with what she saw.

With a slight gesture of her hand, she summoned her older daughter, Munira, who produced a velvet case from her Hermes shoulder bag. "May God's happiness be with you always," Faiza said, presenting the case to Amira. "Wear this on your wedding day with our blessing." She opened the box, which contained a magnificent, diamond-studded platinum tiara.

Amira's breath caught in her throat. She had never seen gems like this before, and for the first time she understood that the life she would lead as a princess was far, far beyond the comfort she had known in her father's house.

"Your blessing is more precious than diamonds. I pray I'm worthy of your generosity."

Faiza nodded her approval of Amira's words. As the aunts oohed and aahed over the gift, pots of mint-flavored tea appeared, along with platters of sweets, the product of hours of baking. First came the *kanafi*, a shredded wheat pastry stuffed with sweetened cream and drizzled with honey. This was followed by *ma'amul*, a rich shortbread filled with dates and nuts, and baklava, made of phyllo dough and pistachios, sweetened with sugar and rosewater syrup.

Amira took a fine porcelain plate from the sideboard, filled it with pastries, and offered it to Faiza, who acknowledged the gesture with a slight inclination of her head.

"Please try the *kanafi*," Aunt Najla urged. "Amira made it herself."

Faiza took a bite, chewed it carefully, then swallowed. "Very nice," she pronounced, "though the syrup could use a bit more rosewater."

Encouraged by this demi-compliment, Najla continued: "The French dressmakers say Amira has a perfect figure. She will look like an angel in her wedding dress."

Faiza's eyes flicked over her two daughters, neither of whom could merit such a compliment. "Physical beauty can be a blessing—or a curse, especially if it leads to vanity."

Aunt Najla retreated.

"My Ali has just been appointed minister of culture," Faiza announced proudly—though in fact the appointment had been made by his own father.

The women murmured their appreciation of this honor.

"It's a position of great responsibility and respect. My Ali will supervise the completion of our new cultural museum. And he will travel all over the world, to England and France and Italy, perhaps even America, to show what is best of al-Remal."

Amira was dazzled. England and France and Italy—storybook countries rich with delights she could only imagine. Perhaps the prince would take her with him. Perhaps they might one day visit Malik and see all the glorious places she'd been reading about for so many years.

"His wife will have to set the highest standard for herself," Faiza continued. "She will have to be chaste and unassuming—and above all, obedient and modest."

Amira lowered her eyes. Was the woman a mind reader, too? Did she suspect Amira's fantasies were not of modesty or obedience, but of adventure? Knowing all too well how powerful a mother-in-law could be—in al-Remal, after all, at least half of the married men still lunched regularly with their mothers—she resolved to be careful to keep out of Faiza's way as much as possible, much as she had tried to do with her aunts.

While Aunt Najla and Aunt Shams engaged Faiza in polite small talk, Amira studied Ali's sisters. Zeinab, who was almost as wide as she was tall, appeared to be rather simple, even by prevailing standards of womanhood. Elaborately coiffed and heavily made up, she wore a flowered dress that emphasized her formidable arms and massive thighs.

With heartfelt sighs of appreciation, Zeinab tucked into the pastries. When she ordered Bahia to refill her plate a second time, her sister Munira asked dryly, "What happened to your latest diet regimen, Zeinab? Only this morning you vowed not to eat more than one sweet a day."

"I did, I truly did." Zeinab giggled. "I know I should be stronger, but I just can't resist such delicious pastries."

"Just pastries? It seems to me, dear sister, that all food is irresistible to you—even after you've consumed enough of it to satisfy two or three women with less . . . hearty appetites."

Faiza shot Munira a warning look, but Zeinab just rolled her eyes and giggled again. "Everything you say is true, alas. But what can I do when Allah clearly intended for me to be plump? I can only be grateful that in his infinite wisdom, the Almighty blessed me with a husband who prefers a well-rounded woman to one who is bony."

"As you say, you are indeed blessed," replied Munira, who, though not unattractive, was both bony and husbandless.

Of Ali's two sisters, it was she who interested Amira more, for although Munira had studied only with palace tutors, it was said she could quote at will from the poetry of Kahlil Gibran, the work of historian Ibn Khaldun, or the writings of the fourteenth-century traveler, Ibn Battutah. These examples of learning met with the king's approval, but Amira's aunts said that Munira often overstepped, citing the works of such Egyptian feminists as Huda al-Sharawi. "The king pretends not to hear such nonsense," Najla had said, "so if the girl makes any subversive speeches, smile and say nothing."

Amira waited eagerly, hoping to hear something "subversive." But after jibing at her sister, Munira subsided, half-smiling as she took in the conversation around her, appraising Amira with her eyes as she expressed her good wishes.

• • •

When the al-Rashad women left, Amira wanted nothing more than to go to bed and dream about the future, but her aunts, still brimming with nervous energy, began dissecting the royals.

"She gives herself a great many airs, our queen," said Shams, "especially when you consider that she came from a very poor desert tribe."

"With nothing more than her beauty for a dowry," Najla chimed in.

"But it's not her beauty that is the source of her power."

"What do you mean?" Najla asked.

Shams put a finger to her lips, as if swearing her sister to secrecy. "Well, you know that our king has a prodigious sexual appetite . . ."

"That's well known throughout the kingdom. I doubt that even he knows how many concubines he has—or how many children."

"What is not so well known," Shams said, with a satisfied smile, "is that the queen herself selects these women."

"No . . . you don't mean to tell me . . ."

"I have it on very good authority. Therefore, it is the queen who controls all who live within the royal *hareem*."

There was a moment of silence. Then Shams moved on. "A bitter young woman, that Munira. Already past her twentieth birthday and without a husband."

"And yet it's well known that the king favors her above all his daughters. He has even been heard to say that she was more than a daughter."

"But certainly less than a son," Shams insisted.

"That goes without saying."

• • •

Where once Amira's days seemed to drag on interminably, they now flew by. The marriage contract, the *katb kitab*, was signed, first by Omar and the king, next by Ali—and last by Amira. But there would be no consummation until the *doukhla*, the party at the royal palace.

Then it seemed as if all of al-Remal came to call, to offer good wishes, to take a close look at the young woman who would marry the ruler's second son. To bring gifts, to take her measure as a soon-to-be princess, and to speculate on how her life in the royal palace would be.

But the best gift of all came just two days before the *doukhla*. As Amira sat in the garden, enjoying the cool breeze that stirred after sunset, a familiar voice called out: "Daydreaming, little sister? I would have thought our aunts would have a million tasks and rituals to keep you busy."

"Malik!" With one fluid movement, she rose from her seat and threw herself into his arms. And then, to her great surprise, she began to weep.

"Amira, what's wrong? Amira, you must tell me. Are you unhappy about this marriage? Because if you are, I'll talk to Father at once. Prince or no prince—"

"No, no," she protested, tears now yielding to laughter. "I'm not unhappy, at least not about the marriage. It's just that seeing you here, now, it stirs up all kinds of feelings."

"I know," he said softly, stroking her hair. "I don't think I'll ever be in this garden without remembering, without wondering . . ."

Wiping the tears from her face, Amira looked up at her brother. He seemed different, yet the same. The lines of his face were harder, yet his dark eyes were filled with the same love she had always seen there.

"So you are happy, then?"

"Yes, brother, yes, of course. I'm about to be married. To a prince. Isn't that enough to make any woman happy?"

"That's a question, not an answer. And you, my dear, are not just any woman. You're my sister and I will personally skewer any man who fails to—"

Amira squeezed his hand. "I know, but I am all right. Truly. I want to be married."

"And I want this marriage to be everything you desire. I need to know that your life is rich with happiness . . . enough for both of us, Amira."

"But surely you have a good life, Malik. Your daughter must be a source of great joy."

"I adore her," he said fiercely. "More each day."

"And your letters are filled with comings and goings."

"Indeed," he laughed. "I'm in perpetual motion, buying and selling and trading, all over the world, little sister. As the Americans say, I have my fingers in a great many pies."

"And what about the rest? When will you take a bride?"

"When I meet someone who touches me as Laila did. Meanwhile, I have acquired a splendid new apartment in Paris. And a new French nanny for Laila." He dug into his pocket and produced a photograph of a chubby little girl laughing as she played with an enormous and expensive-looking doll.

"She's beautiful," Amira said, longing to see her niece, to hold and kiss her.

"One day soon, little sister, one day I'll find a way for us to be together, as a real family should."

• • •

Amira woke at dawn and said her prayer. She slipped into an almond-scented bath prepared by Bahia, who vigorously exfoliated her skin with a loofah, then scrubbed it with French soap. "And now your beautiful hair," the servant said, applying the shampoos that had been imported from America, but using a final rinse of chamomile, just as she had done for Jihan.

Wrapping herself in a thick terry-cloth towel, Amira climbed out of the big marble tub and stretched out on a nearby chaise lounge. Bahia disappeared for a moment, returning with a saucepan filled with a taffy-like substance made of cooked sugar water. Scooping out a ball of this homemade depilatory with her fingers, she began spreading it over Amira's body—her legs, her arms, under her arms, her pubic area. "Your skin will be so smooth, so beautiful, like a baby's skin," Bahia crooned, as she yanked the first strip, tearing with it a clump of hair from the roots.

"Ouch, ouch!" Amira cried out. "That hurts, Bahia, that really hurts!"

"Of course it hurts, young miss. What did you imagine marriage would be?" Bahia smiled, as if to indicate she was joking, then said gently: "Your husband will prefer you this way, and you must learn to please him." When Amira's skin was finally as hairless as Bahia's efforts could make it, the servant massaged Amira with a soothing aloe vera lotion and left her to rest.

• • •

The vision in the mirror was not like any Amira had seen before. In the brightness of the afternoon, with the sun streaming over her shoulder, she looked like a queen—no, an empress. On her hair, which had been gathered into an intricate topknot, she wore her new diamond tiara. From it cascaded a veil of handmade lace that spilled over her shoulders and onto the creamy white richness of her magnificent gown.

Now, discreetly covered by a veil of gray silk, she was on her way to the palace. Accompanied by her father and her aunts, she rode in Omar's prize limousine, a vintage Mercedes. Today he wore his finest *thobe*, a white robe woven of finest Egyptian cotton; over it, a beige linen *bisht* edged in gold. Her aunts, resplendent in silk and lace, were so jeweled and adorned they were almost unrecognizable.

Like a queen, Amira waved to the well-wishers who lined the streets, calling out congratulations and prayers for health and happiness. In al-Remal, celebrations for this wedding had begun at dawn, when, by order of the two fathers, hundreds of sheep had been killed and distributed to the poor.

Though Amira had seen the palace many times before, today it was like a fantasy garden drenched in flowers—tens of thousands of blooms flown in from Holland at dawn. Baskets of tulips, hyacinths, lilies, and gladioli lined every room and corridor; garlands of roses and carnations were draped over doors and windows and stair rails.

Omar escorted his daughter as far as the steps, where a pair of guards stood impassively at attention. Kissing her forehead, he murmured, "God be with you," then returned to the car, to be driven to the farthest reaches of the palace grounds.

There, under brightly striped tents, the men's celebrations had already begun. Amira could hear the sound of male voices raised in song, accompanied by the rhythmic pounding of the drums. She could smell the pungent aroma of lambs cooking over open fires, their juices dripping into huge cauldrons of seasoned rice.

Entering the palace, she was met by a group of young female cousins, who were all dressed in white and carrying tall white candles. When the women had shed their veils, Aunt Najla lit the candles, and the *zaffa*, the procession, began—stately, solemn, the little girls in front, the bride and her aunts behind them. They made their way through the cavernous entrance gallery, down the long marble corridor towards the main reception hall.

Suddenly the sound of a hundred female voices trilling rang out, and Amira felt an answering joy in her heart. As she entered the vast room, which was lit by a hundred crystal chandeliers, all the guests, women and children alike, rose to applaud.

The Lebanese chanteuse Sabah, accompanied by a troupe of male musicians hidden behind a screen, began to sing *"Dalaa ya dalaa"*—"Cuddle me"—as Amira made the circuit of the room, to be admired and complimented, to receive good wishes for the future.

"May you have only sons," one woman called out.

"A thousand nights of love," said another.

"A blessed old age," yet another.

When Amira sat down in a thronelike gilt chair at the head of the room, the feasting began in earnest: caviar from Iran; foie gras from France; lamb, accompanied by rice, cooked a dozen different ways; grilled pigeons and roast chicken; fish from the Red Sea; desert truffles sautéed in butter and onion; heaping platters of fruit from the four corners of the globe; pastries and ice cream; a giant wedding cake flown in from France.

• • •

As the food was served, Sabah sang of love—lost, regained, lost again—her husky voice rising and falling, sometimes breaking, her audience calling out their understanding of the feelings she expressed.

When her set ended, the musicians launched into the folk songs that had been passed on throughout the Arab world, from one generation to the next. The entertainment went on—a troupe of Lebanese belly dancers, a female magician.

The room buzzed and hummed with gossip and laughter. "Amira's not so beautiful," a buxom thirteen-year-old said to her mother. "Why would a handsome prince like Ali al-Rashad choose her?"

"Hush, hush," her mother replied. "Prince Ali is Amira's *nasib*, her destiny. In a year or two, your father may find a handsome prince for you, *inshallah*."

Unfettered and uninhibited, the women traded stories and enjoyed the impromptu fashion show as much as they did the entertainment. On a day such as this, everyone wore her best. For some, that meant the finest of European couture; for others, it was the best effort of local dressmakers who specialized in copying Western fashions from magazine photos. The room fairly glittered with gems—for here was an opportunity to show off not only a husband's wealth but the depth of his affection.

As coffee flavored with cardamom and mint tea were served, a half-dozen guests went to the center of the room. Accompanied by the tabla (a small drum) and oud (a lutelike instrument), they began the local circle dance. Arms at their sides, hips almost still, they took tiny skipping steps, moving their heads and shoulders in small, delicate circles in rhythm to the music. Compared with the enthusiastic gyrations of the belly dancers, their dance at first seemed quiet and measured, yet as it progressed, the subtle movements became sensual, even erotic.

The audience shouted its appreciation, and as the dancers approached Amira's table, their remarks grew louder and bawdier. Amira blushed as the women around her speculated aloud on what she was wearing under her gown—and how quickly her husband would remove it; on the size of the prince's member—and how vigorously he would use it.

Yet embarrassed as she was to receive this kind of attention, Amira couldn't remember so much unrestrained gaiety and laughter. She savored every minute of her celebration, and when her aunts said it was time to leave, she did so with genuine regret.

• • •

Outside the reception hall, her father was waiting. With a solemnity Amira had rarely seen, he extended his arm and slowly walked her through the corridors, up the marble staircase of the palace that was now her home.

He stopped in front of a richly paneled mahogany door, then patted her on the cheek. Though he seemed on the verge of serious words, he settled for an awkward embrace. "May God protect you always, daughter."

Unbidden tears flooded her eyes. Strange, she thought. She had dreamed of the time when she could leave the stifling protection of her father and her aunts, yet now that it was here, she couldn't help but feel the loss of all that had been familiar.

She kissed her father good-bye and stood for a long moment before her husband's door. She had seen fuzzy photos of him, in newspapers and during ceremonial events on television, and she vaguely remembered his face from childhood. But what would he be like now, in person?

She tapped lightly on the door. It swung open immediately, welcoming her to the most beautiful suite she had ever seen, opulent beyond anything she'd known in her own wealthy home. The furnishings were European antiques, the walls almost hidden by paintings she remembered from books—a Picasso, a Renoir, a Signac . . . on and on.

Prince Ali al-Rashad was as elegant as his surroundings. Wearing a monogrammed white silk robe over matching pajamas, he was handsome as a film star, slightly built, not tall, but finely proportioned, with coal-black eyes and dark silky hair.

For perhaps a full minute, he studied Amira, as if she were a painting or a statue. Then he smiled. "May eternity be as beautiful as you are at this moment."

Amira exhaled a sigh of relief.

Ali held out his hand. Obediently and with something very much like gratitude—after all, he could have been old and like Laila's husband—she took it.

He led her into the bedroom, which was dominated by a majestic Chinese bed, hand-carved and decorated in gold. Silently Amira tried to take in the lavishness of her new home.

"Champagne?"

She was startled. Amira wasn't a religious fanatic, and she knew that plenty of people drank in al-Remal despite the strict laws against it. But she had never tasted alcohol herself.

Omar handed her a crystal tulip filled with bubbling gold. He smiled. "Relax, my dear. It won't hurt you. Champagne's not even liquor. It's liquid happiness."

Amira sipped. Her mouth tingled, an interesting sensation.

Still smiling and in the same pleasant tone, Omar said: "Take off your clothes."

Amira froze. This, of course, was expected—but not so suddenly. She knew what she had learned from her aunts, learned all her life, in fact: that no matter what her husband wanted, she must do it. Not just tonight, but always.

Otherwise she could be sent back to her father's house in disgrace. To be ruled by her aunts. To become one of them herself in time. She shuddered at the thought, and Ali, mistaking the cause, laughed. "Is it so terrible to be alone with me? You're my wife, after all."

Blushing, Amira retreated to the marble bathroom. She removed her bridal gown, the layers of silk underwear. When she reached the flimsy teddy, about which there had been much ribald comment at the women's celebration, she stopped.

She didn't want to make her husband angry, but she couldn't stand naked before him, she just couldn't. Timidly she edged back into the bedroom, her bare feet sinking in the luxurious white carpet.

He didn't seem angry or even annoyed as he admired her once again, almost as if she were an artwork.

"You have a lovely body," he said, "lean and supple and strong . . . like a true thoroughbred."

Amira smiled her appreciation of the compliment. Since reaching womanhood, she often worried that she'd grown too tall, that her hips hadn't filled out enough, that she lacked the voluptuous fleshiness that so many Remali men seemed to prefer. Yet from the way he spoke, it was clear Ali was pleased with her.

He led her to the bed and began stroking her, as if she were a kitten. Basking in the warmth of his approval, Amira allowed herself the pleasure of his touch. How lovely it was, she thought, to be petted and caressed.

As Ali brushed her breasts with his fingertips, the champagne-tingle spread throughout her body. *So this is what it was all about*, the whispering and laughing. This warm fluttering, this weightlessness, this was what had been forbidden.

But when Ali parted her legs with his knee, she stiffened.

He stopped, again more amused than angry. "Are you afraid of me, Amira?"

"No," she protested, though she certainly was afraid of disappointing him.

"Then perhaps you simply don't wish to do what you've been told you must do—is that it?"

Amira lowered her eyes. How could she wish or not wish for something she had never experienced?

"If you're reluctant, there's no need to go on."

"But that's impossible," she blurted out. "What about . . ." she trailed off, too embarrassed to proceed.

"Ah, yes." Ali smiled. "The requisite show of blood to prove your virtue. Well, my dear, I have no need of such proof. But if you feel there must be some display, I'm ready to shed my blood in place of yours." From the nightstand drawer he pulled out a jeweled stiletto, rolled up his pajama sleeve, and extended his arm. "Just say the word."

"No! No, I don't want you to . . . I mean, there's no need."

Ali put the knife down. "Well, then, perhaps you require more champagne."

"Yes, please." She stole a glance at her husband as he got up to refill her glass. Above the silk pajama bottoms, his body was well muscled and smooth.

Turning quickly, he saw her looking. "Do I pass muster, dear wife?"

She blushed furiously. "I didn't . . . I mean I wasn't . . ."

"Of course you were," he teased. "There's no need to be so demure—as long as those glances are reserved for me."

She took the glass he offered and drained it quickly.

"Slowly, slowly, Amira. Such pleasures are meant to be savored."

She giggled. Such a lovely feeling, this light-headedness, the cocoon of Ali's bed. He opened his arms and kissed her slowly, deeply.

"That's more like it," he said. "This isn't an execution, you know."

Totally relaxed, she fell back on the bed. He began stroking her again, outlining the curve of her breasts, the swell of her belly. When he reached her thighs, she parted them readily, no longer apprehensive. As his fingers probed her, first gently, then insistently, she felt a liquid heat building inside her.

"Lovely," he murmured, his dark eyes glistening. As her body began to shudder, he straddled her legs quickly and entered her. When she cried out, he stopped for a moment, then began to move inside and against her. The pain gave way to a rush of new sensations, rising and swelling—and when she cried out again, it was from joy and the thrill of discovery.

She did not notice—nor could she have known—that her husband did not reach a climax. She fell asleep peaceful and content, thinking that if this was marriage, everything else was pale and insipid by comparison.

HONEYMOON

"Why Istanbul?" Ali asked when they were airborne in the king's private jet, on loan to the newlyweds for the duration of their honeymoon.

"Because . . . because someone very dear to me went there for her honeymoon. She said it was beautiful—and exciting."

Ali smiled indulgently, as he had done when Amira first expressed a wish to see the place Laila had enjoyed so much. "Well," he said, "to someone who hasn't seen much of the world, I suppose Istanbul can be impressive. But you, my dear, you can expect to see much more, that I can promise."

Amira could scarcely imagine "much more." Here she was, flying for the first time, in a luxurious craft fitted out with a stately seating area, an opulent bedroom and marble bath and a well-appointed dining room, complete with bone china, crystal goblets, and gold eating utensils. And though Ali had insisted on taking the controls himself during the Boeing 727's takeoff, they had at their service the king's most experienced pilot and a flight crew of five.

Being served orange juice in crystal goblets at forty thousand feet made Amira feel as if she were a fairy-tale princess, an impression that lingered long after they landed at the city on the Bosporus. A limousine picked them up at the airport, whisking them quickly to the Hilton, Istanbul's premier hotel, where Ali had booked a penthouse suite.

Amira had never stayed in a hotel before. She thought this one even grander than al-Remal's royal palace, with its lushly landscaped grounds, crystal-clear pools, and inviting tennis courts. And the people who crowded the lobby—Amira could not take her eyes off them—the fair European men, so different from what she was used to; the beautiful women, unveiled, wearing their fashionable clothes for all to see.

As the manager personally escorted them to their quarters, he proudly informed the honeymooners that "the famous American actors Kirk Douglas and Anthony Quinn" had recently stayed there.

Amira was enchanted. American film stars, no less! In this very place. As soon as she and Ali were alone, she dashed from room to room, throwing open the curtains and exclaiming over the dazzling cityscape below.

"Don't be such a bumpkin," Ali said, but with a tender smile that took the sting from his words. "As it is, most Europeans think all Gulf Arabs live in tents and know nothing of indoor plumbing."

"Of course," she said, stopping in her tracks, "of course, you're right." Yet far from upsetting Amira, Ali's words made her feel important, as if she had a purpose outside her own home: to represent her country in a small way, to bring honor to the royal house of al-Remal. She began to walk around the room, slowly and with a measured pace, imitating the elegant European women she had seen in the lobby.

"Brava," Ali said, clapping his hands, "you look like a queen. Let me show you off to the world right now. And while you're practicing your royal walk, let's leave your veil behind."

"Really?" she asked, with some trepidation. "In the streets of Istanbul?"

"Yes, of course. Atatürk did away with the veil when he founded the Turkish republic. You might see it in the countryside, but not here. We don't want to look as if we've come from some primitive backwater, do we?"

So Amira went sightseeing unveiled. At first she felt quite strange, as if everyone were staring. But as time passed and her self-consciousness slipped away, she savored the breeze that ruffled her hair, the sunlight that warmed her skin.

At her request their first stop was the Topkapi Palace. Once the royal residence of the Ottoman sultans, it had been converted into a museum housing dazzling collections of jewels, tapestries, and porcelains. "It's just as Laila said," Amira whispered under her breath as she gazed at the magnificent gems—the imperial diamonds and rubies and emeralds—that had once adorned sultans or graced their favorite wives. She wanted to linger here, as if perhaps she could feel something of Laila's brief presence at a time when she had been a young bride, happy and full of dreams for the future.

But Ali urged her on, studying various exhibits and making notes in his leatherbound notebook. "Hope you don't mind, my dear, but the king will expect some recommendations for the museum project at home."

Amira did not mind. She was impressed by her husband's cultural background and wished her own were not so limited. Yet Ali seemed to enjoy playing teacher and tour guide, as he walked her through the nearby archeological museums, studying the exhibits from the ancient civilizations of Mesopotamia and the Hittites.

Next came the city's great mosques: the magnificent Saint Sophia, with its superb Byzantine interior and immense soaring dome; the Sultan Ahmet, with its sublime blue frescoes; the graceful Suleymaniye, where Suleyman the Magnificent and his wife were buried.

After pausing for lunch at a small waterside restaurant, where they dined on a fine Turkish *meza* and bass steamed in earthenware, Ali took Amira to the Capali Carsi, the vast and sprawling covered bazaar. "Choose as many souvenirs as you like," he said, clearly enjoying her look of wonderment.

"It's like Ali Baba's cave," she said. "I've never seen anything like it in al-Remal."

"That's because we don't have anything like it. I'm told there are more than four thousand shops here. Spread out over sixty-odd streets."

The choices laid out before her were legion: carpets woven of richly dyed wools and precious silks; tapestries from the time of the Ottomans; heavy silver jewelry set with amber and carnelian and onyx; perfumes from Europe; inlaid furniture set with mother-of-pearl; brass coffeepots and trays and candlesticks; bags and shoes made of Kilim carpets; housewares fashioned of copper and brass. So much more, Amira's head was spinning.

Not wanting to appear greedy—or childlike—Amira strolled through the cavernous arcade, admiring a fragment of tapestry here, an intricately carved perfume bottle there. Shopkeepers called out to the couple, entreating them to stop and look, to enjoy a delicious cup of tea. Ali bestowed a princely smile on all. And when Amira lingered over a silk carpet and later an antique writing desk inlaid with mother-of-pearl, he entered into spirited negotiation with the shopkeepers. In spite of his great wealth, he understood, as did Amira, that haggling was an expected—and much-savored—part of any transaction.

"That's all? Are you sure that's all you want?" he asked after the bargaining ritual had been concluded.

She nodded tentatively, wondering if perhaps she'd disappointed him in some way.

He laughed. "Perhaps you haven't spent enough time among other women, learning how to manage a man. Else you'd have been taught to be more demanding."

Amira was silent. Was Ali mocking her? It was certainly true she knew precious little about "managing" a man. She had believed it would be enough to simply bow to his wishes.

"Don't look so serious, Amira. I was just teasing you. I'm very touched, actually, that you require so little by way of material things. That will make it much easier for me to spoil you."

Instinctively—and sensing perhaps that such a statement might diminish her in Ali's eyes—Amira refrained from saying she had little interest in material things. And later that day, when it was time to dress for dinner, she chose what she felt might please him: one of her more elaborate Paris creations and the sapphire jewelry that had once belonged to her mother. She was rewarded with Ali's murmurs of approval.

They dined at the century-old Pera Palace, the most imposing of Istanbul's grand old hotels. "I thought you might like this place," Ali said, as Amira admired the ornate paneling, the majestic dimensions of the main dining room. "Greta Garbo stayed here. So did Agatha Christie, Mata Hari, Josephine Baker, and Leon Trotsky. Not to mention assorted kings and queens. And now you, Amira . . . a royal princess of al-Remal."

Amira clapped her hands and laughed. "How wonderful. But how do you know all this?"

"A chap at the American consulate next door. He brought me here for drinks once. Gave me the entire history of the place, ever since it was built in the late nineteenth century. For the Orient Express travelers, I believe."

How attentive he was, Amira thought. And how elegant, as he ordered a sumptuous meal in impeccable French. No one had ever taken such care to please her before, she realized, as he offered her choice morsels of grilled pheasant before he took a single bite himself.

She wanted to return the favor. So when he asked if she'd like to visit a nightclub—"I warn you, however, that the entertainment will be limited to some mediocre belly dancing and some rather average singing"—she noted that his eyelids were drooping and thought he might be tired.

"Perhaps you'd rather go back to the hotel," she ventured. As soon as the words were out, she began to blush, thinking he might take her suggestion as a sexual overture. When he agreed readily, she became quiet and a little shy, in anticipation of the intimacy they would share again.

Yet when they returned to the hotel and entered the elevator, Ali pushed the button that took them to the casino floor. The place was crowded with men and women in evening clothes and pulsing with the energy of winning and losing. Surely Ali's father would not approve of such a place, she thought, but she said nothing.

With a familiarity born of practice, Ali took a seat at the blackjack table with the highest limit and threw down a thick pile of bills, barely glancing at the pile of chips he received in return. A moment later, a tuxedo-clad waitress appeared at his elbow. "Glenlivet. Bring the bottle."

His movements were languid, almost bored, as he played his hands with careless ease, signaling with a barely perceptible motion of his little finger whether or not he wanted another card. Within an hour he had almost doubled his pile of chips. And though Amira had no idea what the game was, she gathered from the remarks of the people who'd gathered to watch that Ali played in a most unconventional way, taking "hits" when the odds called for standing fast. Soon a crowd gathered to watch the dark, handsome prince in impeccably tailored evening clothes. But Ali's eyes barely flickered.

• • •

Dutifully Amira stood behind his chair, imagining they would soon leave. Yet as he refilled his glass again and yet again, he continued to gamble, tossing chips on the table as if they had no meaning at all. Sometimes the pile grew; sometimes it diminished.

"What nerve," a man at the table murmured, "taking a hit on seventeen."

Ali smiled. The card he'd taken was a three of spades; it gave him a winning hand. Yet to him winning seemed the same as losing, and Amira had no sense at all of what he wanted to accomplish before they could leave. She had been prepared to wait, but now she was tired, so very tired. Finally at about three in the morning, she said very tentatively, "Perhaps we should go now, Ali. It's very late."

A look of molten anger was his reply, so intense yet so fleeting that Amira wondered if she'd seen it at all. A few minutes later, he said, not unkindly, "If you're tired, my dear, perhaps you'd like to retire. I'll be here for a while."

She stood her ground for a while. Was her place here—or would Ali prefer her to go? Fatigue finally made her go.

In their honeymoon suite, the bed had been turned down, her nightgown artfully arranged alongside Ali's silk pajamas. It seemed like a reproach. Why was the appeal of the gambling tables greater than her own? She had no answer. Yet one thing she did know: the story of the *hammam* that Bahia had told. In the days before all the fine houses had private bathrooms, women used the communal bath to perform their grand ablutions, the ritual total immersion that was required after sex. Bahia laughingly said you could always tell a new bride because she would come to the *hammam* every day—until her first child was born, then less and less often as the marriage grew older and the husband's passion waned.

But on a honeymoon—Amira had been told that the appetite of a new husband was insatiable, that she could expect to make love until her body ached from his demands. While she was pondering this against the reality she'd experienced so far, she fell asleep.

When she awakened, Ali was there beside her, fully clothed, his silk pajamas swept to the floor. In spite of her insecurity about what to do next, she was hungry enough to get up. Walking barefoot so as not to make any noise, she went into the living room and called room service, as she had seen Ali do when they'd arrived.

She ordered fresh fruit, pots of tea and coffee, and a variety of toasts and breakfast cakes. She dressed quickly and, when the waiter arrived, had her meal served on the terrace, where she could enjoy the parklike grounds below.

Later, when she thought she heard a sound from the bedroom, she tiptoed inside. Ali was stirring. Softly she called his name. His eyes opened, but they seemed dull and unfocused.

"Shall I bring you some coffee?"

"Whiskey," he said.

She was shocked but said nothing. Ali was her husband, and it was not her place to question him.

"In the West, it's called 'hair of the dog,' Amira. It's like medicine. Nothing to concern yourself about."

She brought him a bottle and a tumbler. He took both into one of the bathrooms. She heard the sound of the shower being turned on. A half hour later, he came out. "That's better," he said with a smile, "don't you agree?"

Amira smiled in return. Her husband did indeed look better, restored to his former self. She hoped he would not drink so much tonight.

The next few days followed the same pattern: a few hours of sightseeing, shopping in the European-style boutiques that lined the Cumhuriyet Caddesi and the Valikonagi Caddesi, splendid meals at fine restaurants. In the evening there would be something for Amira—her first ballet *(Giselle)*, her first opera *(Madama Butterfly)*. Yet later, they would inevitably finish the evening at the casino, with Ali drinking too much and staying out almost until dawn, while Amira slept alone.

On the fifth day of her honeymoon, just when she had resigned herself to this routine, Ali announced that he had arranged for a special evening.

A short time later she found herself aboard a sleek sailing yacht cruising the Bosporus, moving gracefully between the European and Asian sides, Ali pointing out the sights.

"The Dolmabacha Palace," he said, pointing out a white fairy-tale castle in a Turkish-Indian-Baroque style. "It was built by Sultan Abdulmecit as a summer residence, so he could enjoy the same delightful breeze we're enjoying now."

Amira closed her eyes, luxuriating in the moment. It was as if her husband had been away and then returned to her. There was no Scotch whiskey and no casino. Tonight he was choosing to be with her.

A white-jacketed steward served champagne and *borek*, cigarlike dumplings filled with cheese and various fillings. Then came vine leaves and artichokes in oil, followed by lamb kebabs prepared with yogurt. Dessert was flambéed fruit.

"Simple food but quite good, don't you think?"

"Yes," Amira agreed. "If you like, I could prepare this at home."

"We already have a Turkish cook in the royal kitchen," he said. Then, seeing her crestfallen expression, he added, "But it would make me very happy if you were to supervise the menu for our private meals."

"As you wish," she said with a smile.

When the dishes had been taken away, they reclined on cushioned bolsters, lulled into a pleasant drowsiness by the motion of the boat and the wine. He stroked her hair, and as the boat pitched gently back and forth, she fell asleep, wondering how long it would take to understand her handsome but rather puzzling husband.

MARRIAGE

Lazy languid days and long sleepy nights—these were the rhythms of Amira's life in the palace. And how quickly she adapted to it—as if there had always been a masseuse to pamper and soothe her muscles, a fortune-teller to entertain her with predictions and prognostications, a hairdresser and cosmetician to carry out her daily beauty routines.

Life at home had been very comfortable, but this was beyond imagining. It was, Amira decided, even decadent—a word she'd read but didn't really understand until now. Any material thing she wanted was here. If it was lacking, all she had to do was ask, and it would be flown in. Food, clothing, electronic equipment, toys and amusements, they were all hers for the asking.

When Ali went abroad, she went, too. She saw concerts, operas, and ballets, visiting all the legendary places she'd imagined as a young girl, enjoying the freedom of appearing unveiled. These trips were like a dream come true, yet when she returned to her luxurious cocoon in al-Remal, she often asked herself which was reality and which was the dream.

In the palace she was rarely alone but often lonely. The king's various wives and concubines, their daughters and daughters-in-law, all these women were like a country within a country. Even Zeinab, who had a spacious villa of her own nearby, spent most of her days here.

At the heart of the women's country was the queen, Faiza. It was she who had built the communal *hammam*, where Amira now reclined on a bench of marble. The room was large and airy with diamond-cut skylights, the walls covered with intricate mosaic tiles in jewel-like tones of blue and green. There were several tubs for bathing; along one wall, a battery of nozzles regularly released powerful bursts of steam. Throughout the day, an elaborate music system piped in the queen's favorite "easy listening" music.

The *hammam*, Faiza often said, was an old custom worth keeping.

Nonsense, said Zeinab, who reclined on a neighboring bench; the *hammam* was simply another of Faiza's devices for snooping and prying.

During the six months she'd been married, Amira had learned a great deal from Zeinab, who loved to chatter indiscriminately, and who was, even now, confirming the rumors of how her mother regulated the king's philandering.

"Just watch," Zeinab giggled, "and you'll see. When my father becomes irritable, when he begins to lose his temper with no provocation at all, my mother says it's a sign that he requires a new woman. So—that's when she finds a new maid, someone young and pretty and virginal. She sends the young woman to the king's bedroom on some pretext or other, and *voilà*, all is well. When he becomes irritable again, she finds the maid a new position and sends another in her place. It's brilliant, don't you think?"

Was this, then, what Ali had meant, about learning to manage men from other women? Though he did sometimes lose his temper with no provocation at all, she could not imagine searching out other women and sending them to his bed. To her, the queen's machinations seemed rather sad. It was true that in al-Remal, saving face was all-important—but at what price did the queen ransom her pride?

Amira sighed and exhaled as her personal maid scrubbed her back with a loofah, a treatment that kept her skin soft and fresh. Much to her own surprise, Amira had learned to enjoy the ritual of communal bathing.

As her maid applied the henna that gave Amira's hair reddish highlights and body, Zeinab called her son and daughter, who were frolicking happily in one of the enormous marble tubs. "Hassan! Bahija! Come quickly so Nanny can give you a good washing." The children laughed and continued to splash one another.

How lucky they are, Amira thought, *the young ones who could run free, bathing naked together as if it were the most natural thing in the world.*

Suddenly the door to the *hammam* opened and closed. It was the queen, wrapped in a saronglike Turkish towel embroidered with silver and silk. "Any news yet, Amira?"

Amira rose to show her respect, wrapping her own towel around her. "Not yet, Mother, but soon, God willing."

"Let us hope so."

Amira returned to her bench, her sense of relaxation gone. She was not pregnant and therefore a disappointment to her mother-in-law. But how could she tell the queen that it was not her fault? That it was very difficult to become pregnant when sexual activity was so erratic and unpredictable?

In the weeks and months that followed her marriage, Amira had come to believe that Ali had two faces—and as many personalities. Sometimes he was kind and attentive, interested in what she had to say, content to curl up beside her in bed, his body wrapped cozily around hers, talking about the planes he flew or the changes he envisioned for al-Remal. She loved those quiet moments when it seemed they might be friends, and not just husband and wife.

But there were other times when he was moody and withdrawn, when her most innocent actions seemed to offend or anger him, when he came to her bed drunk and brutishly exercised his marital rights as if she were there to serve him, nothing more. Yet since it was those occasions that were likely to give her a child, Amira endured them stoically, as a good wife should.

• • •

The gala to celebrate the opening of the al-Remal Cultural Museum was a glittering but fairly subdued affair. In honor of the Western guests—oil-company executives, foreign diplomats and their wives—Ali had arranged for a British orchestra, but they would play only classical music, for there would be no dancing here, no public touching between men and women. It went without saying that there would be no alcoholic beverages.

Thanks to Ali's powers of persuasion, however, the queen and assorted princesses were also present, albeit properly robed and veiled and segregated from the foreigners. Since Amira could not properly speak to anyone outside the palace group, she tried to engage her sister-in-law, Munira, in conversation. "I've just had a lovely note from Karin Vanderbeek, the woman who used to be my nanny. I want to invite her to tea next week, and I thought you might enjoy meeting her. She's very intelligent and very beautiful."

"A beautiful woman can't really understand the life of the mind," Munira said decisively.

"But how can you say that?" Amira protested. "There have been many accomplished women who were beautiful as well."

"Accomplishments alone are not the hallmark of the true intellectual."

"Well, then, what is?" Amira pressed on, not liking Munira's pontifical tone.

Munira shrugged, as if to say: You couldn't possibly understand.

"Don't mind her," said good-natured Zeinab. "She's just jealous because you're beautiful and married and clever, too. But she can't very well admit that you could be all those things, can she? Then life would be truly unfair."

Munira shot her sister an angry look and said nothing. Reluctantly, Amira accepted Zeinab's explanation, for she had tried hard to win Munira's affection and respect. Ah, well, she thought, perhaps in time she might yet succeed, for Munira would be an interesting companion, someone who might understand Amira's interest in books and learning and the world beyond the palace walls.

At least Ali seemed to be having a good time, she thought. Surrounded by reporters from the foreign language weeklies who served the country's expatriate workers and the cameras of al-Remal's single television station, he was explaining how important the new museum was. "For us in the so-called 'developing nations' it's important to know that on our land once stood a great civilization. By displaying its artifacts and teaching our children the lessons learned from our past, we may yet, *inshallah*, regain our national pride and dignity."

Ali's remarks were well received, and the museum itself—a modern sandstone structure with a vaguely Eastern cast—was enthusiastically applauded by the foreign visitors. By the time the reception was over, Ali was in a fine mood.

"Did you enjoy yourself, my dear?" he asked Amira. "I thought the evening was a great success."

"I think so, too," Amira said. "I just wish . . ."

"What? What do you wish?"

"I don't know. I just wish I could be more . . . useful."

"Why not take those college courses you mentioned?" Ali suggested. "They'll keep you busy. Unless . . ."

"Unless what?"

"Unless you're afraid of offending my sister, Munira," he said with a smile. "She rather fancies herself the palace intellectual, you know. She might not approve of a rival scholar."

Amira laughed. "I'm sure she wouldn't. But what would I do with a degree here?"

"A great deal, Amira. As an educated wife and mother, you'll be even more precious. And one day, if you're patient, you can be part of the changes that are coming. They'll be slow, to be sure, but they are occurring even now. A few short years ago, my father never would have allowed a mixed gathering like the one we had at the museum tonight."

• • •

As if to further prove his point about progress and change, Ali announced that they would be entertaining a foreign guest. "Dr. Philippe Rochon . . . he's come to al-Remal to treat my father. I've invited him to dinner."

Amira was doubly impressed. Dr. Rochon was a well-known internist and diagnostician whose brilliant mind and healing skills were much in demand, not only in his native France but throughout the Middle East.

Normally a dinner like this would be a male-only affair. For Ali to bring him here, to their private quarters, that was indeed progress.

"And you may wear one of those dresses you brought from France," he added. "Without the veil."

Amira was shocked—and pleasantly surprised.

So was the palace staff, especially some of the older ones. The younger ones were simply excited. Amira empathized with both reactions. Regardless of what she did when she traveled abroad, she had never been unveiled in al-Remal, not since she was a girl.

She fussed over the menu and lingered longer than usual with her toilette. As she prepared for dinner, she felt as if she were wearing only a negligee. The feeling gathered force and nuance when the Frenchman arrived.

"Peace be with you, *ya* Ali," he said, his voice deep and rich.

"And upon you. *Itfuddal*, Doctor, you honor our humble home," said Ali. "Allow me to present my wife."

Philippe Rochon was perhaps forty, pepper-black hair just showing the first sprinkling of salt. Not much taller than Ali, but one of those men who seem to gain stature through some special aura, some sheer power of their presence.

More than anything else, it was his eyes, Amira thought. Though he greeted her in good Arabic with conventionally elaborate courtesy—"Your Highness, you do your poor servant too great an honor"—his eyes, the changeable expressive blue of Normandy, spoke far more eloquently.

Later, Amira would remember that first glance as one of the sincerest compliments she ever received. (Ali still called her beautiful from time to time, but too often his voice carried the smug pride of ownership, and his words sounded recited by rote.)

"It is the guest who honors the house," Amira replied, also conventionally courteous.

"No, no," Ali laughed. "This is not a school for diplomats. Tonight, Doctor, we are doing things *à la mode de l'Ouest*. Please call me Ali and my wife Amira."

A Gallic shrug and a smile of helpless acceptance. "Ah, well, then you must not call me Doctor, but Philippe."

Champagne was served, as was Ali's custom with foreign visitors.

"Tell me, Philippe, how is my father?"

The doctor smiled. "The king's problem is one I can do nothing about. Meaning no disrespect, but he eats like a gourmand run wild in a forest of three-star restaurants—and he's not a young man anymore. I'm told he listens to you—perhaps you can persuade him to exercise more moderation. Certainly he pays no attention to my advice."

Ali threw up his hands to indicate his helplessness in this situation. "My father might consider my opinion on some matters, but not when it comes to food. But he has an iron constitution, Philippe. He'll be around long after you and I have gone, I'm sure of it."

Dinner—especially prepared by the palace cook in Philippe's honor—began with foie gras that had been flown in from Strasbourg, followed by quail stuffed with wild rice and a salad of baby greens lightly dressed with champagne vinegar and delicate sesame oil.

"My compliments on a delectable meal," Philippe said to Amira. "I don't believe I've enjoyed anything as much in years."

"You are too kind, Philippe, but I don't deserve your compliments. It was our cook Fahim who prepared the meal."

"Nevertheless, it is you I thank, for I am certain it was your guidance that inspired his efforts."

Amira blushed, lowering her eyes.

"Ali tells me you're taking university-level correspondence courses, Amira. Have you found a particular interest yet?"

"No. I'm enrolling in a general program, some literature, some history, some science, some philosophy. But I feel as if I'm still shopping. That's what it's like, in a way—like being in some wonderful store where there's so much to buy that you can't make up your mind."

Philippe smiled warmly, his blue eyes crinkling as they looked directly at her. "What a marvelous attitude, Amira. I hope you always feel that way. And as far as a specialty, well, there's plenty of time."

Amira basked in the glow of his approval. No one had ever taken her so seriously before. She liked his assumption that she would be continuing her education, even finding a particular specialty.

Over dessert—an Arab-style crepe stuffed with cream and drizzled with rosewater syrup—Ali spoke of Philippe's well-known diagnostic skills. "I've heard you described as a medical Sherlock Holmes."

Philippe smiled. "I take that as a great compliment, Ali, one I try always to live up to. For example, I recently had a fascinating case in Paris. The gentleman was suffering from a near-total paralysis of his left arm, from the elbow downward. Of course, the first fear is a stroke, but there were no signs of that. The next likely possibility was what we called a 'dropped wrist,' something like Bell's palsy, but not in the face. It results from trauma to a nerve—injury in some cases, though a virus can do it, too.

"Sometimes it's called 'crutch arm' because people who use crutches can damage the radial nerve where it runs along the inside of the upper arm. But this man didn't use crutches. What's more, he swore he'd done nothing whatever to put unusual stress on his arm. I'll tell you, I was frankly at a dead end, running test after test and learning nothing. Was it psychosomatic? I just didn't know.

"Then one afternoon, for no good reason, I canceled a nonurgent appointment and went to see my patient at his office. He was surprised to see me—worried, too, I imagine. His office furniture was old-fashioned—massive wooden desk and high-backed chair. I hadn't been there a minute when he had a phone call. As soon as he picked up the receiver with his right hand, he flung his left arm—crippled forearm and all—over the back of that chair and almost hung there, half his weight on it. Obviously an unconscious habit. When he hung up, I asked how much time he spent on the phone every day. 'Oh, hours.' Then he saw me looking at his arm over the back of the chair. We both started to laugh. He recovered full use of his arm in about two months."

Amira started to laugh. "That's marvelous," she said, brimming with admiration. "I wish I could do what you do."

"You could," he said, his expression mirroring hers. "So could many people. I'm just a mechanic, really," he added, turning pensive. "But the real magic is in healing the driver. If I had it to do over again—if I were as young as you, Amira—I believe that I would specialize in psychology."

It was a moment Amira would remember in the years to come, a moment when she glimpsed the future.

She was enjoying herself so much, she wanted the evening to go on and on. But after a second cup of coffee, Philippe said, with obvious regret, that he would have to leave. "An early flight, alas. But please allow me to return your hospitality. I would be honored if you would visit me in Paris." Bending over Amira's hand, he kissed it lightly, his breath like a caress.

Scarcely noticing Ali's searching look, she went to bed reliving that moment, Philippe's touch, his voice, his elegant manner, that special glance from his eyes.

• • •

In the quiet time before dawn, while she was still fast asleep, Amira felt a hand on her breast, fingers trailing so delicately on her skin that she moaned with pleasure.

But suddenly the fingers were no longer gentle. They squeezed and pinched and hurt. She cried out in pain and pushed the hand away. A stinging slap jolted her awake. Ali was beside her, his face mottled red with anger. "Listen carefully, woman," he said between clenched teeth, "and listen yet again. I decide, do you understand? I decide what happens in this bed and outside it, and that's how it will be until the day you die."

Amira listened, eyes wide, scarcely breathing. Why was he so angry? What had she done? Could he possibly know that she had slept with thoughts of another man? That her body had responded to his touch? She searched Ali's face for answers, but found none. Without another word, he got up from the bed and left.

Later that day, she found a sura from the Koran, written on parchment and nailed to the wall of her bedroom: *"If you fear that they (your wives) will reject you, admonish them and remove them to another bed; firmly beat them. If they obey you, then worry no more. God is high and great."*

And for the first time in her marriage, Amira feared her husband.

MOTHERHOOD

"Are you certain, Amira? Absolutely certain?"

"The doctor confirmed it today."

Ali fell to his knees and began kissing her hand. "This is the greatest gift of all, Amira, not only to me but to my father. Now you are truly my queen."

"The king's pleasure and yours are as my own," she said, meaning every word. Now the pressure to conceive was over; now her husband, her mother-in-law—and everyone else—knew she was not deficient in any way.

As she placed a hand on her belly, trying to sense the life inside, she felt an unexpected rush of sorrow, as fresh as it had been years ago. Laila. Poor Laila. How wretchedly unlucky she had been. She had prayed for a boy because she had learned all too well how wretched a woman's life could be. Amira, too, hoped for a boy—because she knew that every man wanted a son—but all that was really expected of her was to deliver a healthy child. And until that day came, she would take good care of herself and fill the hours as she chose.

She chose to immerse herself in studies.

Inspired by her conversation with Philippe Rochon—and the glimmer of hope he'd given that her life might somehow reach beyond the production of children—she added a course in basic psychology to her correspondence curriculum from Cairo University. Her textbooks were like an "Open Sesame" to a world she'd never imagined, showing her the pathways to the human brain, explaining how humans responded to stimulation.

As she studied Freud's teachings on dreams, she half expected to find something like the elaborate, rather baroque interpretations she'd heard growing up. But to her surprise, the analyst seemed to believe that almost every sleeping image—and many waking thoughts—related to sex. Was he right? she wondered. She had never thought of herself as overly interested in sex. Yet it seemed that these days, every time she opened the psychology text, she thought of Philippe, remembered the way he'd looked at her, the way he'd kissed her hand.

And even as she daydreamed about another man, she was very much aware that Ali's sexual demands—erratic at best—had stopped altogether. He didn't want to hurt the baby, he said, though the doctor said there was no risk until her last month. She didn't miss the kind of sex she and Ali had shared, but she did miss the warmth of being held and petted. She tried to content herself with daily lanolin massages, which Zeinab had recommended to prevent stretch marks.

Yet even as he distanced himself physically, Ali pampered Amira in everything else. To encourage her in her studies, he had her bedroom fitted out with bookcases, a handsome desk, and a chair that was custom-made to support her back. He installed a midwife in the palace and had a London specialist flown in every two weeks. "You must have the best of everything," he said. "Anything you need, Amira, anything at all, just ask."

At times she searched her mind for something to ask for, simply because he expected it. All she had to do was mention that it might be pleasant to have a glass of juice, a piece of melon, or a sugar cookie, and someone ran to fetch it. In spite of modern medicine, it was still believed that if a pregnant woman craved something and did not have it at once, her child would be marked.

Noting Ali's overprotectiveness, the queen remarked acidly that he was turning into a woman himself. Ali seemed not to care.

Yet in spite of the excellent care she received, Amira couldn't help but fear the moment when her child would arrive. How could she not, when the memory of Laila's delivery was still etched in her mind?

She knew there were drugs to ease the pain, but comparing the luxury with which she was surrounded to the filth and squalor of Laila's prison cell, she was too ashamed to mention them to her doctor. When he asked whether she preferred "natural childbirth," she answered simply, "Whatever God wills."

• • •

"Wake up, Ali, please wake up," Amira pleaded. She had been wakened moments ago by a mild cramping sensation—and a rush of warm fluid that soaked her nightgown and sheets. It had begun.

Quickly she went to Ali's bed and shook his shoulders.

"It's time?" he asked as his eyes flew open.

"Yes."

Moving with a speed she had never seen, he bundled Amira into a palace limousine and summoned the midwife. Soon they were speeding towards the new al-Remal hospital. As Ali had previously ordered, a suite of rooms had been set aside for Amira. A staff obstetrician was in attendance, and the London specialist—who'd been lodged at the Intercontinental Hotel for the past few weeks—was on his way.

Yet in the end it was far less difficult than she'd imagined. A few hours of discomfort, an hour or so of real pain. A final push and she heard his cry. Her son had been born.

Café-au-lait skin, a shock of black hair, enormous liquid eyes of deepest lapis. "Beautiful," she whispered when the nurse placed him in her arms. "I love you, my son, more than my own life." And when he gave her another lusty cry, she was sure he had heard and understood.

• • •

How did I ever live without him? Amira asked herself as she suckled her baby. She would never tire of looking at her Karim, of touching his silken skin, inhaling his sweet baby fragrance. She wanted so much to take him home, to rock him in her arms, to sing him to sleep, and to wake with his beautiful face near hers. But Ali insisted that they both stay in the hospital for a week. "The doctor tells me that the first few days of an infant's life are the most fragile," he explained, "and the most likely period for complications. I couldn't bear it if anything happened to him. Or to you," he added hastily.

To ease the boredom of her hospital stay, Ali brought in a large-screen television and a collection of videotapes, along with all her textbooks. He filled the room with flowers the morning after Karim's birth. And on the following day, he presented Amira with a small velvet box inscribed with the name of a well-known London jeweler. Inside, against a cushion of white silk, was an antique pendant, an enormous pigeon-blood ruby. Amira had never seen a stone of such size, such richness of color.

"It once belonged to Marie Antoinette," Ali said. "A queen of France."

But such an unhappy one, she recalled—and then quickly banished the thought. The pendant was a magnificent gift, and she thanked her husband graciously.

"It's scarcely worthy of you. You've given me my first son. Nothing, no one, can compare with that."

The ruby was but the first of a shower of gifts. Visitors laden with beautifully wrapped boxes trooped in and out of Amira's room all day long, and she was soon glad of the opportunity to rest. Munira brought an antique engraved cup of heavy English silver and a handful of turquoise beads, to hang on the baby's cradle and his clothes, as protection from the evil eye.

Malik flew in from Paris with an entire carload of handmade toys. He was sleeker, more poised, better dressed—and Amira couldn't resist teasing him. "You're looking very prosperous, brother. Have you really become the hardworking and brilliant businessman Father imagines you to be?"

"I am prosperous, *nushkorallah*, thanks be to God. And I do work hard. But as for brilliance, well, my old friend Onassis insists that making money takes no particular talent. When I told him I was striking out on my own, he said: 'My young friend, I have just one piece of advice for you. To be successful, you must always have a tan and you must always pay your hotel bills.' I have tried to follow this advice—though my tan, of course, is permanent."

"Silly," she said, pushing him playfully. Then she lowered her voice. "Tell me . . . how is Laila?"

The sophistication fell away, and he was a boy again, his eyes sparkling with love, his voice rich with tenderness. "She's wonderful, Amira. She learns something new every day. She hears a new word once, and immediately she knows what it means. Her French is quite amazing now. Her nanny says she has a great facility with language."

Amira's eyes went to her own son, lying in his elaborately decorated cradle just a few feet away.

"They grow faster than you can imagine, Amira," Malik said softly. "And soon you cannot imagine a life without them."

Amira's final visitor arrived on the day she was to return home. Dr. Philippe Rochon. "I've been attending the king this week," he explained, "so I thought I'd look in on you and the baby."

Did Ali know? she wondered, but dared not ask. She was surrounded by hospital staff, and Philippe sat in a chair a full three feet from her bed, yet there was an intimacy to his presence that she had not experienced before.

"The baby is healthy," he went on, "as I'm sure you know. And you, Amira, you . . ."

"Yes?" she asked, holding her breath.

"You're lovelier than ever. If that were possible."

She exhaled slowly. He had crossed a line. A personal compliment. And her husband not present.

"Tell me about your studies," he said, breaking the tension. "Ali tells me you've been very diligent throughout your confinement."

"It isn't diligence. Though I'm often frustrated because there's no one to answer my questions, I love learning new things, or trying to."

"Ah, Amira," he said sadly, "someone like you, a natural student, you belong . . ."

"Yes?"

"Nothing."

"I'm studying psychology, as you suggested. Just a beginning course, but still . . ."

Philippe's blue eyes crinkled with pleasure. "And? What do you think?"

"It's like learning a new language, a new way of thinking and seeing. I don't pretend to understand it yet, but I will, I know I will."

"I wish I could see it all with you, Amira, through your eyes."

Amira was quiet. Too much had already been said. Philippe got up to go, waiting perhaps for a moment to see if she would stop him. She did not. But when he left, the room seemed so very empty. And cold.

• • •

For a long time after Karim's birth, Amira was so involved with him she scarcely noticed that Ali still had not returned to their marriage bed. First Karim was circumcised by the *mutaharati*, one of the handful of old men who specialized in the simple procedure. Then followed a week-long feast, almost as lavish as her wedding. Food was distributed to the poor; gold pieces were handed out to all who came to pay their respects.

Now Amira's days were truly full, nursing Karim, bathing him, making sure he was comfortable and secure. There was an army of maids and nurses living in the palace, but Amira wanted to do as much as possible herself.

Though Ali doted on his own son, he seemed to have little time for Amira, mumbling excuses about business, affairs of state, meetings with his father.

And though he was less important to her than her baby, Ali's indifference reproached her. Surely she must be failing in some wifely duty, she thought. And so she tried to make herself more attractive and went out of her way to make certain the meals they shared were properly prepared. She put together little conversational tidbits to feed him with his grilled fish or roasted quail—and was rewarded with monosyllables and polite smiles.

When the prescribed period of abstinence—forty days—passed, she felt shamed by Ali's lack of ardor, his obvious disinterest. Was something wrong with her? Maybe it was because she'd been fat and ugly for so long. And how would she bear another child, another son, if he never touched her? These were troubling questions, but there was no one she could consult, no one to talk to.

Certainly not her mother-in-law, who believed that her Ali was not just a prince of al-Remal but of the entire universe. Nor fat Zeinab who delighted in telling anyone who'd listen that her husband would just not leave her alone. That he demanded sex at all hours of the day and night, even when she was asleep. That he'd gone so far as to caress her when she was in the throes of labor.

As for Munira, though she was the most intelligent of all, she turned a sour face when there was any talk of men. She seemed to see them as conspirators in a plot to make her unhappy and had managed to persuade her doting father that each and every candidate he suggested was in some way unsuitable or unworthy. No, neither of her sisters-in-law would be of any help.

How she longed for her mother. Though she remembered the time she'd seen Omar trying to force himself on Jihan, surely her marriage must have been happy once. Maybe she could have explained how desire could live for so many years in some marriages—and then flicker and die in others.

And there was more. Her feelings for Philippe, the experience of childbirth, the ripening of her body, all these changes had wakened her sensuality. She wanted to be touched and caressed. Perhaps now she might even find pleasure in the things Ali did to her.

Desperate to bring her doubts and fears to some conclusion, Amira prepared herself as carefully as she had for her wedding, removing every trace of hair from her body, scenting herself with L'Air du Temps. She put on her most provocative French lingerie, and when she heard Ali stirring in his study, she presented herself to him.

"Well, well, what have we here?" He smiled but did not stop pouring his favorite single malt scotch.

Was he teasing her? she wondered.

She walked past him, around his chair, her movements becoming more provocative.

He ignored her. He had no interest in what she offered after she had abased herself like a common courtesan. And the Badir pride flared. "As always your words have been an enlightenment to your poor servant, my husband," she said with sarcastic formality. "But I've interrupted your refreshment too long."

As she turned to stalk away, he was suddenly on her like a madman, knocking her to the floor, ripping away the silk, taking her—raping her, really, for now she wanted no part of him. "Is that it? Is that what you want, sow?" he demanded, his voice hoarse with anger. And when he was finished, he pulled his robe around him and left her, as if she were a common whore.

And suddenly it came to her. Just like Omar, he must have someone he loved more than her. Someone he loved instead of her. *He hates me*, she thought. *He must. That's why he hates being with me. He wants to be with her.*

"Is this what happened to you, Mama?" she said aloud. "Is this how you felt?" Would she become like Jihan? Had it happened—so soon? Already? Amira gathered up the shreds of her little silken fantasy and went to bed.

• • •

The morning light softened the brutality of the night before, made it seem like a bad dream. Like a good Muslim wife, Amira found a way to blame herself: throwing herself at Ali that way when he clearly wasn't in the mood, why wouldn't he be repelled, angry?

The idea that he might have someone else was only an irritating little splinter under the skin now, not the gashing certainty it had seemed in the night. Perhaps he had seen someone while she was pregnant. Men had been known to do that; they had their needs.

But now Amira had given him a son, his first, and no other woman could ever do anything that important for him. Perhaps something was wrong between them sexually, but surely that could work out with time. Even if it didn't, the world would not end. Her life would still be far better than that of most wives, certainly better than Jihan's was (ridiculous to have imagined that she was turning into her mother, like one of those movie tricks where a flower blooms and dies in half a minute).

Leave the bedroom out of it; look at the way Ali treated her everywhere else. He never complained when she buried herself in her books. He not only tolerated her work (the first time she thought of it as that), he encouraged her to do more!

In fact they complemented each other. As minister of culture, Ali had a certain image to maintain, especially among foreigners. So it was a thing of great worth to him to have the best of both worlds—an obedient Arab wife, yet one who was accomplished, educated, who could converse about matters more substantial than the latest fashions or servant problems.

And yet, and yet, even as she tried to catalog Ali's virtues, she remembered Philippe Rochon and knew instinctively that he would never treat a woman as she had been treated, not even in a darkened room where no one else could see.

From the nursery, she heard a beloved cry, and her breasts wept milk in response. Taking her baby to her, she consoled herself with the thought that even if there were nothing else, there would be Karim and her, and that would be enough.

PHILIPPE

Paris

Wrapping her white mohair spring coat around her, Amira stepped out of the George V lobby. Shaking her head at the driver who sprang to attention when she appeared, she turned left and walked towards the Champs Élysées.

This was the third time Amira had been to the city, and she had come to love it more than any of the other places to which Ali's duties had taken them. She loved walking the broad boulevards and picturesque streets. She adored all the typical tourist pleasures, the glittering shops on the Avenue Montaigne, the fabled restaurant atop the Eiffel Tower, the *bateau mouche* on the Seine. But more than that, the sense of freedom, the pure pleasure in living—it was overpowering.

The styles the women wore, and the style with which they wore them; the smell and taste of the food; the play of light along the river; and most of all, for Amira, the fireworks display of ideas she could witness in any one of a hundred cafés and bistros on the Left Bank around the Sorbonne.

Here were young men and women (!) scarcely older than herself laughing, shouting, whispering conspiratorially, arguing and expounding on every possible subject from communism to the *Kama Sutra*, from atheism to the Albigensian heresies, from black holes in space to the Black Panthers in California.

This is paradise, Amira sometimes thought. *I could stay here forever.* She had to remind herself that she couldn't.

Since they'd arrived yesterday morning, the hours had flown by. A new haircut at Alexandre's. A whirlwind shopping trip at Dior. Lunch at the Tour d'Argent. A party at the Remali embassy in Ali's honor.

Visiting Paris also meant a visit with Malik, who had established a base of operations here in addition to those in Marseilles, Piraeus, Rotterdam—name a city, it seemed, and her brother would mention a "deal" he was working on there. And there would be an opportunity to see Laila, nearly old enough for school now. It was easy to arrange—Ali had claimed an important meeting with someone he'd met at the embassy, but Amira knew he had no interest in spending time with Malik.

• • •

The fifteen-room apartment on the Avenue Foch, still smelling of fresh paint, was magnificent. Soaring, elaborately plastered ceilings, fireplaces of the rarest marble, remarkable parquet floors burnished to a golden patina, marble fireplaces—these were but a few of the features that had attracted Malik when he'd begun his search for a new home. The rest—the impeccable French antiques, the English silver, Aubusson tapestries, all the opulent furnishings—Malik had added himself.

"Who decorated this place?" Amira asked as he walked her through the apartment, clearly trying to restrain his pride of ownership. "I know there's a woman here. I see touches . . . those framed photographs on the piano, the antique lace in the guest bedrooms. Surely you didn't do all that?"

"The 'woman' in question is a decorator," he replied. "And she was very well paid for those 'touches.' "

"That's it, then?" she teased. "Your private life consists of *rendezvous* with decorators?"

Before he could answer, a little girl burst into the room shouting, "Papa! Papa!" Her nanny trailed behind.

Malik scooped his daughter into his arms and held her close, his tender expression revealing the depth of his love. With her dark eyes and elfin face, Laila looked like a perfect Parisian gamine whom someone had kidnapped and dressed in the very finest clothes.

Amira sat back and watched them. Her niece spoke perfect Parisian French—with an occasional astonishing Marseillaise obscenity tossed in, at which Malik laughed uproariously. As she told her father everything she and her nanny had done, it was clear that her Arabic, what few words of it she knew, was atrocious.

When she finally turned her attention to Amira, she said in rapid succession, "Did you bring me a present today? I still have the pretty dress you brought last time. Do you have any little girls I can play with? Will you come to see Papa again?"

Amira chose her answers cautiously, so as not to reveal her relationship to Malik. Though Laila knew Malik was her father—he could not bear for her not to know—she was boarded with her nanny, in a comfortable home a short distance away. It was not a satisfying situation, but Malik had hinted he might soon arrive at a solution.

Soon the child skipped off and began to bounce a ball in the apartment. The nanny made as if to stop her, but Malik shook his head. He watched indulgently as she played among valuable artworks and antiques, unconcerned about the material things, seeing only his daughter's happiness.

He's been lonely, Amira thought to herself. *He has so much love to give. He shouldn't be alone.*

With a sister's bluntness, she asked, "When are you going to settle down, Malik? Laila needs a mother. And if you found a woman to marry, you could find a way to live together openly. As a family."

He paused, as if considering the wisdom of speaking frankly. Then he smiled, a shy melting smile that tugged at her heart. "I don't want to say anything just yet . . . it's too soon. But I have met someone. She's had a hard life, Amira . . . and she reminds me of Laila. If things work out, then I'll have some news for you."

She threw her arms around him. "I'm so happy, Malik. And I'll 'think positive.' My psychology text says that positive thinking can accomplish a great deal."

He laughed. "Soon I'll have to be careful what I say in your presence. You'll be analyzing all my secret thoughts." Then he grew reflective again. "And you? Is marriage treating you well? Is Ali a good husband?"

"He . . . I . . . yes. Everything is fine."

Suddenly Malik was hard-eyed. "Is he mistreating you? Tell me the truth, Amira. If he is, I'll put an end to it, I swear."

"What are you talking about? Everything's fine. Ali treats me very well. Everyone says so. And he adores our son."

"Well, then. Good." The moment passed. Much as she wished for harmony between Malik and Ali, they simply did not like one another. Part of it, she thought, was Malik's natural older-brotherly protectiveness. Part, Amira had to admit, was a kind of envy on Ali's part. Malik, younger than Ali, was making a name and a fortune more or less on his own. Ali, although richer by a considerable margin, had traded shamelessly on influence, inside information, and capital borrowed against his father's inexhaustible resources.

Though the bad feelings between Ali and her brother caused Amira some distress, they also gave her a great deal of freedom. All she had to do was say she was spending the day with Malik, and she was free to do as she pleased.

• • •

A few hours later she was seated in a sidewalk café. The sky was blue, the sunlight was warm, the day seemed magical. "I wonder what any of us would be like," she said, "without all this money."

"We would be poor, of course," Philippe said with a smile, his hand closing over hers. "But speak for yourself. I'm only a country doctor who makes house calls and who has to pay French taxes."

Amira smiled back. She knew very well that the "house calls" he mentioned often started with a jet flight to Riyadh or Muscat or Amman. But what she was thinking about was what it would be like if she were away from Ali and everything he represented, if she were just a woman on holiday in Paris, meeting a man she adored at a Left Bank sidewalk café.

In the months since they'd first met, Amira had seen Philippe a half-dozen times, a few hours here and there in al-Remal and once at an embassy party in Paris. Yet he'd been with her in dreams and fantasies. When her bed seemed lonely and cold, she imagined him as he was today, his blue Norman eyes twinkling in the sunlight, the Parisian breeze pushing at his salt-and-pepper hair.

Is this what it's like to love a man? Is this what caused Laila to risk her life and then to lose it?

"What's it like to be veiled?" Philippe asked, suddenly serious.

"I hate it. I've always hated it. At one time I had become used to it, I suppose, but now it seems worse than ever."

"I know you have no choice, but what's the justification for the whole thing? I mean the religious reason."

"Well, the mullahs say it's mandated by the Koran, but my sister-in-law pointed out that the Koran admonishes both men and women to be modest, nothing more. Apparently veiling began as a voluntary practice among upper-class women—to set them apart from the lower classes. Munira says that male-dominated societies used it to keep women separate and powerless." She smiled tentatively, because she wasn't sure she believed everything Munira said.

Philippe listened as carefully as if she were a colleague describing some important advance in medical science. It was typical of him. She remembered the way he'd listened to her that first night in al-Remal. Not that he refused to assume a mentor's role where circumstances warranted it: he advised her which of her biology and psychology books were outdated or mere popularizations and sent her better ones. Once, when she complained of how dull she found chemistry, he reminded her of Freud's own prediction that "the future belongs to the chemicals." But in matters where her knowledge or insight was greater than his, he listened as if she were the teacher.

Now, in the burnished gold light of late afternoon, as Amira's precious hours of freedom drifted away, they talked fitfully and in murmurs, trying to postpone parting. Philippe broke the mood. "I was in a store the other day," he said with a smile, "and I saw a black silk scarf, very sheer. I picked it up and held it over my face and walked around—you could see through it well enough. The saleswoman was in a fine state of alarm. She certainly thought I was mad, and if I hadn't bought the thing, she probably would have summoned the paramedics." He shook his head and looked out at the boulevard, the slanting light accentuating the smile wrinkles around his eyes. "I wanted to see what it was like—the veil."

Amira leaned toward him, and suddenly they were kissing, a long, deep, deeply shared kiss that she wanted never to end.

When he drew away, the look in his eyes was almost more than she could bear. "My apartment isn't far from here," he said quietly. "Will you come with me?"

Her body screamed yes, but she looked down and mutely shook her head, a little gesture that might mean almost anything.

Against the dark screen of her closed eyelids she saw Laila's body twitching to the blows of countless stones.

When she still said nothing, Philippe touched her hand. "It's all right. I understand."

They had approached a threshold and drawn back, as if they'd opened a door, seen a beautiful but dangerous garden, and closed the door again.

"We're still friends," Philippe said.

"Always." More than friends. Matched souls, Amira imagined, an inseparable pair broken apart long ago in some cosmic accident, perhaps in one of those black holes in space the Sorbonne astronomy students spoke of with the icy passion of their science.

A MAN IN THE NIGHT

When she first returned to al-Remal, Amira could not stop thinking about Paris and Philippe. Everything in her daily life—everything except her child—seemed stifling. But daily life weaves a strong web, and within a few weeks it had entangled her; nothing she could do prevented the time with Philippe from losing its urgent reality, becoming a kind of keepsake, a photograph in the locket of her memory, something to be opened to view only once in a while, tenderly and secretly.

Yet she had changed; she could feel it. The small taste of love she had experienced was like the scent of food to someone starving. She wanted more—far more.

It was a desire she tried to suppress. Time and again she told herself that even if her husband was almost a stranger to her, her life still was one that many women would envy. The women's wing of the royal palace might be a cloister, but it was a luxurious one.

On her walls were paintings that, as a girl, she had admired in Miss Vanderbeek's books. True, most of them were abstract, since the royal family officially adhered to the belief that the Koran prohibited artistic representations of the human body or other natural scenes, but they were beautiful, and she could lose herself in them for hours. In a more capricious mood, she could express a desire to update her wardrobe, and the next day Pierre Cardin or Saint-Laurent or Givenchy would arrive with a string of models to stage a private fashion show.

Whatever Ali's faults, he was generous, she had to admit. On their first anniversary, he had summoned her to the living room in the men's section. Some of his kinsmen were there, as were two men in western suits whom Ali introduced as representatives of Harry Winston. The men opened a dozen cases in which diamonds blazed against black velvet.

"Take your pick," Ali told her expansively.

It was in the aftermath of the oil embargo, and money was gushing into al-Remal in unbelievable quantities, but Amira disliked some of the self-indulgence that came with it. She pointed to a lovely little bracelet that would accentuate her hands nicely. In a world where faces, legs, and arms were kept hidden, hands were a major feature of a woman's beauty, and Amira was rather vain of hers.

Ali looked irritated. "Is that a set?" he asked, indicating a magnificent necklace, bracelet, and earrings.

"Yes, Your Highness," one of the Winston men said.

"She'll take that—and the little bracelet, too, of course."

Amira did not have to feign being overwhelmed. Like all Remali women, who in the event of divorce might be left with little but their jewelry, she had an expert knowledge of its value; the price of the diamonds her husband had chosen would approach a million American dollars.

On Karim's first birthday, Ali's gift to the mother of his son was equally impressive: a magnificent emerald said to have belonged to a maharajah. This time he made the presentation in private. Had one of his older brothers objected to the conspicuousness of the diamond showing? Amira took the chance to ask, "Why do you give me such wonderful gifts, my husband? Surely I'm undeserving."

"My wife should have fine things," he said, as if it were self-evident.

"But . . . so much." She trailed off. It was not her right to expect some word of love, she told herself. Ali was not that kind of man. Still, it hurt to be treated as if she were only a prized servant, richly and frequently rewarded but hardly loved. For a moment she saw Philippe's smiling eyes.

As the months passed, Ali's indifference gnawed at her. Everything in her family upbringing, everything in her society, told her that if a man did not love his wife, it was the wife's fault. Perhaps she was being punished for her feelings for another man. Yet sinful though that was, everyone knew of women who had such feelings—and more than feelings—whose husbands nevertheless worshiped them. No, it must be a deeper failing, some fundamental unattractiveness in her. "Good marriages are made by good wives": was it Aunt Najla who was always reciting that old saying?

She began to be obsessed with becoming pregnant again. Things had been so much better when she was carrying Karim, and just after his birth. Surely Ali wanted more children; all men did. Yet how was she to conceive? He came to her so rarely now, and when he did, the act often ended in his failure, accompanied by recriminations against her. Only cruelty seemed to sustain his desire, but even when little tortures of her helped him to a finish, it was usually in a way that was unnatural and painful, and that could never give her a child.

But wasn't that her fault, too—that he did not find her desirable enough to satisfy him in normal ways?

Was he seeing other women, draining his passion with them? And if he were, again whose fault was that? A man had needs. If his wife were not enough for him, the common wisdom was clear as to who was to blame.

Common wisdom had remedies to offer as well, and one night Amira found herself thinking about them. Charms. Potions. There were women—often Egyptians—who sold them. But that was out of the question. If a prince's wife were seen at the door of such a woman, the story would be on every tongue in the palace within hours. She couldn't send a servant, either; they all worked for the Rashads, and only incidentally for her. Perhaps she could go home for a while, ask Bahia or Um Salih.

But was that necessary? Not every love spell was a deep secret. Jihan—an Egyptian, after all—had told her dozens of them. For instance, there was green wheat and pigeon meat cooked with nutmeg. A priapic, guaranteed to turn a man's member as rigid as iron. And everyone knew that a few drops of a woman's menstrual blood, mixed in the man's food, would enslave him to her forever. Maybe combine the two? But how could anyone possibly induce Ali to eat green wheat and pigeon meat?

Suddenly, alone in her room, Amira burst out laughing. Had it come to this? Amira Rashad, with all her education, with her pretensions to Parisian sophistication, Amira Rashad the would-be psychologist, scheming like a desert Bedouin to enchain her husband by superstition and witchcraft! She laughed until the tears came. If only there were someone to share the joke!

There was no one, of course; certainly not her in-laws. To the royal family, a wife who produced only one child was no laughing matter. When Amira had borne Karim, Ali's mother and sisters, previously so cool and standoffish, had almost overwhelmed her with their approval and solicitousness. The first few months of her son's life brought the closest thing to happiness she had known in the palace. Then the respite was over. Soon hardly a day went by without some seemingly casual remark about her next child. Then came the pointed questions and expressions of concern about her health. Finally, not long after Karim's first birthday, Faiza announced that she had summoned the doctor to examine Amira.

Protests were no good—Um Ahmad was in her most regal mood. Soon Amira found herself wearing her veil and little else, being probed and questioned by the same doctor who had failed to help Jihan in her crisis. For once she was grateful for the veil.

"You are in very good health, Princess, praise God," the man informed her when she was dressed. "I see no reason, God willing, that you should not have many children."

"You give me good news. God is indeed compassionate."

"Indeed." The doctor toyed with his stethoscope. He looked uncomfortable.

"Is there something else? Something wrong?"

"Wrong? Nothing at all." He tucked the stethoscope away. "Forgive me, Highness, but in order to be of most value to you, I need to ask some rather personal questions. In strictest confidence, of course."

"Go ahead."

"I know that you have visited Europe several times, with your husband, of course, and I must ask—please don't take offense—if you are taking one of the so-called birth control medications."

"No."

"I thought not. Forgive my asking. I would be remiss if I didn't. It's not unheard of, you know, especially among women who have gone abroad. God knows why."

"Of course."

The doctor nodded. "Only one more question, Highness. Again forgive me—you understand. But is everything . . . as it should be between you and your husband?"

Beneath the veil Amira's skin burned. She longed to tell someone, anyone—even this servile little man—that nothing was as it should be. But she couldn't. The shame was too great. "Everything is fine," she said.

"Yes?"

"Yes."

"Well, then." The doctor brightened and picked up his bag. "It hasn't really been that long, you know, Highness, although certainly I understand your eagerness to have more children. As I said, you're healthy. Be patient, and God willing, you will be rewarded."

After he left, Amira felt like breaking something against the wall. The examination had been humiliating, but her anger was about more than that. She was angry because she had lied. No, because she was in a position where she had to lie. But who was to blame for that? Only she. Nothing would change unless she changed it.

That night she came up with an idea.

"Ali, heart," she said, using her best wheedling voice, absorbed from Jihan, "do you know that soon we will have been married two years?"

"Of course I know. You don't think I'd forget, do you?" He was on his way out—to where?—impatient to be gone.

"Do you know what I'd like for a present?"

Ali shrugged. "Ask and it's yours."

"Only you, my husband. Your face has become a stranger's to me. I know I've offended you."

"Nonsense." He glanced toward the door.

"As a gift, I would like for us to go away for a week or two, love. Just you and me and Karim. Someplace we have never been, where there's not a single embassy party or exhibition opening to worry about. Can we do that?"

For a moment he looked at her so uncaringly that she was sure she had angered him. But then he smiled—the handsome, charming Ali. "Of course we can," he said. "And I know just the place."

• • •

From the air, the Nile Delta was a spill of shocking green across a sand floor, the line between desert and verdure as sharp as if cut with a knife. Then in the distance Amira saw another color, the deep blue of the Mediterranean. As the plane descended, she could make out tiny figures on a grayish beach.

Thc airport was small and had a decidedly bedraggled look. As she stepped from the plane into bright sunlight, Amira braced for the blinding heat she had left in al-Remal, but felt only a cool breeze. The temperature could not have been much more than eighty.

A Rolls-Royce waited on the runway. A customs inspector standing beside it merely saluted, welcomed them to Alexandria, and opened the door. Half an hour later, Amira was strolling the grounds of a seaside villa in a suburb that Ali called Roushdy. Red tiles topped a white-marble house—a small palace, really, and classically graceful. It looked as if it could have been a noble Roman's summer home at Pompeii or Herculaneum in the days when Vesuvius was just a pretty mountain. Bougainvillea bloomed profusely, and a lush lawn flowed down a gentle slope to the beach. A long, narrow swimming pool fitted perfectly into the landscape. From one angle, a trick of design made its blue water appear to merge with the sea beyond. On both sides of the broad lawn, high walls lined with date palms stretched all the way to the sand.

"You can wear a bathing suit in privacy," Ali pointed out. "Just be sure the male servants are warned away first."

"Oh, Ali, it's gorgeous! It must be the most beautiful place on earth. My God, the rent must be a fortune, even for two weeks."

Ali raised an eyebrow. "Actually, I bought it. A good price. It belonged to a friend of my father's in Abu Dhabi." He glanced at his watch. "That reminds me. I have a few acquaintances I need to renew in town. I may as well do it this evening. I'll probably be rather late getting back, but you'll want to rest anyway, after the flight. We'll see the sights tomorrow."

It wasn't what Amira hoped to hear, but for a husband to tell his wife his plans at all was a token of consideration. Besides, she was too in love with this jewel of a place to be disappointed.

Three days later disappointment had set in with a vengeance. She still had not left the grounds. Ali went out each night and came in late, bleary and smelling of liquor, taking a quick swim in the pool before stumbling off to an oblivious sleep from which he did not rouse himself before noon. Whatever Amira had hoped for this holiday together, it was not happening.

The beauty of her surroundings was consolation. She rose early, and, after feeding Karim, breakfasted on her balcony overlooking the sea. Later, while her son napped, she took a book to read by the pool. In al-Remal, serious sunbathing was unheard of, and the American and European compulsion to bake in the full sun was considered sure proof of an essential lunacy. But here, with nothing but a swimming suit between her and the caressing ocean air, the cool water, the sun's warm kiss, Amira found a pleasure that bordered on the erotic.

Still, three days was enough; the villa was becoming a prison. She hadn't even been to the beach, fearing that, as liberal as Egypt might be, an unaccompanied woman might encounter trouble.

That afternoon she took her stand. "Ali, this city is famous for seafood, but all I've had since I've been here is lamb and chicken. I might as well be back home." It was true; they had brought along a sous-chef from the royal kitchen as cook, but the man refused to exercise his skills on the unfamiliar catch of the local fishermen.

"Perhaps tomorrow. I have an appointment tonight." His face, still puffy from the previous evening's drinking, was sullen, his eyes bloodshot.

Amira persisted. "We can eat early. You'll still have time to visit your acquaintances. If you wish."

In the end, perhaps because he was in too much pain to argue, Ali relented. The restaurant was on the Sharia Safia Zaghloul. The drive into town took them along the broad, curving Corniche, the harbor on one side, the lights of the city rising on the other.

The driver, an Alexandrian, pointed proudly toward a long peninsula across the water. "There stood the lighthouse of Pharos, one of the seven wonders of the world." But no wondrous lighthouse shone there now. There was only a massive, squat building that the driver identified as an old fort. That seemed to be the way with much of the city, as far as Amira could tell from the window of the Rolls.

She knew that Alexandria once ranked among the world's capitals, rivaling Rome and Constantinople. In modern times, it had remained an exotic destination—cosmopolitan, more European than Egyptian, and spiced with a reputation for decadence and sin. Now the town simply looked down on its luck.

The restaurant accorded with this general impression. It reminded Amira vaguely of some of the lesser bistros she had seen in Paris, although less crowded. Only a few tables were occupied. The bouillabaisse she ordered was acceptable, nothing more. None of that mattered. She was wearing beautiful clothes, sitting unveiled beside her husband in a public place, and enjoying every minute. She even had a glass of wine.

A middle-aged couple, obviously British, sat at the next table. The man had a vaguely military look; the woman was thin, elegant, handsome. As Amira studied them, she noticed a certain reserve in the waiter's treatment of the couple and chilly glances from one or two patrons.

"Those poor people," Amira murmured. "They can't be very comfortable."

"Ah, yes," Ali said, "the lingering aftereffects of British colonialism. We have long memories in the Middle East. We don't forget. And we rarely forgive. But since I have no grievance with the English, I see no reason why we shouldn't be civil. And hospitable." He beckoned the waiter over and ordered a bottle of red wine for the next table.

When it arrived, the Englishman rose from his chair. "Thank you. Thank you very much indeed," he said to Ali. "You're very kind."

"Not at all. Perhaps you and your lovely wife would like to join us. My wife and I would enjoy the opportunity to practice our English."

"A pleasure," he said, extending his hand. "My name is Charles Edwin. And this is my wife, Margaret."

"Ali Rashad. My wife, Amira. What brings you to Alexandria?"

"Oh, we just came out for a few days to summon up the ghosts of our youth," Margaret answered, her cool gray eyes warming in a genuine smile.

"Ghosts?" Amira asked.

"Charles was attached to the British embassy in Cairo," Margaret explained. "It was a long time ago."

Amira wanted to ask what the Englishman did at the British embassy, but she felt that might be impolite. Perhaps he was a spy, she thought—a bluff, tweedy, balding James Bond.

"And have you found any ghosts?" Ali asked.

Sir Charles laughed. "Haven't encountered many, I'm afraid. Old station's not what it once was. Although I saw a Greek or two on the street today, and even a Frenchman. Maybe they'll let us all back in someday."

"And you?" said Margaret, addressing the question to both of them. "Let me guess—you're on your honeymoon."

"No," said Ali.

"It's our second anniversary," Amira supplied.

"Ah."

"I've bought a place in Roushdy," Ali said. "It seemed a good time to put it to use."

"Roushdy," said Sir Charles. "May I ask which place is yours?"

Ali told him. The older man was clearly impressed. Soon the two of them were discussing the real estate market in various locales in the Middle East. Margaret turned to Amira in the immemorial manner of women excusing themselves from men's talk.

"And are you enjoying Alex, my dear?"

"Alex? Oh, Alexandria. Well, I've hardly seen it. I've—we've—spent most of our time at the house."

"Ah. Well, then, why not let me play tour guide? Charles has some sort of chore in Alamein tomorrow, and I'll be at loose ends. I'd love to show you and your husband the old town, if you don't mind a touch of nostalgia."

"Ali, could we?"

"Could we what?"

Amira repeated Margaret's invitation.

"I'm afraid I may have to do some business tomorrow. But you go, by all means."

"It's all right?"

"Of course."

At the end of the evening they made arrangements. The Edwins were at the Hotel Cecil. "Not what it once was, of course," said Sir Charles apologetically.

"What is, my dear?" said Margaret.

The Rolls was waiting. Ali gave the Edwins a lift to their hotel, then instructed the driver to take Amira home. "I'll find a cab," he told her. "Don't wait up. You'll need to be on your way early."

He was still asleep when she left in the morning.

• • •

"There are still some things worth seeing in Alex," said Margaret Edwin, "but we shan't see them all today. There's an excellent museum, for instance, some real treasures in it, but it needs hours to appreciate it properly, hours and a working knowledge of the history of Macedonia and Rome—and Egypt, of course."

Amira admitted that her learning in those areas was not great.

"Ah. I'll give you some books. Perhaps we'll take in the museum another day. I think we'll skip the Kom es Chogafa catacombs as well. I'm afraid I've never developed much enthusiasm for catacombs."

They were riding along the Corniche in a British consulate car, a uniformed Egyptian chauffeur at the wheel.

"And, of course," Margaret went on, "one trouble with Alex is that there are so many fascinating things one *can't* see, simply because they've vanished."

"The famous lighthouse," Amira volunteered, to show that she wasn't totally ignorant of local lore.

"The lighthouse. Apparently it symbolized the city to the whole ancient world, much as the Eiffel Tower for Paris, or the Empire State Building for New York City. You could ask Charles about the technical side of it. The lantern—the thing that shone the light out to sea—was some sort of magic lens or mirror. One could look into it and see ships a hundred miles away. Not only that, but it could focus the sun's rays on enemy vessels and set them afire. Or so the legend goes."

"What happened to it?"

"The lighthouse? Oh, the usual thing: time. The Muslims who took the city had no interest in Greek science. Someone told the local ruler that there was treasure buried under the lighthouse. The digging caused the lantern to fall. A few centuries later, an earthquake knocked down the tower itself."

A large, rather worn-looking building loomed up on the left, overlooking the Corniche and the harbor. "That's our hotel," said Margaret. "Normally we'd be at the consulate, but—well, actually, the Cecil is where Charles and I spent our honeymoon, twenty-five years ago."

"But that's so romantic!"

"Ah, well. Of course, in the midst of it, Charles is off on some business or other—as your man is."

The evaluating gray eyes seemed to demand a response.

"I never ask Ali about business matters," said Amira. "Almost never."

"Quite." The little smile. "In any case, let's begin our tour. Hamza, take Sharia Nebi Daniel."

The driver turned off the Corniche onto a narrower and poorer street teeming with pedestrians.

"Daniel," Margaret informed Amira, "like Abraham and Moses, is a prophet in both our religions. A remarkable fate for Jews. That mosque just ahead is the Mosque of Daniel. It's said that the remains of Alexander the Great rest somewhere in the cellars. Naturally, no one knows for sure."

"El Iskanderieh," said Amira. It was the Arabic name for the city. "Iskander" was Alexander.

"Cleopatra is also supposed to be buried near here," Margaret continued. "More invisible history. Like the great library of Alexandria. This is where it was—all around us. A university as much as a library. The intellectual center of the world for hundreds of years."

"It burned." Amira remembered from her lessons with Miss Vanderbeek. "All that knowledge lost."

"It didn't burn by accident," said Margaret. "The Christian monks who ran the city in those days burned it. They thought the books pagan. The same crowd killed Hypatia."

"Hypatia?" Amira had never heard the name.

"A philosopher and professor of mathematics whose ideas displeased the monks. Somewhere just along here, in the year A.D. 415, a mob caught her walking home from a lecture and tore her to pieces with shards of building tiles."

"Her? A woman?"

"Odd, isn't it, when young women in this part of the world are struggling simply to be allowed into university, to think that a woman was a professor here sixteen hundred years ago. Ras el Tin Palace, please, Hamza."

Ras el Tin was impressive even to Amira, who, after all, lived in a palace. Built when the Turks ruled Egypt, and last occupied by Farouk, it rose amid formal gardens on the harbor peninsula, the Mediterranean on one side, the city on the other. Its magnificent chambers dazzled the senses: the throne room, seemingly as large as a soccer field, the floor inlaid with ivory and rare woods in peacock-tail designs; the mirrored ballroom, windows two stories tall overlooking the gardens and the brilliant blue sea, the thirty-foot ceiling kaleidoscopic with stained-glass patterns, upstaging the multicolored marble dance floor; the chandelier room, its namesake fixture a ten-thousand-pound galaxy of glittering crystal and gold.

Amid all the opulence, the most poignant object was one of the least spectacular: Farouk's diary, open to July 26, 1952—the day the aging, obese, childish, despised king abdicated. According to a khaki-uniformed guide, the monarch misspelled his own name on the paper by which he surrendered the throne.

They walked through the gardens before leaving. Out to sea, an ocean liner plied westward, a pretty toy ship against the horizon.

Following Amira's gaze, Margaret said, "I believe that's the *Azonia*. She cruises between here and Marseilles, four days each way. How nice to be aboard, eh?" Amira realized that it was just what she had been thinking.

Margaret insisted on buying lunch. She chose a seaside restaurant called Aboukir, a single large room, glass walls all around. Fish of a dozen species swam in tanks, awaiting the customer's choice. "You can't get fresher than that," Margaret observed, "but I think I'll have the *soubia*. It's excellent here."

"I'll have that, too," Amira told the waiter.

Soubia turned out to be tiny octopus cooked in olive oil. She braved a first bite. Delicious.

"Did you notice the so-called shortcut we took getting here?" asked Margaret.

"I noticed we went through a rather rough-looking neighborhood."

"That was a corner of the Mina, the old port. I imagine Hamza was hoping to catch a glimpse of a loose woman. I wouldn't give him the satisfaction of seeming to know, but we passed right by Madame Heloise's, the most notorious brothel still doing business. The whole area was once the fleshpot of all fleshpots, catering to any and all predilections, one hears. It still has a certain reputation—nothing like in the old days, of course. Today the clientele is mainly oil Arabs. No offense—certainly our chaps had their innings."

Amira shrugged. Why should she be offended? Everyone knew what men could be like away from home.

The afternoon was devoted to another place, the Muntaza, a pinkish sand-castle fantasy set in a park of eucalyptus and pepper trees on a cool-breezed hill above a lovely beach. Amira recalled Jihan's stories about the Muntaza, but nowhere did she see the pool where Farouk's naked bathing beauties cavorted. Perhaps it had been filled in, forgotten.

After touring the building and grounds, she and Margaret walked barefoot on the shore, Hamza accompanying them so that there would be no difficulty. It was a public beach but lined with cabanas—comfortable little houses, really—for private rental. Elderly men crisscrossed the sand offering coffee or lemonade to families basking in the blue-and-gold afternoon.

The last stop was the British consulate in Roushdy, scarcely a mile from home, for an elaborate tea. Amira had been in London once; this little corner of Egypt seemed far more English. As the setting sun threw long shadows across the combed lawns, she found herself wishing she could push it higher in the sky to keep the day from ending. It was Margaret, she realized, who made her feel that way.

Amira had been truly close to three women: Laila, Miss Vanderbeek, and Jihan. All were gone. Now, out of nowhere in this foreign place, she had found a little of each of them—the adventurous companion, the teacher, the mother—in Margaret Edwin.

It was time to go. Margaret had sent for the car. They stood at the door making small talk. Yes, Amira might be free tomorrow; she would ask Ali. Good. Perhaps they could see the museum after all.

Then, unexpectedly, Margaret said, "Charles and I had a daughter.

She died in a sailing accident when she was twelve. She would have been just your age. We were talking about it last night, after we met you. Charles said you had a lovely smile, but your eyes seemed sad. I know I'm being presumptuous, but if you need someone to talk with, I'm here—for a few days, at any rate."

"Thank you." Amira didn't know what else to say. Again it was as if the older woman had read her thoughts.

• • •

Ali was lounging by the pool, a tall drink in hand. "Home is the explorer!" he said cheerfully. "Go put on your suit. Take a dip with me."

It was an easy order to obey. When she came down in her suit, he was splashing happily, a fresh drink on the pool's edge.

"You're not going into the city tonight, dear heart?"

"Hmm? I don't know. Maybe give the old town a rest. Make an early night of it."

A pleasant surprise. After a swim they sat by the pool, stars coming out in the delightful evening. Ali mixed another drink and poured a soda for Amira.

"So tell me about your day," he smiled. "Did you discover the remains of Cleopatra?"

She told him about the palaces, the *soubia*, the ultra-Britishness of the consulate. He laughed, asked little questions, made jokes. He was drinking too much, but what did that matter? He was here; at least that was a start.

The change came without warning. Amira was relating what Margaret had said about the Mina. Ali's face had darkened. He stood up unsteadily.

"I don't want you to see that woman again."

"What?"

"You heard me. I forbid it. Sitting in a public place talking about whorehouses!"

"But, Ali, dearest—"

"Don't argue with me. Maybe your family has no reputation to worry about, but mine does."

"But it was only—"

"Will you sit there and dispute your husband? I tell you I forbid it!"

He stalked into the house. She sat in the growing darkness, too shocked to cry. When, much later, she went inside, he was gone.

Margaret called in the morning. She was devastated, blaming herself when Amira told her what had happened. They talked for a long time, Amira trying to explain that it was no one's fault. God's will. Nothing to be done about it. What choice did she have but to obey her husband? "I understand," said Margaret, but Amira could tell that she didn't, not really.

"Good luck, my dear. Good-bye." Those were the last words Amira heard from her new friend.

"God's peace," she said, but the line was already dead.

• • •

Again she had the pool, her books, and nothing else.

"Ali, I want to go home."

"Home? But why? It's beautiful here. Aren't you happy?"

"No. I came here to be with you, but you are never here."

"I'm here right now."

"You know what I mean."

"No, I don't know what you mean. I know that my business in this city is not your business. I know that this trip was your idea. I know that I spent a fortune to buy this place that you don't enjoy. But I don't know what you mean."

A little later she heard the car leaving.

There was nothing she could do. Her idea had failed terribly. Things were worse here than in al-Remal. That night, for the first time, the sea air and the sound of the waves did not lull her quickly to sleep. She paced in her room, wondering what was going to happen to her.

If there were no more love, no more children, would Ali divorce her? She almost hoped for it. She was still young, still had time to make a good match. But what would happen to Karim? Besides, Ali wouldn't divorce her—he had said so more than once, not out of love, but out of vindictiveness, when they were arguing. She would be relegated to some back room of the palace to wither while he fathered children on new wives.

She looked at Karim, asleep in his crib. In a few years, he would go off to the men's quarters; then he would be grown. If she were lucky, he might have lunch with her once or twice a week.

She tried to tell herself that it was all God's will, but the words didn't help. What did it matter whose will it was? If a shooting star fell from the sky and crushed her bones, that would clearly be God's will, but would it hurt any less? If only there were someone to talk to. Philippe. Or Malik. She thought of the *Azonia*. It would be back from Marseilles in another day or two. What if she took Karim and her passport, climbed aboard, bribed the purser? That was madness. Even if they gave her passage, Ali would be waiting at the dock in France.

She curled up on the bed. *Mama, where are you?* she whimpered. Stop it. Jihan was in paradise. Wasn't she? Was Laila there too? What made her think of Laila?

She got up and went through the house to the cabinet where Ali kept his liquor. Without looking at the label, she opened the first bottle and took a swallow. It was like drinking fire. She gagged, held it down, took another gulp. Maybe now she could sleep. Ali slept like the dead. The sleep of the righteous?

She climbed the stairs. They seemed to be swaying. When she lay down, the room whirled. She went to the bathroom and vomited, then, exhausted, crawled back into bed, her hand reaching out in the darkness to touch her sleeping child.

• • •

The moon was high and bright, flooding the room, hurting her eyes. Where was she? Oh yes: Alexandria. What time was it? No idea. Her head hurt. Something had wakened her. Karim? No. Sleeping peacefully. Voices outside. Ali. Who was he talking to? A servant? He sounded angry.

She slipped from the bed and out onto the balcony. In the moonlight below, by the pool, Ali in his swimming trunks was facing a young man whose clothes testified to poverty.

"Excellency," the man implored in a voice that just carried to Amira, "I mention only your promise. You said you would take care of me. But the money hasn't come."

To Amira's astonishment, Ali hit the man with a hard backhanded slap. "How dare you come to my home! I warned you never to set foot here. You know where to meet me. There and only there!"

"Excellency, please listen. My mother is sick. We need money for a doctor, for medicine. I beg you. If I don't please you any longer, let me send my brother. You've seen him, Excellency. He's only thirteen, very beautiful, very pure. You would be the first, as you were with me."

In the warm Alexandrian night, Amira felt as if she had turned to ice. Suddenly it was all clear: Ali's indifference, his moods and unpredictability. His anger that time when she tried to coax him into making love. Her fingers were tingling, her head light. *Don't faint*, she told herself. *Not here, not now.*

"Please, Excellency, just a few pounds."

"Listen, dog, you lose everything by coming here. Get to your kennel!"

But now the young man's cringing attitude changed subtly, a hint of threat in it. Amira realized that he was larger and more muscular than Ali. "Excellency, I never meant for it to come to this, but I have pictures. Perhaps someone would buy them for a few pounds, just enough to pay the doctor. Please don't force me to do such a thing."

Ali's hands actually reached for the man's throat. Then he let them drop. "You're lying, of course," he said in his most aristocratic manner, "but I won't waste more time on this nonsense. Even such a fool as you must know that I don't carry money in my swimming trunks. Wait here."

He turned and disappeared from view, into the house. The young man's eyes followed him—yes, like a dog's, Amira thought. Dully, she pictured herself sunning by the pool tomorrow, Ali coming down bleary-eyed. What would she say to him?

He reappeared below, and she unconsciously shrank back into a shadow. Ali held out a wad of bills in his left hand—an insult, but the young man was not here to boost his pride. Bubbling gratitude, he reached for the money. Ali hit him again, this time in the chest. The young man grunted, sank to his knees, sprawled on his back. Only then did Amira see the knife.

"No!" she screamed, the word tiny in the vast night.

Ali turned to find her, his eyes wild. "You're there? One more word, Amira. One word—do you understand?"

There was no need to answer.

Ali clasped the body by the feet and dragged it down the lawn toward the sea. Amira stood shivering. It occurred to her that this was all a nightmare. In the morning it would vanish.

Ali returned, breathing heavily. He splashed water onto the blood beside the pool, then dived into the pool himself, climbed out, and walked into the house. That was all.

He'll be caught, thought Amira. *He's a murderer and he'll be caught.* But then it came to her that she was being stupid—perhaps it was the liquor she'd drunk. Ali had nothing to fear. Even if the police found him with the knife in his hand and the corpse at his feet, he was a prince of al-Remal, and the dead man had been an intruder. Any difficult questions could be answered with money and, if necessary, the transfer of the questioner to some outpost in the Sahara.

All the same, they returned to al-Remal the next day. On the long flight, not one word was said between them.

Part Five

FEAR

"You're a whore, aren't you, a dirty whore. Admit it."

"Ali, please—"

"Say it!"

He pulled her head back by the hair. The pain was bad, but the fear was worse.

"All right, yes, I'm a whore. Please."

"You want it, don't you? You want it here!"

Fingers of his left hand prodded, stabbed painfully into her.

"Oh. Don't, Ali. I'm begging you—"

"Say it!"

Her scalp felt as if it would tear from her skull.

"All right, for God's sake, yes, I want it there. Please just do it."

He moved against her, and she braced for more pain. But nothing happened. He growled in frustration and shoved her face hard into the pillow. She couldn't breathe. *Am I going to die now?* she wondered. She envisioned Karim's dark eyes looking into hers.

Suddenly the weight lifted from her head, and she heard Ali lurch from the room. She gulped air as his steps receded unsteadily down the hall. He was going to drink more. Good. If he sucked greedily enough at the bottle, he would pass out. But he might take more pills, too—the evil black pills that kept him awake all night. If he did that, he might come back, even more of a madman.

She knew this from hard experience. The two months since Alexandria had been a deepening hell. Ali had never shown the slightest remorse for the killing. Instead, he seethed with anger. The liquor amplified it—the liquor and the pills. (Had he been taking them before? Had she simply not known?) He could still present a smiling, unruffled appearance to the world, but alone with Amira things were different.

Ironically, he now demanded her body nearly every night. That, too, had become a hell. Before, she had endured occasional cruelty; now there was outright sadism. She knew the term from her psychology books, but it had never seemed quite real. How could anyone take sexual pleasure in the pain of others? Well, Ali did. Yet even that was deteriorating. More and more often, like tonight, he could not become aroused no matter how much he abused and humiliated her.

Maybe he would just give up, go back to his boys. No. That wouldn't happen. The violence would grow until, sooner or later, he killed her. She was sure of it. Deep in his mind he wanted it. If for no other reason, wasn't she the only witness to his crime?

What am I going to do? She was more alone than ever, cut off by the enormity of what Ali had done, was doing. If she told the truth, every syllable of it, who would believe her? No one in al-Remal, not even her father. Malik would believe, of course. But she couldn't tell him. She knew how he would react, and she knew Ali's power—the royal family's power. To tell her brother would be to sentence him—as well as herself—to death.

It was the same with Philippe. He would believe her. But what could he do? Nothing. Nothing that wouldn't bring him to harm.

She went to the side chamber where Karim slept when Ali made his conjugal visits. Incredibly, that was just what the child was doing—sleeping. Had he been awake earlier? Other times? What had he heard? What would he remember when he was older, whether he knew that he remembered it or not?

She touched his brow, and he murmured in his sleep. It was not just a mother's prejudice, she thought: he was beautiful. He would grow up to be a handsome young man. Suddenly a thought came to her that she had never had, and it made her nearly sick with fear. Her husband's predilections, the way he treated her: if she was gone, what might he do with Karim someday? No, surely not—not even Ali.

Oh, God, I've got to get us out of here. But how? There was no way. There must be a way. She couldn't think of it tonight. She was too tired, too confused. Sleep. Tomorrow. Tomorrow she would find a way. It was a promise she had made to herself every night since Alexandria. Hating the smell and feel of her bed, she fell exhausted on it. Everything was quiet. Maybe for once the liquor had won out over the black pills. She turned out the light and closed her eyes.

It was al-Masagin again, the crowd in the square, the figure tied to the stake. But the figure wasn't Laila: it was the young man in the night at Alexandria. His eyes turned to Amira. Then, somehow, Ali was dragging Laila's body down a beach, blood trailing. Amira ran behind, begging him to stop. The blindfold fell from Laila's face. It wasn't Laila. It was Amira. The Amira who was watching tried to touch the dead Amira but couldn't. It was as if her arms had heavy weights on them. She looked down and saw two snarling black dogs clamping her wrists in their fangs.

Someone was tugging at her, there in the dark. Oh, God, it was Ali. She could smell the liquor.

"Ali, what are you doing?"

"Teaching you a lesson."

"Please, Ali!" She tried to push him away, but something held her hands. Was she still dreaming? Oh, God, she was tied.

Ali switched on the light. The pupils of his eyes were mad pinpoints; the pills had won.

"Now, bitch," he said. "Now." He showed her a quirtlike whip, the kind camel drivers used.

"No, Ali!"

"Turn over unless you want it in the face."

"What have I done, Ali?"

The whip cut across her breasts. Amira cried out at the fiery pain and rolled onto her stomach.

"You're a sow. Yet you look down on me. I can read your devil's eyes. You dare to look down on me. Your husband. A royal prince. Respect. I'll teach you respect."

Each sentence ended with a lash of the whip to her back, her legs, her buttocks. There was no escaping it. She screamed. Surely someone would come—a servant, anyone. No one did.

In his room Karim howled. Somehow Amira tore one hand free, then the other, skin peeling on the rope. She tried to rush past Ali, but he blocked her into a corner.

"Please, Ali. I can't help it if I'm not a man. For God's sake, just stop!"

He did stop. But only for a heartbeat—just long enough for Amira to realize that she should have endured the whipping. On her husband's face she saw cold, deadly rage. She saw murder.

She tried to shield her face as he came for her, but his fist smashed between her hands. She felt the cartilage in her nose snap. A blow to her cheek sent stars dancing through her brain. The room was very bright and distant. Something slammed into her abdomen, driving the breath from her, and she fell. A liquid warmth touched her thighs. *I've wet myself*, she thought with shame.

The last thing she saw was Ali's foot floating toward her in dreamy slow motion, a child's balloon on a string.

• • •

Cool pastel colors. A woman in white. A touch on the lips, rough, soft, cold. Ice in a cloth. It hurt, but the dampness was heaven. She was dying of thirst.

"God be praised," said the woman. "God be praised for saving Your Highness from such a terrible accident."

Accident? Amira tried to say the word, but the sound that came out was unrecognizable. Her face felt like a melon rotted to bursting. Worse was the burning deep within her. Yet somehow the pain seemed far away. Slowly she understood. Hospital. Nurse. Drugs. She remembered why she was here. She slept.

When she woke, the pain was anything but far away. The nurse, a middle-aged Pakistani, brought a pill. Amira took it greedily.

"My son," she said.

"Your what? Oh, your son. I'm sure he'll be along soon enough, Highness. But we wouldn't want him to see his mommy in her present mussed condition, would we?"

"No."

"But your husband has been here so much that half the patients think he's a doctor."

The nurse gently inserted a thermometer beneath Amira's tongue. "Such a charming man. In case you're wondering, he's not angry about your driving the car. Just look at all the flowers he's brought."

Half a dozen large bouquets crowded the room. Glancing at them, Amira realized that she was seeing with only her right eye. The left wouldn't open. Driving the car.

"No, no, Highness. Mustn't touch the dressings." The nurse removed the thermometer, made a note on the chart, and rattled on in the maternal tone of her vocation. "You were a naughty girl, Highness—you could have died, God forbid. But the merciful God was on your side. It's thanks to Him that Dr. Rochon showed up when he did."

"Dr. Rochon? Philippe Rochon?"

"Exactly. He arrived the very day they brought you in, thank God, and Dr. Konyali asked him to perform the surgery. Not that Dr. Konyali couldn't have done it himself, of course."

The painkiller was taking effect. Amira wondered if she were hearing the woman correctly. "Dr. Rochon is here? And he did surgery on me? What surgery?"

The nurse became tight-lipped. "Best wait for the doctor to discuss that, Highness."

"No. You tell me. I'm not superstitious. I won't blame you for bad news. In fact, I'll thank you. What surgery?"

There was pity in the nurse's eyes. "You had internal injuries, Highness. You were hemorrhaging. They had to operate to save your life. They removed one of your kidneys. And your womb."

How sad, thought Amira. Yet it all seemed so distant, as if it concerned someone else. Thank God for the painkiller—morphine, whatever it was. Her womb. How sad.

"At least you have the son, Highness. And you are alive."

"Do you have children?"

"I've never married, Highness. It's kind of you to ask." The nurse adjusted the seating of an intravenous needle. "Rest now, Highness. I'll be right here in case you need anything. And the doctors will be checking on you. My name is Rabia, by the way."

Amira was floating out on a tranquil lake. The thought that Philippe would be there soon drifted by like a cloud in the sky. "Can you bring me a mirror?" she heard herself ask.

"A mirror? I—I'm afraid we don't have one, Highness. Maybe I can find one for you later. Rest now."

"Yes . . . Philippe."

He was standing behind Dr. Konyali, concern in every line of his face.

Dr. Konyali cleared his throat. "I'd forgotten you knew Dr. Rochon, Highness." The little courtier would not have forgotten such a thing. He was merely glossing over Amira's impropriety in addressing a man so informally.

She could not have cared less. The gaze of her one good eye had not left Philippe. She had never seen him in his medical garb. It made him look more boyish. Yet at the same time he seemed older, frailer.

"Are you well, Philippe? What brings you here?"

His eyes crinkled in a smile. "Am I well? Who's the patient here? How do *you* feel?"

She tried a smile herself. It hurt. "Never better."

"You didn't tell me this patient was suffering from a sense of humor, Doctor," said Philippe, glancing over Konyali's shoulder at Amira's chart. "As for what brings me here, His Majesty had a rather acute episode of his chronic trouble. He asked me to fly down. When I arrived, he had learned of your accident and sent me directly to assist Dr. Konyali."

The Turk fairly preened at the flattery, but Amira had caught Philippe's slight emphasis on the word *accident* and his glance at her when he said it. A single thought cut through the fog of pain and medication: *He knows!*

"We don't want to disturb your rest, Highness," said Konyali. "It's what you need most just now." He shifted uncomfortably. "I gather that Rabia has told you about the various . . . procedures we performed."

"Yes."

"It was absolutely necessary, Highness, I'm sorry to say."

"Not your fault. God's will."

Konyali inclined his head to acknowledge the profound truth in her remark. "Your husband is waiting to see you, Highness. I've told him that we can allow him only a few minutes."

Did her fear show? Philippe was studying her intently. Yes, he knew.

"I hope you won't mind if I look in on your patient now and then, Dr. Konyali," he said.

"By all means, Doctor. After all, she's your patient as much as mine."

Philippe winked at her. "I'll be nearby, Highness. Nurse Rabia can find me anytime."

He was gone before she could say good-bye. Konyali followed after giving brief instructions to Rabia. Then, suddenly, Ali was there. Rabia stood and moved toward the door.

"No, stay, Rabia, it's all right."

The nurse looked at her oddly. "I'll be just down the hall, Highness. Please, Highness sir, only a few minutes. The doctor requests it."

"Of course."

As the door closed behind Rabia, Ali stepped forward. Amira fought an impulse to scream. Then her husband did the most astonishing thing: he fell to his knees beside the bed and kissed her fingertips.

"Thank God! Thank God for delivering you! It's my fault. I would never have forgiven myself. If I'd been a proper husband, you'd never have done such a crazy thing."

"What are you talking about?"

"Why, the accident, of course. You should see the car."

Had he gone mad? Had she?

"No car."

"What?"

"I wasn't in a car."

He patted her hand. "I shouldn't have come so soon. Rest, my dear. I'll be back tomorrow. I promise you, things will be different from now on. Very different."

Was it some kind of extreme guilt reaction? Had he blanked out the truth? Did he simply lack courage to admit what he had done? Or was it something else?

He smiled at her from the door. And there—just there, behind his dark eyes—something flickered, glinting like other eyes entirely, the eyes of an animal in the night. Then it was gone. But she had seen it—and it had seen her.

She was too weak for more fear. None of it made sense, anyway. She was asleep within seconds of Rabia's return.

• • •

For two days Amira hardly moved. She was too weak and in too much pain. On the third morning, Rabia helped her sit up on the edge of the bed, and late that afternoon she took a few steps, feeling like a very old woman or a very young child. That same day, Dr. Konyali removed most of the bandages from her face, and after considerable foot-dragging, Rabia finally produced a mirror.

Amira gasped when she saw her reflection. Her face, still swollen, was virtually a single bruise, which had turned a sickly yellowish purple. Adhesive tape still hid her nose. A black ladder of stitches crawled down her forehead from the hairline. Her left eye was almost fully open but grotesquely bloodshot.

"There will be a scar, not a bad one, here," said Konyali, pointing to the stitches, "and your nose won't have quite its old shape, but there's no permanent damage."

Philippe had come in and watched somberly while the bandages were cut away. Now he smiled and said, "If you're not happy with your new nose, I can give you the name of a plastic surgeon. He can give you any nose you'd like."

"Can he give me"—Amira struggled to think of a French movie star—"can he give me Catherine Deneuve's nose?"

"Why not? He gave Catherine Deneuve hers."

"Would you like your veil, Highness?" asked Rabia.

"Because the bandages are gone? No, it's pointless. These gentlemen know my face better than I do—which isn't very well just now."

"We'll need to monitor the healing process, anyway, and of course remove the stitches," said Konyali. "No one can fault you for immodesty in these circumstances, Highness."

"Thank you, Doctor. How is His Highness, my father-in-law, Phili— Dr. Rochon?"

"Much better, I'm happy to say."

"God be praised," Konyali, Rabia, and Amira herself said.

"He really has no further need of me, so as soon as we have you on your feet again, I'm afraid I'll be heading back to Paris." Philippe said it casually, but his eyes were intense with unspoken communication.

"Well," said Amira, "I hope we'll have a chance to talk before you leave. I owe you—and Dr. Konyali—my life."

"I'm sure we'll have that chance, Highness."

But the chance proved hard to find. Although Amira strengthened steadily over the following days, either Rabia or another nurse was always present; Ali had insisted on it. And often Ali himself was there, so solicitous of Amira—and of Philippe when he appeared—that she wondered if it were possible that he really *had* changed, the way a person's hair supposedly could turn white overnight after some terrifying experience. But no—no, it couldn't be. There was that thing behind his eyes, watching her, almost laughing at her. No: she would be afraid of him forever.

The morning came when Dr. Konyali announced that she would be going home the next day. That afternoon, when Ali had left, Philippe came in to say good-bye. Oddly, at first he seemed less interested in Amira than in chatting with Rabia.

"Dr. Konyali tells me you're well traveled."

"I, sir?" Rabia smiled with shy pride. "Well, Pakistan, of course, then Delhi, then England—Birmingham and London—then here."

"How many languages do you speak?"

"Only my own, and a little English, and such Arabic as I am speaking now, sir."

"Not French?"

"No, sir, not a word, I regret to admit." She looked genuinely rueful at disappointing the famous physician.

"I know a little French," said Amira, catching on, "but it's been ages since I practiced it. Are you going to examine me, Doctor? Ask your questions in French. Tell me where I go wrong."

"Very well."

"You don't mind, Rabia?"

"I mind, Highness?"

"*Bon.*"

Philippe took out his stethoscope and applied the receiver to her back.

"We can't take long," he said in French. "Answer when I ask. Breathe deep. Now exhale. He did it, didn't he?"

"Yes."

"Again. Has he hurt you before?"

"Not like this."

"And again. I believe that you are in great danger."

"I saw him kill a man."

"Once more. You've got to get away from him. I'll help in any way I can."

"There's nothing you can do."

"Lie back. That's it. Relax. I need to palpate."

His touch was firm, gentle, expert. There was safety in his hands, protection.

"Does that hurt?"

"No. If I leave, he'll take my son."

"And if you took the boy with you?"

"He'd hunt me down and kill me."

"And here—any pain at all? Even in France?"

"A little. Like a bruise. Yes. Even there." Was he asking her to leave Ali for him? God, if only it were possible!

"Cough, please. Good. And if the two of you were to vanish?"

"I don't understand."

"Go far away. Become someone else. I have money."

"He'd hunt us down, I tell you. You have no idea."

Philippe leaned close to examine the wound on her forehead, where the stitches had been. "Healing nicely. Just a little scarring."

"I don't think he'll dare anything soon—not after this."

"I hope not. But you've got to get out. I'll try to come up with something. You try, too."

"Please. You can't help. Don't try."

"I'm your doctor, Highness," he said, smiling. "Your health is my concern."

"You don't understand the danger."

"Oh, but I do. Precisely." He stepped back from the bed. "Our patient's doing very well," he told Rabia in Arabic, "and so is her French."

"God is merciful and compassionate."

"Yes. Well, Highness, I leave you in the capable hands of Dr. Konyali. Follow his orders. I'll be checking up on you the minute I'm back in al-Remal."

"And when might that be, Doctor?"

"Why, for the festivities, the semicentennial. His Majesty was so gracious as to invite me. Didn't I mention it?"

Amira's heart leaped. The fiftieth anniversary of the king's ascension to the throne was less than two months away. It would be a nationwide feast that lasted for six days.

"It will be good to see you, Doctor."

Their eyes locked.

"Take care of yourself, Highness. *Au revoir.*"

"Au revoir."

He left with a professional compliment to Rabia, who blushed fiercely.

• • •

"He'll be our guest, of course," said Ali. "It's the least I can do. He saved your life, then left without giving me a chance to reward him properly."

"He might be more comfortable in one of the Western hotels," Amira said, hardly knowing why she said it.

He waved the objection aside. "Every hotel room in the city is taken. I could twist arms, but why?"

He was right. Most of the dignitaries of the Middle East, and many from Europe and America, were coming for the semicentennial. Al-Remal had only a handful of first-class hotels. Hundreds of guests would necessarily rely on private hospitality. Why was she suddenly uneasy about the prospect of having Philippe as a houseguest? In the hospital, she would have sacrificed ten years of life to keep him near her for another week. Was it something in Ali's tone, some hint of hidden meaning?

"In any case, it's done," said Ali. "I called him an hour ago, and he accepted the invitation."

Amira tried to look indifferent. Her husband stepped toward her. She suppressed a flinch, but he merely touched her forehead as if testing for fever. Her skin crawled.

"Are you sure you're strong enough to see to setting up the house? I'll do what I can, of course, but I'm afraid this is a busy time for me."

"I'll be fine."

The house was a large, beautiful place near a small and very ancient oasis just south of the city. Like many of the younger members of the royal family, Ali and Amira were temporarily vacating the palace to make room for favored semicentennial visitors. Amira's bedroom, for example, would be occupied by the wife of the vice-president of the United States.

"I've told some of the servants to begin work this afternoon," said Ali, sealing the arrangement. He glanced at his watch. "I'll be running back and forth all day. Let me know if there's anything you need. The palace will know where to reach me."

"I will."

"Don't tire yourself."

"I won't."

He left with a smile. What was its true meaning? she wondered.

To all appearances, he had become the most considerate husband in al-Remal. It didn't matter. Nothing he did mattered to her. A thousand angels testifying that he was a changed man would not induce her to trust him.

The first weeks out of the hospital had been a time of respite. All that was expected of her was that she rest and heal, and in doing so she was enclosed in an ever-present shell of women: cousins, friends, servants, mother-in-law, sisters-in-law, in-laws she barely knew.

Everyone commented on the terrible "accident," then never mentioned it again. If they had questions, they wanted to forget them. But she had no questions and had forgotten nothing: not the man in the Alexandrian night, not the beating, and most of all, not her terrible vision of Ali and Karim in a possible future. As her strength slowly returned, she wanted nothing further except a way out.

With her recovery, the shielding veil of women gradually lifted. That was fine with Amira. She was ready for a little aloneness, a little privacy, and she was weary of the thing that hung in the air, unspoken but as pervasive as the stench of a snuffed candle, among her comforters: she was an object of pity to them.

After all, she was now barren, a female without purpose or future, a has-been at twenty-two. In a way, in the view of the other women, a part of her *had* died that night, and they reacted as people do to death, with secret gratitude that it had struck someone else.

Ali had not approached her sexually. She was not sure what she would do if he did. She might claim debility, or she might simply refuse and see how thick or thin was the veneer of kindness with which he had disguised himself. But perhaps he would leave her alone for a long time, or even forever. Perhaps he sensed the revulsion his touch caused in her. Or perhaps he was himself repelled by her barrenness.

A few days ago, she had overheard Faiza commenting that Ali would of course take another wife. And of course he would. No one would blame him; in fact, many would fault him if he did not.

Again, it didn't matter. She was waiting for deliverance, nothing else, in whatever form it might take.

She sent for a driver to take her to the new house. In minutes, a servant told her the car was ready. That was one of the positives about the allegedly new Ali: she had freedom to come and go almost as she pleased.

In the few steps between the palace's family entrance and the cocoon of the waiting Rolls, Amira felt the chill of the Remali winter. The temperature had dropped into the fifties; tonight, water might freeze. She hoped that the weather would moderate in time for Philippe's arrival.

The driver, a large, fierce-looking man with a pockmarked face, hurried to help her. Amira knew that, like all his colleagues at the palace, he was an expert in defensive combat and the use of small arms, a variety of which nested near at hand under the front seat.

"God's peace, Highness."

"God's peace, Jabr."

"Shall I turn up the heater?"

"No, it's perfect."

As the luxurious car purred from the palace grounds into the unusually busy city streets, the big man suddenly asked with boyish excitement, "Has Your Highness seen the tents?"

"What tents?"

"Out toward the airport, Highness. The desert people have come in for the feast."

"Show me," she said on a whim.

Several times in her life she had seen little encampments of Bedu, but never anything like this. Hundreds of black tents stretched to the distant low hills. The air was hazy with the smoke of cooking fires. More horses and camels than could be counted stood in little knots among the tents. Men turned to look at the car, then resumed their conversations.

"My people," Jabr said proudly. "I left them when I was twelve to serve His Majesty, by God's will."

"So many!" was all Amira could say. The sight stirred her deeply. Until this moment, she had thought of the semicentennial as a palace party. Now she saw that it was much more than that; it was a celebration of the whole people. Many of these leathery men and black-clad women had crossed hundreds of miles of open desert to be here.

"May God give their numbers increase," said Jabr. "As long as there are Bedu, there will be an al-Remal."

It was true, Amira thought. The desert people, though they were now only a small fraction of the population, were the country's soul.

"It's beautiful, Jabr. I'll make you bring me here again." She would. She would bring Faiza, too. She wanted to see the older woman's reaction, in all her royal elegance, to the life from which she had sprung. Would Faiza's fingers remember how to weave black-dyed goats' hair and wool into a Bedu tent?

Jabr took a last look at the vast camp and turned the Rolls south.

At the new house, there was little for Amira to do. The servants knew their work and constantly urged her to rest. She did oversee one task personally, the hanging of a painting over the bed in what would be Philippe's room. It was one of Henri Rousseau's jungle fantasies. Amira had never seen a jungle. She wondered if the artist had. It looked like a very French idea of a jungle to her. She hoped that Philippe would like it enough to compliment her taste. Then Ali would feel compelled to give the painting to him.

But probably Philippe would say nothing. He knew al-Remal better than any European had a right to know it.

• • •

"Highness, Prince Ali wishes for you to come and greet his guest."

It was about time. Ali had monopolized Philippe for nearly an hour. She followed the servant into the men's quarters.

There he was.

He looked paler than the last time she had seen him. The European winter, she remembered. European skin.

"Welcome, Doctor, to these poor temporary lodgings. You've come to see if your patient survived?"

"Hello, Highness. God willing all my patients should survive so well. I'll be as another Avicenna."

"Spoken like a Remali, Doctor," said Ali with a smile. And so it was, thought Amira, right down to the reference to the great Arab physician of antiquity; most Westerners would have mentioned Hippocrates.

"But all is well, Highness?" Philippe asked seriously. "No problems?" His eyes cut deep.

"Nothing to speak of, Doctor."

"Please," said Ali, smiling again. "Enough of these formalities. Aren't we friends? First names from now on."

Philippe made a Gaelic gesture of willing agreement. Amira said nothing, her assent to her husband's wish taken for granted.

"Philippe was telling me," Ali continued, "about the shah's big bash. He thinks ours will be better."

"You were there, Philippe?" He had never mentioned it to her. The shah of Iran's 1971 extravaganza at Persepolis, celebrating the twenty-five-hundredth anniversary of the Persian Empire, had been the talk of the world.

"Not as an invited guest," said Philippe modestly. "I was merely part of the Pompidou entourage."

"Give us your impressions," prodded Ali.

Philippe shrugged. "It was *de trop,* of course. Actually, what reminded me of it was the Bedu camp I saw on the way here from the airport. That is the real thing. The shah set up tents, too: tents designed by Jansen. Two bedrooms—Porthault sheets. Marble baths. Of course, all of that was for the elite. Most of us were housed in Shiraz, forty miles away."

"My father was in one of those tents," said Ali. "He agrees with you that it was *de trop*. Yet may people even today speak of the thing as the last step to Paradise."

Philippe shrugged again. "Tastes differ. Certainly it was a good show. The entire Iranian army costumed and coiffed like Persian soldiers of old. Every kind of entertainment, never a dull moment. One ate reasonably well, too: the shah brought in the full staff of Maxim's."

"Let me ask you, my friend Philippe: Do you know what the shah spent on his little circus?"

"I've heard the sum of three hundred million dollars tossed around."

"That is approximately correct. But in all the time you were there, did you ever hear a single *sura* of the Koran?"

"Since I'm not of the faith, Highness—"

"Ali."

"—Ali, I wasn't paying much attention to such things. But no, I don't believe I did."

"Neither did my father. And to this day, he says that the shah's irreligion will be his undoing."

Philippe nodded. "It may be. As for me, I found it hard to enjoy the festivities for other reasons. I had just spent several weeks in the Sahel—

the U.N. had asked a group of us to look into the medical situation there. There was little we could do. The drought was at its worst then, if you remember, and people—children especially—were dying like flies. After that, it was difficult to appreciate the offerings of Maxim's."

"Of course, of course," said Ali vaguely. Amira could tell that he saw no connection between the chronic problems of sub-Saharan Africa and a vast party hosted by the occupant of the Peacock Throne.

In a gesture that was becoming habitual, Ali checked his watch. "A thousand apologies, my friend, but duty calls. I'm overdue at the palace. My brother Ahmad is late, too—he's supposed to be here to help welcome you. I'm sure he'll show up any minute. Meanwhile, my home is yours."

Amira looked at him in some confusion. It would be improper for her to entertain a male guest alone.

Ali noticed her uncertainty. "It's all right. As I said, Ahmad will be here any minute—and anyway, we can't leave our guest unattended. Have someone show him his room, let him freshen up. I've talked the poor man to death."

With another smile, he was gone. Amira looked at Philippe and he at her. She wanted to rush to his arms but dared not; what if someone saw?

"It's good to have you here," she said simply.

He looked at her intently. "Do you still want to leave, Amira?"

Her voice sounded tiny when she said yes.

"You're sure?"

"Yes."

"I may have a way. But this is no time to talk about it."

"No."

A moment later Ahmad strode in. If he thought anything about Amira's presence in the room with Philippe, it didn't show. He was as quiet and somber as Ali was effusive. Behind him came two of Ali's cousins. In the crowd of men, Amira felt distinctly out of place, and she quickly excused herself.

In the women's world, she dealt mechanically with the servants. Philippe had a plan. What would it be?

And whatever it was, could she really do it?

Yes, she told herself. Yes, she could.

THE MATAWA

Determination was one thing. Opportunity was another. For three days, Amira never had a moment alone with Philippe. The festival swept along like a hurrying caravan, pausing only for prayer or sleep. The palace grounds were thrown open to the public, fire pits cut into the manicured lawns, and tents set up in which an army of cooks fed roasted lamb and seasoned rice to all comers until the small hours of the morning.

The foreign embassies vied with one another in offering brunches, lunches, and formal dinners to invited guests. There were horse and camel races by day, fireworks by night, hospitality and conversation at all hours.

At midweek fell a Great *Majlis* at which any Remali might raise a grievance before the king himself. On this occasion most of the petitioners brought not complaints but congratulations, every village sheikh striving to put in a few words of praise and fidelity.

Now and then, though, someone stepped forward to beg the king's justice. One old man quivering with awe announced that two of his goats had been killed by a truck, and that far from paying for the goats, the driver had demanded money for the damage to his vehicle. Two witnesses from the man's far desert village supported his story.

The king ordered that the driver pay not only for the goats, but also for the cost of the three men's travels to the *majlis*. The trio, assured of fame in their homeplace for the rest of their lives, departed thanking God and the monarch.

Like smaller jewels among the official events, countless private parties flared and sparkled, relatives and friends visiting and bearing gifts back and forth until nearly dawn. It reminded Amira of the week after Ramadan, only more frenetic. It was entirely possible to forget which party one was attending.

Everywhere, except at some of the embassies and in the most liberal private homes, standard segregation of the sexes applied. Even in her own house, what with the comings and goings of guests and the scurrying of servants, Amira never had a chance to exchange more than a few perfunctory and very public words with Philippe.

What little privacy there had been all but vanished when Ali's sister, Zeinab, showed up with her luggage and her somewhat overwhelmed husband, complaining that the house to which they had been assigned was little better than a shepherd's hut—impossible to remain there another minute.

It was Ali who finally gave Amira her chance. "Our friend isn't feeling well," he told her on the fourth morning of the festival. "He says he's just tired, but I'm not sure he's in the best of health. At any rate, he plans to stay in and rest today."

"I'll tell the servants."

"Good. But we can't leave a guest alone. I'd like for you to stay and keep him company—unless you can't resist another embassy meal and speeches."

"To tell the truth, I'm a little worn out myself." It was a fact; she still hadn't fully regained her strength from the ordeal in the hospital. "But mightn't there be talk? I mean, won't there be anyone else here, besides the servants?"

"I don't know. I can't keep up with Zeinab—enough trouble figuring out my own schedule. But there's nothing to worry about. It's an unusual situation, after all, and you have my permission. Besides, as you said, the servants will be here."

"Well . . ." She didn't want to seem eager.

"I must go. Everything will be fine."

"As you command," said Amira like the good Muslim wife she had once tried so hard to be.

That day after noon prayer, she sat down with Philippe to a light lunch of quail, fried rice balls, olives, dates, and fresh fruit. She ordered a bottle of white wine brought up from the supply Ali kept for foreign guests, a few liberal friends, and of course himself. Philippe seemed pleased by the gesture, although he objected mildly when Amira refused to take a glass for herself.

"It's strange," he said. "To your people, drinking wine is a terrible sin, or at best a kind of naughtiness. To mine, wine is a food. Most of us would never think of having a meal without it."

They were alone in the dining room. Zeinab had whirled in earlier and taken the children, including Karim, to some party or other.

"Many things separate our people," Amira said.

"Only three, really. Language, religion, and the Mediterranean." For a moment, he seemed lost in reflection. "When I was young, I thought nothing in the world did so much evil as religion. I still think that, but as I grow older, I also see the good that religion does."

"I'm sure that's true. Let me refill your glass." Amira was uncomfortable with the topic Philippe had chosen to discuss. Living in the palace, she had developed a sixth sense about when servants were eavesdropping. There was too much silence behind the doors to the kitchen. Most of the servants were tradition-minded. Their tongues would wag for days about Amira's dining alone with an alcohol-drinking foreign male. Freethinking comments about religion would only make matters worse.

"Well, Amira," said Philippe decisively, "we need to talk."

Instantly she lifted a finger to her lips.

After only a moment's hesitation, he nodded. "What I need to know," he continued smoothly, "is whether you and Ali have any travel plans. I long to return your hospitality. Will you be in France anytime soon?"

"France? Well, I'm sure we'll be there sooner or later, but I don't think there are any immediate plans. We'll be touring the Emirates in a couple of weeks. Then, in the early spring, we're scheduled for a visit to Iran—Teheran, with a side trip to Tabriz. There's some talk of going to New York after that. I've never been to the United States."

"Tabriz," said Philippe. "Why would you be going there?"

"There's a mosque there, apparently a great old one, that had fallen into disrepair, then was nearly ruined by the earthquake a year or two ago. Apparently the shah wants al-Remal to lend its money and moral weight to repairing the building."

Philippe smiled. "The shah hopes to appease the fundamentalists nipping at his heels." He mouthed the question, *"Parle français?"*

Amira shook her head. It would seem suspect. Some of the servants might even know a little French.

Philippe took a small notebook and a pen from the pocket of his tweed sports jacket. "I do worry about your health," he said, writing as he spoke. "Are you sure you're recovered from the accident enough for all this travel?"

"Oh, I'm much better, thanks to you and Dr. Konyali."

"Good." He showed the paper to her: *Are you going to Egyptian Night tomorrow?*

She nodded.

"And yet I worry about my patient," Philippe said, writing again. "It would be dangerous to exert yourself too much."

I'll be in the garden when you return, the note said. *I'll wait.*

"I'll be careful, Doctor," said Amira. "I promise."

• • •

For the younger women of the Remali elite, Egyptian Night was a keenly anticipated feature of the semicentennial. It was an all-female party at which they could talk without restraint and wear the most outrageous fashions they owned, changing back to more modest clothes before going home. It was something new; it couldn't have happened even ten years earlier in al-Remal.

The venue was the ballroom of the Hilton, the activities being considered too Western for the palace. In her Givenchy gown, with its fitted sequined bodice and flared taffeta skirt, Amira arrived to find what looked like a very large European dinner party—except that there were no drinks and no men.

Three or four hundred women milled and mingled, drinking sweet fruit drinks and munching hors d'oeuvres amid a cacophony of compliments, jokes, gossip, and laughter. Only a few had been too timid to abandon traditional dress, and even these were unveiled.

As the evening went on, a feeling of camaraderie developed in the room. It was as if what they were doing was very daring and called for openness, one woman to another. Amira heard complaints about men, laws, and Remali society in general that would never have been voiced under other circumstances.

At one point, she was confronted by a princess she hardly knew who demanded, "Amira, tell us the truth: Did you wreck a car or not?"

She was saved from having to answer by a burst of recorded music and an announcement of the main event, a performance by the great *beledi* dancer Sonia Murad. This was one reason why Egyptian Night was too risqué for the palace, and why so few older women attended: their generation had been taught that professional dancers were little better than prostitutes. Amira's own knowledge of *beledi* was limited to the few moves she had learned from Jihan and practiced with Laila. She was about to learn a great deal more.

Sonia Murad was an artist. There was no other word for it. From the moment she took the stage, it was obvious. She had the presence and beauty—not looks, but beauty—of one born to show others the way.

When she began to dance, her personality filled the room like a powerful light. Amira had always thought of *beledi* as sensual at its heart, and perhaps that was true. But there was far more than sensuality in Sonia Murad's dance. There was joy, pain, humor, even fear. Her dance was about being a woman and a human being.

Sometimes the undulations of Sonia's body were so rapid and so perfectly rhythmic as to seem impossible. Sometimes she struck a stillness so profound that it made one think of the stars or of God.

The crowd was hers, clapping and shouting with the music, and when she gestured to one of them, the woman moved toward the stage as if drawn by an invisible cord, and began a dance of her own. Soon a dozen, then two dozen women were dancing at Sonia's behest. It was amazing, thought Amira, how the different personalities were revealed. Then Sonia pointed at her, and suddenly everyone was urging her to dance.

She did. She felt awkward for only a moment, then found herself enjoying a freedom of movement forgotten since the day her father caught her dancing to the radio. But suddenly a sharp pain in her abdomen doubled her; the sliced muscles there had not mended enough for this exertion. A face appeared from the crowd around her: the little princess who had asked about the car wreck. "It's all right, Amira. We know." What did that mean?

The floor shook with the rhythm of the dance. Amira thought of the pagan frenzies of ancient Egypt and Greece. The room was an oven, the air-conditioning overwhelmed. Women were soaked with sweat, makeup streaming down their faces. Someone had opened the sliding glass doors along one wall to let in the cooling night air.

Suddenly there was a disturbance on the edge of the crowd. Women shouting in outrage, men's angry voices. Sonia Murad glanced toward the sound, tried to continue her dance, then stopped.

"It's the *matawa*," a woman near Amira said.

What were the religious police doing here?

"The music!" someone said. "They're angry because they can hear the music outside."

"Females, cover yourselves," a man shouted.

There was near panic. Women pushed toward every exit. Amira, still in pain, moved with a ministampede to the sliding doors. Then she was out under the cold winter stars.

Around her, hundreds of women in the latest Western fashions fanned out into the Remali night. Some were in tears, others laughing; one young woman cursed the *matawa* like a camel driver, a punishable offense in al-Remal. Foreigners coming into the Hilton stood and stared at the mass of jeweled refugees.

Amira sat on a low concrete wall, unable to go any farther. A strong hand gripped her arm. Was she under arrest?

"Come with me, Highness. The car is just over there." It was Jabr, the driver.

He half carried her across the street. A green-turbaned member of the *matawa* approached, saw Jabr's scowl, and turned away. Amira sank into the safety of the Rolls.

"There were rumors among the drivers," Jabr told her. "I came early in case something happened."

"Thank you."

The big man shook his head angrily. "I love God as much as any man," he declared. "But these religious police—what do they have to do with God? Forgive me, Highness."

"There's nothing to forgive, Jabr. Thank you again."

The house was quiet, only a single servant there to greet her. Princess Zeinab was upstairs asleep, the girl explained. Everyone else was still at the festivities.

"And Dr. Rochon?" said Amira. "Is he at the festivities as well?" Only at that moment had she remembered Philippe's promise to meet her in the garden.

"I don't know, Highness. I haven't seen him."

"Go draw me a bath—make sure that it's hot—and lay out my night-clothes. Then make some tea."

"Yes, Highness."

As soon as the girl was gone, Amira slipped out into the garden. No one was there, only the cold moon close overhead, the details of its rocky face etched as if in crystal. Amira shivered, wondering how long she dared to wait.

"Cinderella," said a voice from the shadows, "home from the ball?"

"Philippe! You nearly frightened me to death."

"Ssh. Just stay where you are and act as if I'm not here. We'll talk very quietly."

"All right."

"Amira, I believe that your life is in danger and that you must get away from Ali. Yet I wonder if I'm doing the right thing. I have a plan, but it's a drastic one. Surely there must be a better way. Let me ask you this: What if I were to talk with the king, explain matters. Wouldn't he grant you a divorce?"

"He might. But he would never give up his grandson. Karim would be Ali's. And I cannot allow that."

"And you're certain that if you just walked away—took Karim and went to France, for example—Ali would pursue you."

"Yes. He'd take Karim and kill me as well, if it were necessary. Which it would be."

"You're sure?"

"Yes."

"Then I can see only two possible solutions. One is to kill Ali. I can't do that, and I don't think you can, either."

"No."

"Then the only alternative is to kill you and Karim."

"What?"

"You wouldn't be dead, of course, but suppose that the whole world—Ali included—thought you were. Suppose that you and Karim could start a totally new life somewhere—America, for example. Would you do it?"

"I—I don't know. It's too hard a question."

"You needn't answer it now. But soon."

To leave everything she knew behind: friends, father, homeland, everything. "Would Malik know the truth?" she asked.

"I don't think he should. Not for a while, at any rate—perhaps a long while. Your brother is an impetuous man. He would never tell the secret, but his actions would give it away."

"He would have to think that I was dead?"

"It's cruel, I know, but it may be necessary. In any case, that can be decided later. What you must first decide is whether to take the course I suggest."

"And you, Philippe? Would I ever see you?"

There was a silence in the shadow.

"Ever is a long time," he replied at last. "Who knows what will happen? Let's get you safe first."

The night was turning very cold. Amira shivered in her Egyptian Night gown.

"I can't decide now. I need to think."

"Of course. But the sooner the better. And there are some details to think about, too. Do you have any money?"

"There is some money in my name, but I can't take it out of the bank without Ali's permission."

"Ah. And your jewelry?"

"That I can take anywhere. But it's all I have."

"And probably not salable for more than a third of what Ali paid for it," commented Philippe. "Well, it's something, anyway—plenty for a start. If you decide to go through with this, take all your jewelry when you and Ali go to Iran. And bring Western clothes for both you and Karim."

"Tell me what you have in mind."

"I don't have it all worked out yet. But I know that it can't be done here, or even in the Emirates. Certainly not in New York or Paris or even Teheran. We need someplace out of the way, cut off a bit from the world. Of all the stops on your itinerary, Tabriz is the best choice."

"This sounds dangerous."

"It will be—a little. But not for Karim. Only for you and me."

"You? Why for you?"

"I'll be there, of course. But we've talked enough. Go now, my dear. I see you're cold. Think it over. If you decide to do it, let me know by saying something, anything, about Tabriz. Even if you can't make up your mind before I leave, you can still use that signal—in a postcard or something."

"Oh, God. It's just so hard to believe, Philippe. This life of mine."

"I'm sorry. You deserve better. Go, my dear. We have several days yet. Perhaps we can talk again. But the decision will still have to be made."

"I don't know what I'll do—it's too much for me, just now. But I do know that I can't thank you enough, Philippe."

"It's not necessary to thank me at all. We have an understanding, do we not? A friendship. Good night, my dear."

Turning to the house, Amira took a last glance at the crystal moon. As she did, she caught a glimpse of movement at a second-floor window. A curtain closing? Perhaps it was just a reflection, or her imagination.

"Good night," she whispered back into the shadows of the garden. "Good night—my love."

MORNING VISITORS

The festival was over, the Bedu vanishing back into the desert, the foreign guests crowding the airport, but Ali insisted that Philippe stay for another day or two.

"Right here in this house," he said. "I'm keeping it for a few days, so as not to put you to the trouble of moving to the palace or to a hotel. So you see, the plans are already made."

His enthusiasm seemed excessive to Amira—surely he had demonstrated his gratitude and hospitality to anyone's satisfaction—but if he had an ulterior motive, she couldn't imagine what it might be.

Philippe seemed to resist the invitation, pointing out that he had a practice to maintain in France, but a call from the palace decided the issue: the nonstop feasting had caused yet another onslaught of the king's gout; Dr. Rochon's services were urgently desired.

"You see that God is wise," said Ali with his best smile. "Even my father's affliction brings some good."

"Tomorrow is Saturday, in any case," said Philippe. "I'd only be puttering around my apartment or loitering in some bistro, while here I'm in the best of company. But I absolutely must leave by midafternoon Sunday. *Inshallah*," he added with a smile.

"If it must be, it must be, my friend, although we'll be sad to see you go."

Amira silently thanked God for the extension of Philippe's stay. It would give her another chance to talk with him, she was sure. She needed his thoughts, his advice. She needed him, she realized, to make her decision for her.

It didn't work out that way. She spent most of Saturday helping Zeinab move out. There was a great outcry about a pair of earrings that Zeinab was sure she had left on her dresser. After an exhaustive search, they were found in her jewel box.

Philippe was at the palace all day. He returned at dark looking worn, and went to his room to rest. Ali left for some appointment and later called to say that Amira and Philippe should dine without him. They sat together at table—again shocking the servants, Amira knew. Philippe had no appetite. He drank a glass of wine while she ate. They exchanged small talk. There was nothing left to say except the word Tabriz. It hung unspoken in the air. She couldn't say it. Not yet.

Karim was brought in from the nursery. He sat in Amira's lap, then slid down and toddled around to be bounced on Uncle Philippe's knee. In the middle of this activity, Ali arrived, buoyant and loud. Had he been drinking?

"What a domestic picture!" he laughed. "I thought I had wandered by mistake into the house of a rich European and his beautiful young wife and child."

"It might be," said Philippe, "but where is the rich European?"

Ali laughed again. "I have something for you, my friend," he said. He left the room and came back with a gift-wrapped box. In it were a beautifully made *thobe* and *ghutra*, and a black *agal* with solid-gold fittings. "First there was Lawrence of Arabia," Ali observed. "Now there can be Philippe of al-Remal."

Philippe brought out presents in return. For Ali, there was a leather flight jacket, an exact and expensive replica of those worn by American pilots in the Second World War. For "the house"—since it would be improper to give anything directly to Amira—there was a brace of miniature doves exquisitely carved in ivory.

It was a pleasant moment on the surface, but the hypocrisy of it made Amira want to scream. Why couldn't she just say what she wanted to say: "I'm leaving and I'm taking Karim." Why couldn't Philippe step up and add, "And don't try to stop us, my friend."

Because of the consequences, of course, which would be terrible. But still, living a charade was maddening.

The little celebration was brief by Remali standards. Philippe was clearly exhausted, and Ali announced that he himself would need to rise early for yet another appointment. "But certainly I'll be back in time to see you off, my friend."

Philippe, mumbling thanks and apologies, trudged off to bed. After a few minutes' play with Karim, who was cranky with sleepiness himself, Ali, too, went upstairs.

Amira was the only wakeful one. Long into the night, she stared into the darkness of her bedroom. She felt like a desert traveler when the stars are hidden. Movement was vital, but in what direction? It was nearly dawn when, repeating over and over that it was all in God's hands, she lulled herself to sleep.

• • •

She woke with the vague sense that something was wrong. The house was very quiet, but that was logical: Ali undoubtedly had gone out already. Philippe was probably still asleep. Zeinab and her tribe had departed.

Karim slept peacefully. Yet it was *so* quiet. She dressed quickly and went downstairs. Where were the servants? She called and got silence for an answer.

She was about to call the servants' quarters for an explanation when she saw the little chambermaid, Hanan, dressed in her best clothes, crossing the garden toward the side gate.

"Hanan! Come here. Where is everybody?"

"Why, I don't know, Highness. Master sent some of us to the palace to prepare for your return. And some of us he gave the day off—because of our hard work during the festival. I'm one of those, and I was just on my way to visit my mother."

"But there's no one left!"

Hanan said nothing. Disputes between the master and his wife were none of her business.

"When did he order all this?"

"Why, just this morning, Highness, just before he left." Hanan looked faintly guilty. "I could stay, ma'am, if I'm needed."

"No. No, go and enjoy your day off."

"Thank you, Highness." The girl headed for the gate before Amira could change her mind, but she turned long enough to call, "I'm sure some of those at the palace will be back soon."

"I'm sure you're right. Thank you, Hanan."

In the kitchen, Amira searched for coffee. Surely Philippe would be awake soon. She found fruit and bread, and there were eggs in the refrigerator—should she try to make an omelet? It pleased her to think of preparing breakfast for Philippe and sitting down to it with him, just the two of them. Yet she was irritated with Ali. Why would he send away all the servants with a guest in the house? It made no sense.

Then suddenly, it did. Amira stood stock-still. No, she told herself; no, not even Ali would try that. It would be like a bad joke. She almost smiled, but the smile never came. Of course Ali would try it, and it would be nothing at all like a joke.

Under Sharia law, a woman accusing a man of rape needed the directly corroborating testimony of four witnesses. But a man accusing his wife of adultery had only to demonstrate a pattern of incriminating behavior. To be alone in the house with Philippe was damning in itself. Amira had also dined with him in her husband's absence—and someone, she remembered, had seen them in the garden late at night.

There was no time to waste. She needed to act—now. Her first instinct was to warn Philippe, but she stopped in her tracks even as she turned for the stairs. The last place on earth she needed to be was in Philippe's bedroom. Even to go upstairs would be sheer folly.

She could leave, she told herself—just walk out. But how would that look? How could she explain it?

The phone. She could call the palace, order some of the servants back. But would they come? How soon? What if one or more of them were in on it? They wouldn't even have to be in on it—the truth would be damaging enough. She pictured little Hanan testifying before a *qadi* in a Sharia court: "I offered to stay, Excellency, but she ordered me to go."

Think, Amira.

She went to the telephone and dialed her father's number, praying that someone other than Omar would answer.

"The peace of God." It was the ancient manservant, Habib.

"The peace of God, Habib. It's Amira. Please don't disturb my father. I need to speak with Bahia."

"Yes, miss—I mean Your Highness."

Hours seemed to pass before Bahia came on the line.

"Bahia, don't ask questions. Just get your daughter and any other woman servant you can find and come here now, immediately—don't waste a minute. If anyone asks what you're doing, say that Karim and I are ill, and all of our servants are on holiday."

"I'm coming," Bahia said simply and hung up.

Amira paced in the kitchen. If Philippe came downstairs, she would send him out of the house instantly. Someone—one of Ali's relatives, for instance—might walk in at any time. Someone might be on the way at this very moment, for the exact purpose of finding her alone with the foreign male guest.

She returned to the phone and tried Farid. He wasn't in. Several more calls failed to locate him. There was nothing further to do but wait. Why didn't Philippe come down? Or was it better if he didn't?

There was a rattle at the servant's gate. Amira let in Bahia and her daughter. "I couldn't find anyone else on such short notice," Bahia apologized.

"Don't worry. You're both angels from Paradise. Come in, come in. What I need right now is for you to look busy. Make coffee, start putting breakfast together, do whatever else needs doing. I want it to look as if you've been here all morning."

As they set to work, she explained about the illustrious house guest, Dr. Rochon, the mysterious decampment of the servants, and her natural concern under the circumstances. She left out only her fear that Ali was behind it all.

Bahia asked nothing, but gave her a long look. "Nothing will come of it, God willing," she said. "But you did well to send for someone. Where is Karim?"

"Asleep upstairs."

"Maryam, go and fetch him."

"The third door on the right," said Amira.

When Maryam returned with the sleepy little boy, Bahia had coffee ready.

"Go out on the patio, Highness," she said, using the honorific for the first time, "and we will serve you in style."

She had hardly said it when they heard male voices from the front of the house and someone cried out, "Woman, veil yourself."

Bahia and Amira exchanged a glance. Both had noticed the use of "woman," not "women."

Ali's cousin Abdul burst into the kitchen. Three other men followed. Two of them Amira had never seen; the third seemed familiar, although she couldn't quite place him.

"Amira, what's going on?" Abdul seemed surprised to see Bahia and Maryam.

"What do you mean, Abdul?"

"We come to visit your husband, and the front door is open."

"Naturally we feared something might be wrong," said the man Amira couldn't quite recognize.

"Yes, we thought something was wrong," echoed Abdul.

"The door was open? You mean ajar?"

"Yes."

"Ali must have left it open on his way out."

"Your husband isn't here, then?" The familiar-looking man had hot, hard, inquisitorial eyes.

"He had an appointment early this morning. But I'm sure he'll be back soon. Please make yourselves at home. I'll have Bahia bring you coffee. Have you eaten?"

"And your houseguest?" asked Abdul. Amira had never liked him, and even the familiar-looking man looked pained at his lack of subtlety.

"Dr. Rochon? What about him?"

"Where is he?"

"Why, asleep, I suppose. I haven't seen him this morning."

"Is that so?"

"Yes, it's so. Abdul, what are all these questions? Is something the matter?"

"Who are these women? They aren't your regular servants."

"My husband saw fit to dismiss the regular servants for the day. Bahia and Maryam have been servants of my family all my life, and I asked them for help."

"Loyal servants, who will do anything for you, are a blessing from God," said the familiar-looking man.

"When did they arrive here?" Abdul pressed.

"They've been here almost all morning."

"*Almost* all morning," said the angry-eyed man.

Amira had had enough. "Gentlemen, I'm only a woman, but I must remind you that I am the wife of a royal prince, and this is his house. Abdul, you should appreciate that as much as anyone. You say you came to see my husband. I suggest that you save your questions for him."

"What questions? What's going on here?" It was Ali. He stood in the doorway, face flushed as if with excitement.

"That's what we were wondering, cousin," said Abdul. "We came to see you and found the front door ajar. When we entered, we discovered your wife alone—or, rather, alone except for these women, who are not the regular servants."

Ali glanced at Bahia and Maryam. Was there a trace of anger in his expression? "Well, I know them," he muttered.

"We asked about your distinguished guest," Abdul blundered on. "Your wife claims that she hasn't seen him all morning."

"Dr. Rochon is, as you say, my guest. I dislike insinuations against him."

It was a slip, thought Amira. No one had insinuated anything against Philippe. The whole business had the feeling of a play in which Bahia and Maryam's presence had disrupted the actor's lines, forcing them to ad lib.

"She says that he is asleep," prompted the angry-eyed man. The other two men had said nothing. They were simply witnesses, Amira realized.

"It's late for anyone to sleep, even a foreigner," said Ali. "I'll check on him myself."

He was gone for longer than it should have taken. In the kitchen, no one spoke. The familiar-looking man glared at Amira. Suddenly she knew who he was. She hadn't recognized him without the green turban. He was the *matawa* man who had approached when she was leaning on Jabr's arm during the Egyptian Night catastrophe.

Ali returned. "He isn't there," he said. "Where is he, Amira?"

"I don't know, my husband. I haven't seen him at all."

"Perhaps he left a note or—or something," said Abdul.

"I looked," said Ali irritably. "There was nothing."

"Nothing? I could help you search."

Even the *matawa* man appeared nonplussed by this exchange.

"*Bonjour*, my friends. A lovely morning. Am I intruding?" Philippe stood smiling in the doorway. He wore the typical walking clothes of the European tourist, and his pale skin showed a faint touch of sunburn.

"We—we were just looking for you," said Ali lamely.

"Ah! I've been out. I slept poorly, woke early, and saw that it was a beautiful day, so I went for a walk. In fact, I left just behind Your Highness. I thought to call out to you, but you seemed to be in a hurry."

"You've been out all morning?" asked Abdul obtusely.

"As I said." Philippe shrugged. "I had a pleasant walk, then took an outdoor table at a coffeehouse and watched the world go by."

"What coffeehouse did you visit?" inquired the *matawa* man casually. "We have so many."

"I didn't notice the name."

"Ah."

"But if you really want to know, you could ask my host's brother Ahmad. He and his entourage passed in the street. He was kind enough to spend an hour with me."

How much did Philippe understand of what was going on? Amira couldn't tell, but the fact that he could call on Ali's brother to account for his whereabouts ended the little inquisition in her kitchen. Ali made some remark about the mystery being solved and herded his visitors toward the men's quarters.

"Have Bahia bring us coffee," he told Amira. "I hope we haven't disturbed your reunion." His smile was so disarming that Amira wondered if the only danger had been in her imagination. Or was the smile that of a duelist who has lost the first touch but knows that he will win the duel?

That afternoon they drove Philippe to the airport. In the crowded concourse, the two men embraced like brothers. Listening to them exchange thanks, compliments, and cordial promises of future hospitality, Amira again wondered if she hadn't been paranoid about the empty house.

The farewell was interrupted by the public-address system paging Prince Ali Rashad.

"Always something," said Ali. "I'll be right back."

Philippe watched him go. "We have only a minute," he told Amira. "I'm the one who had him paged. I called from the house before we left. Amira, do you know what was happening this morning?"

"I think so. I didn't know if you did."

"It was a stage piece—what the Americans call a 'frame-up.' Just as I said, I woke early and decided to take a walk. While I was dressing, I dropped some coins. One rolled under the bed. When I reached for it, I found a bottle of whiskey, half empty. It wasn't mine—someone had to have put it there. I became worried and searched the room. What do you suppose I found tucked into a corner of the bed, under the sheet? A piece of lingerie—very attractive, I might add. Provocative. I don't know, but I imagine it would have fitted you perfectly."

"Oh, my God." She had been afraid that morning, but only now did she understand how great the danger had been. In al-Remal, evidence like that could send a woman to her death.

"I hid the bottle and the lingerie in my pocket—and then threw them away as soon as I got far enough from the house."

"Thank you for that. But what—"

"Amira, you can't wait too long to decide. If it's to be Tabriz, I'll need time to make plans, set things in motion. If not . . . well, I fear for you, my dear. You must get away from this somehow—before it's too late. I'll help in any way I can."

Before she could reply, Ali rejoined them with a joke about confusion in the paging system: "Too many princes named Ali." At that moment, Philippe's flight was called.

They walked him to the gate. Passengers were boarding in a line. Philippe said good-bye.

This might be my last minute with him, Amira realized. The words were out before she could think about them: "I almost forgot to ask, Philippe, but haven't you been to Tabriz?"

"Tabriz? Did you say Tabriz?"

"Yes, Tabriz. Ali and I are going there. We've never been. I thought a traveler like you might have been there—to Tabriz."

"Yes, I've been there," he said, and in his eyes she saw his promise reaffirmed. "They say that Tabriz is the unfriendliest city in the Middle East, but I've found good people there, very helpful. I'm sure your visit will turn out well."

Then he was gone.

PRODIGAL'S RETURN

Spring was coming. The nights were cold but the days pleasantly warm. One afternoon half an inch of rain fell in half an hour. Women as well as men ran into the streets to savor the sweetness of it. To the younger children, who had never seen water fall from the sky, it was a miracle.

Karim splashed in a muddy puddle, his face raised to heaven, blinking and giggling with delight as raindrops hit his eyes. When the brief storm ended, he pulled at Amira's *abeyya*. "Make it more, Mommy, make it more." Faster than she could believe, he was changing from a baby into a little boy.

Ali missed the cloudburst: he was in America for two weeks, training in some new fighter plane. He came home moody and withdrawn, as he usually did from places where morality was freer than in al-Remal. Amira no longer cared why this might be.

Just over a month remained before Tabriz, but she felt no particular fear or even anticipation. In fact, she was having trouble making the whole thing seem real. She had no information. What was Philippe doing, what was he planning?

He had written only once, the letter addressed of course to Ali, who passed it on to Amira as a matter of minor interest. It expressed conventional thanks for their hospitality, mentioned bits of personal news and international gossip, and then, almost as an afterthought, gave the names of several acquaintances of Philippe's they might want to look up on their visit to Tabriz.

In her room, Amira memorized the names, then pored over the letter word by word in search of any hidden message. She found nothing. It was maddening. She was angry with Philippe. She didn't expect details, but couldn't he have slipped in some tiny reference that only she would understand, some reassuring little code word? Didn't he realize that her life was at stake?

Or maybe nothing was happening. Maybe the plans had all fallen apart. Maybe there had never been any plans.

The next morning, a servant brought her a telephone as she sipped her coffee. "It's long distance, Highness. France."

Amira forced herself to reach languidly for the receiver, as if she were utterly weary of calls from France.

"Bonjour."

"Is this Paris?" said a man's voice in heavily accented French.

"This is al-Remal."

"Peace be with you," said the man in Arabic. "Please hold for Paris."

There was silence, then a dial tone.

"Good God!" She almost threw the receiver at the wall. Billions of dollars in oil money, and the phone system was a joke. Two companies, one Belgian, the other French, had built it. Rumor said that Malik had helped broker the French contract and had harvested a none-too-small fortune in commissions. If so, Amira could at this moment happily have broken his neck.

The phone rang again.

"Operator, I was cut off—"

"Little sister? Is that you?"

"Malik, I was just damning you to hell, God forbid."

"What? Speak up, can you?"

"I said—never mind. How are you? Is something wrong?"

"Wrong? No, not at all. I have news for you—good news. And a favor to ask."

"Tell me."

"Little sister, I'm married!"

"What! My God! When? Who is she?"

"She's a wonderful woman. French. Just a few days ago. Four days. I can't wait for you to meet her. She'll be a wonderful mother for—for the children we hope to have."

She understood his caution about mentioning Laila. Anyone—the operator, a servant, even Ali or Faiza—might be listening on the line.

"I don't know what to say, brother. My God! It's wonderful news. God's blessings on you both. It's just such a surprise. You've told Father, of course."

There was a brief silence. "Well, little sister, that brings me to the favor. No, I haven't spoken with him. I know, I know: it's not right. But to tell you the truth, I was afraid he might try to forbid it. For one thing, she's Christian."

"Ah." That might indeed be a problem—but not nearly as bad as presenting Omar with his only son's marriage as a fait accompli.

"Don't worry, I'll call him. I'll call him today. He'll erupt, of course, but that's all right. What I need is for you to help Farid calm him down before we actually arrive."

"And when will that be?"

"This weekend, God willing."

"*This* weekend?"

"I know it's not much time, but the sooner the better, don't you think? I'm calling Farid the minute we hang up. You know how he can twist Father—like a goldsmith braiding wire. He'll take care of it, don't worry. All you need to do is back him up—you know, the tactful remark at the right time. He's like anyone else in al-Remal—the opinion of someone in the royal family carries weight, even if it's his own daughter."

Amira sighed. "I'll do what I can, brother, as God allows."

"Thanks, little sister. I . . . it hasn't been easy, you know . . . for me to find someone."

"I know. Tell me about her."

"Her name is Genevieve."

"A beautiful name."

"Not as beautiful as she is," Malik said, with a tenderness that convinced Amira her brother was truly in love.

"Naturally. It goes without saying that you would marry a beautiful woman."

"It's not like that, Amira. It's not just the way she looks. She's been good for me. She makes me believe that life is good. And she makes me laugh. It's been such a long time . . ."

"I know."

"And she's said she would consider converting to Islam . . . after she learns more about it, of course."

"And what does she do, this perfect woman?" Amira teased.

There was a brief hesitation. "She's a singer. A nightclub singer."

"Ah."

"You may as well know it all. She's a bit older than I am. Not much. Just a few years."

Some of this, they agreed, could be passed along more or less unabridged to Omar. Some—Genevieve's age, for example—need not be reported with perfect accuracy. Some, such as her religious views, could be cast in a positive light. And some—her profession, especially—ought not to be mentioned at all.

When Amira hung up, she was as nervous as a bird. She couldn't seem to focus on any single thought. Malik was coming this weekend. Malik and Genevieve. Tabriz was a month away. Philippe. Malik. Omar. Ali.

She paced in her room. The palace was a prison. She couldn't even walk in the garden, closed to women this morning, a ceremony of some kind. Malik. Philippe. Tabriz.

She buzzed the chamberlain on the intercom. "Send a car for me."

"Yes, Highness."

Ten minutes later, Jabr was holding the door of a Silver Dawn.

"Peace be with you."

"And with you, peace."

"Morning of goodness, Highness."

"Morning of light, Jabr."

It felt good to exchange the formal greetings. The world might be blowing away, but the old words were like small, tough roots that no wind could dislodge.

"To where, Highness?"

"My cousin's," said Amira, for the benefit of the listening doorman.

Once behind the wheel, Jabr glanced in the mirror. "Which cousin, Highness?"

"No cousin. Drive somewhere. The desert. I need to think."

His reflected eyes met hers, concerned. "The hills will be better for thinking, Highness. The desert begins to be hot."

"The hills, then."

The place was a shaded notch in a high ridge. A thousand feet below, the desert glared like an endless, motionless sea, but here the air was cool. In sheltered places, tiny flowers bloomed. How long had they waited, Amira wondered, for the rain to bring them from the dust? How long would they wait again?

The silence was immense. She could hear the tiny pops and pings of the car's engine cooling a hundred yards below and behind her. Jabr waited in the car. There, no matter who might see him, he was only a driver obeying orders. A few steps up the slope toward Amira and he might be accused as her lover.

What would it be like to be loved by a man like Jabr—loved simply and completely, for the woman she was, nothing else? Amira tried to imagine it. She couldn't. There had never been anyone like that for her. There might have been Philippe, there would always be Philippe, but that was different.

Maybe someday there would be someone, after Tabriz . . .

And there it was, the real question: What *would* happen after Tabriz? She had no idea—only vague impressions, hardly more than daydreams. Would Philippe hide her away in some château in the countryside of France? Would he ship her off to Tahiti, where Karim would grow up like a little native, running naked on the beach? Or maybe he had secretly bought a *finca* in—where did they have *fincas*? Argentina.

But then there was Philippe's idea that her disappearance must be total, that people would have to think she was dead. All the while that she was hiding, everyone she knew—everyone except Philippe and Karim—would think that something terrible had happened. She pictured Malik, her father, her aunts, even Bahia, all in mourning. How long before she could let someone know? Philippe had said a long time. How long? A year? Two?

Suddenly it all seemed like madness, an impossibility. Yet she had to do it. If she stayed with Ali, she would be dead—not just in people's minds, but really and truly. She could feel it as surely as she could feel the heat of the sun climbing above the ridge. Yes, she had to do it. Unless . . . unless Malik could think of something.

If anyone could find a way out, a way that didn't mean running and hiding, her brother could. The problem was that she couldn't tell him the truth, not a word of it. He was too impetuous, as Philippe said. But what if she were to disguise the situation, weave a tale of some other royal wife who was in danger from a sadistic husband? She would have to be careful: if Malik even suspected that she was talking about Ali, it would be catastrophic.

Perhaps it was the vast silence of the desert, perhaps it was the hope that her idea had given her, but she felt better, calmer. In any case, there was nothing to do about any of it until Malik arrived. Meanwhile, she had a favor to do. She returned to the waiting Rolls. "My cousin Farid's," she told Jabr.

• • •

The marriage of Omar Badir's eldest son was a momentous event. Amira had never seen her father's house so crowded, not even on the day Jihan died. Both the men's and women's sections buzzed with guests, and the air was rich with the smells of spiced coffee, roasting lamb, incense, and perfume. Omar had gone all out, once he made up his mind—inviting virtually every friend, associate, and casual acquaintance he had to celebrate Malik's marriage.

"In business," Amira had heard him tell Farid, "when you are trapped in a bad deal, you must appear not only to welcome it, but to have planned it. It's the same with this. God is all-knowing; it will all turn out for the best."

It had taken masterful persuasion to bring him to that point. Farid had carried it off brilliantly. The problem, he and Amira agreed, was not so much that Malik had married an infidel—although that was bad enough—but that he had done so without asking Omar's permission and blessing. That was unforgivable. "There's only one way that the unforgivable can ever be forgiven," said Farid, "and that's if one admits right away that it was unforgivable. Such is human nature."

"Malik was wrong," he told Omar, "completely and unremittingly wrong. You know it, I know it, and he knows it. He told me so himself when he called. No, no, Uncle, don't say it: he should have called you, not me. But that's the whole point—he's too ashamed to speak with you."

Before it was over, Farid made it seem that Malik's action, terribly misguided though it was, actually stemmed from his tremendous respect for his father. "He was so afraid of offending you, Uncle, that he committed a far worse offense. Do you remember the truck driver who swerved to avoid a donkey and crashed into Prince Mubarak's Ferrari?"

"Which are you likening me to, nephew—a car or a donkey?" But Omar was smiling.

"Forgive me, Uncle; I'm clumsy with words. So let me ask you straight out: Will you let me tell Malik that he has your permission to call and apologize?"

Omar sighed. "Yes. Yes, of course, nephew. But first tell me what you know about this woman."

Farid was an artist, carefully choosing the colors, the areas to highlight and shadow, in his portrait of Genevieve. Amira, listening outside the door, found herself half convinced that a lapsed Catholic Parisian cabaret singer in her late twenties was actually a shy, virginal girl who might have become a nun had she not fallen in love with Malik and taken a deep interest in Islam.

And so they were all here today, eagerly awaiting the groom and his bride, excusing the unconventionality of the occasion by agreeing that Malik lived in Europe now, and when in Rome . . .

And as painstakingly as Farid and Amira had built it, just that quickly it all collapsed.

As Amira learned later—when everyone was talking about it—it started with a remark by Ali's cousin Abdul. "So now the Badirs have a celebrity in the family."

"What do you mean?" someone asked. Everyone said it was Omar's old friend Fuad Muhassan who had overheard.

"Why, the woman's a movie actress," said Abdul. "I thought everyone knew that."

"I would not call any man a liar," said the older man sternly, "when I lack the facts myself. But I've known Omar Badir all my life, and he would never let his son marry a woman of that kind."

"As you say, you lack the facts," Abdul replied flippantly.

"Young man, you need to learn respect—"

"Gentlemen, gentlemen." Ali himself stepped in, ever the diplomat. "It's all a misunderstanding, nothing more." By now others were listening. "My cousin is mistaken," he continued. "The young lady was never in a movie."

Abdul looked betrayed. "Well, she had the chance to be in one. You told me so yourself."

"I told you that in confidence, cousin," said Ali reprovingly. "It's true that she was offered a role, because of her fame as a singer, but she turned it down."

Now half the room was listening, including Omar.

"A singer! What's this you're saying, Ali?"

"It's nothing, my father-in-law, nothing at all," said Ali apologetically.

"You said a singer. What kind of singer?"

Amira, noticing the break in the rhythm of conversation, slipped in from the kitchen.

"It's nothing," Ali repeated. "The kind of thing many young women do in Europe, while they're waiting to find a husband."

"A singer!"

"Please, Father-in-law, forget I mentioned it. It's nothing."

"Where do you hear this?"

Ali looked uncomfortable. "From friends in Paris. But it's nothing, really. She sings only in the best places, none of these dirty little *boîtes*. My friends say she's quite good, a regular songbird." He smiled his famous smile. "I'm sure you've heard some of this from Malik. Personally, I congratulate you on your liberal outlook. I know from my own father that many men of your generation—"

"Farid! Where is Farid? I want the truth about this!"

"He went to the airport," someone said, "to meet Malik and— They should be here any minute."

"Bah!" Omar was fuming. Everyone present understood his predicament: in front of all his friends, he would have to either reject his only son's wife or allow a woman of loose morals—an infidel at that—into his home and his family.

Amira knew her father well enough to have no doubt which way he would choose. Something had to be done.

"Father," she said, moving to his side, "you can see that there must be some mistake. It's someone else, I'm sure of it."

"You contradict your own husband?"

"No, I—"

"This is none of your business, young woman. Go back to your place!"

She retreated toward the kitchen, as did the other women who had filtered out to see what the trouble was. They never made it there, for just at that moment Farid pushed open the front door and called for God's blessings on Malik and his bride.

Genevieve had tried, thought Amira, she had really tried. She wore an *abeyya* and veil and walked behind Malik like a good wife. But rather than being shapeless and concealing, the *abeyya* had too much of Paris about it, showing the curves of her body, and from beneath the edge of the veil a lock of dark blond hair had slipped, as brazen a provocation as a bare arm. If that were not enough, she had the terrible habit of European women, looking frankly and directly at the faces of the men in the room instead of demurely lowering her eyes. Given what had just been said, it was the worst thing she could do.

Omar needed only an instant to make his decision. "What is this woman that you bring into my house?" he demanded.

"Father, this is my wife," answered Malik. Amira could tell that he already knew the situation was hopeless, though not why. Farid had gone ashen. Genevieve, who obviously did not understand Arabic, merely looked nonplussed.

"Tell me the truth," said Omar, his voice shaking. "Does your *wife* sing in front of men, in a place where men go to drink alcohol?"

Malik glanced at Amira. What had gone wrong? She shook her head, unable to help.

"Yes," Malik told his father. "In France."

"Then let her be your wife in France. She is no one's wife here—not in al-Remal and not in this house."

Malik's eyes swept the room—did they linger for a split second on Ali? "Someone has poisoned your thoughts, Father." His voice was shaking too.

"Yes, and it is you. You have neglected a son's duty, you have lied to me, you have dishonored me and all your family. Yet you are my son, and so I give you a choice: Send that woman away and remain my son, or leave with her and never return."

There was not a drop of blood in either man's face. Malik spoke with deadly quietness: "God is One, and my wife is my wife everywhere. If we are not welcome here, you need not order us to leave, or fear that we will ever return. Good-bye, Father."

With that he turned and guided Genevieve out the door. Farid stared wildly around the room for a moment before following. Amira could not believe what was happening. "No!" she screamed, and although someone shouted behind her, she ran after her brother.

They were already piling into the car. "Malik! I don't know what happened!"

"Me either, little sister. But do you see now? Do you remember what I've always told you?"

She had no idea what he was talking about.

"Don't take a plane, not yet," pleaded Farid. "Stay at my place. Let me talk with him."

"No," said Malik. "Start the car."

Amira leaned in the window to keep them from pulling away.

Genevieve, more blond hair tumbling around her face, pushed back her veil and, to Amira's surprise, smiled.

"You must be Amira," she said in French. "I've looked forward to meeting you. But it seems"—she gestured toward the house—"I've come at a bad time."

"Oh, Genevieve, it's horrible. I'm so sorry."

"It's not your fault. The story of my life. I make a terrific impression wherever I go." She smiled again, more ruefully. The expression reminded Amira of Philippe. She liked this woman, she realized. Would she ever see her again?

"Go back inside, little sister," said Malik. "Don't get caught up in my trouble. Drive, cousin."

"*Au 'voir, petite soeur,*" said Genevieve.

Then they were gone.

Amira stared after the car until it disappeared. Guests were spilling out of the house as fleeing a fire. She hardly saw them, hardly heard the women's words of sympathy.

Tabriz, she thought.

Tabriz and Karim.

They were all she had left.

ESCAPE

Something was wrong in Iran. Amira felt it the minute she and Ali entered the Teheran airport. They were met by the Iranian minister of culture—a tall, rather urbane man—and a handful of other dignitaries, but the welcome seemed staged, the welcomers preoccupied.

Perhaps it was because they were all but surrounded by a cohort of hard-looking men in trenchcoats and sunglasses—SAVAK, Amira knew, the shah's secret police. One of the sunglassed men escorted her, Ali, and Karim to a line of large black American cars. A driver who made Jabr look like an oversized schoolboy held a door for them.

The SAVAK man slid into the front seat, spoke in Farsi into a handheld radio, and gave the driver a curt order. The limo pulled out in convoy with the others.

Teheran was as unprepossessing a large city as Amira had ever seen, an endless agglomeration of concrete structures softened by the backdrop of snow-capped mountains to the north. The air was a yellow haze, dimming the sparkle of the distant peaks.

Amira's eyes watered. "Is there a fire somewhere?" she asked.

"Smog, Highness," the driver replied in accented Arabic. "If you think this is bad, come back in the summer." He translated for the SAVAK man, who gave a grunt of laughter.

The city was as flat as a table until the northern suburbs began to rise gently toward the mountains. The line of cars turned in at a large, elaborate gate to grounds on which not just one but several large and not-so-large palaces were visible. The driver pointed out the shah's nephew's palace and the shah's mother's palace. There was no need for him to announce which was the ruler's own palace: a huge statue of Reza Shah Pahlavi said it for him.

With another flowery speech of welcome, the minister of culture turned them over to a factotum who led them to their rooms on the second floor.

Though the palace was furnished with a richness that far surpassed anything she had seen in al-Remal, it was the artistry of the carpets—hand-woven in classic Persian designs of timeless beauty—that most impressed Amira.

A maid reminded her of the hour of the formal reception that evening. Amira nodded. The reception was her excuse, if she should need one, for bringing along every carat of jewelry she owned. After the servant left, she took out the jewel case and poured the brilliant earrings and bracelets and necklaces on the bed. Karim played with them, making little piles and from time to time choosing a particular piece to call "pretty."

She was in Teheran. In forty-eight hours, she would be in Tabriz. Not long after that, Karim and the jewels might be all she had in the world.

Or maybe nothing would happen in Tabriz. There had been only the one letter from Philippe. Maybe it had all been only talk.

Ah, well—it was in God's hands.

Wasn't it?

"Pretty," said Karim, holding up the pigeon-blood ruby that had once belonged to Marie Antoinette.

• • •

"Caviar, Highness?" said the handsome man with graying temples. He was a minister of something-or-other that had to do with oil.

"No, thank you," said Amira. The great ceremonial hall on the palace's ground floor was practically buried in caviar. She must have eaten a half pound already, and she didn't even like the stuff.

"It seems as if this is the only place in Iran where you can find good caviar these days," said the man, "even though we're famous for it. Almost all of it leaves the country. I bought a few tins in Toronto last week—a good price, too."

It was perhaps the fifth time that Amira had heard about the scarcity of Iranian caviar in the land of its origin—and at least the tenth that someone had alluded to a recent trip to Toronto or New York or London or Zurich. Wealthy Iranians seemed to be exceedingly diligent about maintaining contacts abroad.

As always before an official trip, Amira had received a briefing on the host country. She knew that there was unrest in Iran, that much of it was being stirred up by fundamentalist mullahs. But these were not subjects she or Ali would discuss with anyone they might meet. They, after all, were here on a cultural mission involving the restoration of a venerable mosque in Tabriz.

Amira looked around the great hall. Were all these rich, powerful, smiling, laughing men and women—with the army, SAVAK, and even the Americans on their side—secretly terrified of a group of elderly clerics brandishing the Koran? Was that what the bank accounts in Switzerland and the luxury apartments in Manhattan were for, in case of the midnight alarm and the rush to catch the last plane out? Well, why not? She thought of the way the rulers of her own country—the royal family to which she herself belonged—walked on eggs around the fundamentalists.

There was a stir and then a hush. The shah entered with his wife, Farah Diba. They were far later than expected, the delay unexplained.

Amira would not have recognized the shah. The handsome, commanding, middle-aged man of the newspaper and magazine photographs looked shrunken, sallow-skinned, and old. Farah Diba, on the other hand, was even more beautiful than the images Amira had seen. In her thirties and the mother of four, she nevertheless had the glamour of a movie star.

Ali and Amira were honored guests, but not the most honored in the glittering crowd, and it was some time before they stood face to face with the shah and Farah. Through an interpreter, the shah and Ali exchanged conventional diplomatic greetings, and the shah made a little speech. After that, there was little to say, and Amira understood that it was time for them to move on.

Then suddenly Farah said, "You're Karim's parents! I should have known. I saw him upstairs with his servant. What a heartbreaker! Of course, the Remalis are famous for their looks."

The Remalis were famous for no such thing, but Amira was charmed nevertheless. So was Ali, she could tell. Even the shah seemed buoyed by his wife's enthusiasm.

A few more words, a little discussion of the mosque at Tabriz, and the audience was over. The American ambassador materialized to buttonhole Ali. Soon the two were engaged in a discourse about aircraft. Amira, worn from the day's journey and feeling distinctly peripheral, wished she could slip away to sleep.

"Highness," said a familiar voice over her shoulder, "how good to find you here."

"Philippe! What on earth—"

"Highness, Mr. Ambassador," said Philippe to Ali and the American, both of whom greeted him by name.

"Well, this is amazing," said Ali. "What brings you here, my friend?"

"I was about to tell the princess. I'm an interloper, I'm afraid—a party crasher, as you say, Mr. Ambassador? A colleague asked me to Teheran to consult on . . . on a particularly complicated case. When I learned that my old friends would be here tonight, I wangled my way in."

Amira forced herself to stop staring at him, to play the part of the pleasantly surprised international acquaintance.

"Well, it's certainly a small world," said the ambassador affably. "And your patient? I trust he's doing well?"

"Ah, my friend Elliott, surely you're not one of those obnoxious persons who insist on making us physicians discuss bunions and gallstones in our few moments of leisure."

"Sorry, Doctor. Just curious."

The ambassador allowed himself a speculative glance across the room at the shah. So, Amira noticed, did Ali.

It might be: the Shah was the kind of patient Philippe would travel thousands of miles to treat—the shah or cholera-stricken villagers in the back of beyond. But surely Philippe was in Teheran for another reason—wasn't he?

"You're here for long?" Philippe asked Ali.

"Only through tomorrow."

"Then we go to Tabriz," volunteered Amira.

"Ah. Yes, I think you mentioned that the last time I saw you. I leave tomorrow myself."

What did that mean? Amira searched his eyes. She saw nothing except that his pupils seemed unnaturally dilated, and his face was flushed.

"Please excuse me," said Philippe. "I haven't had a chance to eat since this morning."

He wandered away in the direction of the food tables.

"The doctor looks a little unsteady tonight," commented Ali.

"The French," said the ambassador, rolling his eyes. The two men returned to their discussion of the F-14.

Amira felt as if she were going to explode.

"Husband," she ventured, "forgive me for interrupting, but may I bring you something? I'm going to get a little bite for myself."

"I'm glad to see your appetite has returned," he said with a half-smile. "But nothing for me."

She found Philippe examining the vast carpet that formed the centerpiece of the ceremonial hall. He had a plate loaded with canapés but was not eating.

"Ah, Princess. Someone told me that this carpet is more than two hundred square meters. I've seen smaller casinos."

"Philippe, it's—"

"Did you know," he interrupted her, "that the Persian weavers always include a flaw in their work? The idea is that only God should be perfect."

He cut his eyes sideways. A few steps away stood a lone man in a tuxedo. Was he studying his drink too intently?

"It's a principle that French carmakers seem to have carried to an extreme," said Philippe. "At any rate, I'm not going to try to find the flaw in this monster."

He was steering her gently through the crowd. The man in the tuxedo did not follow. Paranoia?

"I didn't expect to see you here," she said. "I didn't know what to expect."

The noisy chatter of a large group nearby made a good screen for her words. Philippe had time to lean close to hear.

"I would have come anyway," he said. "The medical call was a piece of luck. Or maybe not so lucky, since it subjects me to a certain amount of scrutiny. The patient, as I'm sure you've gathered, is an important one. Are we still on for Tabriz?"

He added the question so casually that Amira almost missed it. This was the moment, she realized: the moment to say no, to forget this crazy scheme, to commit herself to going home and trying to fight Ali on ground she knew.

"Yes," she said.

"Listen carefully," said Philippe, smiling as if they were sharing an amusing reminiscence. "Someone will contact you in Tabriz. Do exactly as you are told. Exactly and immediately, do you understand?"

"Of course."

"Have one small bag packed—no more. Two changes of clothes for you and Karim. One traditional, one Western. Whatever personal articles you absolutely need. And your jewels. You have them?"

"Yes."

"Good. That's all."

"You'll be there?"

"Yes. No more now. It's dangerous. The shah spies on everyone—on principle or just out of habit, who knows? Say it's been a pleasure and you hope to see me in al-Remal."

"How good to see you again, Doctor. You must promise to visit us when you're in al-Remal."

"With pleasure, Highness. Please convey my regards to your husband again, in case I don't see him. I'm afraid it's bedtime for this poor carcass of mine."

A few words of good-bye and he disappeared in the crowd. He hadn't touched his food, Amira thought irrelevantly.

Once, in France, she had gone to a circus. There was a trapeze act in which a woman swinging from a bar high above the ring suddenly threw herself astonishingly into space. For one heart-stopping instant, she seemed certain to hurtle to her death—and then she was caught by the strong hands and powerful arms of a man swinging to meet her.

Now, in the ceremonial hall of the shah's palace in Teheran, Amira felt as if she were flying out on the thin air, the deadly earth rushing to meet her. Only Philippe could catch her, only he could save her. She was trusting him with her life.

• • •

Amira had expected an exotic town of old Persia, narrow streets within ancient walls, a suitable setting for intrigue. In reality, Tabriz was a city of several hundred thousand, as modern and nearly as sprawling as Teheran.

They were greeted by the mayor of Tabriz and the governor of Azerbaijan-Sharghi province. Clearly, the Remali minister of culture was considered a very important guest. Amira and Ali had connecting suites that occupied most of the top floor of the Hotel Tabriz, with several of the hotel's personnel assigned as servants. They also had their own SAVAK man lingering in the hallway.

The first order of business was an official lunch. The women ate separately from the men. Despite the city's reputation, Amira could not say that the citizens of Tabriz were less friendly than people elsewhere; they simply smiled less. They also had the sense to provide good local cuisine rather than to attempt cosmopolitan delicacies.

The main dish was *abgusht*, a stew of potatoes, lentils, and thick chunks of fatty mutton. It tasted better than it sounded, although there was a trick to eating it: a mortar and pestle were provided for mashing the meat and potatoes to just the right consistency to mix with the broth. The governor's wife showed Amira how to do it, but the too-polite cheers of the other women convinced her that she hadn't got it quite right.

After lunch, there was an inspection of the Blue Mosque, the structure that Ali's father, as a goodwill gesture to the Shia minority in his own country, had volunteered to restore. Amira did not enter the mosque, of course; she waited in a car with the governor's wife and the wife of the mayor. Only a small part of the majestic building was open; the rest had an air of damage and neglect verging on ruin.

"It was built a little more than five hundred years ago, by the grace of God," said the governor's wife.

"What happened to it?" asked Amira. It took an effort to show interest. More than half of her mind was on the contact Philippe had mentioned. Where? When? Who? Was it one of these women?

"Earthquakes, mainly," said the governor's wife. "We have them often here—a very bad one just two years ago. But also invasions, fires—the usual thing."

Ali was to meet all afternoon with various civic and religious officials. Amira and the two wives, accompanied discreetly by the SAVAK man, went to see some of the sights of Tabriz, among them the teeming bazaar, which was every bit as winding and medieval as she had imagined the entire city to be. Another place that she would remember ever after was the Arg-Tabriz, the remains of a huge ancient fortress that had crumbled to ruin about the time the first stones of the Blue Mosque were laid. She would remember it because of a story.

"In the old days," said the governor's wife, "they executed criminals by throwing them from the top of the Arg into a ditch. There was a woman sentenced to death for adultery, but when they threw her from the heights, her *chador* billowed out around her and caught the air like—like one of those things the military use."

"A parachute," said the mayor's wife.

"Exactly. It broke her fall and saved her life, God be praised."

"She was allowed to live afterward?" asked Amira.

"Of course. It was God's will."

Back at the hotel, Amira collapsed on the bed and stared at the ceiling. She was exhausted. In a few minutes, she would have Karim brought to her . . . in a few minutes. Just now she needed rest.

There was a soft knock at the door. A hotel maid entered.

"I'm sorry to disturb you, Highness, but I'm to tell you that I'll be your servant for the night. My name is Darya. Is there anything I can bring you?" She was Amira's age and size and coloring; they could have been taken for sisters.

"No, nothing," said Amira.

"Perhaps your Highness would like some music?" Darya indicated the suite's receiver and tape deck, very new.

"No," said Amira patiently. "Nothing at the moment."

The maid came close and mouthed the word *yes*. Amira couldn't understand the girl's temerity. Then the awareness ran through her like an electric shock: this was it, the contact.

"On second thought," she said as calmly as she could, "a little music would be nice."

"Thank you, Highness." Darya tuned the radio, raised the volume, and returned to Amira. "Are you ready?" she asked quietly.

"Now? Right now?"

"No. Later tonight. But are you ready?"

"Yes."

"Good. You're going to the affair?"

"What? Oh. Yes." A celebratory dinner was scheduled; apparently the conclusion was foregone that al-Remal would help restore the mosque.

"All right. Go as if everything were normal, but if you can, convince your husband to leave early rather than late. Plead sickness, exhaustion, whatever."

"That will be easy enough."

Darya did not smile. "As soon as you are back here, have your son brought to you. Is it likely that your husband will . . . visit you before he retires for the night?"

"No. Very unlikely."

The girl nodded as if confirming something she already knew. "His room is stocked with liquor—a special service the hotel offers some guests. Will he drink before going to bed?"

"Yes. I think so."

"Good. There'll be something extra in each bottle. He'll sleep very late tomorrow and appear to be drunk when he wakes."

Amira said nothing. Everything was moving so fast.

"Be ready to go at a moment's notice," Darya instructed. "When it's time, I'll knock. Just one knock. Bring your things and follow me without a sound. Keep the boy quiet."

Amira was trying to sort it out. "Won't they know? I mean, won't they find out about whatever you put in the liquor? Won't they know who did it?"

"So what? We'll all be far away."

"Where will you go?"

Darya looked at her with something like contempt.

"I'm sorry," said Amira. "It was a stupid thing to ask."

"I won't tell you where, but I'll tell you a little about why. I want you to know that we're not doing this for you, or for your friend, and certainly not for money."

"Then . . . why?"

"It may not have occurred to you, Highness, but your disappearance will embarrass the shah—and perhaps strain relations between him and your father-in-law. Creating problems for the Peacock Throne is the cause to which I—and many like me—have dedicated ourselves."

"You're a fundamentalist?" asked Amira.

"Hardly. Do I strike you as one of those? But we work with them when it suits our needs." Darya paused. "I'm talking too much. Rest, Highness. You have a very long night ahead. Call the front desk if you need me."

After a while, Amira turned the radio down. She had heard revolution spouted by students in the cafés of Paris, but she had never met a real revolutionary. Now, suddenly, she was a pawn in someone's deadly chess game against the shah.

It had to be God's will, she thought, for never could she have willed it herself.

• • •

Karim was asleep. Amira waited in the traveling clothes she had worn on the flight from Teheran. From time to time, she heard the soft footsteps of the SAVAK man patrolling the hall. What would be done about him?

There was no sound from Ali's suite. Earlier she had heard faintly through the door the familiar tink of bottle against glass, followed after a time by noises of clumsy stumbling. Now nothing.

For the dozenth time, she checked to make sure that the jewel case was in her bag. It was. *Stop being obsessive, Amira. Just wait calmly. It's in Philippe's hands. And Darya's. And God knows who else's.* Had she remembered her passport? Yes, there it was. Would she even need it?

She listened. Something was different. The hall was quiet now, but someone was there. She could sense it.

The single knock seemed as loud as a pistol shot. Surely Ali had heard it. She scrambled for the bag, dropped it, picked it up again, and cradled Karim in her other arm.

Darya opened the door and whispered, "Hurry!" Amira followed her to a door at the end of the hallway. Darya used a key to open it. A stairway. Amira's heels clacked loudly, echoing in the stairwell. They went down several flights. Another door, another key. They were out in the night, in some kind of alleyway.

"Damn it!" said Darya. "He should be waiting."

"Who?"

"Your friend. He's late."

"Women," said a heavy voice behind them, "what are you doing out in the night?"

They both froze.

The SAVAK man stepped from the shadows. "You'll have to come with me and explain yourselves," he said.

It's over, thought Amira.

Darya flew past her with animal speed and clawed at the man's face. Cursing, he knocked her aside, but suddenly there was movement behind him. Amira heard a slapping thud, then another, and the SAVAK man's legs gave way. Two young men stood over him.

"Are you all right, Darya?" one of them said.

"Yes. Damn! Where did that son of a bitch come from?"

"God knows. What do we do with him?"

"Let me think."

"What is it, Mommy?" said Karim, half asleep.

"It's all right, baby."

"There's only one place to take him," said Darya. "If we can get him there." She looked down the alley. "Damn it, Princess, where's your friend?"

"I don't know."

"Look, maybe the best thing for you to do is go back upstairs. Try to get into your room without being seen."

"I can't. I left my keys. I didn't think I'd be back."

"God! Here—take mine. One of them is for your room. Wait! Who's that?"

A tan vehicle had pulled into the alley.

"That's him! For God's sake, Highness, go!"

"I want to thank—"

"Go!"

She ran to the car, a battered Land Rover. Philippe pushed open the door and pulled her in.

"I'm late—sorry," he said. "Trouble there?"

"Yes."

"Tell me about it later. For now, let's get out of here."

It must have been around midnight. There was little traffic, but the sidewalks were crowded with men out on the town. Amira felt as if every one of them were staring at her, memorizing her face, as Philippe pulled onto the boulevard and accelerated.

BROTHER PETER

Philippe drove west on a cobblestone boulevard through the heart of the city, counting cross streets under his breath as he passed them. Amira did not interrupt his concentration. She wanted only to be far away from this place. Karim woke long enough to say "Hello, Uncle Ph'lipe," then drifted back to sleep in her lap. Around them cars sped slapdash, threatening to demolish clopping two-horse *droshkys*.

Philippe turned right and crossed a river. A few blocks farther on, he cursed in French, turned left, and crossed and recrossed the same river at a large traffic circle. Soon they came to another bridge, and a broader stream slipped beneath them.

"The water's high," said Philippe. "The spring thaw in the mountains. I hope it won't be a problem later."

Signs for the airport appeared, then slid behind. Amira looked questioningly at Philippe.

"We're not flying," he said. "We're driving out."

"They'll be watching the airport," said Amira.

"No. They won't be watching anything for hours."

"Where are we going?"

"To Turkey, for a start. We ought to reach the border by daybreak."

"*Inshallah.*"

"Yes, if God wills it and this old Rover is worth half what I paid for it. I bought it in Rezaiye, across the big lake. The ferry had engine trouble. That's why I was late getting to the hotel." He glanced at Amira. "What happened back there?"

Amira told him about the SAVAK agent.

"That's not so good. I was counting on Darya to do something for us in the morning. Ah, well. It's not critical, and maybe she'll do it anyway."

"Do what?"

"You don't want to know yet. When we're out of Iran."

"What will happen to him?"

"The SAVAK? At best, he'll have a very uncomfortable day or two. At worst, he'll turn up in that river we crossed."

"We're part of that?"

"Indirectly, anyway. And it may happen, I regret to say. But you didn't ask him to follow you. Remember that—and what he would have done to you and Darya."

Amira remembered Darya clawing at the SAVAK agent like a leopardess. She had never seen a woman physically attack a man—not like that. Even more astonishing, when she thought about it, was the fact that Darya was obviously the commander of the little revolutionary group, the two young men deferring to her.

They were beyond the city now, among mountains in the high desert. The road was dirt. Tabriz itself was nearly a mile high, and they had been climbing steadily ever since leaving it. A surprising amount of traffic, mainly trucks, moved north with them, a red chain of taillights in the night.

Philippe reached for the old-fashioned black medical bag that he always carried. "Hand me that water bottle, will you, my dear?"

He took two pills from a vial and washed them down. "Methamphetamine," he explained. "Unfortunately, I need it to keep me going. I haven't slept since I arrived in this country. Don't worry. I tell you only so that if I start seeing dragons in the road, you'll understand."

In the glow from the dash, his face was both haggard and surprisingly youthful. Amira thought that she had never seen him so handsome, not even that afternoon at the café in Paris.

"How did you do all this?" she finally asked.

"Money. Old favors. Old friends. I'm using up all three at an amazing pace."

"And why? Why are you doing it?"

"You know why."

"Yes. Thank you."

"Don't thank me. Do you have your passport?"

"Yes."

"We'll lose it somewhere before the border. Open that compartment."

There were two French passports, one for her, one for Karim. Philippe turned on the map light for her.

"So I'm *femme* Rochon, and this is little Karim Philippe Rochon."

"At least until we're in Turkey, at a place called Agri. Then you'll be someone else."

"These look real."

"Done by the best forger in France, which is saying something. One reason he's the best is that only a select clientele know he's the best."

"How did *you* know?"

"One of those old favors. Or two."

"Is it safe to use your name? Won't they be looking for us?"

"As I said, they won't be looking for anyone until morning, and maybe not for several hours after that. The SAVAK is a complication, though. It's best that we reach the border early."

There were a hundred questions to ask. Amira let them all evaporate. She should have been exhausted, but instead a deep and almost radiant elation filled her. She had her child, and beside her the man who was the love of her soul, running with her in the desert night through one foreign land toward another, from known danger to danger unknown.

Free.

The word came to her as if whispered by a secret voice. Never in her life had she applied it to herself.

Free.

It was like honey, the first taste demanding the next.

A low haze of road dust dimmed the taillights ahead, but the stars burned bright and endless above.

"Whatever happens," Amira told Philippe and the universe, "it was worth it."

• • •

Dawn caught them at Maku, a town huddled in a valley hardly wider than the road, under a huge overhanging cliff. They had been delayed at a bridge—not much more than a culvert, really—that a swollen mountain stream had torn away.

Philippe parked the Land Rover behind a truck.

"I'll be back in a few minutes. What would you like to eat?"

"Anything."

"And Karim?"

"I'll feed him while you're gone."

He looked confused, then nodded. "I'd forgotten how late you wean in al-Remal."

"Bring him something sweet, if you can. He eats solid food, too, you know."

He came back in twenty minutes with bread, cheese, kabobs, and a thermos of coffee. There was a cup of honeyed yogurt for Karim.

"Maku," said Philippe. "Do you know what it means?"

"How would I?"

"The story goes that in ancient times a general had to move his army by night. They marched by moonlight until they came to this place, where the mountains, that cliff there, blocked the sky. The army was stumbling around, disintegrating, in pitch blackness, and the general cried out, *'Ma ku? Ma ku?'* It means 'Where is the moon?' "

"Where did you hear this?"

"It's well known among civilized people everywhere—although it obviously hasn't reached al-Remal yet." He grinned. "Actually, I've been here before, here and across the border, in Turkey. Long ago, when I was very idealistic, fresh from medical school. It was the usual horror: an earthquake followed by an epidemic. I was here for the epidemic." He gazed into the distance. "Death isn't the enemy," he said unexpectedly. "Death will always be there. What wears one down is the weight of ignorance, as massive as that mountain above us. Cholera everywhere: 'What measures have you taken?' 'Oh, we're eating garlic.' A child wasting away with diarrhea: 'I put a charred peach pit in his navel, Your Honor, but he doesn't get better, by God's will.' I'm sure it hasn't changed a centime's worth all these years later."

"Neither have you, my friend. You're still the idealist. And still young," she added, because in the growing light, his weary face did not look young at all.

"Hah! So young that I'm going to need another of these to get me to the border." He took out a pill and swallowed it with coffee. "We're only half an hour away. Don't worry, nothing's going to happen. They may ask me some routine questions, but they rarely question women. Don't worry about Karim, either. If he calls me Uncle Philippe, no one at the border will know it doesn't mean 'Daddy' in French." He started the Land Rover and winked at her. "*Allons-y.*"

As they came out of the valley, a high mountain capped with snow came into view, bright as a bride in the sunrise.

"Ararat," said Philippe. "Noah's Ark."

Amira nodded. She was familiar with the story.

At the border, the traffic was backed up for a mile. It took more than an hour for them to reach the Iranian guard post. There a harried-looking soldier waved them through after a quick glance and a few words. Crossing the no-man's-land to the Turkish side, Philippe let out a long breath. "That was the big moment. They haven't heard a thing. The Turks won't know, either."

But at the Turkish post, after studying their papers, the guard ordered Philippe to pull the Rover aside. Moments later an officer appeared. He motioned Philippe out of the car. The two men exchanged a few words that Amira couldn't understand; then Philippe followed the Turk into the building.

Five minutes. Ten. Fifteen. Fretting in the Land Rover, Amira invented a game of popping little balls of bread into Karim's mouth. Twenty minutes. Twenty-five. What was wrong? It was full morning. What was happening back in Tabriz? By now, someone must have noticed that her room was empty. Was Ali awake yet? What if the SAVAK man had escaped from Darya's friends?

Philippe emerged from the building, the officer following. The two were smiling and chatting, an obvious exchange of mutual esteem. When Philippe at length started the Land Rover, the officer stepped back, saluted, and made a show of halting a truck so that he could turn back onto the road.

"What happened?" asked Amira when the border was behind them. "Was something wrong?"

"I don't know. I had the feeling he suspected something. Maybe the pills—border officers develop a sixth sense for drugs. Or maybe it was just the usual grab for *baksheesh*. But I played my trump card and ended up having tea with him."

"What trump card?"

"When I was here before, I worked with a young Turkish lieutenant. We became friends. We still write every year or so. He's a general now. So I asked the captain if he happened to know my old friend. He does—and fears him, too, I'd say."

Amira laughed. It was hard to stop laughing, her relief was so great. "My God, Philippe, is there any place on earth where you *don't* know someone?"

"One never regrets kindness," said Philippe. "Always remember that, my love."

"Those pills are turning you into a philosopher."

Now Philippe laughed, too.

• • •

They crossed rolling hills, surprisingly green under a cloudless sky. Here and there sheep grazed on new grass. Every time a flock appeared, Karim pointed happily: "Sheep!" Philippe said that the countryside reminded him of Montana, a place he had visited in the United States. Ararat rose on their right, dominating the horizon.

Forty-five minutes from the border, the first town came into view, a bare-bones scatter of three or four hundred ugly stone houses. As plain as it was, it thrilled Amira because the clothes of the men she saw were unmistakably European: shirts, sweaters, pants, wool jackets, and caps. Though the women were unveiled—as the founder of modern Turkey, Mustafa Kemal Atatürk, had decreed they should be decades ago—they were conservatively dressed, their heads covered with scarves.

• • •

"They're conservative out here," Philippe explained. "In the cities, certainly in Ankara, you can almost imagine you're in New York, but here they cling to the old ways."

To the west the land changed. There was less green, and plowed fields began to appear. Ararat slipped behind, fading and diminishing with distance.

"Tell me what we're doing," Amira said.

Philippe nodded as if to affirm that it was time for an explanation. "It's not the greatest plan, but fortunately, we're dealing with rather predictable people. Very soon now your husband will wake with the worst hangover of his life, and soon after that he'll learn that his wife is missing. The hotel staff may already know that you're not in your room, but no one will do anything without Ali. After all, you might be in *his* room. Once it becomes clear that you're gone, there will be a flurry of phone calls to al-Remal and Teheran. Everyone will have one main desire: to keep the whole thing quiet as long as they can. Sooner or later, it will come out—but with luck, nothing will become public for at least a day or two."

"And then?"

He ignored the question. "Meanwhile, they'll be looking for you—quietly. Not the regular police. SAVAK. And if Darya was able to complete her task, they'll stumble onto a false trail."

"What do you mean?"

"The plan was for her to take the early flight from Tabriz to Teheran. She should have landed an hour ago. You may have noticed that she looks a bit like you, and she was to specify that a child was traveling with her. If someone asked on the plane, she could say that she had decided to leave the child with an aunt. But he would be on the flight list. And she would be noticed. Someone will remember when SAVAK comes asking."

"It sounds dangerous for her."

"Less dangerous than staying in Tabriz, now that she's kidnapped a SAVAK agent. At any rate, in Teheran, she'll go through the same charade at two different airlines, buying tickets for al-Remal at one and London at the other. And there the trail will end, because she won't catch either flight. She'll simply leave the airport and disappear in Teheran."

"They'll know she didn't take either of the flights?"

"Eventually, but it will give them plenty to chew on for a day or more, and even then the logical place to look will be Teheran."

"And what are we going to do while all this is happening?"

"Right now we're going to meet a man in a town called Van. He'll get you safely out of Turkey while I go back to Ararat and lay the second false trail."

It was as if the world had tilted. "You're leaving me?"

He shook his head as if denying it. "I have to, my love. Remember the plan: you and Karim aren't just running away, you're disappearing for good. I'm going back to wreck the car in a river in the mountains. It will look as if the bodies washed away."

"Why can't we go with you?"

"Because the three of us could never get away from there unnoticed. I . . . I'll get away."

"But what then? Are you going to disappear, too?"

"Yes. Don't worry, my dear. All will be explained later."

"When will I see you again?"

"I don't know, my love. Perhaps not for a very long while."

Those words again. "I don't like this, Philippe."

"Neither do I, believe me. But there's no other way now. Sooner or later, some genius in SAVAK will decide to check the border posts. When my name comes up, a red light will go on. They'll start gearing up for a covert search in Paris, which is where they'll figure we've gone the minute we reached an airport in Turkey. But then the wreck will be found, and the red light will go off while they hunt for the bodies. It will give you an open window to slip into Paris."

"I'm going to Paris?"

"For a little while. Then to America."

"America!"

"Yes. As I said, it will all be explained. Just get to Paris safely."

"Who is this man? The one we're meeting."

"He may be the best man I've ever known. His name is Brother Peter."

• • •

The air was thin and cold. Sheep and goats grazed among patches of snow, and the low mountains were still coated in white. Here and there crouched stone houses with huge haystacks atop their flat roofs. Farmers drove wagons or led heavily burdened donkeys along the muddy, rutted road.

Amira stared moodily out the window. Philippe's plan was too complicated. Or maybe it wasn't. It didn't matter. What mattered was that he wasn't in it. Why was he abandoning her—her and Karim? Why couldn't he come with them—to Paris, to America, wherever? Where would he go? Wherever it might be, was someone else waiting for him there?

She had no right to ask such questions, but she couldn't help thinking them. The sweetness of her newfound freedom had vanished, leaving a bitter aftertaste. The taste of loneliness. The taste of fear.

The Rover topped a rise, and a town appeared ahead.

"Agri," said Philippe. It was much larger than Dogubeyazit, but the people looked the same, the odd combination of Western-dressed men and conservatively garbed women. A sizable mosque dominated the middle of town. Philippe parked on a busy street nearby. "I'll get some food. Walk around if you like. No one will object."

She led Karim around a little square and quickly found herself surrounded by a knot of curious, smiling women. She couldn't understand a word they said until one of them shyly managed a little Arabic: "Where are you going? Where are you from?"

What was a safe answer? "I was born in Egypt, but I live in France with my husband. We're driving from Teheran to . . . to Istanbul. It's a dream of his."

Heads nodded when this information was translated. Everyone could sympathize with a woman whose husband had strange ideas.

Philippe returned, followed by several men vying with one another to help him. One carried the thermos, another a basket of food. A third knelt to inspect the Rover's tires and nodded in apparent satisfaction at their soundness. When Philippe at last was able to shepherd Amira and Karim into the vehicle, someone passed a bottle through the window. There were shouts of "*Sagol!*"

"*Sagol!*" Philippe replied. As they drove away, children ran beside them. "I'd forgotten how friendly the Turks are," Philippe mused.

"What does *Sagol* mean?"

He laughed. "It means 'long life.' "

Amira uncovered the basket: a split loaf of dark, fresh bread serving as plates for cold vegetables and chunks of grilled lamb. Philippe handed her the thermos.

"It's only tea. It seems there's no coffee in Turkey. It's like caviar in Iran. They sell every ounce for foreign exchange."

"What will I do in America?" she demanded suddenly. She had meant to sound angry, but the question came out merely petulant.

For the first time since Tabriz, he touched her, the backs of his fingers light on her cheek. "Don't be afraid, my love. What will you do in America? It's up to you. It's a country where a person with intelligence and dedication can become whatever he wants. Or she wants. But I've taken the liberty of arranging an opportunity, if it interests you. Would you like to go to Harvard?"

"Harvard? The university?"

"Of course."

"As a student?"

"What else?"

"But I'm not qualified," she protested. "And there's Karim—what about him?"

"You're qualified. And Karim will be fine." He took his hand from her cheek. "This isn't the time for details. You'll get those from a friend of mine in Paris. His name is Maurice Cheverny. He's a lawyer. Contact him before you do anything else. Call him from the airport. He's expecting you."

At an intersection, he turned left. In minutes they were out of Agri, heading south.

A university student! It was a far better dream than hiding away in a château or *finca*. It was something she had wanted almost as long as she could remember.

But it was so far away, in so unknown a place.

"Come with me, Philippe." There, she had said it.

He smiled sadly. "I wish I could, my love, but I can't. Someday you'll understand—trust me." He uncapped and sniffed the bottle that the man in Agri had given them. "Raki. One swallow and I'd be comatose. Well, maybe just one." He took a drink and fell into a coughing fit. "God—just as bad as I remembered it."

A few minutes later, he was humming softly.

In midafternoon, they reached a small town with a vast sheet of blue stretching beyond it.

"Is that the ocean?" Amira wondered, as she had forgotten her geography.

"Van Golu—Lake Van. It's salty; that's why there's nothing growing along the shore." He talked for some time about the saltiness of the lake. Amira had seen the effects of amphetamines; she knew that the pills were wearing off.

Van, a city of perhaps a hundred thousand people, lay an hour down the road. Philippe had trouble finding the hotel he wanted. Finally, they happened on it almost by chance. They registered as M. And Mme. Rochon and child and turned over their passports. The hotel, a pleasant medium-sized place called the Akdamar, apparently had few other guests.

"Cold," said Philippe.

"You're cold?"

"Too cold for tourists. They come for the lake. But not until summer."

In the room, he tipped the porter, closed the door, leaned against it, and fainted. Amira gasped, but knew intuitively that she must not call for help. Somehow she lifted him onto the bed. Karim watched awestruck: this, with absolute certainty, was a matter for adults. A damp cloth to Philippe's forehead opened his eyes. "Amira, my love. I'm sorry. I wanted to spend these last few hours . . . you know: talking, listening. But I have to sleep. Or I won't make it to Ararat. Wake me when it's dark."

"Just sleep."

"At dark: promise me."

He slept. Karim climbed onto the bed. "I take care of Uncle Ph'lipe." Soon he was asleep, too. Amira allowed herself to lie down beside them—just to rest a little, she told herself.

She woke with a start. A glance at the window told her that night had come. Philippe was dead to the world. Trying to rouse him was like trying to wake Ali when he had drunk too much. After a long effort, she got him to a sitting position.

"What time is it?" he mumbled.

"I don't know."

He looked at his watch as if it contained a great mystery. "Ten o'clock," he finally said. "Not too late." He pushed himself to his feet, went to the washstand, and splashed water on his face.

"Not too late for what?"

"I have to go out in the town and make my presence known. Then we'll have a visitor." He found his medical bag and took a pill. "Two left," he said to himself. "That should do."

"Philippe, you're exhausted. Can't whatever you're planning wait till morning?"

"No. This is the dangerous time. It's possible that they're already looking for us in this country. We have to move fast."

He pulled his coat on and left. He was gone for an hour. When he returned, he seemed to have regained his energy.

"Brother Peter will be here soon. You'll go with him tonight. By morning you'll be in Erzurum. There's an airport—one flight a day to Ankara." He tore loose the lining of his coat and produced some papers. "Your plane tickets. Erzurum to Ankara, Ankara to Istanbul, Istanbul to Paris. All return tickets. And here is your new passport, and some papers for Karim."

She looked at the passport: Jihan Sonnier. Spouse of Dr. Claude Sonnier.

"Not quite two years ago," said Philippe, "an earthquake killed fifty thousand people in the district north of Lake Van. There are many orphans.

Karim is one of them. You're here to adopt him and take him home to France. You . . . you can't have children of your own."

Amira nodded. That much, at least, was true.

"Brother Peter has been closely involved in helping the earthquake victims, especially the children. He can answer any questions that anyone in authority may raise. And he will never betray you."

Amira looked at the passport again. "*Jihan* Sonnier?"

"Your mother's name came to me when I was instructing the forger. Is it all right?"

"Yes."

There was an almost inaudible knock at the door.

The man who entered was small and wiry, with thinning brown hair, sunburnt skin, and faded blue eyes. His clothes resembled those of the Turkish man Amira had seen. He and Philippe embraced like long-separated brothers.

"I thank you for this, my friend," said Philippe in English. "You know I wouldn't have asked if it weren't life or death."

"No apologies, mate. I'm a grown man."

Philippe introduced Brother Peter to Amira. "Forgive his abominable English—he's Australian."

"Australian," said Brother Peter amiably. Then he turned serious. "I hate to rush things, but we need to get started."

"Ah. Yes, of course. Well, we're on your ground. How do you want to do it?"

"I don't want Amira—Jihan—or the boy to be seen with me anywhere near Van. Too many people know me. Too much chance someone will notice and make a connection. As we get west of Agri, it won't matter."

"You're saying that she and Karim should stay hidden?"

"I'm using the mission's panel truck. I've made a cubbyhole in back under some blankets and cartons. It won't be comfortable, but it's only for a few hours. Can you keep the boy quiet if need be?" he asked Amira.

"I'll give him a mild sedative," said Philippe. "He'll sleep for at least eight hours. Will that be enough?"

"Should be plenty."

"Good. What else?"

"What are you driving?"

"A tan Land Rover."

"Go north, back toward Agri. Take it slow so I can catch up—I'll leave twenty minutes behind you. If anyone stops you, you're tourists enjoying a lovely moonlight drive along the lake."

"All right."

"Somewhere north of the lake and south of Agri, I'll blink my headers three times. Pull over and we'll make the switch." He looked at both of them. "Any questions?"

"Why are you called 'Brother'?" said Amira.

Peter smiled almost bashfully. "Philippe didn't tell you? I'm with a mission. A service order, actually. Very small."

"You mean Christian?"

"Yes. I know it's odd, but we've been here since Atatürk, and they still tolerate us. We're quiet. We don't proselytize. We just try to help. Well, then—are we ready?"

"Why not?" said Philippe.

• • •

With the headlights cutting the night, Van was a dream, Tabriz a distant memory, al-Remal forgotten. The road was familiar, the road was home. She had been in the Land Rover all her life.

Karim slept, having taken a spoonful of sweet red liquid from Philippe's bag. Philippe kept thinking of things to caution her against. "Remember: call Maurice Cheverny before anything else. And try to be sure no one follows you from Orly—they won't do anything in the airport itself. If they try something in the city, scream for the police. If the truth comes out, ask for political asylum. It's the best chance. My God, I almost forgot: here's money—more than enough to get you to Paris."

At two o'clock in the morning, Brother Peter blinked his signal. Philippe stopped and opened the door. In the cabin light, his face was sickly gray.

"Are you all right?"

"What? Yes. A bit worn out. Don't worry."

Brother Peter pulled up alongside and got out. "Well, old frog," he said, "this seems to be it. I don't know what you've got planned, but be careful about it."

"And you. Thanks again—for everything."

"Thank only God, my friend, not his poor servant."

Philippe turned to Amira. To her surprise, tears were streaming down her face. He held her so tightly it hurt. "Good-bye, my love. I wish . . . I wish it had been different."

"It will be different. Everything will be different. But don't say good-bye, my heart. It's only *au 'voir*, isn't it? We won't lose each other, will we? Promise me?"

"We won't lose each other. We can't. *Au 'voir. Au 'voir*, Amira."

Brother Peter carried Karim to the panel truck. "In here, my lady."

Her eyes met Philippe's one last time as she wedged herself in with her sleeping son. Then Brother Peter rearranged boxes and blankets, shutting out the world.

"Go first and go fast," he told Philippe. "I want to be well behind you at Agri."

She couldn't make out Philippe's reply, only the sound of the Land Rover pulling away. In a moment the panel truck grumbled to life.

"Comfy?" called Brother Peter.

"I'm all right."

"Good. Next stop, Erzurum."

It was pitch black in Amira's little cave. Time lost its shape. Had ten minutes passed? An hour?

"Brother Peter?"

"Yes."

"Why are you doing this?"

A silence. "Because I believe it's what God wants me to do."

"You and Philippe must be very good friends."

Another silence. "I owe him my life—and a great deal more."

That was all. Much later Brother Peter said, "Agri," and the motion of the vehicle changed. After that, there was only a dark eternity.

She woke because they had stopped. A door opened, the blankets flew back, and blinding light flooded in: morning.

"Up front quickly," ordered Brother Peter. "We're nearly to Erzurum. There'll be a checkpoint in a few miles."

Karim had wet himself in his sleep, but there was nothing to do about it here. Amira, using the truck's side mirror, freshened up as best as she could.

"Do you have a scarf?"

"Yes."

"Use it like a veil. Cover your hair and part of your face. Don't worry: European women often do it out here. When in Rome, you know."

Armed soldiers manned the checkpoint. Brother Peter answered their questions in Turkish. One of the men gave an order. Brother Peter slid over on the seat. A soldier opened the door and climbed behind the wheel.

"No fear, Mme. Sonnier," said Brother Peter, seeing Amira's expression. "Erzurum's a military zone. All foreigners have to be escorted by a soldier. So we have a chauffeur."

At the airport, she changed an irritable, half-asleep Karim into his one fresh set of clothes. A crackly loudspeaker announced the Ankara flight.

"On time," said Brother Peter. "I've always wanted to witness a real miracle, and here it is. A good sign, Mme. Sonnier."

He and the soldier saw her to the plane.

"*Sagol!*" said the soldier.

"*Sagol* to you, too. And you, Brother Peter."

She was in Ankara by noon, in Istanbul by evening. That night she slept seven miles above the earth on a jet bound for Paris.

M. CHEVERNY

Customs at Orly came as a welcome anticlimax; a yawning official barely glanced at her papers before stamping them.

She was in France.

The airport teemed with arriving passengers. Amira towed Karim with one hand, clutching the bag containing all she owned in the other. If they were hunting her, they would be here. Who might be a hunter? A Turkish-looking man scanning the crowd—had he lost someone, or was it an act? A couple who might be Iranian conversing near a ticket counter—did the woman glance Amira's way? A blue-jeaned young man lounging on a bench reading a textbook—wasn't he a little old for a student?

She found a telephone, changed a ten-franc note, and tried to remember which coin was needed. Suddenly someone was beside her.

The man in blue jeans.

"Mme. Sonnier?"

Should she deny it? Run? What?

He smiled. "My name is Paul. I work for Maurice Cheverny. You are calling him?"

"Yes." Thank God.

"Go ahead." He inserted a coin for her.

Cheverny's voice was rich and cautiously cordial. "Welcome to Paris, Mme. Sonnier. You had a safe journey?"

"Yes."

"Good. We have work to do, but there's no rush now that you're here. Will tomorrow be soon enough? I imagine you need rest. Paul is with you?"

"Yes."

"Let me speak with him."

She handed over the receiver. Paul listened and said, *"Ça va,"* then *"Non,"* then *"Oui, m'sieur,"* and hung up.

He had a car. As they pulled away from the airport, Amira could not help glancing over her shoulder.

"No onc is following," said Paul. "There was no one watching you in the airport, either."

"How do you know?"

He shrugged. "Part of my job." He was tall and thin, almost frail, but somehow he reminded her of Jabr.

"What do you know about me?"

"Only that someone is looking for you—someone with the full resources of a foreign government—and that M. Cheverny does not wish for you to be found."

"Where are we going?"

"A hotel that M. Cheverny sometimes uses for clients who require . . . privacy. Small, very discreet, quite nice."

It was more than nice; it was a quietly elegant jewel a few blocks north of the Seine.

"It's a pity to miss spring in Paris," said Paul after checking the security of her suite, "but please don't leave the hotel. Call the concierge if you need anything. By the way, the room service is the best in the city."

When he was gone, Amira kicked off her shoes and luxuriated on the bed.

The phone rang. It was the concierge.

"What a shame, madame, that the airline should lose your luggage. All your wardrobe? If you will tell me your sizes and needs, I will have some things brought over for your selection."

"How kind. But I'm carrying only a few thousand francs."

"Do not disturb yourself over such matters, madame. It's all arranged."

Coffee. She would have coffee. And a real meal. And a long, lazy rest. But before any of that, a long, hot bath. "Come on, young man," she told Karim. For once, he didn't object.

• • •

A gourmet lunch. New clothes for herself and Karim. A visit from Paul, who played with Karim and told amusing stories about Paris. A delicious dinner. Television—not readings from the Koran, as in al-Remal, but little movies, including an inscrutable American dream called *Dallas*.

Where was Philippe now? Was he safe? Had he made his way out of the wilds around Mount Ararat? That night she dreamed that she was drinking tea with him in a peasant's mountain hut, snow everywhere around. The peasant smiled like J.R. on *Dallas*.

Maurice Cheverny called at nine in the morning. Could she meet with him at eleven? Good; he would send Paul.

A maid brought coffee, croissants, and *Le Monde*. As Amira spooned jam onto Karim's plate, a headline caught her eye: "French Physician, Philanthropist Dies in Eastern Turkey."

She dropped the spoon and ignored her son's outcry.

> Dr. Philippe Rochon . . . died Tuesday in an apparent accident south of Kars, Turkey . . . body found in a wild mountain river downstream from his wrecked car . . . search efforts under way for a woman and child believed to be traveling with him . . . extremely rugged terrain . . . Dr. Rochon, in addition to being one of the most esteemed members of his profession, endowed more than 100 scholarships to universities in France and abroad.

It couldn't be true. It had to be a mistake. What had happened? What had gone wrong?

She called Cheverny.

"I've just seen it myself, madame. Paul is on the way. I've canceled my other appointments."

• • •

Maurice Cheverny's office overlooked Paris from one of the city's new skyscrapers. The attorney was a balding, heavyset man in his early sixties. What remained of his hair was still black, slicked straight back. He wore bifocals.

"I tell you frankly, madame, that I am uncomfortable in this situation. I do not know if Jihan Sonnier is your true name—do not tell me—but I believe I can guess. In strict duty, I ought perhaps to alert the authorities to your presence. But I have my client to think of, and his instructions were quite specific."

He unlocked a drawer and brought out a large envelope and a small one. He handed her the large one. "Dr. Rochon left this for you. He told me openly that it is a substantial sum of money, in cash—American dollars—and that I was to advise you to be very careful with it. He also instructed me to put you in touch with a plastic surgeon whose name he gave me. If you wish, I will call the man, and Paul can take you to him. Finally, there is this letter for you." He handed over the smaller envelope.

The letter explained everything. *"Pancreatic cancer . . . six months, no more—not good months, either . . . and this way, they will believe it."* Through her tears, Amira read the end of the letter. *"I do not believe in an afterlife, but who knows? I'm not one of those doctors who can never be wrong. Perhaps we will meet again after all. Meanwhile, keep me alive in your heart. Be safe and happy, with your son. Good-bye, my love."*

"Do you want to read it?" she asked the attorney.

"No. But tell me what you can. Use general terms."

"He was dying. He gave his life to help me and my son escape from . . . from great danger."

"You were there when it happened?"

"No."

"Ah." He removed his glasses and wiped them with a tissue. "Philippe Rochon was like a son to me," he said simply, the lawyerly tone gone for an instant. He cleared his throat. "There is one more thing, madame.

Philippe—Dr. Rochon asked me to see to your acceptance at an American school, Harvard. I've corresponded with an old friend of mine, an assistant dean. I know nothing of your academic abilities, of course . . . Well, that's neither here nor there. In this and all else, I'll help you in any way I can. Do you want to see this surgeon?"

"Yes. As soon as possible."

He reached for the phone.

ENEMIES

Barely a kilometer away, in the converted ancient régime *hôtel de ville* that served as his Paris office, Malik stared at the *Le Monde* article. He knew it by heart now but still couldn't make sense of it. Before, he at least had been able to make assumptions about his sister's disappearance, to envision a pattern. Now he felt like a man stumbling in the dark who suddenly finds his foot hanging over empty space.

For the dozenth time, he went over it all from the beginning. His spies in Ali's entourage had informed him of his sister Amira's escape almost as soon as it occurred. He probably learned of it, he reflected with some satisfaction, before Ali himself did. He had learned about the search, as well, the dead end in Teheran. Then, yesterday afternoon, word had come that Philippe was involved, and the trail led to Turkey. But even then, he had expected something, a dash to Ankara or Istanbul, a private jet to—where? Rio?

Nonsense. Philippe might be a romantic, but he was no idiot. He would bring Amira to France, fight—if he had to—on home ground, where he had friends and power. Resources. Besides, this was no mere affair of the heart, of that Malik was sure. Amira was running not to someone, but from someone. Malik had long had his suspicions, his spies' reports of Ali's idiosyncrasies. What had happened only confirmed his thoughts—and fueled his anger.

All in all, he had assumed that Amira and Philippe would be in France at any moment, and that sooner or later she would contact him. He was her brother; he was powerful; he could protect her.

But now this. Death in some godforsaken mountain gorge in Turkey. It made no sense at all.

"Amira," he said aloud, "little sister"—and in that moment felt again the odd reassurance he had experienced when the news article was first brought to him an hour ago. He couldn't explain it: it was mystical, religious perhaps, or maybe genetic, blood thicker than water. It was the certainty that Amira was alive. He knew it. If she weren't, he would know that, too.

He summoned an aide and gave orders.

Twelve hours later he stood on a bare mountainside in Anatolia. With him were two bodyguards, a translator, a colonel in the Turkish army, and the local headman of the remote area where the car—and Philippe—had been found. Two hundred yards below, by the fast waters of a narrow river, a pair of soldiers stood desultory guard over the smashed remains of the Land Rover.

The leathery headman, who might be any age from forty to seventy, looked like a cross between a goatherd and a bandit. Probably, thought Malik, that was exactly what he was. The man's counsel was simple: Malik's request was a waste of time. If Amira and her son had been in the car, they might have been killed and swept downriver; no one could have survived such a crash. Even if, through some miracle, they survived, they could not have gone far in these mountains; his men or the army would have found them, or their remains, by now—unless, of course, wolves or a bear had done so first. Either way, Malik was looking for something that was not there.

"Where, then, should I look?"

The man gazed diplomatically into the distance. "I do not speak of your woman, of course, but when ours stray from the path, it is in the cities that we find them."

Malik already had agents in Van, where Mr. and Mrs. Rochon had stayed briefly in a hotel, but the man's wording confirmed a fear he had harbored from the first: Ali was hunting Amira, too, and his operatives were painting her as a runaway wife. Even if Malik could match the royal billions bribe for bribe, no good Muslim would help him in the face of a husband's rightful demands. And if Ali were to find her first . . .

But no one found her. Malik's and Ali's men crisscrossed eastern Anatolia—Kars, Van, Agri, every town of any size—bribing, cajoling, intimidating airport personnel, bus drivers, cabbies, private citizens who owned automobiles, anyone who might have helped a woman and child leave the area. There were countless false trails, but even with the full cooperation of the police and the army, who were being bountifully paid by both sides, nothing concrete led beyond the hotel in Van or the wrecked Land Rover.

It was as if Amira had disappeared from the face of the earth.

Eventually, even Malik had to give up. On the plane back to Paris, he remembered the icy chill of the snow-fed river. Was that where Amira and Karim slept? If not for his inexplicable certainty that his sister was alive, he would have despaired. But surely that feeling was true, he told himself. Surely he would see her again.

• • •

Ali had no parapsychological intuition concerning his wife. His feelings were simple: rage and fear. Rage at her betrayal—if she turned up alive, he would certainly kill her. Fear that if she were dead, so must be his son.

It had been nearly noon on the day following her escape when he awoke, half-poisoned, to learn of it. His first instinct had been the same as Malik's: the local airport. Much time was wasted in trying to find a woman of Arab descent and child who left Tabriz on an early-morning flight to Teheran. Nothing came of the effort, and when a steward from the flight was found and questioned in Basra, he swore that the woman had had no child with her. More time was spent investigating a European-looking man and his Arab wife and child who had flown from Teheran to Istanbul. They turned out to be a Belgian businessman and his family on vacation.

Late on the second day, the body of a SAVAK agent who had been watching Amira was found on a dung heap south of the city. The search took on a new seriousness. The next morning someone discovered that a Mr. and Mrs. Rochon had crossed the Turkish border at Bazargan. Philippe Rochon! Ali reflected bitterly that the trap he had tried to set in al-Remal had, in a perverse way, sprung on his own hand.

Rochon's involvement made Paris the most likely destination for the trip. SAVAK agreed, but with the death of their colleague, the secret police had grown decidedly cool toward Ali. He wanted his own men in Paris. The Remali intelligence service was practically an arm of the royal family—one of Ali's uncles was its director—and its best agents in Europe were rushed to the French capital to wait and watch. Ali had no way of knowing that the two who were assigned to Orly arrived just as Paul and Amira were driving away.

The more Ali thought about it, the more he was convinced that his brother-in-law was behind it all. He had never liked Malik. The man was a commoner, after all, like his bitch of a sister, no matter how rich he was making himself, and he apparently fancied himself a European, enlightened, superior—the same delusions that afflicted Amira. Undoubtedly, the gigolo doctor—who was finished, Ali would make sure of that—was just a dupe, a pawn, an excuse.

Then came the news from the wilds of eastern Anatolia. At first, Ali believed that Amira and Karim must indeed have died with Rochon in the wreck, and his hatred of the woman alternated with grief for his son. But at heart, he had never trusted anyone, and there were many things to doubt in the accounts coming out of Turkey. He sent men to investigate, and soon they told him that Malik was there.

To Ali, there were only two possibilities. The first was that something had gone terribly wrong with Malik's plan and that he was in Turkey to find out what had happened. The second was that the plan had come off perfectly, right down to some treachery that had left the French doctor's corpse as a smoke screen, and that Malik's presence on the scene was merely added smoke.

If the first, Amira and Karim were probably dead. If the second, they were certainly alive. In either case, Malik was to blame for everything—and for that Ali would take vengeance, in his own way, in his own good time.

He swore it to himself and to God.

A NEW WOMAN

Amira followed it all in the newspapers and on television. It had taken the press only a few days to connect her with the woman missing in Philippe's accident. There had followed a field day of speculation about the mystery of her disappearance. There were quotations from Malik and from Ali, from her father, even from Farid. The event commanded the same kind of attention that, a few years earlier, the disappearance of one of the Rockefellers in New Guinea had occasioned.

She was glad, for once, that she came from a culture that officially frowned on photography. The news stories carried over and over again the same wedding portrait, partly in profile and not a very good likeness. Of Karim, there was only a baby photo. Not that it mattered: she was in a place where no reporter could have reached her; moreover, any reporter who did could never have recognized her.

The place was a château in Senlis. It was a recovery house for women who had had cosmetic surgery and could afford absolute secrecy, and during the first week of her stay there—the time when her wedding picture was on every newscast—Amira looked worse than she had after Ali's beating.

The surgeon had explained that what was needed was not a complete change of her looks, even if that were possible. For one thing, she was presumed to be dead. For another—and more important—recognition depended on only two or three key features.

Her nose needed repair anyway, after Ali had flattened it. The surgeon would also rearrange the cast of her eyes slightly, and she would wear contact lenses that changed the color from light brown to a deep green. He would also remove the scar from her forehead.

It sounded simple and rather delicate; it left her looking temporarily like the victim of an airplane crash. After a week, though, as the swelling subsided and the bruises cleared, she could see the face of a new woman emerging, familiar yet different.

Two weeks later the surgeon himself took photographs. Two days after that, she had a French passport bearing her new likeness and her new name: Jenna Sorrel. Karim kept his first name—it was Jenna's wish, against the surgeon's advice. That was the only part of the matter that was overtly discussed. Philippe was mentioned only indirectly, as a fine man and a wonderful friend.

One month from the day she entered France, Amira—Jenna—left from Le Havre as a passenger on a freighter bound for New Orleans. The mode of transportation represented a last bit of caution: someone—probably Philippe—had decided that it offered the least likelihood of scrutiny.

The crossing was difficult. The only woman aboard, she felt exposed—naked—to the gazes of the crew. The captain, a fatherly Greek, apparently understood the situation and gave orders. After that, there was no more overt leering, although the men's sidelong glances could not be misinterpreted. Yet all that was hardly more than an embarrassment. Far worse was her growing sense of guilt over Philippe's sacrifice. And there was Malik. By now, he must have accepted her death, must be grieving for her. Should she let him know that she was alive? Just a note?

No. Better for now that he know nothing at all.

At New Orleans, she filled out papers for status as a foreign student. She found a hotel that had child-care facilities, then went out to find a jeweler. The town did not match her picture of America—certainly not the America of *Dallas*. It was more Mediterranean, rather like Marseilles.

She passed the shop on Royal Street three times before going in. The name on the window was Jewish, raising prejudices with which she had been instilled since birth, but she liked the look of the place. The jeweler rosc from a table to greet her, his loupe perched above his right eye.

"I want to sell some jewels," she said simply, and emptied her case on the counter.

The old man looked for a moment, then said, "This is quality. This is beauty. May I ask your name, ma'am?"

"Sorrel."

"Sorrel. Harvey Rothstein. A pleasure. Your name is French?"

"Yes. I'm French by marriage."

"I see. Well, Mme. Sorrel." He lowered the loupe and inspected the jewels. Now and then he sighed with pleasure. At length, he said, "I will buy these, even though I'll have to borrow to do it."

He named a figure. It seemed terribly low to Amira. She bargained. He raised the price, but not greatly. "You won't get more," he told her.

Something about the man, his open admiration of her jewels, made her trust him. "Very well. I'll take it."

"Come back tomorrow morning. I'll have a cashier's check." He looked at the jewels for a moment more. "Mme. . . . Sorrel, you must know that I'm offering only a fraction of what these pieces are worth. That's only fair—first, because I must make a profit; second, because there are certain . . . risks involved. But this one, no." He pushed the pigeon-blood ruby toward her. "That's not part of the price. I recognize it, and so would any other fine jeweler in the world. Keep it. Forgive me if I predict that there will be better times for you, and you will have it then."

The next afternoon, she caught a plane for New York with a connecting flight to Boston, where, on the recommendation of M. Maurice Cheverny and after an interview and a special placement test, she was assured of a place at Harvard for the fall term. She would major in psychology.

Part Six

AN ALL-AMERICAN BOY

"What happened?" Jenna Sorrel demanded.

"Nothing," said Karim unconvincingly. His left eye was blackened. A streak of blood had dried under his nose.

"The truth, young man."

"I had a fight, okay?"

Jenna heard shame and pride mixed in her son's reply. He was nine years old, she reminded herself.

"No, it most certainly isn't okay. What happened?"

"Josh was calling me names."

"Josh Chandler?" Half of Karim's fourth-grade classmates seemed to be named Josh, but Jenna recalled the Chandler boy as one with whom her son did not get along well.

"Yes."

"What kind of names?"

"Just . . . names."

Jenna remembered the insults thrown at Middle Eastern students during her second year at Harvard, when the hostage crisis had broken out in Iran. Now and then Karim's first name and his café-au-lait complexion had subjected him to similar cruelty from his schoolmates.

"Names are no reason for fighting. You know that, don't you?"

Karim nodded, close to tears.

"Your father always said that most fights happen because someone is afraid not to fight. He said that what takes real courage is to walk away. And he was a brave man."

Karim nodded again. The father he had never known was his greatest hero. Unfortunately, that father was a lie: Jenna had created him, worrying all the while about the psychological implications of the act and cautioning herself not to build a role model too perfect to emulate. Physically, the man she invented was smaller than average, as Ali was and Karim himself promised to be. In most other ways, he resembled Philippe. He was not a physician, though: Jenna had feared that someone someday might link "French doctor" with "vanished princess." So Jacques Sorrel was a ship's captain who had died bringing medical supplies to an epidemic-stricken port in Africa.

"Come on," she said briskly. "Let's go solve this problem."

She knew the Chandlers slightly from school functions. They lived in elegant Beacon Hill, a brisk walk from Marlborough Street.

A maid answered the door and ushered Jenna and Karim in. Carolyn Chandler appeared, tall, blond, tennis-fit, and smiling graciously, if a bit nervously. Behind her big Cameron Chandler loomed up like a cordial but concerned bear. The Chandlers appeared to be in their mid-thirties.

"I understand there was some trouble," said Cameron. An indulgent smile indicated that he didn't think the trouble very serious.

"There was. And I've come to get your assurance that there won't be more." Jenna did not smile.

"But," interjected Carolyn, "I think your son hit ours first."

"If that is so he was wrong and will apologize. But from what I hear, Josh was attacking Karim's heritage—his ethnic heritage. And that must stop. I'm sure you agree with that."

Cameron Chandler nodded. "Of course we do. Unfortunately, boys will be boys. Josh, come in here."

Josh was inches taller and twenty pounds heavier than Karim. He had a badly split lip.

Cameron took charge. After a few blunt questions elicited what was probably very close to the truth of the episode, he ordered the boys to shake hands and forget the whole thing. Jenna wasn't sure she agreed with his method, but it seemed to work.

"Want to shoot some baskets?" Josh asked Karim.

"Sure. Can I, Mom?"

"Just for a little while."

The two scurried away from the council of adults. Feeling at loose ends, Jenna gratefully accepted Carolyn's offer of coffee. Cameron joined them with a drink in hand.

The Chandlers didn't exactly pry, but Jenna soon found herself reciting the fiction of her past, so well rehearsed now that it seemed almost like the truth. About her hosts, there seemed to be little to learn. They were what everything about them proclaimed them to be: old Boston society. Cameron was an investment banker; Carolyn devoted her spare time to tennis and charities. He was aggressively friendly, she cool and diffident.

Jenna intuited a certain distance between them, something in their body language. Perhaps they had argued over Josh's behavior.

"So you're a psychologist," said Cameron.

"Yes."

"Of course!" said Carolyn, suddenly animated. "*That's* who you are! Why didn't I make the connection?"

"Who?" said Jenna, almost afraid to ask.

"You have a book out, don't you?" Carolyn bubbled on. "I've been meaning to buy it. I saw a very nice review of it somewhere. *Ancient* . . ."

"Ancient Chains," Jenna said with relief. "I'll bring you a copy if you'd like." The book had been a sweet surprise. A reworking of her doctoral dissertation, it had been published in a print run of a thousand by a small university press in the Midwest. There it might have died like countless other scholarly monographs except for a brief but very positive notice in the *New York Times Book Review*. Now it had sold thirty thousand copies, and there was talk of a paperback.

"Chains," said Cameron. "Sounds kinky."

"Some of my colleagues agree—too Jungian. The publishers chose the title."

"What's it about?"

Jenna sighed. "The relationship, in psychological terms, between male dominance mechanisms and female survival strategies in selected cultures over time."

"Yow!" said Cameron. "Does it come with English subtitles?"

Even Jenna had to laugh. "Sorry. It's hard to explain in one sentence. Let's just say it's about the ways women have adapted to various forms of discrimination and abuse."

"A hot topic," said Cameron. "Hot enough to send me back to the liquor cabinet. Get you anything?" He didn't ask Carolyn.

"No, thank you. Actually, I'd better be going. I've taken up a lot of your time."

The Camerons made conventional protests. Carolyn walked her out. Under a backyard goal, the boys were playing one-on-one, to all appearances best friends. Jenna watched for a moment. She knew nothing about basketball, but it was obvious that Josh's size was a great advantage, which Karim countered with agility and deception. Where had he learned all those feints and fakes, clever little lies told by the body? She shrugged off a shiver. The quick knife in the night in Alexandria.

Walking home, she glanced sidelong at her son. Love and sadness welled in her; he was growing up so fast! Only yesterday, he had been a baby. Then, in those first years when they were learning a new world together, they had been as close as two people can be. And now—too soon!—she could sense the beginnings of distance between them; already in his face, with its heartbreaking black eye and its newfound secrecy, there was the outline of the man to come.

She reached out and tousled his hair. He squirmed away but grinned. It was an American moment, she thought, like a snippet from some TV commercial. In al-Remal, a mother wouldn't treat a male child so familiarly, not at Karim's age. But, of course, Karim knew nothing about that. He was an American. She was one herself—or nearly one. My God, she had even become a Red Sox fan. Her English carried hardly a trace of accent, and most of that vaguely Dutch, from Miss Vanderbeek. Karim had an accent, too: pure Boston.

An all-American boy. But had she done wrong? she asked herself for the thousandth time. She had gone to the Chandlers to defend her son's heritage, but hadn't she robbed him of that far more fully than any schoolboy insult could? Karim knew nothing of his nationality.

As for religion, there were mosques in Boston, but she had never taken him to one. She had taught him a little about Islam—but a little about other religions as well. Then there was his personal birthright: he was a royal prince, yet far from knowing that, he did not even know his true father.

She had enrolled Karim in the prestigious Commonwealth School, which, ironically, accepted him readily because it was hungry for "minority" students. But she understood that in some way this was a concession to the remnants of her aristocratic memories and fantasies. Karim had no such illusions.

Someday she would tell him the truth, she promised herself. Meanwhile, what was the point in questioning herself this way? She had done what she had to, and it was done.

"What do you think, kiddo?" she said, trying to shake off the mood. "Should we stop by the bookstore and see if they have any new puzzles?" Karim shared her passion for large, fiendishly difficult jigsaw puzzles. She liked to think that it meant their intellects were alike, attuned to solving problems.

"Can we order a pizza, too?" Karim asked eagerly.

"Great idea."

And just like that, for the moment at least, the distance was gone; he was her little boy again. They were Jenna and Karim, together against the world.

GENEVIEVE

Wednesdays were a challenge because of Jenna's three afternoon patients. It wasn't that their problems were especially tricky, although Colleen Dowd's was certainly difficult. The trouble was that Jenna personally liked all three women and found it hard to maintain objectivity.

Colleen Dowd was forty-five, several years divorced, no children. She suffered from agoraphobia. The term, a combination of Greek words meaning "fear of the marketplace," had once signified an irrational fear of open places. Now it was applied to a spectrum of phobic reactions to various circumstances, which usually involved being out of one's accustomed sphere. Colleen had panic attacks whenever she went more than a short distance from home.

Over the years she had circumscribed her life ever more tightly to avoid them, even relocating her business to a storefront on the same block of Hanover Street as her apartment. At her first appointment, she had been triumphant at having accomplished the short cab ride to Jenna's office. Ironically, she was a travel agent.

Barbara Aston presented a quite different set of problems. She was an alcoholic who also depended heavily on prescription drugs, especially Valium—a dangerous combination. She was also addicted—the word was quite accurate—to cosmetic surgery.

At forty-three, in a desperate effort to stay thin and young for fear of losing the husband she professed to adore, she had already undergone a dozen procedures ranging from breast implants to a facelift and from a tummy tuck to two separate nose jobs.

Before attacking the deep insecurity that underlay all this, Jenna was attempting to deal with Barbara's chemical dependencies, which not only interfered with other therapeutic efforts but were potentially life-threatening.

The final Wednesday-afternoon patient, Toni Ferrante, was thirty-five, married for fifteen years, the mother of two sons a bit older than Karim. She was also a lesbian, a fact she had finally admitted to herself only a year earlier. The problem was that she could not admit it to her husband, her boys, or—especially—her parents. From Jenna's point of view, Toni was a difficult patient simply because there was nothing wrong with her.

Unlike Colleen and Barbara, she was not in the grip of some disorder. In coming to a psychologist, all she was seeking was a confessor who would not condemn her while she struggled to choose between living the truth and living a lie.

It was a choice Jenna understood only too well, and often she felt like a hypocrite, even a charlatan, presuming to help others face up to their problems while she hid from hers.

That very afternoon, at the end of their session, Toni had stepped across the patient-therapist boundary. "Hey, Jenna, you know, I saw your book in the store. How come you don't have a picture of yourself on it?"

"Well, it started out as a scholarly work, and they often don't have author photos."

That was true—as far as it went. But something skepical in Toni's expression made Jenna go farther. "Then too," she said, stepping over the boundary herself, "my father was a strict Muslim who disapproved of photography. I suppose I never really overcame his judgment."

Toni grinned. "Still trying to win old Dad's heart, huh? I can dig that."

In truth, Jenna had refused repeated requests from the publisher for a photo; it was just too risky.

Living a lie.

Toni left. It was four o'clock. Karim would be at soccer practice—he showed surprising skill at the game—for another hour. Jenna looked at the paperwork that needed doing; soon she was going to have to hire a secretary. She looked at the pile of forms, bills, and letters again and decided on a cup of tea at the Village Greenery instead.

On the way she stopped at a newsstand for the *Star* and the *National Enquirer*. A man buying a Boston *Globe* looked at her purchases with amused disdain. She was accustomed to the reaction, but she had learned that the tabloids, travesties of journalism though they might be, were the most likely source of news about her brother.

At the coffeeshop, a hand reached out to open the door for her: the man with the *Globe*. A few years earlier, she might have panicked. Now she merely nodded thanks. The man took a table and was soon absorbed in his paper. Not a spy, not a hunter—just another tired professional, maybe even a shrink, off work a bit early.

She ordered Earl Grey with a croissant and jam, and settled into the scandal sheets. Disappointingly, she found nothing about Malik. Usually there was at least a gossipy teaser suggesting his romance with this or that model or movie star, although, when quoted, he always pointed out that he was happily married.

For years now, the stories had identified him as "one of the world's richest men." Lately they had begun dropping "one of" and making it "man," singular. He owned a shipping fleet that would have rivaled that of his old mentor, Onassis; held investments in enterprises of a dozen kinds all over the world; and—in the dark speculation of the tabloids—might or might not be earning huge brokerage fees on billion-dollar arms sales in the Middle East and elsewhere.

Once in a while, the stories mentioned the tragic death of Malik's sister, the Remal's princess.

Twice there had been photos of Genevieve, smiling and a bit heavier than Jenna remembered.

Once there had been a picture of Laila, tall for her age, thin, and looking almost angrily at the camera.

Jenna had never let Malik know that she and Karim were alive. It was the hardest thing in her life, a knife that made a new cut every day. But she was afraid. After seven years, she was still afraid.

The early days had actually been easier. Then, there had been no question of telling anyone anything. She had lived as a fugitive, pure and simple. If someone stood for a few minutes across the street or walked behind her for two blocks or merely gave her a long glance in Harvard Yard, she wondered if Ali had found her.

That kind of fear—fear she woke with and went to sleep with and dreamed—was past. She still took precautions, such as not having a photograph on her book, but she no longer suspected that every odd click on the phone meant a wiretap.

Yet she couldn't bring herself to contact Malik. He was too flamboyant, and too beset by hungry reporters and wolfish paparazzi, for the secret to remain secret for long. And if it came out, what then? Malik was wealthy, but his millions—or billions, if the press could be believed—were nothing against the vast fortune of the Remali royal family. Could he protect her and Karim from Ali? For how long? Could he even protect himself?

Better to let things remain as they were. By now, surely, her brother had reconciled himself to her death. So had her father, her aunts, Bahia, everyone she had known in her old life.

Everyone except Ali.

From the same tabloids that told her about her brother, she knew that her husband had married again and fathered at least one new son. But that wouldn't matter if he discovered that she and Karim were alive. He would be as implacable as a falcon—and as deadly.

Far better to let the truth lie quiet.

Still, she hurt.

"Jenna? May I join you?"

She looked up and recognized Carolyn Chandler.

"Of course. What a nice surprise."

"I'm not interrupting your . . . reading?" Carolyn indicated the *Star* and *Enquirer*.

Jenna laughed. "You've caught me. I admit it. It's my only vice. Or my worst one."

Carolyn sat down. She was wearing a black skirt and gray silk blouse that gave her a businesslike look. "I sneak a read myself now and then," she confessed. "Did you see the one last week? 'Aliens Kidnap Cows for Love'?"

"No. God, those aliens. You'd think I'd get one or two of them as patients, with the problems they have."

"Or at least the occasional traumatized cow," said Carolyn. She looked around. "It really is a small world. I've never been in this place—just popped in on impulse. Do you live nearby?"

"Walking distance. But my office is just down the block."

"So you're really a practicing psychiatrist, besides being an author."

"Psychologist."

A waitress appeared. Carolyn ordered a cappuccino.

"Have you noticed," she asked when the girl was gone, "that our sons have become inseparable?"

Jenna smiled. "I *have* heard quite a bit of 'me and Josh' lately."

They were at a window table, and the late-afternoon light warmed Carolyn's tennis tan, accentuating her hazel eyes. She seemed so much friendlier than at their last meeting, thought Jenna. Of course, she had been on the defensive then, about Josh.

"Isn't it amazing," Carolyn said as if reading Jenna's thought, "how little boys can try to beat each other's brains out one minute and be Damon and Pythias the next? Grown men, too. I swear they're a different species—maybe the notorious aliens. In middle school a girl named Sarah Stubblefield slapped me once. I've hated her ever since. And, of course, when a man hits a woman, it's never forgiven, is it?"

"No," said Jenna, although it wasn't that simple. "But even between men, it's not the same everywhere, you know. Where I grew up, if one man struck another, they were enemies for life—and one of them might not live very long." As soon as she said it, she remembered Malik flattening Ali in her father's garden, and Amira Badir twisted Jenna Sorrel's fingers into a sign against the evil eye under the table at the Village Greenery.

Carolyn shook her head. "I still say they're aliens. How did we get on this depressing subject?" She took a pack of Virginia Slims from her purse, but her cappuccino arrived before she could light one.

Jenna checked her watch. "I hate to do it, but I need to run. There's a stew in the Crock-Pot that may have turned into a brick by now, and Karim will be home any minute. He's like a locust after soccer."

"Josh, too," said Carolyn. "Wait till they hit puberty. We'll be setting out shovels and pitchforks instead of flatware."

"It was good to see you. I'm glad you had that impulse."

"Me, too. Listen, we're having a little brunch party Sunday, very informal, just some friends and acquaintances. We'd love to have you. Bring Karim—Josh will be eternally grateful."

Jenna hesitated. She accepted few social invitations. It was a habit born of the old fear: in a crowd of new faces, who might at last recognize hers? Over the years, almost without realizing she was doing it, she had made her son and her work into a twin-towered castle from which she rarely ventured.

"I know it's short notice," said Carolyn.

Jenna decided. "Not at all. It sounds nice."

"You'll make it nicer. Bring a guest, too. The more the merrier."

"I think Karim will be enough. Thank you. I look forward to it. What time should we be there?"

"Elevenish. As I said, it's very casual. Most of us will be wearing workout clothes, old college sweats."

Walking home, Jenna already felt uncomfortable about accepting Carolyn's invitation. What had persuaded her to do it? The other woman seemed personable enough, but what did they really have in common except that Karim and Josh were classmates?

Maybe it was just a matter of being tired of living like a recluse.

Bring a guest. If only Carolyn knew what a sad joke that was. In her seven years in Boston, she had never had a real relationship, hardly even a date. It wasn't for want of opportunity; in college, a dozen young fellow students—and a couple of not-so-young professors—had made overtures. She had brushed them off. In those days it seemed to her that Ali and Philippe had ruined men for her, the one by his cruelty, the other by providing an example no one else could match.

But time had passed. She was thirty, and she felt something missing in her life. She wondered if there could be someone for her someday despite everything, despite the fact that, after all, she was still a married woman.

Maybe that was why she had decided to go to the party, she thought as she turned in at her door. Maybe she was hoping for something new, something good to happen. And why not?

Home. Entering her apartment always filled her with a sense of pride and security. She had moved in a year earlier, after her practice had gotten off the ground. Two bedrooms, with a third converted to a workspace. It was expensive but not outrageous, unlike the first place she had taken in Boston.

What a poor little rich girl she had been! Accustomed to luxury, she had viewed the typical student apartments of her classmates as little better than hovels. After considerable searching she had found a palatial five-bedroom place on Commonwealth Avenue, which very much resembled a French boulevard. In one bedroom she had installed a nanny for Karim, in another a live-in maid who also did the cooking. That had seemed like a reasonable minimum of servants—no need to call attention to herself through excess.

Looking back, she had to laugh at that Jenna. Her ignorance had been appalling. She had no idea how much food cost or what a plumber did, no awareness that servants in America expected regular days off or that landlords, even of luxury apartments, wanted the rent on the first of the month. After a year and a half, she had finally confronted the fact that she was running through her money at an alarming rate, and that there was no wealthy father or husband to replace it. She took a two-bedroom apartment a mile from the campus, dismissed the cook and the nanny, and learned about day care and supermarkets.

She and Karim had lived happily in that apartment for nearly five years.

The stew was simmering nicely, tender and tasty. Its aroma made the new place feel even more like home. *Bring a guest.* Did she really want to leave her warm and cozy castle for the cold wilds outside?

She heard the beep of the soccer-team minibus from the street, followed by Karim's footsteps on the stairs.

"Hey, Mom! Guess how many goals!"

"Two?"

"Three!"

"Who was the goalkeeper?"

"Josh."

"Uh-oh. Is he upset?"

"Huh? Nah. We're pals. Besides, it's not his fault the other guys can't stop me."

"Whoa! Superstar!"

Karim ignored the mild rebuke of his boastfulness. "Can we eat early, Mom? Do I have to do my homework first? Something smells great, and I'm *starv*ing."

"All right. I'll watch you eat, though. I snacked after work."

They sat at the kitchen table talking of school and soccer while Karim devoured two bowls of stew. It was a cozy scene. It felt right. They were the smallest possible family, but a family nonetheless. At times like this, Jenna could say that she was truly happy.

"Can we watch TV, Mom?"

"Nice try. Homework first."

"Awww . . ." But he dutifully retrieved his bookbag and hauled it to his room.

Jenna had a half-dozen library books herself, along with two hundred new, blank index cards, but somehow she couldn't generate the energy for doing research tonight. When Karim vanished into his cave, she puttered aimlessly around the apartment. *Bring a guest.* She wouldn't, of course. But if she were to invite someone, which of her male colleagues and acquaintances would it be? No one. Very well, if she could invent someone, what would he be? No one. Very well, if she could invent someone, what would he be like? She couldn't form a picture. Yes, she could: Philippe. Suddenly, the longing for him hit her like a physical blow. *We won't lose each other*, he had promised. Was there something of him out there still, knowing her loneliness, her love?

Stop it, she commanded herself. Of all the emotional reactions she encountered in her work, the most common and the least productive was self-pity.

Wanting to shut out thought, she switched on the evening news. Dan Rather and various correspondents were discussing a compromise between President Reagan and the Democrats in Congress. Jenna half listened, convinced that she would never grasp the nuances of American politics. The two parties opposed each noisily, but what was the real difference between them? She was searching for the *TV Guide* when she became aware of a woman's face on the screen. It looked so much like—

"Tragedy today in France," Rather intoned, "where Genevieve Badir, wife of international financial magnate Malik Badir, died in a road accident. According to French police, her Mercedes was struck head on by a produce truck near the town of Saint-Tropez, where the Badirs had one of their many vacation homes."

Jenna clawed for the volume control as the story continued: "Madame Badir, a former singer remembered by friends as a woman of simple tastes and warmhearted good humor, was driving alone to a favorite restaurant. A source close to the family told reporters that Malik Badir would normally have been in the car but had been called away unexpectedly on business.

"Badir's name has been linked with intrigue at high levels of the military and government in France and elsewhere, but authorities stress that they do not suspect foul play in his wife's death. The truck driver, who was also killed, was said to be, quote, 'profoundly drunk.' Genevieve Badir, dead at thirty-six in France."

The images of Rather and Genevieve dissolved to a commercial. Jenna stared numbly. "No," she heard herself say, "no, no, no!" She was too shocked for tears. Poor Genevieve. Except for that brief moment of kindred feeling in al-Remal, Jenna had never known her sister-in-law, and now she never would.

She flipped through the channels, hoping to learn more about the accident. Finding nothing, she replayed the story from memory. One thing especially struck her: Malik might easily have been in the car. If so, he would have died believing in her own "death." The idea filled her with unbearable guilt.

Turning off the television, she rummaged through her desk until she found some plain white stationery and wrote:

> Dearest brother,
>
> My heart aches for you. I can only try to imagine your pain and your loss. I wish I could kiss and comfort you. But I cannot. I beg your forgiveness for causing you sorrow. That choice was not lightly made, and I can only hope that you understand how necessary it was.
>
> Life has been lonely and hard, but I am well, thank God, and so is Karim. I have established a successful career in work I love. That and my son sustain me. I hope that you, too, can find solace

> in your daughter's love and in knowing that your sister thinks of you often and wishes with all her heart to see you once more.

She would mail it in the morning—first thing, before she could lose her nerve. But when morning came, so did doubt and fear. If she simply dropped the letter in the nearest mailbox, the Boston postmark would give her away. She should drive to some little town in the countryside, maybe even across the line in Rhode Island or Connecticut. Maybe even New York. She slipped the letter into her shoulder bag. She would mail it, she promised herself, definitely she would. But not just now.

CAROLYN

Preoccupied with Genevieve's death and how it must be affecting Malik and Laila, Jenna would have forgotten the brunch invitation had Carolyn not called to remind her, and she would have canceled if she could have invented a plausible excuse on the spur of the moment. As it was, she promised to be there.

It turned out to be an anticlimax—pleasant, but hardly the adventure Jenna had half hoped for and half dreaded. The guests all seemed to have gone to college together and to know the same people and the same stories. A faint aura of Beacon Hill hung over the whole scene. The lone single male, a corporate lawyer—rather transparently a pairing for Jenna—drank several Bloody Marys and became sentimental about his ex-wife; it was, apparently, the first anniversary of their divorce.

Carolyn called later to apologize. She made several wicked comments at the lawyer's expense. Jenna couldn't help laughing. That was the real beginning of their friendship.

It was an unusual one. Carolyn, a few years older, tried to be a mentor, instructing Jenna in subtleties of American—or at least Bostonian—tastes in dress, makeup, and interior decoration. She even prodded Jenna to take up tennis, and Jenna, eager to please her new friend, went so far as to take lessons. It was a disaster; as the pro put it on the morning that he advised her to try almost any other sport, "Jenna, you simply have no concept of racket hitting ball."

At the same time that Carolyn took a dominant role socially, she also leaned on Jenna emotionally. It was obvious that she badly wanted a confidante, preferably one from outside her accustomed circle. Yet her confidences were slow in coming, delivered in little bits and pieces. They had to do, of course, with her husband.

Cameron Chandler was a mystery to Jenna. His demeanor toward her was at first cordial, then merely indulgent, then almost hostile. She suspected that he was threatened by her closeness to Carolyn; many men felt that way about their wives' friends. She finally mentioned it to Carolyn.

"Please, Jenna. It's the same way he reacts to my family. He feels insecure around them, and so he makes up reasons to dislike them. God, the nonsense. It's a real problem."

"Why should he feel insecure?"

"Do you really want to know? I wonder if you'll understand. What it comes down to is that his people have been better-fixed financially over the last couple of generations than mine, but mine have been in Boston two centuries longer."

It was no news to Jenna that discrepancies in family prestige might contribute to marital discord, although when she was new to the country it had come as a surprise to her that Americans could concern themselves with such matters almost as much as Remalis. The Americans she had known in the Middle East had never mentioned their ancestors farther back than a grandparent or two, and even then their stories often seemed to emphasize how poor their families had been. In any case, the idea of the ancientness of Carolyn's line versus the wealth of Cameron's as a major cause of strife rang untrue—more likely it was only a symptom of a deeper problem. Nor did it explain Cameron's obvious resentment of Jenna.

As more months went by and Jenna's friendship with Carolyn deepened, it became clear that something was seriously wrong between the Camerons. Little hints disguised as conversational slips, little shades of intonation, pointed to a deep lack of respect on both their parts, as well as a clinging, almost desperate possessiveness. It did no good to ask probing questions. Carolyn could demonstrate a true New England reticence when she wanted to. And any suggestion that professional counseling might be a solution met with immediate dismissal: "Please, Jenna, we don't do that in our crowd. If someone goes loony, we just ship 'em off to New York or Provincetown, where nobody will notice."

On the other hand, she could be positively voluble in making excuses for Cameron after having disparaged him. A favorite theme was the pressure of his work. "You know, when Cameron started in banking, not that long ago really, it was still a gentleman's business—in Boston, I mean; I can't speak for anyplace else. But now all of a sudden there are these dozens of bloodthirsty yuppies with the MBAs and ugly power ties, working twenty hours a day and coming up with schemes that would have got them thrown in jail a few years ago. It's hard on Cameron. Thank God his father's on the board. Of course, he won't be there forever."

One bright spring day Jenna found out just how much she and Carolyn had in common. It was at a soccer game. Josh, with his long reach, was playing goal. Karim, to even Jenna's surprise, showed every sign of becoming a star striker, fast, sure with his feet, agile as a mongoose, slipping by larger defenders as if they were anchored in cement; his only flaw, according to the coach, was a reluctance to pass the ball to his teammates.

The game was an exciting one, but despite several spectacular saves by Josh, Carolyn hardly stirred from her perch on her old-fashioned, British-style shooting stick with a fold-out leather seat on a single tubular-steel leg. Undoubtedly, her great-grandfather had used it while big-game hunting with Teddy Roosevelt, but it was not the most stable of foundations, and at one point Carolyn leaned too far and had to brace herself. When she did, she gasped in pain and fell to her knees.

Jenna was right beside her. "My God, are you hurt?"

"Just help me to the car," whispered Carolyn between clenched teeth.

In the front seat, she began to cry. "That bastard! I think he's broken my ribs!"

"Cameron? He hit you?"

"Yes, he hit me. Where it won't show. That's his little trick."

Jenna couldn't believe what she was hearing. "You mean he's done it before?"

"Yes." But Carolyn's face already was showing the familiar signs of closing the subject.

"Carolyn, listen to me. You've got to get help—you and Cameron both."

Carolyn said nothing.

"I *know* about this," Jenna stressed, then added, "I've seen this among some of my regular patients. You need to get out immediately—you're in real danger. After that, the two of you can get help."

Carolyn turned on Jenna with something very much like hatred in her eyes. "I'm not a patient at the free clinic. And I don't need help. What I need is for my husband to be the man I married."

The sense of déjà vu was almost sickening. How many times had Jenna—Amira—thought the same words about Ali?

Carolyn would say no more. By her standards, she had gone too far. For a week, when Jenna phoned, the maid answered and said that Mrs. Chandler was out. Then one night Carolyn called. She talked about trivia. It was clear that she wanted to pretend nothing had happened. When Jenna tried to broach the subject of Cameron, Carolyn said with brittle finality, "Everything's fine." The message was unmistakable: Don't mention it again.

After that, Jenna and Carolyn did the old things together, going to the theater, to soccer games, for tea and cappuccino at the Village Greenery, but it was never quite the same. Jenna kept hoping for an opening, some way by which she could lend Carolyn her experience and her expertise, but Carolyn would never let it happen. At least—as far as Jenna could tell—Cameron had not attacked her physically again.

Jenna had her work. Carolyn had tennis and fund-raisers.

Gradually the two friends became more distant. Gradually they became hardly friends at all.

INCIDENT IN TORONTO

Ancient Chains had made Jenna a minor celebrity in academic circles, especially among feminist scholars. One result was a steady stream of invitations to conferences and symposia. She always turned them down.

Even though the media generally ignored the small, insular world of academia, any public exposure seemed risky to her. But when she was asked to sit on a panel discussing "Women, History, and Therapy" at a convention in Toronto, she decided to accept. The topic was important, and the city was, after all, in another country.

After her years in Boston, she found Toronto remarkably clean and orderly, its citizens polite and quiet, and the whole experience rather dull. If the city lacked the dirt and danger of its American counterparts, it also seemed to lack their capacity for the serendipitous encounter with something new and excellent.

The restaurants where Jenna and her colleagues dined were all tasteful in their decor and commendable in their cuisine, but hardly memorable. The university reminded her less of Harvard than of the pictures Malik had sent home from the manicured grounds of Victoria College. And why did the Canadian professor who seemed to be making a pass retreat so meekly at the first sign of her habitual reserve?

All in all, when the time came to return to Boston, she was more than ready.

And then, at the airport, there was one of those small, chance occurrences that change more lives than wars, epidemics, or natural disasters. Jenna's flight was delayed, and she went to a coffee shop. Sipping her tea, wondering what Karim was doing, she couldn't help overhearing the two men in the next booth. They apparently were business acquaintances whose paths had crossed here in their travels. After some chat about wives and children, one man—he had a British accent—said, "I must tell you I had a bit of a turn in Rome two days back. I'd taken a client to Checchino dal

1887. We'd just ordered when all hell broke loose. Gunfire all over the place, people diving for the floor—including me, you can be assured."

"My God. What was it? Mafia?"

"A kidnapping attempt. Some bloody billionaire was in the place with his daughter. Apparently she was the target. Badir, whatever his name is."

For Jenna, everything else in the restaurant vanished.

"So what happened?" said the second man. "Why all the shooting?"

"Apparently someone's bodyguard outside spotted the kidnappers going in, and one thing led to another. Frightening, I can tell you. I've never been in a war, but . . ."

"Anybody hurt?"

"The two kidnappers shot up rather badly. And I believe a policeman and two or three patrons were wounded, including this Badir chap."

Jenna whirled around. "Malik was shot?"

"I beg your pardon?"

"Malik Badir—he was wounded?"

"Yes, but not too badly, I believe."

"And Laila—is she all right?"

"Laila?"

"The girl. The daughter."

"She wasn't hurt. Rather shaken, I imagine. You talk as if you know these people."

"I . . . I'm an acquaintance of the family. Are you sure he wasn't badly hurt?"

"Well, I don't have all the details, naturally. It was rather hectic there in the restaurant. Actually, most of what I know comes from *Le Monde*—I left Rome for Paris that night."

"It was in *Le Monde*?" She had to find the paper. Surely there was an international newsstand in the airport.

The Britisher was rummaging in his attache case. ". . . may still have a copy. Yes, here it is." He handed the newspaper to Jenna. "Please keep it, since you have a personal interest in the matter. If I may ask—"

"Thank you," said Jenna before he could ask anything. "Thank you so much."

In the concourse she read about the kidnapping attempt. It was as the man had said. Laila was unharmed. Malik had a "painful but not dangerous" wound to his arm.

Her flight was called. As she checked her purse for her ticket, the letter to Malik caught her eye. She had never mailed it. A bookshop had stamps, and the cashier directed her to a mailbox. She dropped the letter into it before second thoughts could take hold.

There, she had done it, she thought as she hurried for the plane. But what had she done?

LAILA

In the weeks that followed, Jenna often wondered what effect her letter had on Malik. Had he simply been relieved that she was alive? Furious at being deceived? A little of each? If she were to see him, would he still be the Malik she knew? Or would he be a stranger? And what would Laila be like now, having grown up in the perpetual pageant of her billionaire father's life?

The tabloids had become strangely silent on the subject of Malik. Perhaps, thought Jenna, he was sheltering himself and Laila after the trouble in Rome. Then, two months after the shooting, Jenna read that her brother had acquired yet another lavish residence, an apartment at the Pierre Hotel in New York. The brief article—a regular news item in the *Boston Globe*—noted that Malik was still recuperating from the attack in Rome and that "a source who asked not to be named stated that Badir believes his daughter will be safer in the United States than in Europe."

That might be true, thought Jenna, but she couldn't help wondering if her letter had something to do with Malik's decision. Could it be that he was reaching out, just as she had?

Despite her education, she still harbored an ingrained belief in portents and in destiny, and when, a month later, she read in the *New York Post*'s "Page Six" that Laila had been enrolled at the Brearly School, she was sure it was a sign, fate calling out to her. Should she answer? Dared she?

• • •

Squeezed into a cramped seat on the Boston–New York shuttle, Jenna tried to convince herself that she really *did* need to keep in touch with colleagues such as her old Adlerian-theory professor, now in private practice in New York, with whom she had a lunch date. In rebuttal, the remnants of her objective, analytical powers delivered a more succinct, if unprofessional, opinion: *You're crazy, Jenna, absolutely crazy.* But her heart, not her head, had all the votes.

Donald Weltman's offices, off Park Avenue, could have belonged to one of the neighborhood's star plastic surgeons. The former professor wore an Armani suit rather than the patchy tweeds Jenna remembered from the lecture hall. His iron-gray hair, flyaway at Harvard, was elegantly coiffed. Obviously, he was doing very well.

He had a reservation at the L'Argenteuil and insisted on picking up the tab. For much of the meal, he was still the lecturer and she the student, although instead of Adler, the topic was the beauty of private practice in Manhattan.

"And you, Jenna?" he said over dessert. "I hear you're developing a good young practice."

"I can't complain. I have enough paying customers to make ends meet and still have time for a little research."

"A new book?"

"No, not yet. Just general research. And I do some volunteer work at a shelter for battered women." It was something she had just started, driven by Carolyn's experience—and her own.

Donald frowned. "That's fine, of course, but you don't want to go too far along those lines. One thing I've learned"—and now he smiled—"is that rich people have problems just like poor people."

"That's certainly true."

He glanced at a chunky gold Rolex and said, "I have to get back to the mines. But what's your schedule? Maybe we can get together later, talk over old times when we're not so rushed."

"I wish I could. I'd love to see Robin again." Robin was Donald's wife.

"Actually, she's out of town—a family emergency."

• • •

Jenna took a taxi to the Brearly School, stationed herself outside—and waited. Would she recognize the little girl she had helped deliver on a bed of straw?

She did. Dark hair, almond eyes, the older Laila's heart-shaped face, something, too, of Jihan Badir. A touch of Malik, of course, but harder to define than mere resemblance: something in the set of the girl's shoulders, something brave yet vulnerable that reminded Jenna of Malik as he had been a long time ago.

Laila stood apart from a clutch of her schoolmates. A bit of a loner? *Nothing to be alarmed about*, Jenna-the-psychologist assured herself; *she's still the new girl.*

A stretch limousine pulled up. Jenna's heart leapt. She was sure she would see her brother, catch a glimpse of the face she'd missed for so long. But no, the man who stepped out of the car and greeted Laila wasn't Malik, only a chauffeur whose thick shoulders and watchful eyes practically shouted "*bodyguard.*" A few moments later, he and Laila were gone. Jenna stood there, staring at the space where her niece had been, as if to somehow prolong the all-too-fleeting vision.

Well, now you've seen her, she told herself, as she finally forced herself to leave. *That will have to be enough.*

• • •

But it wasn't enough, and a few weeks later, she found another pressing reason—a bit of library research that could have been done by telephone—to go to New York. And once again she stationed herself outside the school. She would look, nothing more, that's what she had promised herself. No danger in that, either to her or to anyone else.

After a short wait, she saw Laila talking with several other girls. Good—her niece had made some friends. No chauffeur this time—good again. The little group left the school, walking west. Against all reason, Jenna followed.

Kidding and laughing like any teenagers, the girls turned south on Fifth Avenue. They stopped at Bergdorf Goodman, Jenna slipping in behind them. In twenty minutes the little group collectively spent a sum that, Jenna estimated, many of her clients would be happy to earn in a week. Unconsciously she shook her head in disapproval.

The group moved on to Saks. They went inside, Jenna entering behind them. This time they seemed inclined just to look and were soon headed for the door. But wait, what was happening? A man moved quickly, grabbed Laila, and pulled a silk scarf out of her bookbag. She had been shoplifting—and now she was caught!

Laila began to protest, then to cry. The other girls had vanished, melting into the crowd of shoppers. Without a moment's thought, Jenna moved into action, not knowing what she was doing yet knowing she must do something. She stepped between Laila and the man. "What are you doing, sir!"

"Who are you?"

"I'm this young woman's mother. Who the devil are you?"

"Store security."

The manager appeared. Jenna turned to him, trying her best to put on a show of indignation and injured innocence. "I asked my daughter to meet me here, to pick up the scarf this man is holding. It's just like the one I have at home. I'm sure she was looking for me when he . . . when he jumped her! Is that how you treat valued customers, sir? Because if it is . . ."

The manager looked Jenna over. A stunning woman and obviously affluent, the very picture of a valued customer. But he knew all too well that shoplifters came in many guises. Still, the girl hadn't left the store. The security guard, a new man, should have waited till she was outside—the point at which she could safely and incontrovertibly have been charged with stealing. The manager yielded. Jenna produced her Gold Card and paid for the scarf.

Laila looked bewildered, but didn't make a sound. Jenna could see she was terrified. Even when it was clear she was being rescued, she didn't relax.

Once outside the store, Laila whispered, "Thank you." And then, "Who are you? Why did you do that?"

"I might ask you the same question," Jenna responded. Taking charge, just as she did with clients who were too distraught to think for themselves, she led her niece to a nearby coffee shop. Without asking, she ordered two cups of tea. "I'm Jenna Sorrel. I'm from Boston. I'm a psychologist." Jenna didn't know why she added this information—perhaps from a need to say something.

"A psychologist," echoed Laila.

Jenna smiled. "It's OK. I'm off duty." She couldn't take her eyes off the girl, drinking her in, seeing the young woman she would soon become. Jenna had missed her family—the idea of family—for so long. And here was Malik's baby, her niece, the child she'd helped deliver.

"You're here for a convention or something?" asked Laila.

"No. Just visiting."

"I'm new here myself."

"Oh yes?"

"Yeah. I'm from France."

"Your English is wonderful." It was true. The French accent was almost imperceptible. Far stronger was the Valley Girl patois that had spread across America—even to Boston—from California. The girl must have a good ear.

"Well, we've traveled a lot," explained Laila. "And I've had lots of American friends."

"That's good. Good to have friends, I mean." *Careful, Jenna*, she warned herself, *you have no right, no right to do this*. But she couldn't help herself.

"But I don't have any friends here. Like at school. Not yet, anyway."

"No?"

"No," said Laila moodily. "I don't know what I'm doing wrong. Sometimes I think it's because I'm different. I mean, I'm from France, and my father's from al-Remal, and I . . . look like him."

"There must be other people from different backgrounds in the school, no? More likely it's just that you're new. You've seen that in other places, haven't you? Everyone's slow to warm up to the new kid?"

Laila didn't answer. "Maybe it's because Papa is . . . I won't tell you his name, because you might know it. But he has *lots* of money. Some of the other kids' parents have money, too, but not as much as Papa. I try to be nice. I buy presents for everyone. They seem to like them, they thank me, but then . . ."

Jenna said nothing. This wasn't the time to point out that the worst way to make friends was to try to buy them. Sooner or later, Laila would see that for herself.

"And then today. That was like a chance, you know, to be part of things, to belong. That was the whole idea. They said I had to prove myself. I had to steal something from Saks." Watching Jenna's face for signs of disapproval, she hastily added, "All the other girls have done it. It's like a club, you know? Nobody ever got caught before."

"I see," said Jenna neutrally. So lonely, she thought. The girl needed someone—her father, obviously, but if not him, who?

"And now I've screwed up," Laila concluded, tears in the corners of her eyes.

"Maybe you didn't really want to do it," Jenna offered.

An unhappy shrug.

"Did you ever notice," Jenna went on after a sip of tea, "maybe in sports or dancing, that when you try too hard, you . . . screw up? It's the same way with making friends. Sometimes the worst thing you can do is to try too hard."

"But what can I do except try?"

"Just be yourself. Take an interest in other people. Give them the chance to get to know you."

Jenna knew the words weren't enough. No words could be. Sitting across the table was a lonely child, a child who had lost her mother and who—from all accounts—didn't see nearly enough of her father. Before she could think about the wisdom of what she was doing, Jenna blurted out, "Perhaps we could see each other again. Would you like that?"

"How much do you charge?" Laila asked.

"Charge?"

"You're a shrink. How much do you charge? If it's a lot, I'll have to ask Papa—and I'd rather not."

The question broke Jenna's heart. Was everything in Laila's life bought and paid for? "I wasn't talking about seeing you professionally. I meant . . . as a friend."

Laila pulled back, her eyes narrow with suspicion. "Why?" she asked.

Of course, Jenna thought, after all that had happened to her, she was bound to question a stranger making overtures. "There's an old Oriental proverb that says if you save a person's life, you're responsible for it from that moment on. I didn't exactly save your life, but I think the same principle applies. I just want to know that you'll be all right. Besides, I've enjoyed our talk."

Laila cocked her head, then bobbed it. "Okay. But if Ronnie sees you, he'll ask a lot of questions and tell Papa."

"Ronnie?"

"My chauffeur. And kind of a guard."

"I certainly don't want to get you in trouble."

"Oh, don't worry. He's not around *all* the time—just when Papa's worried." Laila put on a serious look. "I told Papa that I need some *space*, you know? To be myself, like you said." Her glance wandered to a clock on the wall. "Oh, my God. I've got to go. Sure, I guess it's okay if we get together again. The best place to find me is at school. We get out at three. It's the Brearly School. Do you know where it is?"

"Yes."

"So come by sometime."

"Well . . . thanks."

"Thank *you*. For . . . you know—what you did. By the way, my name's Laila."

"Jenna."

"See you, Jenna."

And she was gone.

• • •

Two weeks later, Jenna again made the trip to New York. She felt guilty about getting to know Laila under false pretenses, but at this point false pretenses seemed to be the only ones available. Besides, she rationalized, she really meant it about wanting to make sure Laila would be all right. How could she not?

"I was surprised to see you," Laila said as they walked along peeking into shop windows on Madison Avenue. "I thought you might have, you know, disappeared. Like maybe I imagined you or something."

Over tea in an unpretentious little restaurant, she talked freely about her father, although still concealing his last name. When he wasn't caught up in business, which often meant travel to far places, they went to the theater, made shopping expeditions, and sometimes took wonderful holidays aboard his yacht. "It's just that he's . . . so busy," she ended wistfully.

Jenna wished she could call Malik. Or write him an anonymous letter: *"Your daughter needs more of you. Now, not later, not when you have time, but now. In another two or three years, she'll be her own young woman."* But of course she couldn't do that. But why couldn't she?

"I hope you didn't come down just to see me," Laila was saying.

"What? Oh . . . no. I had some research to do."

"I'm glad, because I have to go. A friend of mine asked me to her house to study together."

"A friend? From school?"

Laila grinned. "Yeah. Things are getting a little better. Like maybe you were right, you know?"

"I hope so. It would be nice to be right once in a while."

Laila put on sunglasses. "Sometimes people recognize me," she explained. "Like photographers. Because of who Papa is."

"Ah."

"I'm sorry to rush off. I enjoyed this. Can we do it again, say another two weeks? I'll make more time."

"Why not?" said Jenna happily.

• • •

Back in Boston, in free moments between patients or while doing some mindless household task, Jenna found herself fantasizing about her niece. She envisioned them visiting museums and art galleries, sharing long walks in Greenwich Village and Soho. She imagined drawing the girl out, listening to her problems, offering help and advice (not minding if it wasn't taken, she cautioned herself) when a boyfriend broke off with her or she with him. She saw herself praising Laila's achievements at school, supporting her dreams.

She knew that she was picturing herself in the role of a parent. But so what? Laila needed someone. Of course, there were risks. But wasn't there some way to carry it off? What if she swore Laila to secrecy? What if they made it an adventure, like spies, never meeting in the same place twice? Laila needed her. And Jenna was so very hungry for the family she had left behind.

But before fantasy had a chance to become anything more, the past again stepped in. The tenth anniversary of her disappearance was approaching. A Reuters reporter, doing a standard follow-up, discovered that someone else had been investigating the nearly forgotten case. It was Ali, of course, although the reporter's inquiries through the Remali royal press secretary met the long-established official response: What Princess Amira had been doing in Anatolia was a mystery, perhaps part of an elaborate abduction scheme; she was assumed to be dead, although the prince still held on to his faint hopes.

It was enough for an item on a television magazine show, full of speculation and rumor that Amira might still be alive. The writer was astute enough to suspect that Prince Ali Rashad was not so resigned and disinterested as he wished to appear, and this suspicion was voiced in his story.

When Jenna read a sensationalized version—"Have You Seen This Princess?" complete with an old photo—in one of her habitual tabloids, she felt the old fear as if it had never left her. After all this time, all this deception and disguise, she still wasn't safe.

Her self-deception ended. She couldn't continue to see Laila—it might endanger both of them. Even as it was, the girl had to dodge paparazzi, and certainly Ali could employ more subtle methods.

She could easily vanish from Laila's life. The girl didn't even know her last name. But she couldn't do that, just couldn't.

Feeling a wrenching sense of loss—it wasn't fair, she thought, yet again to have to let go of someone she loved—Jenna kept the appointment Laila had suggested. They went to a diner—a trendy Upper East Side version—and shared an oversized cheeseburger and a platter of french fries. To anyone watching, thought Jenna, the two of them must look very much like a mother and daughter from the upscale neighborhood. It made what she had to say all the harder.

"I'm afraid I won't be able to see you so often," she began. "In fact, not very often at all. I've been neglecting my patients. And I have a book contract that's going to eat up every free moment." None of it was quite true, but there was enough truth in it that it wasn't exactly a lie, either.

Laila's eyes reproached her, then turned away. "That's okay," the girl said with forced casualness. "I always wondered how you found so much time for me. And to tell you the truth, I had to lose Ronnie today to see you. These last few days, I don't know why, but Papa's become really worried about me. So it won't be easy for me anymore, either. No wonder nobody wants to date me," she added morosely. "It's like going through Israeli security."

Jenna smiled in spite of herself. Imagine Malik, the old rule-breaker, now the rule-maker. Yet it wasn't so funny, not from the standpoint of her niece's happiness.

She tried to think of something to say, something that didn't sound pat and professional, something that would tell her niece she really cared. But nothing safe came to mind. "Maybe later, when we're both freer," was the best she could do.

"Could I have your phone number?" Laila asked suddenly. "I'd like to talk to you once in a while—if that's okay."

Jenna couldn't resist. "Of course it's okay. Anytime. But will you promise to keep it just between the two of us?"

"Be, like, secret friends?"

"Yes."

Laila laughed. "Sure. Besides, it's not like I'm going to run home and tell Papa about the lady who rescued me in Saks."

Jenna laughed, too. "I never thought of it that way. So, have you decided on a college yet?" Anything to prolong the moment, the talk, the presence of her niece.

"Columbia. Papa's been hinting he'd like me to go to the Sorbonne, but I'd much rather stay in New York. I love it here."

Did Laila's choice have just a little bit to do with her? Jenna wondered. It was a pleasant thought, a consolation prize.

They shared something called a Chocolate Crisis for dessert. When the last morsel was gone, there was no avoiding the fact that their time together was ending, too. The decision had been made. But Jenna's heart pleaded for a reprieve, for a few minutes more.

"Shall we walk a bit?" she asked. She would miss her plane. Too bad.

"Sure," said Laila.

They strolled down Fifth Avenue, along Central Park. The sun was bright, the sky was blue, Jenna tried to pretend this wasn't the last time she would see Laila. Maybe it wasn't. Maybe . . .

When they reached the Plaza, they hailed two taxis.

"Well . . . *ciao*," Laila said, trying to smile.

Forgetting caution, Jenna threw her arms around her niece and held her tight. "Good-bye," she said. *Good-bye, my dearest Laila.*

CAMERON

The call came on a cool September night.

"Can you come over, Ms. Sorrel? Like right away?"

"What's the matter, Josh?" His voice had changed so much she hadn't recognized it for a moment.

"My dad kind of hurt my mom. He's gone now, and she asked me to call you. I—can you hurry?"

Jenna did. At the Chandler house, she took one look at Carolyn's face and went to the phone. Apparently Cameron had forgotten his "little trick" of hitting where it didn't show.

"What are you doing?"

"Calling nine-one-one."

"No." Carolyn pulled the receiver from Jenna's hand and hung it up.

"Carolyn, please try to understand. You may be badly hurt. You're certainly in danger. Will he be back tonight?"

Carolyn shrugged. "Probably." At least she didn't appear to be in shock.

Jenna tried to think. "Was he drinking?"

Carolyn didn't answer. Jenna turned to Josh. He looked at his mother and said, "Yes, ma'am. He was."

"All right. What I should do is walk out of here and call the police and an ambulance from the first pay phone. But you don't wish me to, and I'll respect your wishes. You respect mine. You're spending the night at my place, both of you. Get whatever you need, right now, and let's go. In the morning we can deal with this better."

To her surprise, Carolyn simply nodded and said, "OK. That's not a bad idea."

At her apartment, Jenna doctored her friend's face as best she could. The wounds were mainly bruises and welts. There seemed to be no broken bones, no cuts that required stitches.

Carolyn talked about Cameron in an oddly matter-of-fact way that troubled Jenna. "He just needs something that he can control, that he can dominate. Unluckily, that happens to be me."

In the kitchen, Josh and Karim sat exchanging a quiet word now and then—almost like grown men already, their closeness expressed more through silence than through speech.

It was two in the morning before everyone was ready for sleep. Carolyn shared Jenna's bed; Karim gave his to Josh and took the sofa.

A half hour later, Cameron rang the bell.

"I know my wife's here, Jenna. Let me talk with her."

"Go home, Cameron." She kept the chain on the door.

"Jenna, Jenna, please. I know I screwed up. It's all my fault, I admit it. Just let me talk with her."

"It's really late, Cameron. Go home. Tomorrow you can talk."

"Jenna, I'll go down on my knees." To her horror, he did. "Just let me talk with her."

"Cameron, if you don't leave now, I'll call the police."

He got to his feet. Something about him made her close the door and lock it.

"Go ahead," he said loudly. "You call the police. I'll call my lawyers. And they'll slap a lawsuit on you so fast your head will spin. How does alienation of affection sound?"

"What are you talking about?"

"You and my wife, lady."

"You know better than that, Cameron."

"This isn't France, or Egypt, or wherever the hell you come from. This is my town. You interfere with my life, you'll regret it."

Call the police, she told herself, but she hesitated, ashamed of the fear she felt. It *was* his town, and she wasn't from France, or from Egypt, either. What would happen if he carried out his threat?

At that moment Carolyn swept by her with Josh in tow. "Thank you, Jenna, but it's best that you stay out of this."

"What are you doing?"

"I'm going home with my son and my husband."

"Carolyn—"

"Jenna, I appreciate your kindness and your good intentions. But this is between Cameron and me. It's really none of your business."

She unlocked the door, fought with the chain, and went out into the hallway.

"Oh, babe, I'm so sorry," said Cameron in a wheedling voice. "Are you OK? Are you OK? My love, I'm so sorry."

Josh turned back and looked helplessly at Jenna and Karim, then followed his parents.

It was the end of Jenna's first real friendship in her new life. Jenna stood silently and watched Carolyn go. There was a wall between them, put in place by Carolyn and never to be breached, like the glass between prisoner and visitor in a jail.

It was a turning point for Jenna, although it took months for her to see it. It gave direction to her work. She might have failed her best friend, but if she worked hard enough, studied hard enough, learned enough, perhaps she could help other women facing the same agony.

One morning she woke with the theme and the title of the next book she would write: *Prisons of the Heart: Women in Denial.*

She even had a dedication, although she could never use it: To Ali A. and Cameron C., who made it all possible.

Meanwhile, unknown to her and in a corner of the world she preferred to forget, a man to whom she was truly thankful was about to touch her life again, for the last time but with fateful effect.

MUSTAFA

Brother Peter was dying. He had gone to Zaire to explore the possibility of establishing a mission there, but an epidemic of some kind had broken out, and he had not been permitted to visit the town where the brothers hoped to work. Back in Van, he had suddenly developed a blinding headache, followed by nausea, fever, and fierce thirst.

A local doctor, unable even to diagnose the illness, loaded Peter with antibiotics and advised wrapping him in wet sheets during the worst of the fever, but it was clear that he had no hope for his patient. Brother Peter knew nothing of this: he was lost in delusions by the time the doctor was summoned.

The mission was nearly deserted. Another earthquake had struck to the north, and most of the little detachment of brothers had gone there on their work of faith and mercy. The deathwatch over Brother Peter fell mainly to Mustafa, a native of Van who served as a handyman and local factotum for the mission. He wore a surgeon's mask and gown given to him by the doctor along with emphatic instructions on sanitary measures. No telling what kind of African plague this might be.

It was ten o'clock at night. For hours, Mustafa had watched and listened while Brother Peter slipped in and out of intelligibility. At the moment, the dying man was raving again. Something about Joseph, Mary, and Jesus' flight into Egypt. Hard to follow, even though the name of Jesus, an early prophet of God, was certainly familiar to Mustafa.

"Herod, Herod sent his men after them. Don't you remember? Don't you remember? But Herod was a Jew, wasn't he? These were Arabs. Remember them, mate? Rich, rich Arabs."

Mustafa listened more closely. He remembered when there had been rich Arabs in Van, asking questions.

"Running from them. Mary and baby Jesus. No more Joseph. Joseph died on Mount Ararat looking for the Ark." Brother Peter shook his head fiercely. "Not Joseph. French name. Philippe! Yes, great man. My savior. Where is he?"

Mustafa sat very still. The Arabs, he recalled, had offered large amounts of money for information about a woman and child who had been with a man named Philippe.

"Then Joseph died," Peter went on wildly. "So Peter had to take them. Peter. On this rock will I build my church. Took them in the van, remember the van we had? The van from Van."

"Where did you take them?" ventured Mustafa.

"Egypt! Herod's men hot after us. Was it Egypt? Bloody ugly city, it was."

For a while, Mustafa interjected questions, trying to channel Peter's ramblings. It was like conversing with a sleepwalker, but at last he had the bones of the tale. It was Brother Peter who had smuggled the rich man's wife and son out of Van those many years ago, taking them to Erzurum—or maybe Ankara—in the mission's old panel truck. No one around Van would have thought twice about seeing it on the road; it was as familiar as dust. To the airport in Erzurum. Or Ankara. Something about papers, new papers.

That was all Peter had to tell, now or ever. Toward midnight, with one last shout for Jesus, he fell silent. Then he was gone.

Mustafa did as he had been told. He did not touch the body, but locked the room behind him, removed the mask and gown, drenched himself in a fluid that smelled of alcohol, and called the hospital. Told to wait, he did. Hours later, to his astonishment and great fear, two foreigners—European doctors working for something called the U.N.—arrived. They praised him for following orders; he might have saved many lives, they said. Then they confined him to a room in the mission.

He was there for a month, wondering often if he would die in this infidel place. Sent home at last, he tried to ignore his wife's cries of gratitude to God and went to search for the card that one of the rich Arabs had given him—"in case you think of anything later," the man had said. Praise God, there it was. Never throw anything from such a rich man away. The name of a local hotel on one side; on the other, a phone number in al-Remal. Mustafa stared at the number for a long time. The call would cost him a month's pay. He hoped that what Brother Peter had said was still worth something.

ALI

Abdallah Rashad, head of the agency that most Remalis called simply Falcon and which combined the functions fulfilled in America by the CIA, FBI, and Secret Service, closed the folder on his desk and waited for his nephew's reaction.

"You believe this peasant, this Turk?" said Ali.

"He might be lying in hope of a reward, but so far as it can be checked, his story holds up."

"So the bitch is alive," said Ali.

"It seems probable," Abdallah replied quietly.

"And my son as well."

"God willing."

"Where are they?"

Abdallah decided to ignore the tone of demand. "That, of course, is the question, nephew. I've reviewed the entire file in light of the new information. I've also initiated new inquiries. It seems likely that she and the boy went to Paris. They probably stayed in a certain hotel there. She may have seen a lawyer named Cheverny, but he died two years ago. So far, that is where the trail ends. They could be anywhere in the world now, under almost any identity."

"Find her."

Abdallah looked aside in embarrassment; Ali's terseness verged on disrespect. "If she makes a mistake, we will," he said more quietly than ever. "If not . . . Time is like the sand, nephew. In the end it covers everything."

"I don't need—" Ali controlled himself with visible effort. "Thank you, Uncle. God willing, she'll make that mistake, and you'll find my son. If anyone can do it, it's you."

"God willing, we will."

Ali rose. "I thank you again, Uncle. It's been good to see you. Unfortunately, I must go. Another appointment . . ."

"Of course, of course. I know how busy your schedule is. But perhaps just one more word, while I have the pleasure of your company."

"Certainly." Ali did not sit down. "What is it?"

"Just this, nephew. It is my deepest wish that you be reunited with your son. At the same time, if he and his mother are found, it would reflect badly on al-Remal—and on the royal family itself—if anything . . . untoward happened."

"What do you mean, Uncle?"

"Appearances, nephew. Sometimes it seems as if the great world revolves on them. Imagine the talk if something happened to the woman after we located her. Even something as innocent as, say, a car accident."

"Well, that seems obvious. But what does it have to do with me?" Ali's face was a portrait of surprised innocence—like many guilty men's, reflected his uncle.

"Nothing at all," said Abdallah. "Just a thought that came while we were talking. Please, I've kept you long enough. Peace to you, nephew. May we see more of one another."

"God willing. Peace to you, Uncle. Oh, by the way, does anyone else know of this?"

"No."

"Not even the king?"

"No one."

"Good. Probably best not to trouble him, in his present condition."

"Of course." The king, after a lifetime of self-indulgence, was at the edge of death, his heart, kidneys, and liver failing together as if in a conspiracy.

Abdallah saw his nephew to the door. He disliked Ali's quick temper, his duplicity, and much else of what he knew about him—and he knew a great deal. At the same time, he did not want Ali for an enemy.

• • •

There were many things to think about. Decisions to make. Returning to his office, Abdallah opened the safe that contained his most secret files.

In the hall, Ali cursed under his breath. That strange little warning at the end of the conversation—had the old goat been saying what he seemed to be saying? And if so, where had his information come from?

Oh, well, did it really matter? So what if the old man knew, as long as he did his job and found Karim—and the bitch. Once that happened, who cared what his opinion might be? His whole generation was coming to its end.

Finding Karim. Ali savored the thought. His second wife, although he had come to detest her, had at least given him two more sons, as well as a daughter. But the loss of his firstborn had been the greatest of his life. And now there was a chance that he would get him back. What would the boy—almost a man—be like now? Ali could only picture a younger version of himself.

As for Amira—yes, let Abdallah find her. And then let him choke on his warnings. Ali had a right to punish the bitch. With deep pleasure, he began to imagine the details of his vengeance.

• • •

Abdallah pressed the tape deck's Play button. He had not listened to the cassette in many months, but his talk with Ali caused him to want to hear it again.

"God's peace be with you, Highness."

"And with you, Tamer. How good to see you again."

"And to see you, too, Highness."

The voices were those of Ali and Tamer Sibai, who sounded nervous even in ordinary greetings. An interesting fellow, thought Abdallah. Everyone knew him, of course, as the brother of a woman—Laila Sibai—executed in a famous adultery case. Tamer, the oldest brother, had thrown the first stone.

Abdallah compressed his lips in sympathy and respect for a man who could carry out such a duty.

"Please—no need for formalities when it's just the two of us. Call me Ali."

"As you wish, Highn—Ali."

Abdallah knew that Tamer had reason to be nervous. The man's present was considerably murkier than his past. He owned several businesses—his card described him as an investor—but by far the most profitable of them had come to Abdallah's attention by way of requests for information from various drug-enforcement agencies in Europe and the United States.

"You'll do me the honor of having coffee with me?"

"The honor is mine."

"I'll ring. You know, I was thinking the other day of you—how we used to play together as boys."

"I can't imagine that you'd remember me. I remember you, of course."

"And I thought, 'How is it that I don't see my old friend Tamer anymore?' Ah, the coffee."

Abdallah fast-forwarded the tape through the small talk and coffee that Remali custom required before any discussion of serious business.

". . . and yet, as great as the pleasure of seeing you again, my friend Tamer, I'm afraid I must spoil it with bad news."

"Bad news?"

"I hope you won't blame the messenger for the message."

"No, of course not."

"Very well, my friend, here it is: Through no wish of my own, I have had the misfortune to learn who dishonored your sister."

"Name him and he dies, even now."

Abdallah nodded in approval. Whatever else Tamer Sibai might be, he was a man of honor. Nervousness and servility had vanished completely from his voice.

"Ah, my friend, you speak like a man, as anyone who knows you would expect.

Yet forgive me for saying that even honorable courage must be tempered, as a blade is tempered in the fire. Otherwise it may betray you. One must not forget all caution, even in matters of this kind. A man like you must not needlessly expose himself—and his country—to the prejudice of the great world that does not understand the Remali meaning of honor."

"I thank you for your concern. Who is he?"

"Malik Badir."

A pause on the tape before Tamer spoke again.

"I always thought it was him."

"You did?"

Even on tape, Ali's surprise was palpable. Abdallah almost laughed, recognizing what had happened: Ali had invented the story about Badir, probably expecting to have to convince Tamer, who instead had leaped to the bait. Abdallah had seen the same thing happen in interrogations.

"Yes. And now I know. Again I thank you."

"There's no need to thank me for doing what friendship and respect require. But I hope you understood what I said just now. Badir is a citizen of the world these days. I ask you not to . . . handle the matter in a way that compromises our country."

"I know of only one way to handle the matter. What did you have in mind?"

"Ah. You cut to the heart of the matter. I thought that perhaps a third party, an independent contractor, as it were, could be engaged. Forgive me for saying it, but I've heard that you have certain . . . contacts in Corsica."

"My business takes me to many places."

"Of course. Again, forgive me. I know that I'm asking you to forgo a duty that may seem purely personal. But I ask it for al-Remal. And for that reason, I will gladly pay any costs that . . . engaging someone might involve."

"That's appreciated, but unnecessary. I can take care of the arrangements myself."

"As you wish, of course. But if any extra expenses arise, please allow me to help meet them. Meanwhile, I've taken the liberty of making certain inquiries that may save you some time and effort. For example, I've learned that at this time of year Badir and his wife vacation at a villa in the south of France, and that twice a week they drive to a bistro in a nearby small town. His car is easily recognized—I'll give you all the details—and the road is lightly traveled. If there were an accident . . . a shame, of course, since an act of honor cries out to be known. But there is the country to think of."

"I understand. A third time I thank you, Ali Rashad. I'll never forget this."

Abdallah stopped the tape. He could easily imagine how it might have been done: an assassin who won the confidence of some poor truck driver, got him drunk, crashed his heavy vehicle into an oncoming Mercedes, expertly broke the passed-out trucker's neck, and simply walked away across country.

Abdallah Rashad's life's work was secrets—sometimes the unraveling of them, sometimes their keeping. Here was a secret that he and perhaps three men knew: that Genevieve Badir had not died by accident, but by murder. He had kept the secret because it was in the best interests of al-Remal to do so. But that might soon change. The king was dying, and Ali's brother Ahmad would succeed to the throne.

Ahmad was as practical as Abdallah himself, as practical as Ali was impetuous. Ahmad neither liked nor disliked Malik Badir, but considered him a potentially valuable asset to the kingdom. Perhaps he should be told that his brother's personal enmity had endangered that asset and might do so again. Ahmad would be grateful for the information.

As for Ali, there was no need to lose his favor, either—as long as he could be persuaded to exercise restraint. All Abdallah needed to do was unravel yet another secret—the whereabouts of Amira and Karim Rashad.

KARIM

"Americans have no understanding of the Arab world. Their foreign policy in the Middle East is bankrupt. Their arrogance in presuming to know what is best for us is both hypocritical and destructive. And their so-called peace initiatives will prove to be temporary at best."

Good Lord, thought Jenna. She'd never heard such a soapbox speech—at least not in her own living room, and certainly not from a teenaged girl.

The speaker was Jacqueline Hamid, daughter of Professor Nasser Hamid, a well-known Egyptian novelist at Boston University. She was a classmate and, it appeared, a special friend of Karim's. He sat at her side hanging on every word.

Now he nodded vigorously, eyes shining with admiration. "Exactly. Even you can't disagree with that, can you, Mom?" It was a challenge.

How to respond? Jenna not only disagreed but also found Jacqueline pompous, opinionated—in short, insufferable. But to express that opinion would surely alienate her son, who was clearly enthralled by the petite, dark-haired beauty with pouting red lips and enormous jet-black eyes.

"I heard your father's lecture on Egyptian feminism," Jenna said, dodging Karim's question. "It was very informative. But I wonder why he's not alarmed by the resurgence of the veil in a big city like Cairo, even among university students."

"Perhaps you don't fully understand the implications of current socio-religious movements in Egypt," Jacqueline said primly. "You've been in this country a long time, and Karim tells me that you grew up mainly in Europe. You're Westernized. You've lost touch with your Egyptian identity."

Jenna was shocked. Although Karim spent much of his free time at the Hamid home and was constantly quoting either father or daughter, it hadn't occurred to her that she was being discussed with Jacqueline—and found wanting.

Taking Jenna's silence to mean she had seen the error of her remark, Jacqueline launched into a defense of Arab customs in general and the veil in particular. "In conservative countries—like in al-Remal, for example—women enjoy a level of protection and respect that Western women have never known. All that the so-called feminist movement has done in the West is to turn women into second-class men. I'm not at all sure I prefer that."

Jenna's blood ran cold. How foolish young people could be—and how dangerous, especially when they were so sure they knew all the answers. Didn't this overprivileged girl realize how lucky she was? How blessed that she could open her mouth and say what she pleased? Didn't she know that she could be punished, perhaps even killed, for doing that in a conservative Arab country she so admired?

"I think life in places like al-Remal isn't nearly as romantic as you imagine it to be," she said evenly. "Women aren't allowed to drive or to travel without a brother or husband. They have no civil rights, and they need male permission to do virtually everything that matters."

Jacqueline was not impressed. "I think some of those so-called rights you mention are not especially relevant in a setting like al-Remal," she said dismissively.

"Well, what about the right to live?" said Jenna, her voice rising a little despite her effort to control it. "What about the young woman who was shot by her brother—fifteen times—because she failed to meet his standards of modesty? Or the wife who was stabbed to death by her husband simply because she wanted a divorce? Are those relevant enough for you?"

Karim and Jacqueline stared at her, Karim looking especially surprised and appalled by her passionate but obviously benighted response. "You seem to have heard some sensational stories about al-Remal," said Jacqueline. "Have you ever been there?"

"I . . . I've read a great deal about the Arab world during the years I've lived here," Jenna said lamely, dodging another direct question.

"Reading and living are two different things," Jacqueline sniffed, smugly confident again. "Most articles and books about the Middle East are written by Westerners. They have no feeling for our values, our Eastern soul."

"I agree that there's a certain amount of blindness to other cultures—on both sides. Would you like some tea, Jacqueline? Or coffee?" It was prudent to forfeit the debate. Jenna feared that she had said too much already, and in any event, Jacqueline was not going to be persuaded by a woman whose "Eastern soul" had atrophied. As for Karim, he was obviously so infatuated with the girl that he would happily join any jihad she wished to declare.

• • •

"Isn't she great, Mom?" he asked after returning from walking Jacqueline home.

"She's . . . she's a very interesting young woman."

"And her dad, he's brilliant. He knows so much about Egypt. He asked me all kinds of questions about you. I told him we'd all get together sometime soon. I'll bet he knows some of the people you grew up with. Wouldn't it be great to find out how they are? What they're doing?"

Jenna grimaced involuntarily. She couldn't imagine anything she desired less than a chatty little get-together with Professor Hamid. How many more lies would she have to tell? Could she invent relatives and friends who weren't there? Convincingly enough to satisfy someone who knew intimately the country that was supposed to be her home? And what if she slipped up, got caught in a lie? What then?

Silently, she cursed the day Karim had met Jacqueline. And yet, to be fair, she understood that his attachment to the girl wasn't simply a symptom of rampant teenage hormones. The two seemed to be genuinely close, bonded not only by a common Arab identity but also by a mutual sense of loss. Karim believed that his father was dead. Jacqueline had not seen her mother in years. An American graduate student who met, married, and eventually tired of Professor Hamid, the woman had simply walked out one day. At last report, according to Karim, she was living with a television producer in Australia.

Undoubtedly that explained some of Jacqueline's bitterness toward "Western" ways and women's liberation. In therapy it would stand out like a flashing light. But Jacqueline wasn't a patient. She was Karim's new constant companion. And in that context she was a royal pain.

• • •

Karim's fascination with Jacqueline wasn't the only sign of his struggles at the border between childhood and manhood. As his voice had cracked and deepened, as his bones and muscles thickened, he had begun to question, argue, sulk, rebel at every turn. It was typical teenage behavior, but like Jacqueline's it was a pain.

There was the night when a call came from the Sanctuary, the battered women's shelter where Jenna worked as a volunteer.

"It's Tabetha Coleman," said Liz Ohlenberg, the shelter's hotline operator, also a volunteer. "She's under arrest, or at least being detained. The story was kind of cloudy."

Jenna recognized the name of a former client, a young woman who hadn't appeared at the shelter for several months. "What happened?"

"She shot her husband."

"Dead?"

"No. In the leg. I gather he'll be okay."

"Why did she shoot him? I mean, what were the circumstances? The last I heard, she'd moved out of their house."

"She says that he showed up at her new apartment drunk and demanding to be let in. She called nine-one-one, but he started breaking down the door before the police arrived. She'd got a pistol somewhere—didn't say where—and shot him right through the closed door. Says she only meant to scare him off."

"It sounds like self-defense."

"I don't know. As I said, she wasn't very clear. I get the impression that the gun is a problem. It's illegal, naturally."

"Does she have a lawyer?"

"I left a message on Lou Leahy's machine. If he doesn't get back to me soon, I'll try Angela Trosclair. But Tabetha asked specifically for you. I know it's not one of your nights, but do you think you could go down there?"

"Yes. Yes, of course I'll go. What precinct?"

When Jenna hung up, Karim was standing there. Apparently he'd been listening to her end of the conversation.

"What was all that about?"

She summed it up.

"Mom, do you believe in right and wrong?"

"Yes, of course. Why?"

"Well, then, how come you help people who break the law?"

She had asked herself that question early in her practice. Her answer had been to remember Philippe, who had taught her what a healer should be—humane, tolerant, never judging but simply trying to help.

"Mom?"

"I'm sorry. I was thinking about what you said. I believe that my work isn't about right or wrong; it's about trying to ease human suffering."

Karim scowled as if she were a schoolgirl who'd given the wrong answer. "Well, what about Josh's mother, then? She's supposed to be your friend. You said you wanted to help her. But you hardly see her anymore."

The criticism stung—because she'd leveled it at herself more than once.

"It's not that simple, Karim," she said finally, wanting him to understand. "Josh's father has a very serious problem. Unless he gets some help, it will only get worse. You know he hurt Carolyn, and it could happen again. I wanted to help them, but Carolyn . . . well, she just won't admit that she needs help."

"So you think she should just leave him?" Karim's expression was a strange mixture of curiosity and contempt.

"I told you, it's not that simple," said Jenna, wondering why her son seemed to misunderstand everything she did these days—and why she was always so defensive. "I think she needs to protect herself. To get back her self-respect. She wouldn't be much good to herself or her son if she got killed, would she?"

She had become shrill. Karim's look of disgust could have come straight from his father.

"I won't be long," she promised, gathering coat and purse. "Here's some money for a pizza."

He looked at the bills and turned away.

Hurrying to the corner to find a cab, she felt an all-too-familiar frustration. Once again she'd misstepped without really knowing how or why. It was as if her little boy were disappearing into the body of an argumentative, sneering stranger. *Count your blessings*, she told herself. Karim was an excellent student and a star soccer player. Compared with many other parents she knew, she was lucky. And yet she longed for the days when her child believed she could do no wrong.

• • •

"So you're Jenna Sorrel! What a pleasure to meet you at last!"

"I'm pleased to meet you, too, Professor Hamid."

"Please, call me Nasser."

It was easy to see Jacqueline Hamid in her father.

Physically the man was not unattractive, with enormous dark eyes that some women might have considered "soulful." At the same time, there was something overly ingratiating in his manner, a hint of oiliness better suited to a peddler in the souk than to a distinguished academic.

"You must tell me all about yourself," he said.

"I'm afraid there's very little to tell."

"I don't believe you. My friend Naguib Mahfouz once told me that behind every truly beautiful woman's face is an interesting story. Your story must be very interesting indeed."

"You're very kind." An acquaintance with Naguib Mahfouz, the Nobel Prize-winning Cairene writer, was certainly something to be proud of, but Hamid's compliment would have held more charm if he hadn't been so eager to name-drop.

"Are you enjoying our little *mahrajan*?"

"It's wonderful," Jenna answered honestly. The *mahrajan*—folk festival—was being held in a Veterans of Foreign Wars post near the North End. Despite the somewhat incongruous setting, Jenna had been floating in a near-trance of nostalgia from the moment she and Karim had entered. The sound of spoken Arabic warmed her, and the pungent fragrances of lamb and allspice and cinnamon drifted through the crowded hall. My God, how long had it been since she had last savored these familiar sensations?

Even the attentions of Professor Hamid seemed rather pleasant—up to a point.

"I understand you're quite a cook yourself," he was saying now. "*Adas biz-ruz* and *ruz bel shaghia*—all the good things from home."

"My son has been talking," said Jenna, flicking a mildly accusatory glance at Karim. It was true that she had tried her hand at some of the popular Egyptian dishes that supposedly had been the food of her childhood.

She had done it as a way of reaching out to Karim in his newfound interest in all things Arab. For the same reason, she had bought some cassettes—the old songs of Asmahan and Abdul Wahab—from a small downtown shop and played them for him.

Her gestures pleased Karim, and when Professor Hamid had invited them both to the *mahrajan*—he was one of the organizers—there had been no way of begging off.

"It's good that the boy should know his heritage," said Hamid. "Speaking of which, you must tell me more about yourself. Perhaps we have mutual friends."

"Mmm," murmured Jenna, digging into the plate of food before her, using the pita bread to scoop up the *hummus* and *tabbouleh*, as she'd been taught as a child.

She caught Karim looking at her.

"What?" she asked. "What's wrong?"

"Nothing," he said. "I've just never seen you use anything but a knife and fork."

"You've never seen me eat a hamburger or a pizza?"

"I mean . . ."

"I know what you mean. When in Rome, as they say."

"I find your way with food charming," interjected Hamid. "Utterly charming."

Jenna looked up from her meal to glimpse Jacqueline and Karim exchanging secret smiles—like matchmakers. *Oh no*, she thought, almost laughing aloud. Professor Hamid *was* going to be dangerous, but not in the way she'd imagined.

Mercifully, the conversation broke off as a popular Syrian recording star appeared on the makeshift stage. His voice was clear and pure as he sang a classical *qasidah*, an elaborate technique with sustained floating vocal and instrumental improvisations that dated back a thousand years. The crowd stamped and cheered. Jenna smiled at the eclectic musical heritage of the East: it would be as if the Rolling Stones were to dazzle a crowd with a medieval chanson.

The next performer was Hanan, a singer who had starred in some of Lebanon's earliest films and who now belted out a medley of traditional songs in a rough-edged voice that suggested years of sorrow and hard living. Hakki Obadia from Iraq played a short, classical-style *taksim* improvisation on the violin, and Abdul Wahab Kawkabani sang and accompanied himself on a beautifully inlaid oud.

When there was a break in the music, Hamid resumed his attempt to charm Jenna. She tried to be pleasant, but not too pleasant. Polite, but not encouraging. Luckily, he seemed to have forgotten his desire to hear all about her—perhaps that had been no more than a well-practiced line. Instead, he wanted to talk about people and places he knew in Egypt. She tried not to wince as he waxed eloquent about the "decadent charm" of

Alexandria, the "mystic grandeur" of Sakkara. Why on earth, she wondered, had he spent most of the last dozen years in America?

When the professor paused—to make a second trip to the buffet—Karim whispered, "Isn't he a great guy, Mom? I can tell he likes you."

"Mmm." *Careful,* she told herself, *be very careful. Karim likes these people.*

Now the musicians launched into a rhythmic village folk song created for dancing. Karim took Jacqueline's hand and led her into the center of the room. Jenna watched, amazed, as they led an ever-growing group in the *dabka*, a popular circle dance.

"Nabila, is that you?" It was a woman's voice, and it came from the next table.

"Excuse me?" Jenna said, panic-stricken, though she had no idea who Nabila might be.

"Nabila Ajami," said the woman, who seemed to be about Jenna's age. "From Homs. My name is Fadwa Kabbash. We grew up in the same neighborhood, don't you remember?"

"No," Jenna protested, "no, you must be mistaken. My family is Egyptian. I've never been to Syria. I'm very sorry."

The woman seemed unconvinced, as if Jenna's failure to be her old neighbor was somehow a personal affront. She stalked over to a crowd of laughing, eating people and began to speak with great animation, pointing in Jenna's direction.

Though she had no idea who Nabila might be, the old fear crept from its hiding place like some night animal. The hall was too crowded, too close. She needed to breathe. She hurried outside and huddled in the shelter of a hidden doorway. Then the tears came. A fugitive forever, that's what she would be. Afraid of even the most innocent questions, because even if she wasn't Nabila, she was certainly not Jenna Sorrel. Not for the first time, she wondered if perhaps she should never have left al-Remal, surrendering to whatever fate had been written for her on the day of her birth. And what about Karim? Would he be better off living the life he'd been born to?

"Give me a break," she muttered reproachfully. She wouldn't put up with such whining, such self-pity, from a patient. Why should she indulge in it herself? *Just do the best you can, Jenna. And hope that it's good enough.*

TRAVIS

The group who sought refuge at the Sanctuary—the shelter where Jenna did volunteer counseling twice a week—was as varied as America itself. Rich, poor, black, white, young, and old, the women had only one thing in common—spouses and lovers who used their fists to abuse and intimidate.

Now, as Jenna moderated the shelter's Tuesday night group session, she encouraged Pamela Shields to go on with her story. Pamela, who reminded her so much of Carolyn, was an affluent matron who a short time ago had lived in a sumptuous home. But when she'd finally decided not to tolerate her husband's assaults any longer, he cut her off financially, leaving her nearly destitute.

"I never realized that nothing was in my name," Pamela said. "As long as I did what Burke wanted, money was never an issue. If I wanted new clothes or new jewelry, I just told him, and the money was there. It was only . . . only when I couldn't go on the way we were that I realized he controlled everything." Wiping her eyes with a shredded tissue, she sighed raggedly and went on. "He says I'll have nothing if I try to divorce him. He says he'll take our children and make sure they see me for the no-good mother I am."

"Bull!" shouted Polly Shannon, a diminutive blond of fifty. "Just because he says that doesn't make it so. He has money? Good! The law will make him share it with you. And there's no way on God's earth the law will give him your kids—especially not if you get it on record that he beats you up."

"I don't know . . ."

"Just look at me," Polly insisted. "I whipped Kevin's ass in court. He took so much away from me, but I finally said 'no more.' Now he's in jail—and I'm starting to put my life together again."

"Not everyone is as strong as you are," Pamela murmured.

"It's not about strength," Jenna said gently. "We're not in a weightlifting contest here. It's about what can be done, and how we can help each other to do it." Why couldn't they see that? Why did she have to keep repeating it? She loved her work, but there were times when it wearied her, made her feel as if she was fighting a losing battle. This was one of those times. Besides, she had another reason to wish the session was over: tonight she would see her brother's face and hear his voice. So would millions of other Americans. Malik was going to be on television, interviewed by Sandra Waters on her magazine show.

Connie Jenks, a young sound engineer who dressed in high grunge style, raised a hand like a schoolgirl. "Yes, Connie?" said Jenna, although she could have recited what was coming.

"I want to say something," Connie said. "What it is—what I keep hearing—I mean, it's like all of you ignore me just because I'm trying to make my marriage work. You act like divorce or jail are the only ways to deal with a man who . . . has problems. Well, Steve is working on his problems just like we are, and I hope to get back with him once he gets himself straightened out. Which he will. Do you know what he's been doing? Sending flowers. Twice a week. What about that? Why don't we talk about that—I mean, about positive things—for a change?"

Jenna managed to sneak a glance at her watch without being caught. "No one is saying problems can't be worked out," she told Connie. "But flowers and apologies won't do it, I promise you. First, he has to admit that he has a problem—his problem, mind you, not something *you* did or something you *made him* do. Then he needs to get counseling. Steve's taken those first steps, and I hope he succeeds. But until you see and hear something very different from what's been happening for the past three years, it's best that you take things very, very slowly."

"You always sound like you know so much about this stuff," said Polly. "I mean really *know*. Were you ever with that kind of man?"

Jenna chose her words carefully. "Someone very close to me was. She felt as Pamela does, that her husband had all the power and she had none."

"So how did she handle it?"

"She left him. It was very hard. She took their son and moved to another . . . state. She changed her name so the husband wouldn't find her."

"And how did she make out?" Polly demanded. "Is she okay?"

"She's okay. She has a job. It's working out for her."

"Another man in her life?"

"No," Jenna said, feeling the tiniest twinge of regret. "But let's move on." She felt uncomfortable talking about herself even when she pretended to be talking about someone else.

• • •

At a newsstand Jenna picked up her latest ration of tabloids, although recently she'd found it easier to track Malik through the business pages of respectable newspapers and magazines, where she'd read of the leveraged buyout of a British automaker and the purchase of a German movie-theater empire.

A different kind of story caught her eye. An unemployed Syrian had killed his estranged wife and fled with their children, apparently back to the Middle East. It was a terrifying reminder of how deadly a determined man could be. Even an ordinary man without the kind of power Ali possessed. Jenna didn't want to think about it—no more of that tonight. She hurried home, slipped a blank tape into the VCR, and settled in her favorite chair.

The phone rang. Jenna hesitated for a moment, then picked up the receiver with a sigh. The caller was Toni Ferrante, who after years of intermittent therapy and emotional struggle had divorced her husband. "I'm sorry to call you at home," she said. "I know this number is supposed to be for emergencies. But, Jenna, I don't know how long I can go on like this." Her voice broke, and Jenna could hear her pain. "I thought to myself: 'Maybe this weekend I'll finally tell the boys I'm gay. And maybe they'll try to understand because they love me.' But today they came home from school talking about fags and dykes in the cruelest, ugliest way. And I knew I'd just been trying to kid myself. They won't understand if I tell them I'm one of those dykes. They'll hate me."

Jenna said nothing.

"Tell me I'm wrong, Jenna. Please."

Jenna sighed. "I can't, Toni. You're an intelligent woman. You know the boys will be angry. Maybe they'll even think they hate you for a while. But . . ."

"But what? They'll get past that? They'll love me the way they do now?"

"You know better than that. Nothing stays the same. But what's the alternative? You're miserable now."

"I know you're disappointed in me, Jenna."

"This isn't about pleasing me. It's your life, Toni. I just want to help you live it the best way you know how."

"And honesty is the best way."

"You said that, I didn't."

There was a long silence. "I'll see," Toni said heavily. "I'll just have to see if I can find the courage."

"I'd be happy to schedule a family counseling session if you need one," Jenna offered. But she hung up feeling like a hypocrite. How could she urge Toni to be honest when she'd been lying to her own son for years?

• • •

Even Sandra Waters seemed impressed as she strolled, the camera following her, along the decks of the *Jihan*. "She measures three hundred feet from stem to stern," Sandra said. "The price tag? Forty million dollars. Another thirty million for decorating. Put it all together and you have what may be the most luxurious private vessel the world has ever seen—a floating pleasure palace with its own movie theater and film library, a beauty salon, and a helicopter landing pad."

File footage showed the yacht at sea. "With fifty luxury cabins and a crew of sixty, the *Jihan* can cruise eighty-five hundred miles—once across the Pacific and twice across the Atlantic—without refueling. Her converters produce almost ten thousand gallons of fresh water a day from seawater. Her six king-size refrigerators carry a three-month supply of food."

The video returned to Sandra, entering a cabin. "But perhaps the most dramatic features of this vessel," she said with the enthusiasm of a real-estate agent, "are the bathrooms. This one," she pointed out, "shaped like a scallop shell, is carved and polished from a single block of onyx. The fixtures are twenty-four-karat gold. And this one," she continued after a jump cut, "features a huge white onyx bathtub, Chinese jade fixtures, and its own twin waterfalls."

Waters opened the door of an even more extravagant suite. "Here we have an elmwood latticework ceiling and electronically operated secret doors. A hot tub. Eight-foot circular bed. A salon that replicates a suite at the Plaza Athenée. And more and more and more. It all belongs to this man, the owner of this humble little vessel—Malik Badir."

"Good evening, Sandra," Malik said a bit self-consciously, rising to greet his interviewer. "Welcome aboard the *Jihan*."

Maybe it was the lighting, but to Jenna he looked tired, dark shadows under his eyes. Yet there was still the familiar smile, the well-remembered swagger, as he answered Waters's questions.

"You launched the *Jihan* a year ago. I've heard that the christening party lasted a full week. True?"

"Oh, yes. In fact, I'm not sure that some of the guests aren't still here."

"And your date for the party was—"

"Yes." There was no need to mention the name of the recently divorced and very famous film star Malik had been seeing at the time; everyone watching knew the story.

"Are you two still . . ."

"Oh, we see each other often. We're friends—maybe best friends."

"But you have other . . . friends."

Malik smiled. "Thank God it's not against the law to enjoy the company of beautiful women. Otherwise I could be arrested for this visit with you, Sandra."

Sandra Waters positively simpered before catching herself. "But there's no one special person in your life?"

"Many special people. But what you're asking, I think, Sandra, is whether I'm on the verge of marrying someone. I'm sorry to say no." He did look genuinely sad. "I have no plans in that direction. No one, really, could replace my beloved wife."

The newswoman respectfully recounted the story of Genevieve's accident. "Then there was another brush with tragedy," she said to Malik. "You were shot in a kidnap attempt on your daughter. You lost an arm."

Jenna gasped. She hadn't really noticed the way Malik's jacket fell; it looked casually draped over his shoulders. Now she saw that the left sleeve was simply empty.

". . . told me the wound wasn't dangerous," her brother was saying, "although the bone was smashed. But then there were complications, infection. Nothing to do but lop it off."

My God, thought Jenna, *how could this happen? Why didn't I know?*

"Would you say that your success, your vast wealth, has been a mixed blessing?" asked Sandra Waters, reaching out to touch Malik's good arm. Jenna would have given one of her own arms to trade places with her at that moment.

Malik merely shrugged.

"And now there's another difficulty in your life," Waters went on. "I'm sure you know what I mean. Rumors are rampant that you're about to be charged with violating French espionage laws for your part in the sale of Mirage jets to a third-world nation—the aircraft then being resold to the kingdom of al-Remal?"

Jenna hadn't heard of this, either.

"A misunderstanding," said Malik, "which will soon be cleared up."

"Just a misunderstanding?"

"Of course."

"Would you care to elaborate?"

"No. But trust me, it will be cleared up soon."

Jenna was watching so intently that she hadn't noticed Karim entering the room.

"Do you know him?" he asked, a bit too casually. "Malik Badir?"

"Why do you ask?"

"I don't know. Just the way you looked. I thought maybe he was someone you'd met."

"Does he seem like someone I'd be likely to meet?"

"I don't know. Just asking."

• • •

For two days Jenna worried about her brother's legal problems. She had to know more, more than he was willing to say on television. Finally she decided to call Laila, just this once. She had heard from her niece twice since their last meeting, then nothing. Jenna couldn't blame her, not after she had broken off their budding relationship with lame-sounding excuses. Besides, Laila must have a hundred better things to do than call a woman she scarcely knew.

Laila, still at the Pierre, didn't seem surprised by Jenna's call. "How have you been?" she asked.

"Fine, fine. And you? Are you enjoying Columbia?"

"Yeah. A lot."

"Let's see . . . you must be a junior now."

"Senior."

"Ah. And your father," said Jenna as casually as she could. "I don't want to pry, but there have been stories . . ."

"You mean the Sandra Waters thing?"

"Well . . . yes."

"That's nothing to worry about. Nothing he can't handle. He has a lot of enemies, you know. They started this whole business. But he'll get it all straightened out. He told me he would."

Jenna could almost hear Malik—confident, even arrogant. A far cry from the young man who'd fled al-Remal to save his life and that of his daughter. And yet, she thought, Sandra Waters had been right. There was so much his money couldn't buy. Genevieve was dead. And Laila—would she not have been happier, safer, with a simpler life, a simpler father?

The call ended with mutual promises to be in touch, but Jenna could tell that Laila's thoughts were elsewhere—on a boyfriend, perhaps? She tried to picture Malik's attitude toward his little girl's growing up. Would the aging rebellious son approve of the same tendencies in his daughter? She had to smile at the thought.

• • •

Chance. Serendipity. That was all it was.

Jenna almost canceled out of the conference, even though she was one of the presenters. She simply had too much work to do, she told herself, to fly off for a long weekend in Puerto Rico.

It was Karim who finally convinced her to go. "All the kids I know, their parents take vacations," he said. "You never take one. You *need* some R and R, Mom, even if it's just hanging out on a beach with some other shrinks." It wasn't a self-serving argument aimed at getting an unsupervised weekend. Karim would be spending the time with the Hamids at the professor's cottage on the Cape.

"Maybe you're right," she admitted. Lately, even with her work and her worries about Malik—or perhaps exactly because of those things—she had felt as if her life was stagnating. A tropical beach sounded good.

As she settled into a comfortable business-class seat on the early-morning American Airlines flight to San Juan, she debated whether to review the paper she would be presenting. *Let it go, Jenna. You know the material like the back of your hand. Just relax and enjoy.* Her duties at the conference would require, at most, half a day. The rest of the time would be hers.

Her moment of pleasant anticipation was broken by a deep, gravelly voice, answered by a woman's laugh. She opened her eyes. The flight attendant was fairly fluttering around the man she was ushering into the seat next to Jenna's. He was lean and deeply tanned, with rather weary-looking gray eyes and blond hair lightly streaked with gray.

"Can I get you a magazine?" the young woman asked breathlessly. "Something to drink?"

"Aw, darlin', I promised my Mama never to drink before noon. But then, I promised Mama all kinds of things. How 'bout a Bloody Mary once we're in the air?"

The flight attendant laughed again, as if this were the wittiest human speech she had ever heard.

Really, Jenna thought, *how obvious could a woman get?*

"Travis Haynes, ma'am," drawled her seatmate, turning towards Jenna, waiting for her to supply her own name.

"Jenna Sorrel." She said it as unencouragingly as possible.

Mr. Haynes seemed not to notice. "Pretty name," he said.

As soon as the Fasten Seat Belts sign winked off, the flight attendant was there with his drink. "Could I have your autograph, pretty please?" she pleaded, batting her eyes in a way that Jenna had thought existed only in television sitcoms.

Travis Haynes signed a napkin. "Maybe this lady would like something, too," he suggested pointedly.

"No, thank you," said Jenna.

"Thank *you*, Mr. Haynes," the young woman gushed as she departed.

"An old-time stew," Travis commented to Jenna. "It's kind of like a Harley-Davidson. You might not want to drive one, but it's sorta nice to know they still make 'em."

Jenna had to smile despite herself. Coming from some men, the remark would have been offensive. Travis Haynes made it sound innocent and—well, funny. Who was this man with the most obvious kind of charm and a southern accent so thick that at first she could hardly understand him?

"She certainly seems to think highly of *you*," she pointed out.

"Occupational hazard," Travis replied.

"What occupation would that be?" Did she really want to know?

"Oh, I get up on stage and grunt and groan, and some people call it country singin'. I reckon not everybody has heard of me, though. That's okay," he assured her, although she had certainly not apologized for her ignorance. "I have a way of dropping out of the public eye just when I have a chance of making myself a household name."

"Really? Why do you suppose that is?" Jenna was professionally curious. Besides, she found the man's self-deprecating manner oddly appealing, a pleasant change from the average Bostonian. Here, evidently, was the species Americans called a "good ol' boy."

"Damned if I know. But my agent sure as hell has some ideas. None of 'em are too flattering, though."

"Such as?"

"Oh, she used to say I was a damn fool and let it go at that. Now she's into some kind of '*ther*apy' "—he made the word sound like witchcraft—"and she says I have a fear of success."

"And do you believe that?" Jenna asked, wondering if the agent was simply an agent or perhaps something more.

"Can't say I do. Otherwise, I wouldn't be on my ninth or tenth comeback."

"Wouldn't you?" The professional again.

Travis noticed. "You ask a lot of questions. What do you do for a living?"

"I'm a psychologist," she said, wondering why she sounded so apologetic.

He grinned wide, his gray eyes sparkling with amusement. "Well, I'll be damned. I sure know when to open my mouth. So have you been shrinking me, Doc?"

Jenna smiled and said nothing.

"Well, okay, then, if you won't answer that question, I'll try another. How about taking in my show at the Hilton tonight? Ringside seat, champagne—the whole nine yards."

Jenna was startled. It had been a while, a long while, since anyone had asked her out. Her manner and demeanor didn't normally encourage flirtation or banter.

"I'm going to be very busy," she said with a polite smile. "I don't think I'll have time for any shows."

But she had underestimated Travis's persistence. Before the meal was served, he had cajoled her into agreeing to see his "ninth or tenth comeback." And by the time they'd landed, she had learned a few basic facts of his life. He was forty-one, younger than he looked. He'd been singing since he was twelve—"for pay, that is. Just singin' for fun, I been doin' a lot longer than that." Although he'd never been a star of the first magnitude, Travis had made lots of money, spent it, made more, spent it again. "I guess I do that so I have to keep working," he explained. And Jenna allowed that he might be right.

• • •

Is this really me? she wondered as she sang "You Are My Sunshine" with Travis to the accompaniment of the karaoke in the Hilton lounge. It certainly wasn't Amira Badir. And as for Jenna Sorrel, had she ever been this silly, this giddy? She hadn't—and yet she was enjoying every minute of it.

The show had been great fun—the sequined dancers, the so-so magician, even the corny ventriloquist. She had enjoyed the meaningful smiles Travis had aimed in her direction when he sang, the squeals of delight emitted by his female fans. And she could not deny she was flattered when he introduced her at the end of his set as "my beautiful lady friend from Bah-ston."

His easy, guileless enthusiasm swept her along to an impromptu party in the lounge, Travis singing his personal favorites for the crowd that gathered happily to hear him. And when he'd had enough of singing, he took Jenna by the hand and showed her around the casino, encouraging her to try her hand at roulette and blackjack and craps.

It was all very different from her experience in London and Monte Carlo with Ali. Travis made it all seem like a big joyful game for overaged children. When he lost, he moaned and groaned dramatically. And when he won, he whooped and shouted and ordered drinks for the table.

Is this really me? she wondered again later, in his arms. Could there be a more mismatched couple? But differences didn't seem to matter when they walked the beach at dawn, when they swam at sunrise and kissed just before falling asleep in Travis's enormous king-size bed.

For the rest of her all-too-short stay in Puerto Rico, Travis courted and wooed Jenna as she had not been courted before. With flowers and compliments, and laughter. He gave her fun by day—the kind she might have known as a teenager, had she grown up in America—and tenderness by night. And though she slept very little, she felt refreshed and renewed.

When it was time to go, she felt awkward. Had this been the beginning of a relationship? An interlude? What did she want it to be?

They separated at the airport. Travis had one more week in San Juan, then an engagement in Los Angeles.

"I want to see you again," he said solemnly.

She nodded and gave him her card.

They kissed good-bye.

On the flight home, the whole weekend seemed almost like a dream, something far removed from the reality to which she was returning. How on earth could she explain Travis to Karim? Or to herself, for that matter? All she knew was that he'd been like the proverbial breath of fresh air, bringing a new dimension to her monastic life.

She tried to think of ways to prepare her son. "I had a lovely time," she told him. "Puerto Rico is beautiful."

"Uh-huh," he replied.

"I met a lot of new people. Nice people."

"That's good."

She needn't have worried. It was more than six weeks before she heard from Travis.

"I'm doing two nights in Toronto," he said without prelude or apology, as if they'd spoken a day or two ago, "and then two nights in Boston. I'd like to come see you, if that's okay."

"All right," she said, not at all sure it would be. Once again she tried to pave the way by telling Karim that a friend would be coming by that weekend to take her to dinner. "His name is Travis Haynes."

"A man? You're going out to dinner with a man? When did all this happen?"

"There is no 'this,' " she said, trying to remain calm. Maybe her son was deliberately kidding her, but his proprietary attitude reminded her too much of his father.

Travis arrived on a Friday night, still wearing his stage costume: a cowboy suit of white satin embellished with rhinestones. Karim and Jacqueline were in the kitchen making popcorn. Karim scowled as he was introduced. Jacqueline smirked.

"I've got a present for you, darlin'," Travis said, handing Jenna a big, brightly wrapped package.

"Oh, you shouldn't have," she said. And when it turned out to be an outfit that matched his, she repeated the sentiment, not daring to look at either Karim or Jacqueline.

As quickly as politeness would allow, she whisked Travis away from the apartment. Once they were away from disapproving eyes, she relaxed enough to enjoy mussels and pasta in the North End and coffee and dessert at the Copley Plaza, where Travis was staying. She could not, however, relax enough for anything more.

"I can't," she said, not altogether regretfully, for what seemed right in Puerto Rico just didn't seem appropriate in Boston. "Karim just wouldn't understand."

"Well, if he won't, then I guess I'll just have to," Travis drawled, and Jenna kissed him for that.

• • •

"He's not right for you," Karim pronounced the following morning, sounding so much like a parent that she would have laughed had she not been so annoyed.

His reaction was normal enough. Karim had never had to deal with the prospect of sharing her with anyone else. It didn't take a degree in psychology to understand that.

But when Travis called several times over the next few months, it was clear Karim's objections were more specific: "If you have to date someone, why don't you date an Arab man? Are you ashamed of what you are?"

"I wasn't searching for anyone to date," she explained patiently. "I just met a very nice man while I was on the plane. Don't you think I should have any life of my own?"

Karim glowered at her. Again, for a terrible moment, she thought she glimpsed Ali.

• • •

Travis's schedule—and his natural inclination to roam—did not allow him to be a constant presence in Jenna's life. And, in truth, this suited her. Though it wasn't the kind of emotional connection she had made with Philippe, Travis had brought her out of her self-imposed isolation. He had allowed her to play, to be less serious, less intense, to laugh at herself once in a while, and at life. To be young. After she jokingly referred to their part-time love affair, Travis wrote a song called "Part-Time Lover" and dedicated it to her.

• • •

"Badir Fined, Ending Mirage Case" read the headline in the *Wall Street Journal*. After months of murky revelations about dubious international banking practices and the business and personal habits of several high

European officials, the investigation into Malik's business affairs ended with a series of low-level results. Several minor bureaucrats were forced to resign. Malik, except for the fine—which was huge—got off unscathed.

Elated and relieved that Malik would be all right, Jenna was in a celebratory mood. Unfortunately, she couldn't tell anyone why. Probably it was her mood of willfully suppressed happiness that caused her to say "Why not?" when Travis called that very night and invited her to accompany him on part of his summer tour. She could easily manage a couple of weeks' vacation in August, especially since Karim had already made plans to spend most of the month at the Chandler home in Newport.

Yet no sooner had she said yes than Jenna began to have second thoughts. She had never spent more than a weekend in Travis's company. What would they do for days on end? And how would she adapt to his gypsy lifestyle?

Don't be ridiculous, she told herself. *We'll have a great time. It will do me good to break out of my routine.*

But her concerns turned out to be well founded. The tour wasn't the fun interlude she had expected. It was more like nonstop madness. Worse, Travis's drinking, gambling, and partying weren't as charming to her on a daily basis as they'd been for a night or two snatched here and there. And Jenna's interest in intellectual topics didn't fascinate Travis over the long run as much as it had in short installments.

As August ended, it was clear to both of them that their peripatetic love affair was over.

Their parting was neither bitter nor angry.

"Still friends?" Travis asked with his trademark grin.

"Always," Jenna promised, feeling both sad and relieved. She had been raised to believe that relationships were a serious matter. And she had never been really comfortable with the idea that sex—or a man—could be simply for recreation. Yet . . . what it amounted to was that, before Travis, she had never really known how lonely she was. And now she knew.

Ironically, their breakup made Travis's career. He wrote a bittersweet song about their parting titled "That's You and Me All Over." It hit the top of the country charts, the first of his songs to do so. After nine or ten comebacks, he was at last a star.

• • •

That same August brought the Iraqi invasion of Kuwait, and the winter that followed, with Operation Desert Storm, was the winter of Karim's greatest discontent. It was not that he favored Iraq and Saddam Hussein, but he fervently believed that Egypt had been coerced into the war on the American side and that Americans had no understanding of or sympathy for the Arab world.

It was strange to hear all this from a boy who still had a poster of former Red Sox third baseman Wade Boggs on his wall and who spoke in a pure Boston accent. But in fact Jenna could agree with him up to a point. The problem was that she had seen Middle Eastern politics from backstage and was far less inclined than Karim to draw hard moral lines.

Unfortunately, any word of moderation from her led to torrential idealistic arguments from him. Part of the problem, she was certain, was Karim's continued hero worship of Nasser Hamid. Under the influence of Jacqueline's father, Karim had been reading voraciously about the Middle East in general and Egypt in particular. He had decided that the history and politics of the region would be his area of specialization in college. Perhaps he would become a diplomat—a career that would bring him a sense of connection with what he believed were his roots.

"Don't diplomats have to learn to see both sides of issues?" she asked pointedly.

"Not all diplomats are cowards," he answered.

Like his anger, Karim's plans made Jenna feel guiltier than ever. Her son was building on something that never was. Well, his grandmother was Egyptian—at least that part was true, wasn't it?

Not good enough, her conscience responded. *You've cheated the boy. You've filled his head with fairy tales when he is, in fact, a royal prince.*

But it couldn't be helped. It just couldn't be helped.

EVASIONS

In al-Remal the weather rarely changed in any way except slowly and gradually. In Boston it could go from warm sunlight to icy storm in a matter of minutes. Living with Karim was a bit like living with the Boston weather.

For example, there was the morning the car arrived. It was a Saturday, and Jenna had made Karim an enormous brunch. They had eaten in relative peace, exchanging a few innocuous comments about the colleges he was considering: Harvard, Yale, Dartmouth, and Brown.

A car horn broke the stillness of their quiet, sedate street. It didn't sound like the usual angry signal that someone was double-parked, blocking the signaler. The honking was enthusiastic, exuberant. Jenna went to the window. A bright red Corvette sat at the curb. A young man in a sports coat and tie was looking for someone else—there were, after all, four other apartments in the building. Then her bell rang, three staccato bursts.

"Delivery for Dr. Jenna Sorrel," said the voice on the intercom. "You'll have to come down to accept it, though."

"What's up?" said Karim from the table.

"A mistake of some kind. Come down with me, would you, Karim?"

Karim took one look at the Corvette and delivered an "Awesome" that sounded genuinely awed.

With an elaborate flourish the sports-coated stranger led Jenna to the car, then presented her with keys and the title paper. On the windshield was a note: *"The gift tax is paid, too. I couldn't have done it without you. Love. Trav."*

When Karim saw the note, the sun-to-ice change took place. He glared at his mother and at the car, his expression that of an executioner. "What," he demanded, "did you do to earn this?" He went inside without looking back.

For a moment she debated sending the car back. She could call Travis, explain it in a way that wouldn't hurt his feelings. But, damn it, this was *her* gift, and she wasn't going to let her son spoil it. If she started running her life according to his moods, she would be institutionalized in a week.

"Hop in," she said to the young man. "I'll give you a lift back to your shop."

When she returned, Karim was in his room, the door shut tight.

It was one episode among many. Jenna missed the easy closeness she and her son had once shared. Where had he gone, the good-natured boy who believed she could do no wrong? And how long would the new one be in residence, the one who argued, criticized, disapproved?

She understood that this was normal teenage behavior. Her son was testing his limits, extending his boundaries, reaching for adult status. Being angry with your parents, disapproving of them, was part of growing up, of making the separations that pave the road to independence. It was natural.

All well and good. But as a mother, Jenna simply wanted her son to behave as if he loved her.

Ah, well; if the change was inevitable, it was also probably temporary. Someday, when Karim was secure in his own adulthood, they would come together again, on a new and more equal basis. Wouldn't they? Surely they would.

It was a comforting assumption. How could she know that in a few short seasons it would be blown away like chaff on the wind?

• • •

Another sudden storm, this time over Jenna's avoidance of the Hamids, *père et fille*. Professor Hamid was hosting a small party, mainly for his faculty friends, to whom he would show slides from his last trip to Luxor. Jenna, Karim emphasized, was especially invited.

She begged off, pleading work to do. Karim went alone, in a huff.

What could she have done, Jenna wondered guiltily. She couldn't tell her son that if there was anything she dreaded, it was being in a room full of specialists on her alleged country of birth. She couldn't tell him that Professor Hamid's unctuous flirtations made her skin crawl. And she most certainly couldn't tell him that she heartily disliked Jacqueline's air of superiority and almost everything else about her. Almost everything. At least the girl didn't use drugs, and she didn't appear to be sexually precocious. To the contrary, Jenna observed, she apparently had a zealot's aversion to the pleasures of the flesh. And heaven knows, she was politically correct.

To assuage her guilt over the white lie about work, Jenna called Toni Ferrante to ask how she was doing.

"I had brunch with the boys on Sunday," Toni reported. "They're still living with their father, but they said they'd spend the weekend with me."

One for the good guys, Jenna thought. Maybe Toni's years of suffering and self-doubt were at last leading to a positive outcome. Jenna felt a satisfaction that was as much personal as professional, for she had really come to care for Toni.

There was one genuine piece of work to do—keying in and printing out a grant proposal she had prepared on behalf of thc Sanctuary. Jenna had labored long and hard on her plea for funds. She considered her work at the shelter as important as anything she'd ever done.

She had never ceased to wonder how many American women—often capable, talented, otherwise independent women—suffered abuse in their personal lives. She felt an ongoing frustration at this dark, dirty little secret that so many women carried alone for so long, the shame they suffered, the feeling that the abuse was their fault—and somehow even deserved. What made Jenna's work harder was the lack of empathy and compassion. Even professionals in other fields would ask, "Why don't these women just leave? What's wrong with them? Why do they stay with men who beat them?"

There were so many answers, Jenna tried to explain. Fear of the unknown. Fear of enraging the violence-prone spouse. Low self-esteem. A sense that there was no place to go. And in the end, sometimes there were no easy answers at all. Because while there were women who stayed and stayed, beyond daily abuse until their own deaths, there *were* others who left. Some came to the Sanctuary or a thousand other places like it. Some simply ran, as Jenna had done, with no idea where their stories would end.

When the doorbell rang, she assumed it was Karim, habitually forgetful of his keys.

It was Laila.

"Hi," the girl—the young woman—said, as if it had been only yesterday that they'd parted in front of the Plaza.

Jenna stared for a long moment, almost overcome by a rush of tenderness. She found her voice, trying to keep her manner light. "Laila! What a surprise. How good to see you! What brings you here?"

"Well, I . . . actually, I came to say good-bye. Not good-bye exactly, not forever, but I'm going away."

"To France?" Jenna's heart sank. Though she hadn't seen her niece in—God, how long?—it had been a comfort to know that she was in New York, within easy reach. They had talked a couple of times on the telephone, and Jenna had tried to make that enough.

"No. Nothing like that. I transferred to UCLA. I'm going to study filmmaking. It's a really good school for that, you know."

"So I've heard. But what about New York? I thought you loved being in the city. Come in, Laila, don't stand in the doorway. We can talk inside."

Laila took a few steps forward, then stopped. "I can only stay a minute. I have a ride—some friends who dropped me off. They just went to the deli. They'll be back any second."

"You came all the way to Boston to stop by for a minute?" Jenna couldn't make any sense of this.

"I was visiting these friends. From school." Laila looked around the apartment, not really taking it in, avoiding Jenna's eyes. She swallowed hard. "I was raped, you know," she said, her voice so low it could hardly be heard. "Four months ago. No, don't look like that. I'm all right. Really."

No, please no, Jenna begged a distant and remote God. *Not my beautiful niece.* "I'm so sorry," she said, struggling to maintain control. "What happened?"

Laila shrugged, a gesture belied by the pain that showed in her face. "It was someone I knew. I even kind of liked him." She shrugged again. "There's no point in going over it. Talking can't change what happened."

Jenna yearned to hold her close and comfort her, but everything about Laila said she wanted distance. *Not good*, Jenna thought, making a professional observation. *And the flattened affect, that's not good either.* "Have you seen anyone? A therapist?"

"Yeah, sure. She helped some . . . I guess." Laila seemed to be studying her shoes. "You know, I thought of coming to you, but it would've been like, I don't know, going to see my mother. Maybe that sounds silly, but . . ."

"No, no it doesn't." It was all Jenna could do to hold back her tears.

"But I'm okay now. It's just one reason I transferred. I wanted to get away."

Though Jenna understood all too well the needs that drove a woman to flee, she wanted to tell Laila that running away wasn't always the answer. "Are you sure—" she began, but at that moment, Karim appeared.

He looked at Jenna, then at Laila. His expression asked: What's going on? But he would never be so blunt with a stranger. He simply smiled and waited for his mother to speak.

Not knowing what else to do, Jenna made the introductions.

"Laila Badir?" Karim repeated. "Are you related to Malik Badir?"

"He's my father."

"Wow. I mean . . ."

"I know," Laila said softly. Obviously, it was a reaction she'd seen many times before.

• • •

But Karim's reaction went deeper than Laila could have suspected. *What are you doing here?* he wanted to ask, frustrated that his mother had given no explanation. He had the oddest sensation that he knew Laila Badir—not just knew who she was, but knew *her.* It was something he couldn't explain.

I'm staring, he realized. But just as he thought it, she suddenly gave him a small, sweet smile. For a moment, it was as if they were the only two people in the room.

"Would you like something to drink?" he asked, feeling awkward. How could his mother have failed to offer their guest any refreshment? Had she forgotten her manners completely? And why did she look so uncomfortable?

"Actually, I'd like some water, thank you."

Karim hurried to the kitchen and put a Perrier with lime on a tray.

"Thank you," Laila repeated. Still standing, she took a few polite sips, then said to Jenna, "I have to go. Really. But like I said, it's not really good-bye. I'll write, call. I'll probably be in New York now and then. And you travel, don't you? You'll be out on the Coast sometime, right?"

"Laila, you must call me if you need . . . anything. Anything at all."

"Sure. Well, *au 'voir.*"

Suddenly they were hugging each other tight. Karim saw the tears in his mother's eyes. When did she meet this girl? Why did she never tell him? And why had she said she didn't know Malik Badir?

"I'll walk you downstairs," he suddenly said as Laila turned toward the door.

Again the little smile. She was years older than he was, a grown-up, really, but somehow the smile made her seem closer to his age.

Her ride hadn't come yet. He was glad.

"You're going to California?" he said for want of a better opener.

"Yes. In a few days."

"Where are you from?"

"France."

"Your father's from al-Remal, isn't he? Did you ever live there?"

"No. I've never lived anywhere in the Middle East. I know a little about it from Papa, I speak serviceable Arabic, but that's about all."

"Oh." He didn't know why he'd expected it to be otherwise. Maybe just the way she looked.

"These days I feel more American than anything else."

A car approached. Her ride? No, it passed. Laila seemed disinclined to say anything more.

"What's he like, your father?" Karim asked to break the sudden silence.

"He's . . . I miss him. He's away a lot."

"How do you know my mom?"

For a moment he was afraid he had said something wrong. Then Laila shrugged. "I met her in Saks in New York."

"Saks Fifth Avenue? The store?" He couldn't remember his mother taking any shopping trips to New York. In fact, even in Boston, she complained that she never had time to go shopping.

Silence. It was as if Laila had gone a little distance away from him. "You were shopping?" he prompted.

"What? Oh." She looked him in the eyes. Again the feeling of recognition. Did she feel it, too? "Actually," she said, "I was shoplifting."

Shoplifting? The daughter of the world's richest man? "But why?"

"It's a long story. But she rescued me." She outlined the events in Saks.

Nothing about it sounded like his mother, who was always so insistent on right and wrong. Something was going on here. Something was being withheld from him.

"Then you're not one of her . . ."

"One of her patients? No."

A car pulled to a stop.

"My ride," said Laila. "Thanks for waiting with me."

"I'd like to see you again," Karim blurted.

She looked startled. "It's not a good time."

"I didn't mean it that way."

Her face softened. "I know. It's just that I'm leaving."

He thought for a moment that she was going to touch him—his arm, perhaps his face. But she didn't.

"I'll send you both my address in California," she said.

Then she was gone.

• • •

In the apartment, Jenna had managed something like calm after Laila's bitterly unexpected news.

What had Karim thought of the visitor? With luck, maybe nothing too hard to explain. If anything, he had seemed rather puppyishly smitten with her.

He came back in, his expression one that was new to her, a mixture of puzzlement and—what? Hope?

"How do you know Laila Badir, Mom?"

"She was a patient. Not for long."

"Do you always cry about your patients?"

"Sometimes."

But now his expression was one she knew very well. She had seen it on his father a hundred times.

Eyes flat and blank, as cold and distant from her as some outer planet, he slowly shook his head and disappeared into his room.

• • •

After a night of broken sleep and a brusque "See you later" from her son on his way out in the morning, Jenna was trying to concentrate on her first patient's troubles with his brother when Barbara, her new secretary, buzzed.

Jenna's policy, like that of almost all her colleagues, was that sessions were to be interrupted only for emergencies.

"Yes?"

"Jenna, there's a police officer out here. She says it's important."

Jenna's first thought was Karim. Then, for some reason, Laila.

The woman was in plainclothes. "Detective Sue Keller," she said, showing a Boston badge. "You're Dr. Jenna Sorrel?"

"Yes. What's the matter?"

"You know a Mr. and Mrs. Cameron Chandler?"

"Yes." Oh, God. What now?

"Either of them a patient of yours?"

"No."

"Then I may ask you for a statement later. Just some background information."

"Tell me what's happened."

"Mrs. Chandler is in Mass General. She's in pretty bad shape."

"How bad?"

"She's a good friend of yours, ma'am?"

"Yes."

"Then you might want to get over there. It's bad."

BRAD

Carolyn was in a coma, with massive injuries to her body organs and brain. Cameron was in jail, charged with attempted murder. Jenna knew that much from Sue Keller.

In a waiting room, Josh Chandler looked near shock, as if he had walked away from some terrible accident. "I was going to call you," he said distractedly. "But after I gave the police your name, I didn't know what was right."

"It's okay, Josh. Your mother—have you heard anything?"

"No, I don't know, Miz Sorrel. Oh, God. I . . . I don't think it's good." He choked back a sob.

"Have you seen her?"

"Not since they took her into surgery."

"Josh, what happened?"

"Like I told the police, I heard them arguing—fighting—this morning, early. I guess Dad had . . . just come in. It was worse than . . . I should have done something, but, you know?"

"I know. I know. You didn't do anything wrong."

"Then it quieted down. I went back to sleep. I mean, it's happened before. Not like this, but . . ."

"It's not your fault, Josh. What happened then?"

"Nothing. I mean, I woke up and started to get ready for school. And Mom and Dad's door was open, and I looked in and saw Mom on the floor—" Josh's voice broke. "And Dad—Dad had all his ties spread out on the bed. He was like, trying them on. He said, 'You'd better do something about this, Josh.' And I called nine-one-one."

"Do you have anyone, Josh? Relatives?"

"Grandmom—my mom's mom—she's on her way from Connecticut. I think she'll stay at the house until . . . whatever happens."

"That's good. But if you'd like to stay with Karim and me, you're more than welcome. Just pack a bag and come over."

"Thanks, Miz Sorrel. Maybe I will. But not tonight. Tonight I want to stay with Mom."

"Okay," said Jenna. "I'm going to see what I can find out."

But all she could learn, even after rather deceptively identifying herself as *Dr.* Sorrel, was that Carolyn was still in surgery. Only hours later did a nurse finally give her the word: "She's in Intensive Care now, Doctor, if you'd care to look in for a minute. Room two-six-two-three."

• • •

Against the crisp white linen of her narrow bed, Carolyn looked frail and utterly fragile, her swollen face the texture and color of rotten fruit. Plastic tubes everywhere. *That's how I looked in al-Remal*, Jenna thought. *Philippe came for me. I was lucky. I lived. God willing, God willing, Carolyn will be lucky too.*

"Dr. Sorrel?" A sallow, weary-looking man in surgeon's green.

"Yes."

"Stan Morgan. You're the primary care?"

"No. Just a friend of the family."

"Oh. Well, Doctor, I don't know how much you want to know about this."

"Just the prognosis."

Morgan grimaced. "Not good, I'm afraid, although it's still early. We could lose her. Even if we don't, we may be looking at wysiwyg here."

Jenna understood just enough computerese to know that "wysiwyg" meant "what you see is what you get." "Irreversible coma?"

Morgan rattled off some technical details of trauma, hemorrhage, oxygen deprivation. What it amounted to was that if Carolyn lived at all, it would be in a vegetative state.

A death sentence, Jenna thought. And all because Carolyn had loved Cameron Chandler.

• • •

Josh had been joined by Carolyn's mother, a petite, delicately lovely china doll of a woman. Jenna hugged the boy, feeling she had let him down, and murmured a few empty words of comfort to his grandmother.

"You and Carolyn must be good friends," said Margaret Porter.

"I . . . yes, we're good friends." She said it more to comfort Mrs. Porter than to ease her own conscience. She knew all too well how Cameron had isolated Carolyn from anyone who wanted to be her friend—anyone who might interfere with his control.

"I'm glad," Mrs. Porter sighed. "She'll need her friends around her if she . . . when she . . ."

"I know," Jenna said softly. "And her friends will be there for her, I promise."

"She was such a good girl," Mrs. Porter murmured. "Never any trouble."

Don't talk about her that way, Jenna wanted to say. *It sounds as if she's already gone.* But she simply nodded. "I think they'll let you see her now. Just be prepared. She's very badly hurt. But sometimes these things look worse than they are." Words, empty words.

• • •

Night. The lights of the city looked like close but intensely lonely stars.

Visiting hours had ended. Josh and his grandmother were going to the Chandler home after all; the hospital discouraged overnight stays by patients' relatives, and it was clear that they could do nothing more here. Karim had arrived after school and was going with his friend.

Exhausted both mentally and physically, Jenna stopped in the hospital cafeteria for a desperately needed cup of tea. But the steaming liquid did little to soothe her troubled spirit or ease her guilt.

As she rose to leave, she noticed a man nursing a cup of coffee a few tables away. A beautiful patrician face, close-cut dark hair, blue-blue eyes. And the saddest expression she'd ever seen. What was his story? Jenna wondered. Was a loved one upstairs fighting for life? Was there still hope? Or had the battle been lost? Those blue eyes were so expressive—so like Philippe's.

The following day she stopped by the hospital during the lunch hour and hurried back as soon as she had finished with her last patient. Mrs. Porter's husband had arrived, and the couple sat mournfully in a corner. Karim was there to provide support and companionship for Josh, whose eyes were red-rimmed and puffy.

Nothing had changed for Carolyn except that the prognosis was now more certain: irreversible coma.

For hours, Jenna kept watch beside the empty shell that had once been her friend. The boys left the hospital at dinnertime, and the Porters retired to the waiting room. Jenna stayed at Carolyn's bedside as if through sheer presence and devotion she could remedy the past, restore the future. She massaged Carolyn's hands, even talked to her, giving little bits of news and encouragement. Maybe, just maybe it would help.

Once again, she ended her vigil with a trip to the hospital cafeteria—and once more the sad-looking man was there. Khaki pants and a crew neck sweater over a white oxford shirt—like an aging college boy, Jenna thought, finding the image sweet and somehow vulnerable. Impulsively, she put her cup of tea on the table next to his. "I hope you don't mind," she said, "but you look as sad as I feel. It might help to talk about it."

The man tried to smile but failed. "My wife's upstairs," he said in a soft, slightly hoarse baritone. "She has cancer."

"I'm so sorry," Jenna murmured. "But this is a good hospital, one of the best. I hope . . ."

The man shook his head. "No," he said heavily, "I'm afraid not. It's just a matter of waiting. And saying good-bye."

Jenna couldn't bring herself to utter more platitudes. After a few sips of her tea, she left with a murmured "Good night."

The following night, as if by agreement, they had their coffee and tea together. She told him about Carolyn. He shook his head in sadness and anger when she described the beating.

"And your wife?" she asked. "Any news?"

"Nothing good. But it won't be long now." For a few moments, he seemed to drift away. "I'm sorry," he said finally. "I seem to have forgotten my manners. My name is Brad Pierce."

"Jenna Sorrel. Do you work nearby?"

"I own a pharmaceutical company, out on route one-twenty-eight."

Though he did not elaborate, Jenna made the connection at once: Pierce Pharmaceuticals was one of the largest in the world.

"It's ironic," he was saying. "No, it's . . . cruel. The things we're researching now, recombinant DNA, we're learning something new about the immune system every day. In five years, I believe, maybe less, we'll have something that could have saved her."

Then it was Jenna's turn to tell something about herself. When she mentioned the Sanctuary, she saw a flicker of interest in the blue eyes.

"You might want to get in touch with the Pierce Foundation," Brad said. "We fund a lot of charities and causes."

"Thank you. We depend on donations and grants to keep afloat—but somehow there's never enough to help everyone who needs it."

He nodded, as if he'd heard the story before. "The foundation was really Pat's idea," he explained. "She's been far more active in it than I have. This is the kind of thing she'd support one hundred percent." He sighed wearily. "I need to get back upstairs. It was nice meeting you. I'm serious about contacting the foundation."

"Thanks. It was nice meeting you, too."

His interest seemed so genuine that the next night Jenna brought along some public relations material on the Sanctuary, as well as a few newspaper stories on the work they did. But, to her disappointment, Brad Pierce was not at his usual spot in the cafeteria. Odd how she had come to expect him, almost as if it were a rendezvous. Something must have happened, she thought, but feeling it would be intrusive to inquire, she simply went home.

• • •

The *Boston Globe* devoted a half page to Patricia Bowman Pierce's obituary, listing all her charitable works and noting her many awards from philanthropic organizations. The accompanying photograph showed an attractive woman with an open, friendly expression and a trusting smile. "*Mrs. Pierce is survived by her husband, Bradford,*" the obituary concluded, "*her parents,*

Mr. and Mrs. Colin Bowman, a sister, Karen, and a brother, Dexter." No children, Jenna noted. How sad that must be for Brad.

Though her appointment book was crammed with obligations, Jenna took the time to write him a note. "*We don't really know each other,*" she began, "*but my thoughts and my sympathy are with you today. I know what it's like to lose someone very precious and very dear. If there's anything I can do to ease your pain, please let me know. Sincerely, . . .*"

In the days that followed, she thought often of Brad, wondering how he was coping with his loss, remembering the tenderness with which he spoke of his wife, the love that was there in his face for all the world to see. When a white vellum envelope from "B. Pierce" arrived, she was oddly disappointed that it contained only a conventional thank-you note—polite but brief—the kind of acknowledgment Brad must have sent to hundreds of people.

Well, what did you expect? she chided herself. *Why should he remember a few brief conversations in a hospital cafeteria? This isn't like me*, she thought, *this feeling of unfinished business—words unspoken, deeds not yet done—with this near-stranger who has just lost his wife.*

The feeling gradually faded in the turmoil of her own life. There was Karim, who would soon be starting his freshman year at Harvard. Although Jenna had persuaded him to live at home the first year, he would soon begin a life of his own, away from her. Then she would be alone.

And there was the loss of hope for Carolyn: with every passing week, the chances of her recovery grew slimmer, until finally there was no hope at all. Her parents, devout Catholics who could not bring themselves to request the removal of life-support systems, were moving Carolyn to a private nursing facility in Connecticut.

• • •

"We can't go on like this," said Helen Schrieber, one of the Sanctuary's newer counselors. "We're running out of space. We're doubling women and children up in rooms meant for one."

"I know, I know," Jenna said, "I'm working on it. And I hope to have some news soon." In front of her was a copy of the proposal she'd sent to the Pierce Foundation, describing how the Sanctuary served the needs of women and children who had nowhere else to go. An excellent new space was about to come open in the neighborhood. The Sanctuary had taken a ninety-day option. Would the Pierce Foundation help?

She fully expected a call in response to her plea, but none came. Instead, she received a formal letter from someone describing himself as the foundation's executive secretary requesting detailed information on the cost of acquiring and renovating the new space.

Jenna sent the documentation, the money came, and construction on the Patricia Bowman Annex began. That was all there was to it.

I could call him, Jenna thought. *I could thank him personally*. But it was obvious, wasn't it, that he didn't want that kind of contact? She let it go.

Yet when Brad did call—a full five months later—she knew who it was the moment he said hello. She was so thrown off balance that she began to babble about the grant. "We're all so very grateful. We'll be opening the Bowman Annex in a matter of a few weeks. You'll be the guest of honor, of course, and—"

"You're entirely welcome," he cut in. "And I'll be at the inaugural ceremony. But what I've called about is to ask you if you'd like to have dinner with me. Friday evening—or at your convenience."

"A date?" she blurted, wishing the moment she heard her own words that she could yank them back out of the phone.

He laughed. It was a good sound. "Yes," he said. "I suppose that's what it is."

• • •

It was as if she'd never been out with a man, never dressed up to look her best, never been told how beautiful she was. Jenna littered the floor with the contents of her closet, found fault with every garment she owned, then started all over again. She ended up in the most expensive boutique on Newbury Street spending an outrageous sum of money on the kind of outfit she hadn't bought in years—a creamy gabardine suit that lightly caressed the contours of her body. Not particularly suitable for work, but just right, she hoped, for her first date with Brad Pierce.

They met at Locke-Ober's on Winter Place, with Brad apologizing for not picking her up and Jenna assuring him she didn't mind making her own way there.

"But I mind. I'm an old-fashioned guy—like this place," he said, indicating the dark-paneled woodwork, the traditional elegance of the private room he'd reserved. "I meant to come to your door with a bouquet of posies in my hand, but my meeting ran so long, and I didn't want to just keep you waiting, so . . ."

"It's all right," she reiterated. "I'll take the thought for the deed. At least this once," she added boldly, wondering what on earth had gotten into her.

A tuxedo-clad waiter who looked as venerable as the establishment itself hovered discreetly at Brad's elbow. "Shall I serve the wine, sir?"

Brad nodded. "I took the liberty of ordering ahead," he said to Jenna, "but if you'd prefer . . ."

"No," she said, "I like surprises."

Deftly and without showy fanfare, the waiter served the meal: consommé, green salad, grilled game hen accompanied by a fine Côte de Beaune.

"I've passed this place dozens of times," Jenna said. "I never realized it was so . . . so quaint."

"It was my father's favorite restaurant. I brought my first important date here."

"Your wife?" Jenna asked, pleased to follow the tradition of Brad's "first important date."

He nodded. "We met in high school. And there was no more need to look around. I knew it and so did Pat."

"That sounds rather . . . old-countryish."

"I told you—"

"Right," she laughed. "You're an old-fashioned guy." They continued talking over coffee—he, reminiscing about his marriage and apologizing for boring her, she, enjoying his memories and assuring him she wasn't the slightest bit bored.

"You never had children."

"No."

"And you didn't mind." Despite her years in America, Jenna still reacted as a Remali would, finding it remarkable that a man so desirable continued to love a woman who bore no children.

"We both minded. Very much. But . . . Pat couldn't. We sublimated, I guess. Then we talked about all the needy and unwanted children in the world. That's when we started the foundation. Pat traveled to Africa, to India, wherever kids were starving and in need of medical attention. She established group homes in places where kids were living on the streets. And in the last ten years or so, she'd been doing volunteer work with AIDS babies, you know, holding them, cuddling them, helping them feel that someone cares. In fact, she organized a whole army of volunteers to cover all the hospitals in Boston."

"She sounds like a remarkable woman."

"Oh, yes." Brad's eyes glistened as he retreated for a moment into memory. Jenna reached across the table and put her hand over his. The gesture felt right. Strange, she thought, to be drawn to a man *because* he had loved his wife. And yet not so strange; as a psychologist, she knew very well that Brad's devotion to Pat gave testimony to his own capacity to love.

When she noticed the septuagenarian waiter glance at his watch, Jenna looked at her own. "It's awfully late," she said reluctantly. "I think the old gentleman would like us to leave."

• • •

"May I kiss you?" he asked at Jenna's door.

"What?"

"First date," he mumbled.

"My God—you *are* old-fashioned." But Jenna was charmed. "I think," she told him, "I'm old-fashioned, too."

His lips brushed hers; his hand gently stroked her cheek. An undemanding caress but filled with promise, it evoked distant memories of being cared for and loved. She wished it could go on and on.

* * *

She discovered that they had more in common than loss and loneliness. They both loved the North End and the Isabella Gardner Museum; hated diets and much of what passed for modern art. But most important, they discovered that they were easy in one another's company. Whether they were at a Red Sox game or strolling the banks of the Charles, conversation seemed effortless. The silences they shared seemed cozy, not at all like empty spaces needing to be filled.

One Saturday afternoon, after they'd browsed through the cookbooks at Waterstone's and shared a club sandwich at an outdoor café, Brad said, "I'd like you to come to tea. Tomorrow. At my mother's house."

"Your mother?"

"Sure. Bound to happen sometime. I think you're going to be an important part of my life. So we might as well get meeting my mother out of the way. Besides, it could be fun."

Jenna was touched and flattered. But remembering her mother-in-law, the formidable Faiza, she very much doubted that such a meeting would be "fun."

She was right.

Abigail Whitman Pierce was as impressive as her name. Slender, ramrod straight, with crispy gray hair and steely gray eyes, she presided over an antique-filled Beacon Hill home that could well have been a museum.

As she kissed her son on both cheeks in the European manner, there was a softness in Abigail's gray eyes. A moment later, when she turned to Jenna, it was gone.

"Did you know Patricia, my dear?" Abigail asked over crustless watercress sandwiches and Darjeeling tea.

"No," Jenna replied. "But I know she was a very special woman."

"Indeed. She was one of a kind. A perfect wife for Bradford. Irreplaceable, I might add."

Jenna smiled politely, understanding exactly what Abigail meant.

"And where is it that you were from, my dear?"

"Egypt. Cairo. I grew up mainly in France."

"My late husband and I traveled throughout Egypt, let me see, it was about thirty years ago. A colorful place, fascinating history. And the natives . . . so picturesque."

Jenna smarted under Abigail's patronizing manner. *All right*, she thought, *she's a typical mother—like Faiza. No one is good enough for her beloved son*. And yet Patricia Bowman had been good enough.

• • •

"Catastrophe," she said to Brad as they left the Beacon Hill house. "Total planetary destruction."

"Not nearly so bad as that," he argued. "Mother can be daunting, but a sense of humor helps a lot. How do you think I cope with all her subtle little attempts to set me up with what she thinks of as suitable women?"

Jenna was not amused. So Abigail was ready to accept a "suitable" woman. It was Jenna Sorrel she had no use for. *All right*, she told herself, *Abigail doesn't like you—you'll both have to live with that. You don't like Jacqueline, but because Karim does, you've had to tolerate her.*

So she tried not to mind when Abigail turned up at the opening of the Bowman Annex and spent a full half hour telling the *Globe* reporter what a saint Patricia had been—and pointedly ignoring any references to Jenna and her work.

When Brad mentioned that his mother was having a "small gathering" later that evening, Jenna begged off. She'd had enough of Abigail Pierce for one day.

"Oh, come on, be a good sport," Brad coaxed. "We'll wear her down if we work together, Jenna. You'll see."

"Why am I unconvinced?"

"Don't you think I'm worth a little discomfort?" he teased.

She did.

The expression on Abigail's face told Jenna she had neither been invited nor expected. If Abigail was surprised, she recovered quickly, and with one swift authoritative sweep of her arm moved Brad away from Jenna and toward a striking redhead. "Winky's been waiting for you, Bradford," she said smoothly, just as if Jenna hadn't been there. "She's been very patient, and now I think you should make her a martini. I'm sure you know exactly how she likes them."

For a long awkward moment, Jenna didn't know what to do—especially after the redhead threw herself into Brad's arms and began kissing him with noisy exclamations of joy. *All right, Jenna, keep calm.* Forcing a smile, she strolled into the front parlor and tried to mingle with the other guests. Seeing an elderly man standing alone in a corner, she introduced herself.

"What's that?" he shouted, touching his ear to indicate he was hard of hearing.

"Jenna Sorrel," she repeated, raising her voice.

"Jenny who?"

"Sorrel, Sorrel, Jenna Sorrel!"

"I see you've met Eldon," Brad said, suddenly materializing at her elbow.

"Not exactly," she said peevishly. "We still haven't gotten past my name."

"Ah. Well, then, Jenna Sorrel, meet Eldon Baker. Eldon retired from the state senate fifteen years ago. I think he's kept his hearing aid turned down to low ever since." Brad winked at the old man. "I think Eldon's heard enough nonsense to last a lifetime."

Eldon smiled broadly, as if he'd heard and understood every word.

So who's the redhead? Jenna wanted to ask. But she didn't. She wouldn't.

"Are we having fun yet?" Brad whispered in her ear.

"Not yet."

"Okay, let me start introducing you to some of the other nice people here." Taking her by the elbow, he worked his way around the room, making introductions, exchanging politenesses with people he'd clearly known for years. Jenna tried to continue smiling at the mention of names and places she'd never heard before. The smile grew very strained when the redhead joined them, linking arms with Brad and launching into a series of reminiscences that he apparently found hilarious.

Already feeling out of place, Jenna saw just how unwelcome she was when dinner was announced. According to the place cards—done by an expert calligrapher—Brad was seated next to Winky Farrell. Jenna's card, hastily improvised in pencil, had been placed alongside that of Eldon Baker, the old man with the hearing problem.

Anger bubbled up, pushing aside good intentions. She grabbed Brad by the sleeve and dragged him out to the foyer. "That's it," she hissed. "I get your mother's message loud and clear: I'll never be the person Patricia was. And I can't be *Winky*, either! Well, I don't want to be like any of those people your mother likes. I can only be me, and if that's not good enough, then we won't be seeing each other again."

The outburst felt good, even cleansing. In al-Remal, her family had been among the elite, and even here, she was a respected professional. So how dare Brad's mother treat her with such disdain!

But after she slammed her own front door and flung her handbag against the wall, her sense of righteousness began to evaporate. The Badir temper burned hot and cooled quickly. When reason returned, there were sometimes regrets. Yes, it was true, Brad's mother had behaved very badly. But was Brad's own behavior bad enough to warrant storming out of Abigail's house? Without even having a bite to eat? Jenna almost laughed at herself, for she now realized how hungry she was.

The refrigerator had little to offer, and as she rifled through it, trying to assemble a meal from odds and ends, she came up with some limp lettuce, a small tomato, a piece of cheese. Not very appealing.

The doorbell rang. Jenna pushed the intercom. A rough voice: "Pizza delivery."

Had a genie conjured a meal for her? Had to be a mistake. "I didn't order a pizza."

"I got a pizza for this address, lady."

Something about the voice. She went downstairs and looked through the peephole. Brad—with a large pizza.

She opened the door. "You're lucky I'm hungry," she said, unwilling to let him know how relieved she was to see him, how very glad she was that he didn't just let her go.

Sitting in her kitchen, she devoured the everything-but-anchovies pie, letting him do the talking.

"Jenna, we don't really know each other that well. Is your mother still alive?"

"No. She died when I was a teenager."

"Ah. That must have been hard. I'm sorry." Brad touched her hand. "Let me ask you this, then: If she were still alive, wouldn't you put up with all kinds of silliness on her part, just because she was your mother and you loved her?"

Jenna had to admit she would.

"Okay. It's no different with me. Look, the lady I was so subtly paired with tonight—"

"Winky," Jenna noted acidly.

"Yes. Winky, God help us. Gwendolyn's her real name. We've been buddies since we were six."

"Yes?" Jenna's best professional listening attitude.

"And that's it. We were having such a hoot today because . . . well, because we know each other so well. Listen, she wouldn't mind me telling you this—everybody in Boston but Abigail knows anyway—she's in love with her doubles partner."

"I see."

"I'm not sure you do. I'm not talking about mixed doubles."

Suddenly they were both laughing.

"By the way," Brad said, "maybe we should get Abigail and Karim together. They seem to have the same opinion of our seeing each other."

Jenna laughed even harder. It was true. Her son, now a Harvard scholar and at the flood stage of his Egyptophilia, showed Brad only a dry-ice politeness. But now Karim's disapproval no longer upset Jenna. It wasn't that she didn't care what her son thought, she did. No, it was that Jenna felt a rightness about this relationship that she hadn't felt before.

Brad kissed her, without permission this time, their lips lingering, tasting, exploring. "Does this mean we can go steady?" he asked, his blue eyes serious now.

"Go steady?"

"No more Winkys. Or anyone else."

"Yes," she answered, pushing aside fear and conscience, ignoring the nagging voice that reminded her that according to the laws of the United States and al-Remal, her rights to a relationship were limited in the first instance and nonexistent in the second.

• • •

Going steady meant someone to talk to, to share with. Someone who was on her side, who would rub her back when she was tense, who would fix an omelet when she was almost too tired to eat. Someone who cared.

How did I get along without him? Jenna wondered almost every time she looked into those blue-blue eyes.

"I have a cottage in Marblehead," he said one Wednesday night as he tinkered with Jenna's computer, trying to recover a file that had apparently disappeared. "I think you'll like it. Why don't you come up there with me for the weekend?"

"All right," she said, though she knew there was more ahead than a simple summer weekend at the beach.

• • •

"Cottage?" Jenna exclaimed, marveling at the sprawling oceanfront Victorian with gingerbread woodwork, ornate plaster ceilings, and handmade brass fixtures. "You New Englanders certainly believe in understatement."

"The Puritan influence. We feel guilty about having so much, so we pretend we don't."

As he gave Jenna the grand tour of all eighteen rooms, Brad pointed out portraits of his ancestors, the saints and sinners and those who fell somewhere in between. "We even have a pirate somewhere in the bunch. But my grandfather Benjamin—he's the one who built the house—he refused to display the rascal's portrait. He said Kincaid Pierce was hanged once and that should be enough for any man."

Jenna laughed. "I love this place," she said. "It has a lot of character. Like you."

"I'm flattered. Is that a personal judgment—or a professional one?"

"Both." It was true. If she had ever been certain about anything, it was that Brad was one of those very rare individuals: a truly good person. Which made her feel miserable about deceiving him.

Though the house's refrigerator and freezer had been fully stocked by the caretaker, Brad insisted they should have lobsters—"not in a restaurant, but cooked with our own two hands over a driftwood fire, the way God intended."

Everyone in the quaint seaside town seemed to know and like Brad—the policeman who patrolled the streets on foot, the greengrocer who sold them freshly picked corn, the owner of the lobster pound who deliberated at length before selecting two prime specimens. "The best of the lot," he assured Brad, as if nothing less than the best would do for Mr. Pierce.

This is what living with him would be like, she thought. *Relaxed and easy and familiar. Stop it*, she chided herself. *You have no right to that dream.*

"You seem very much at home here," she observed. "Even more than in Boston."

"When I was growing up, we spent every summer here, lots of weekends, too. I always felt that only good things happen here." He paused and squeezed her hand. "I thought you might feel that way, too."

I wish, she thought, *I wish it were that simple.*

"Why did you wait so long?" she asked, as they cooked the lobsters and corn over a wind-fanned fire on a hidden cove of the rocky shore. "To ask me out, I mean."

For a moment, he seemed to go away a little. "I guess I'm a traditionalist," he said. "A mourning period for someone you love is a tradition, and it seemed right to me."

She liked his answer. "Where I was born, we didn't mourn the dead, at least not formally. It's considered irreligious. But, knowing you, I think it's a beautiful custom." She hesitated a moment. "But why me? Why not one of those suitable women Boston seems to be full of?"

The blue eyes twinkled. "Because you're a good listener. Because you're beautiful through and through. Because you seemed to care about me when we were just strangers. Because," he paused, smiling mischievously, "Pat would have liked you."

They made love that night in a big feather bed, a candle burning on the bedside table, casting flickering shadows on the walls. As Brad caressed her, murmuring endearments and promising to love her forever, she gave herself without fear or hesitation. Perhaps for the first time. It was like coming home.

• • •

"I want to marry you," he said as they snuggled together, limbs still intertwined. "It's going to happen sooner or later, so why waste time?"

Jenna was speechless, joy and dread intermingling. Joy that he loved her. Dread at what she would have to say.

"I've learned how precious life is," he continued. "Losing Pat, realizing how quickly it can all slip away."

"But we don't . . . we don't really know each other well," she protested weakly.

"That's what the next fifty years are for. Because I want to know all about you. I want to know where you go when you get so quiet. I want to know why you don't trust our love . . ."

"But I—"

"Hush," he said, gently placing a finger against her lips. "You don't have to explain anything. Not until you're ready. But I want to be with you, Jenna, while you work through whatever it is that stands between us. I don't want to be someone who just waits . . ."

Like a parent comforting a child who has nightmares, Brad spoke eloquently and persuasively. But in the end, it didn't matter. His proposal touched her heart—and broke it into a million pieces.

Because Jenna had to say no.

MIRAGES

The little room off the main lobby of the al-Remal International Airport was clean and not uncomfortable, but there was no mistaking its function: it was a cell. Waiting for the self-important man with the familiar name to return, Laila, like many prisoners, could hardly believe that this was happening to her.

It had started with a phone call.

David Christiansen was a new force in Laila's life—a force and an anchor. She was beginning to believe that he was the one man, besides her father, she could rely on.

She had been running on the edge for a long time when she met David. Recovering from the shock of rape—the outrage, the self-blame, and finally the psychological numbness—had been like going through a dark tunnel, and when she came out on the other side, it was hard to take anything very seriously.

She lived one day and one night at a time. Parties and new faces carried her through to more parties and new faces. Only once did she leave herself vulnerable, becoming infatuated with a young actor, talented, impossibly attractive, as self-centered as a shark. For six months, her world revolved around him. Then one day she overheard him talking with some of his hangers-on. What he said about Laila made her sick with shame: what he said about Malik's money, on the other hand, was highly complimentary. She walked out without a word.

After that she began to drift away from the glitter-world of Hollywood, Topanga, Malibu. Not completely; she could still show up at the latest hot spot and be welcomed to the party. But that was no longer what she wanted.

One day, for no reason that she could think of, she went down to the waterfront, a marina she had never visited. One boat caught her eye: schooner-rigged, maybe sixty-five feet, lines like a seabird in flight. The *North Star*.

While she admired the teak decks and sparkling fittings, a man emerged from a hatch and rummaged through a tool chest. He noticed Laila, gave her a sun-crinkled smile, and turned back to his work.

"She's beautiful," said Laila.

"Thanks. You sail?"

"Some. I'm not Columbus."

"Who is? Come aboard if you'd like. Dave Christiansen."

"Laila Sorrel." It was the name she chose—after the woman who had once rescued her—when she didn't want a stranger to know who her father was.

He showed her around the *North Star*. The boat was his—"mine and the bank's, that is." He sailed day cruises and charters. "Catalina, the other Channel Islands, once in a while down the Baja. Hawaii twice." Sailing was his life: "I grew up in Madison, Wisconsin. When I was fourteen, a kid I knew took me out on Lake Mendota in a little Sunfish. From then on, I never thought about doing anything else."

When it was time to go, she thanked him for the tour.

"Listen," he said, "I'm doing a group tomorrow, an overnight to Catalina—assuming I can fix the water pump on the auxiliary by then. Want to come along? As honorary crew, I mean. No charge. No pay, either."

Why not? "Sure," she said. "Sounds like fun."

"Some work, too. Eight o'clock tomorrow morning?"

"See you then."

They took twenty paying customers out to the beautiful little hill-ringed harbor of Avalon. Laila slept on deck under the stars. The next morning, they ran before the wind back to the mainland, where Laila, David, and the first mate, a serious young black man named Roy, toasted a successful voyage with icy bottles of beer.

Sun darkened, exhausted, muscles aching, Laila couldn't remember when she had felt so good.

After that, she was on the *North Star* often. There came a time when everyone thought of her and David as a couple, and there came a time when they were. He wasn't like the men in her social set, whether in France, New York, or Los Angeles. He was as calm, confident, and strong in a storm at sea as when he was holding her close. He wasn't brilliant or witty, but his dry, easygoing sense of humor didn't wear thin.

On the night he told her he loved her, she told him who she really was.

"You're kidding," was his first reaction. When she convinced him that she wasn't, he laughed. "Well, it's not going to change my feelings any. But it must complicate yours."

"What do you mean?"

"Well, I say 'I love you,' and you say, 'But my daddy's a billionaire.' " He laughed again. "Hey, I'm not a total dummy—I know what the whole world will think. Who cares? What matters is what you think."

"I don't think you're after my money, if that's what you mean."

He grinned. "Now there's a declaration of undying love if I ever heard one."

"I'm sorry. It's just that you're right. My feelings *are* complicated. By a lot of things." It was true. She wasn't sure how she felt about David. He was a harbor after a storm, and deeply valued for that. She liked, admired, and in a very real sense needed him. But did she love him? Could she love anyone? Did she dare? Her feelings for this man raised so many danger signals from her past, small-craft warnings fluttering in the winds of emotion.

"It's okay, Laila," he was saying now, completely serious. "Take your time. I'm not going anywhere."

It was a few months later, on a midweek sail out to Santa Rosa, just the two of them at an anchorage David knew, that he asked her to marry him. "You don't have to answer until you're ready," he added. "I just want you to know how I feel."

Two days after that, she invented an excuse to go to France. She needed to be away from David for a while, she told herself—a couple of weeks, a month—to sort things out. She needed to remember what life had been like without him.

What she discovered was that life without him no longer existed. In the Louvre, a Monet seascape reminded her of the *North Star*. Over dinner with friends at Le Carré des Feuillants, she found herself wondering if she could prepare an amateur version of the meal for David. At a party, she wished he were there so that they could laugh later about the idiosyncrasies of this or that Parisian video artist or fashion designer or politician's mistress.

When he called, it was a comfortable thing, as if she were just across town and seeing him the next day. Then, in one conversation, he asked as an afterthought whether she had her birth certificate in California.

"No. Why?"

"I just thought of it. You ought to pick it up, or get an official copy, while you're there. Never know when it'll come in handy. Who knows, you might want to get married someday."

Despite that last comment, the birth certificate didn't seem like pressing business, and it slipped her mind for days. Then, one afternoon, she remembered and decided that she might as well have it. It would be right here in the Paris house—in the wall safe where Malik kept personal papers. He was in Marseilles at the moment, but she knew the combination from years of watching him open the safe.

She had no intention of prying; the birth certificate should be easy to find. But as she went through the sheaf of papers, some items naturally tugged at her attention.

Photographs of Genevieve brought tears to her eyes. And here was a picture of her father as a boy—how mischievous he looked. Who was the little girl with him? Funny, she looked a little like Jenna Sorrel. A few letters that meant nothing to Laila. An odd one from someone named Amira, extending condolences about Genevieve and adding that Amira herself was well and doing work she loved. Vague explanations of why she hadn't written before. Karim was fine, too. Karim? Well, the name was common in the Arab world. Probably this was some old flame of her father's, hoping to slip back into the picture after Genevieve's death.

Another photograph, a formal portrait, but small, the size a man might carry in his wallet. A striking young woman in Remali dress. Oddly familiar. Where had Laila seen that face? Suddenly a chill ran up her spine. My God, it was like looking in a mirror!

Laila spread the papers on her father's desk and went through them more carefully. There was no birth certificate, but she found a marriage license for her parents. They had married when she was four years old, nearly five. And there was a little ledger with a record of monthly cash payments to someone in al-Remal—a name Laila didn't recognize, in a town, if that was what it was, she'd never heard of. The first payment had been made the month she was born.

She looked up from the desk. On the facing wall was an oil portrait of her grandmother, Jihan, who had posed for it against her husband's wishes and had given it to Malik to remember her by in France. Laila had always studied the face, searching for signs of Jihan's tragic fate, but now she noticed the hands—and a ring, a star sapphire in an unusual setting. She had seen that ring before. Jenna Sorrel had been wearing it.

Suddenly it all began to make sense. And yet it didn't. It couldn't. It would mean that her whole identity was a kind of illusion. She wasn't who she thought she was, and never had been. Her father had lied to her. Her mother, too—if Genevieve was, in fact, her mother. And Jenna—or whatever her real name was.

Yet it was Jenna she decided to call. There was no answer at the apartment in Boston. Laila tried the office. Dr. Sorrel was out of town. No, she couldn't be reached. Was this a patient? No? Well, was there some emergency? If so, the names of other therapists could be provided.

Laila hung up. She couldn't call Malik. She wouldn't call David. He would think she was crazy. Maybe she was.

Among the documents in the safe was her Remali passport. As the child of a Remali citizen, she was a citizen herself, and her father, a great believer in dual or even multiple citizenship, had insisted on her having the passport. She was glad of it now. She booked a seat on the first flight to al-Remal.

• • •

The man at the car rental agency looked at her with disgust and anger. Didn't she know that it was illegal for a woman to drive in al-Remal?

She wandered through the terminal. Men stared at her. One said, in heavily accented English, "Cover yourself, woman!"

She found a taxi and gave the driver the name of the town from the ledger.

"A little village on the southern outskirts," he said. "I will take you there—but not dressed as you are. Dressed as you are, I will take you only to the Hilton."

"Take me to the Hilton."

At the hotel, she instructed the driver to wait.

"Forever, if you wish—and are paying."

She took a room and sent out for suitable clothes. A maid brought two horrible dark robes of some kind, at a price that must have been ten times what they were worth. Laila didn't care. "Show me how to wear this," she ordered.

The driver was still waiting. He nodded approvingly at her new garments, but seemed offended when she immediately agreed to the price he asked for his services. Too late, she remembered Malik's saying that a Remali enjoyed haggling more than he would enjoy having his first offer met. Well, too bad. She was in a hurry.

The village was an ugly place of poor mud-brick houses baking in the sun. The Arabic that Laila had learned from her father was serviceable, but it took her efforts and the driver's to find a house that went with the name in the ledger.

Inside were a very old woman and one who appeared merely old. The room was dark after the blinding desert brightness, and Laila instinctively pushed back the obscuring veil. The older woman screamed and rocked back as if about to faint. Then she made a sign against evil—Laila recognized it as one Malik superstitiously used—and scuttled out the door. The other woman stared, came closer, stared harder.

"Are you who I think you are, young miss?" she asked Laila in Arabic.

"You tell me. Who am I?"

"If you are who you seem to be, you are the child I nursed for the first year of her life."

Laila's eyes widened with horror. "My mother?" she asked, nearly gagging on the words.

The woman seemed shocked.

"Are you the one to whom my father has been paying money?"

"No. That was Um Salih, gone to Paradise five years now, by the will of God. Since then the money has gone to another aunt of mine—the woman you just saw."

"Why was she afraid of me?"

"She thought you were your mother come back from the grave." She shook her head. "A nuisance. The whole town will know by now."

"Um Salih was my mother?"

"No."

"Who was?"

"So many questions, miss."

"I know I'm rude. I'm sorry. I need to know."

"Then I will tell you."

She told the story bluntly and quickly. When it was over, Laila felt nearly as shaken as the old aunt.

"My mother was killed with stones because of me?"

"Because of the law and God's will, miss, not because of you." The old wet nurse had become increasingly nervous with each passing minute. Clearly, she was anxious to have this sudden guest leave. "Miss, your father had been generous over the years. You have money for me?"

"Money?"

"Miss, by coming here you may have killed me. I must go somewhere, somewhere far. Do you have money for me?"

Laila gave her every rial she had. "I didn't know I was putting you in danger."

"You beware too, miss. Here is not a good place for you. Not just this poor village, but al-Remal."

A small crowd had gathered outside. Laila drew her veil. The driver forced their way through. Back at the hotel, Laila used a credit card for more cash and tipped the taxi man exorbitantly.

From her room, she called California. She needed David's voice, his calm, his love. The marina manager told her he was on a weeklong cruise down the Baja.

She reserved a seat on the morning flight to Paris, went to bed early, slept fitfully, and was at the airport two hours before departure time. While she waited, two men who were obviously police approached.

"Laila Badir?"

"Yes."

"Come with us, please."

They took her to the little room, where she met the man with the oddly familiar name: Prince Ali al-Rashad.

• • •

"You are Laila Badir, and your father is Malik Badir?"

"Yes. What's all this about?"

"About violations of our law, Miss Badir." The prince, a short, slight, distinguished man about her father's age, seemed pleased with himself.

"What violations? What laws?"

"That will become clear later."

He would say nothing more definite, and after taking her passport, he left her alone in the room.

What had she done? Was it that she had violated the dress codes? No, they wouldn't send a prince for that. It had to be something big, something about her visit to the village. But why should that bother anyone? It came to her that she was the daughter of an executed criminal—if the village woman had told the truth. Maybe that was all it amounted to—she was being detained while they checked her out.

None of it felt right. She tapped at the door. A guard opened it.

"I need to go to the bathroom."

He thought it over, then accompanied her and stationed himself outside while she went in.

Thank God, there was another woman there. Laila scrawled her name and the number of Malik's office in Marseilles on a one-thousand-rial bill.

She handed the bill to the woman. "There'll be much more if you call this number and tell whoever answers that I'm in trouble here," she said.

The woman took the money without a word.

Back in the detention room, Laila waited for what seemed like hours. The guard brought her tea, but nothing to eat.

At last Prince Ali swept in again. He smiled and tossed her thousand-rial note on the table. "You may keep your money. And don't worry about your father. He's on his way. It's so very like him to come in person."

"You know my father?"

"We are old . . . acquaintances."

At last she realized where she had heard his name before. Malik had spoken it with anger and contempt. So this man was an enemy of her father's.

"I want a lawyer," she said. "I demand to know why I'm being kept here."

"Why would you need a lawyer? You're not accused of a crime. You're being held more in the nature of . . . evidence."

"Evidence of what?"

"Of various crimes. Kidnapping, for example."

"What kidnapping?"

"Your own." He smiled again. "I see that you are confused. Let me explain. Long ago a crime was committed in our country. It was a crime that requires two criminals, a male and a female. The female was caught and executed. The male was never found out. For years, I've had my suspicions as to the guilty party, and by your coming here and going where you went, you've allowed me to confirm them. So now we're awaiting the arrival of the second criminal."

So that was it: she was being used as bait to draw in her father. "I'm a citizen of France as well as of al-Remal," she said as haughtily as she could. "I have the right to contact the French embassy."

The prince waved a hand. "In good time."

One of the guards entered. "The control tower says he's coming in, Highness."

"Good. Come with me, Miss Badir. You'll want to remember this event."

They went to an arrival bay with a view of the runways. Several aides joined the prince. On the tarmac, a dozen men who appeared to be plainclothes police waited in a loose knot.

"There," pointed one of the aides. Laila recognized the flamboyant markings of her father's private 747 as it touched down.

"Always show, always extravagance," said Ali to the aide. "We'll confiscate the plane, of course."

The jet was taxiing toward the terminal. The plainclothesmen spread out in a semicircle.

There was nothing Laila could do.

A truck rolled onto the tarmac and pulled to a stop just as the big jet did.

Soldiers piled out and formed a line facing the plainclothesmen.

"What is this?" said Ali.

"I don't know, Highness."

Behind them there was a disturbance. A group of men in military uniform approached.

"General, what is the meaning of this?" Ali demanded of their leader.

"Your Highness, I am ordered to escort this woman to that aircraft."

"Ordered! By whom?"

"By the king, Highness."

"The king!" Laila saw the prince's lips tighten with rage, but he said nothing more.

"This way, mademoiselle," said the general. He led her down a ramp to the waiting 747. An attendant sealed the door behind her. The pilot had never cut the engines, and the plane was moving immediately.

Laila saw Malik coming toward her, his face a sculpture of fatherly concern. As he tried to hold her, she half responded, half pushed him away.

"Oh, Papa!" she heard herself saying. "Oh, Papa, I hate you!"

• • •

In the terminal, Ali was on the secret line to the palace. His brother Ahmad—the king since their father's death—answered immediately.

"I demand an explanation, brother," fumed Ali. "I've been humiliated here. Absolutely humiliated. And a criminal has been allowed to go free."

Ahmad's tone was dry. "You are too eager in your duty sometimes, brother. I should have been informed of this, instead of having to hear it secondhand."

"And what would you have done then?"

"Just what I have done now. Do you remember the Mirages, brother? We wanted those planes badly, and a certain individual helped us to get them—against your counsel, if I recall correctly. And in a year or two, God willing, he will help us to buy some American F-fourteens. So I do not wish for him to be interfered with."

"But—"

"Come to dinner this evening, brother. We can talk. It's been too long since I've had a private hour with you."

The phone clicked dead. Distantly, Ali could hear the roar of the 747 as it began its takeoff run.

Part Seven

TRUTH

The thump of the plane's tires on a runway woke Jenna. The red-haired man sat across the aisle watching her.

"Sleep well, Princess? Get you something? A cup of coffee for the ride?"

"No, thank you."

"Some orange juice, maybe?"

"No."

The jet taxied to a halt.

"Well, here we are. End of the line. Steady there—legs not quite awake yet, huh? Wouldn't want a lawsuit, now would we?"

She ignored his offer of help but followed him to the door. What else was there to do?

The sunlight was blinding as they stepped from the jet. The surroundings confirmed Jenna's fears: a private airstrip in the desert. A limousine was waiting. The red-haired man opened the back door for her. A glance at the driver told her that he was an Arab. Of course.

The redhead climbed into the front. "Off we go," he said cheerily.

"How much is he paying you?" she asked. Idle conversation. Whatever it was, it was more than she could match. Not that it mattered now.

He laughed. "Enough. I never thought I'd hear myself say that, but this client pays enough."

Was Karim safe? Of course he was. No one was out to hurt him. What would he hear of this, what would he know? Would he hear anything at all?

They were speeding along a two-lane highway. She recognized neither the road nor the landscape. In fact, there was something distinctly off-kilter about the whole scene. The desert itself didn't look right—not the sand, nor the scraggly plants. And now ahead there were houses. Big, American-style ranch houses. Even in the oil enclave, there had been no such houses in al-Remal. Could it have changed so much?

In the mirror she caught the driver's eyes. A hint of a smile. Something familiar . . . It couldn't be. But he would be older, and—

"Jabr? Jabr!"

"At your service, Highness."

"What are you—?" She turned to the red-haired man. "What is this? Where are we?"

"The right side of the tracks, Princess. Palm Springs, California. We're just coming in the back way."

"Jabr, you tell me, please—what are we doing here? I'm afraid."

The amusement in his eyes turned instantly to concern. "But don't you know, Highness? We're bringing you to your brother."

"Malik? He's here?"

"You didn't tell her?" Jabr demanded of the redhead.

"Hey, I've got orders. I work for him same as you."

Jabr muttered a few words in Arabic that Jenna had no intention of translating. Evidently, there was no love lost between the two men—but that hardly concerned her at the moment.

"Malik's here?" she repeated. She felt light-headed. The whole thing had the surrealistic aura of a dream.

"That's his humble abode straight ahead," said the red-haired man, nodding toward an enormous contemporary wood-and-glass house. They pulled through a gate and up a long drive.

A short, roly-poly man, obviously Remali, hurried down the steps to meet them.

"Oh, this is crazy," said Jenna. "Farid? Is that you, Farid?" She was out of the car, hugging her cousin for all she was worth.

"You've brought the wrong woman," Farid scolded Jabr and the redhead. "Far too young. Besides, Amira was beautiful, but nothing like this."

"Liar! My God, this is too much. Where is Malik?"

"So soon you wish to leave me for your tiresome brother? Very well. This way."

He escorted her into the house. "In there, little cousin. Surprise him—he doesn't know you're here yet."

The door he indicated led to a large room opening onto a vast patio and swimming pool.

Malik was standing with his back to her at the sliding glass door, looking out, apparently lost in thought. It had to be Malik, even though his black hair had gone to salt-and-pepper.

"Brother?"

He turned. "Little sister!"

He rushed to her, and they held each other close. Suddenly she was crying. So was he.

"When I doubt that God is merciful, let me remember this moment," Malik said fervently. "Ah, Amira!"

She pushed him away. "But wait, but wait. Why did you drag me here like this? You scared me to death! Until ten minutes ago, I thought Ali had caught me."

"I had a reason—ten minutes ago, you say?"

"Yes. Until I recognized Jabr, I thought—"

"Well, that's not right. You were supposed to be told while you were on the way, in the air."

"I wasn't told anything. I was asleep most of the time. They gave me some sort of sedative, I think."

Malik frowned. "Ryan was supposed to tell you. Maybe I should have given more specific orders. These guys love to act like they're in the movies. On the other hand, I didn't want him to tell you right away. I meant to show you something—to teach you a lesson."

"You mean you terrorized me on purpose? I should slap you, brother." She half meant it.

"The lesson," he said seriously, "is that if I can do this so easily, others can, too."

She thought it over. "And exactly how did you find me?"

"It wasn't easy. Your letter—sending it from Toronto was a master stroke. So many Arab expatriates end up there. We spent months, years combing Canada—and finding nothing, of course. Then one day Ryan—he's a private detective, in case you haven't guessed—said maybe we should try the United States. I told him, 'Canada's been a silver mine for you. Now you want a gold mine, too.' Maybe that's why he gave you a hard time. He made a fortune looking for you. Once you were found . . ." Malik laughed a little ruefully.

"But how *did* he find me?"

"We had two main things to go on. One, of course, was that you had a son—although we never dreamed he'd still have the same name. The other was what you said about 'success in work I love.' I knew it had to be something that called for education—those books you were always reading, even as a kid. So Ryan started with the colleges, alumni publications, yearbooks, stuff like that. He and his whole agency. Give him credit: even with computers it was a massive job. I must have looked at a thousand pictures. No luck. Then, just when we were both ready to give up, he had the idea of finding out what professional conventions were in Toronto when the letter was mailed. There were a dozen, but the psychologists were the ones who seemed most likely. And . . . voilà!" He laughed. "When he showed me photographs of you, I told him he was crazy. He had to explain about plastic surgery. I was naive, I suppose. We went to Boston, and I spied on you from a distance. I knew right away that it *was* you—something in the way you walk, more than anything else. That was two years ago."

"Two years! Then why did you wait till now—with all this nonsense that I still may slap you for? Why didn't you say anything, contact me?"

"I almost ran up to you right there on the street. But something told me to wait. 'She's been hiding for this long,' I thought. 'She must have a reason.' I didn't know what it might be. To tell the truth, I thought it might have something to do with Philippe's death. So I waited."

"Then why now?"

"Partly because I couldn't wait any longer. But partly because things have changed."

"What do you mean? What's happened?"

He waved a hand. "Later. Let it wait a bit, now that you're here. Relax. You must be tired."

"I slept well enough, thanks to your man Ryan." She realized that she was staring at the empty sleeve. "Your poor arm, Malik. I saw the Sandra Waters interview. I felt so—I don't know: I just wanted to take care of you."

His dark eyes smiled. "The usual reaction. Don't worry, baby sister, it hasn't cramped my style. The illustrious Dr. Kissinger was wrong: power isn't the ultimate aphrodisiac; pity is. The maternal instinct. I was never able to excite it before. Now I can hardly shut it off."

"Idiot," she said hugging him again. "Dear idiot."

"One piece of bad news," he said quietly. "I may as well tell you now: Father died."

"No! Oh, my God!"

"Yes. A bad stroke, and then he just slowly . . . fell to pieces."

A terrible wave of guilt swept over Jenna. "Oh, Malik, he never knew that Karim and I were alive."

"Yes, he did. We had reconciled—at least partly. When he was near the end, I told him . . . what I could. I'm not sure he understood it all, but he did know that his grandson and daughter were alive and well. Ah, but Amira, how I wish you had come to me for help, back then. Why did you go to the Frenchman instead? And what went wrong?"

She told him as much as she dared. Even now, she feared igniting a vendetta against Ali, a fight that Malik could only lose. She settled for describing the murder in Alexandria, including the circumstances that led up to it. "I couldn't live with him after that. But I just couldn't leave, either—he would have hunted me down. Then Philippe came up with this idea."

"It must have been brilliant, seeing that it got him killed."

"Please, brother, don't be sarcastic. Just listen for a while."

She told the story of Philippe's help and heroism. When she had finished, Malik sat quiet for a moment, reflexively rubbing the empty sleeve. "This makes a difference—a great difference," he said at last. "I had come to hate Philippe. Now I see that . . . well, what can I say?"

"No need to say anything, brother. How could you have known?"

"As for Ali, I knew about his preferences, of course. Such things can't be kept totally secret. But of this killing—nothing, not even a whisper. I'm glad to know of it—it may be useful someday. But right now we need to deal with the present." He leaned forward. "Listen carefully, baby sister: You can't hide much longer. Ali knows that you and Karim are alive. He's known it for some time. And all that time he's been searching for you, quietly but very persistently." He smiled grimly. "I haven't been much help to him, I'm afraid. I have certain . . . contacts in his camp—Jabr was one of them, before he came under suspicion and I had to get him out—and I've been able to feed Ali false clues now and then. But it's only a matter of time until he finds you, just as I did. The question is, what will he do then?"

"You're asking me?"

"Yes."

"I don't know. For years I assumed he'd take Karim and have me killed. Or maybe drag me back to al-Remal to be tried for stealing his son—I thought that was what Ryan was doing. But to tell the truth, I don't know. It's all gone on for so long."

"Do you think he would settle for having Karim back?"

"I won't give him back. Never."

"Karim is almost a grown man, little sister," said Malik gently. "Before long, he'll go where he wants."

"Then he can go. But not till then." She heard the childishness in her reply. Jenna, the psychologist, knew quite well that Jenna, the mother, was in denial on the whole matter of growing independence.

"All right, then. Let me give you my ideas. First, you and Karim could live with me, under my protection. I've become very rich, little sister—ten times richer than Onassis ever was. I can hire all the security you'd ever need, give you anything else you might want, and never miss the money."

"I know it, brother. But I have my own life. I wouldn't want to give it up. I don't think Karim would, either."

"That leads us to the second option: You go on as you are, but I provide protection. I can place men directly in the building, both where you live and where you work. The same with Karim. Something like the Secret Service."

Jenna stared at him. "I can't treat patients with a private army hanging around the door."

"It would be more subtle than that, but still . . . I understand. So let me suggest something else. What if we go public with the whole story—newspapers, TV, the works? That might be the best protection of all. Our friend Ali has very serious political ambitions. Once the truth comes out, can he afford to let anything happen to you?"

"Malik, we're talking about Ali. Who knows what he might do?"

He grimaced. "Of course nothing's certain. Maybe we should do both: let the truth come out, then guard you like the crown jewels anyway. But believe me, Amira—Jenna—you're going to have to make some decisions soon. Just promise me that you won't disappear again. I always knew you weren't dead. I just knew it. But what I went through, wondering where you were, whether you were sick or well, how you were managing, alone with a child."

"Don't worry. I couldn't go through it again myself."

He nodded, then smiled. "You'd probably like a shower, maybe even a swim. You'll find some fresh clothes in your room. I try to keep a few nice things available for my guests. You'll need more. There's a personal shopper that I keep on retainer."

"Malik! How long do you expect me to stay?"

"We'll talk about it."

"I have patients, brother, a practice to maintain."

"It's Saturday. Lots of time. We'll talk later."

As he ushered her from the room, she noticed a piece of furniture that took her instantly back to childhood.

"Father's chess table," she said.

"Yes."

"It's smaller than I remember it, but just as beautiful." The table was a work of art, a masterpiece of inlaid wood in intricate geometric patterns.

Jenna remembered the day Malik had flattened Ali among the scattered pawns and knights and rooks. "Do you still play?" she asked. As she said it, she idly opened the table's drawer. Instead of chess pieces, it held a squat black revolver.

She looked at her brother in alarm. He gently pushed the drawer shut. "Unfortunately," he said with his most charming smile, "the games I play these days can be rather dangerous."

• • •

Lunch was a very California affair involving a cactus-bud-and-persimmon salad, grilled rabbit, and kiwi sherbet. Afterward Jenna, Farid, and Malik lounged by the pool. At least Jenna lounged: Farid jumped to answer the poolside phone every few minutes. Sometimes he handed it to Malik; more often he asked questions and gave orders himself. Obviously, her cousin was her brother's top aide.

She still felt as if she might be dreaming. After the long years on her own, her old life buried deep, how utterly strange, yet familiar, to be with the boys of her childhood, her closest relatives now that her father was gone. She wished Karim were here. And where was Laila?

"I need your advice about Laila," said Malik, as if clairvoyant.

Jenna summoned her courage for a confession. "Did you know that I'd seen her?"

"Not at the time. I found out later. I kid Ryan about it. The great detective is looking all over the continent, and my little girl has already found you."

"I knew I shouldn't do it. I knew I should stay away, not just for my safety, but for hers—and yours. But when I saw her, I couldn't help myself."

"Of course, of course." Malik's soft smile seemed to say *How could anyone not love my Laila?* Clearly, she was still the sun, the moon, and the stars for him. Then the smile faded. "You know about . . . what happened to her?"

"I know she was raped."

A tiny wince at the word. "Yes. That was the start of it. Not that long, really, after Genevieve was killed. I thought she came through that in one piece. But the . . . the other thing. She hasn't really been the same since."

"I should have done something. But when she left New York and came out here . . ."

"It's not your fault. I blame myself. For everything. I should have had bodyguards with her twenty-four hours a day. In fact I did—for a while. But she kept begging me to let her lead a normal life. And"—his voice broke—"it's very difficult for me to deny her anything."

He gazed out over the pool to the desert landscape. "That boy, for example. I thought he was all right. He looked me in the eye and called me 'sir.' A good family. And then . . ." His hand clenched, unclenched, clenched again, relaxed. "She wasn't even going to tell me. She was afraid I would judge her."

"It's a common reaction to rape. The victim feels that the attack has diminished her, made her worthless, and that others will think so, too."

"I'm sure you're right."

"What happened to the boy?"

"Ah, the boy. I wanted to kill him, of course. But . . . well, this isn't al-Remal. Instead, I considered bringing charges, as Laila's therapist suggested. That's when I found out how the law works in this country. From the first, the prosecutor told me how difficult the case would be to prove. He told me how the lawyers on the other side would handle it: blame the victim, make Laila look like some kind of—well, like a whore. Then, on my own, I found out that they knew about some of the gaps in her background, and that they even planned to suggest that our relationship was . . . not what it should be. I couldn't expose her to that. We dropped the charges."

"So he got off free?"

Malik was silent for a long, long moment. "It's interesting," he finally said. "A few months later, he was in a minor accident, and some drugs were found in his car. Not much, and they gave him a slap on the wrist—a good family, as I said, and no criminal record. But soon after that, somebody tipped the police, and he was caught with four kilos of cocaine and a large amount of unexplained cash. Right now he's serving about the same sentence he would have gotten for what he did to Laila. Justice, wouldn't you agree?"

Jenna wasn't quite sure what she was hearing. She decided not to ask.

"Not that it helped Laila," Malik continued. "Her eyes—the light was gone from them. I tried everything to bring it back. Everything. I left my business—just left it, indefinitely—and took her on a cruise. She used to love ships, the sea. But she hardly spoke the whole time. I finally cut the trip short because she seemed so miserable. That's when she came out here. I built this place"—he waved his arm at the house—"so I could be near her if she needed me."

Why, Jenna wondered, did her brother believe he needed a mansion in order to be near his daughter? "Didn't you get help for her?" Her tone was sharper than she'd intended, but he didn't seem to notice.

"Oh, yes. Three different psychiatrists. Laila quit them one after another. Then she changed again. Became one of these wild California kids. Every night a party, just drifting—I couldn't stop her. Worthless so-called friends." He lifted a hand. "Don't say it: I know that my own life hasn't always been exemplary. But at least I've learned which people to value. These people cared nothing for her."

Jenna nodded.

"But then," Malik continued, "she met this boy, this young man, and everything changed again." He told the story. Laila had finally found someone, fallen in love—for the first time, really. A young man who captained a full-rigged schooner that carried charter passengers on cruises to Catalina, Mexico, even Hawaii. And slowly, love had brought her back from the edge.

Jenna had a dreadful feeling that she knew where this was going. "Don't tell me he dumped her."

"What? Oh. No, not at all. What happened was that she found out the truth."

"The truth about what?"

"About me. About you. About her real mother. About herself." He recounted Laila's discoveries in Paris and her journey to al-Remal.

"My God," said Jenna when the reality sank in. It was a worst-case situation. The knowledge that one's mother was not one's mother would traumatize anyone. For someone in Laila's unstable condition, it would be catastrophic.

"I don't object to Ali's interference in my business dealings," Malik was saying angrily, still caught up in the scene at the airport. "A man is free to do as he wishes in such matters. But his treatment of my daughter—for that, he'll pay. I swear it." He sat silent for a moment, visibly working to calm himself. "When I got her out, we had a terrible scene. Right on the plane. She said things about me, about you, even about Genevieve. Eventually I had to admit the truth, or most of it, about her mother, her true mother. But telling her the truth seems to have been a mistake, too. I thought she'd storm off to her fiancé. But she's cut him off as well, claims he's just another liar like the rest of us. And instead of running away as I feared, she shuts herself in her room like a hermit."

"Here?"

"Yes, right here."

"She's here now? In this house?"

"Oh, yes. That's the new thing. She shuts herself in her room, hardly comes out, sleeps all day, sits up all night."

Jenna shuddered. The behavior was all too familiar, chillingly reminiscent of Jihan's.

"I'm hoping," Malik concluded helplessly, "you'll be able to do something."

A deep breath. "What have you told her about me?"

"Just that you are indeed my sister, who vanished long ago and let everyone think she was dead, for reasons that I don't fully understand. Which is basically the truth. Of course, to her, it makes you a liar, too."

And she's right, thought Jenna. Hardly the ideal beginning for a therapeutic relationship.

"I'll do what I can," she said, "but it may not be much. Don't look for a miracle."

"I stopped looking for miracles a long time ago. In al-Remal. You remember the occasion."

"Can I see her now?"

"Why not?"

• • •

The woman who opened the bedroom door bore little resemblance to the fresh-faced girl Jenna had rescued in Saks. Laila was only in her mid-twenties, but she looked aged, tired, remote—very much like Jihan in her last days.

"Well, look who's here. My secret friend."

The little flare of bitterness encouraged Jenna: where there were living emotions, even negative ones, there was hope.

"Yes, it's me. And I *am* your friend, as well as your aunt. I'm sorry I didn't tell you the last part. I didn't think I could. Maybe someday you'll let me tell you my reasons."

"I don't want to hear them."

A mechanical response, but the choice of words was significant. Jenna would make notes as soon as she could. She had already decided to stay, at least until she found a suitable therapist for her niece. She couldn't treat Laila herself; she was far too involved for that. But perhaps she could be of value as a nonjudgmental female friend and relative, someone who would listen and understand.

"I'll come again tomorrow, Laila. About this time. Why don't you think about what you'd like to talk about? I'll tell you anything you want to know."

"I don't want to talk."

"Just think about it. I'll see you then—or whenever you'd like."

Jenna had her own patients to think of. First she called the Sanctuary hotline and let Liz Ohlenberg know she would not be in for at least a week. She gave her answering service the same message.

• • •

For much of the next day, Jenna called patients, rescheduling some, turning others over temporarily to colleagues.

Again and again, as she punched in the 617 area code, Jenna thought of Brad. Call him? But what could she say? She had no answer for his question. And if she told him the truth—well, she couldn't tell him the truth.

That afternoon, Laila was deeper in her shell, her responses even more monotonal.

"All right," said Jenna. "I'll do the talking. I'll tell you all about Amira Badir." And she did.

• • •

On Monday, she contacted a Los Angeles psychiatrist highly recommended by several colleagues in Boston. She explained the situation and liked the man's analysis of it. They agreed that even though there was some danger in the present situation, the best prospect lay in getting Laila's approval for starting therapy.

That afternoon Laila was still uncommunicative but seemed to be waiting for Jenna to begin. Jenna took a chance. "Would you like to hear about the woman who gave you birth? She was my best friend—Amira's best friend." And she went through it all, including, as gently as possible, the last night and day of the older Laila's life.

When it was over, Laila went into the bathroom and vomited. When she returned, pale and shaking, she said, "Do you know I went there, to al-Remal? I found this woman who had nursed me, or so she said. A poor woman. Shriveled up early, like so many of the people in that village. God, I hate that place! And do you know what I was thinking? I was thinking, 'Is this my real mother? Did my father . . .' " She broke off. After a time, she lay down on the rumpled bed and slept.

The third day, Laila refused for a long time to open her door. When she finally did, Jenna greeted her but then sat in silence.

"No more stories?" Laila finally asked, her tone surprisingly like that of a little girl being tucked into bed.

"I've been jabbering for two days," said Jenna. "Highly unorthodox in my line of work. Maybe you'd like to tell me how you feel."

"A shrink for sure," Laila said bitterly. " 'How do you feel about that?' " Her face contorted. "How do you think I feel? I feel like one of those stupid toys you knock down that bounce back up. 'Your mother's dead, Laila, only she wasn't your real mother—but that one's dead too. Oh, by the way, that woman you met, your so-called friend, she's really your aunt.' Damn you, damn you! Damn you all!" She was punching the bed with her fist. "Knock me down. But this time I won't get up!"

You're already up, thought Jenna with relief. *Now the job is to keep you up*.

• • •

Over the next few days, Laila gradually came out of hiding. One night she appeared at dinner. The next, she put on makeup. She hinted that she would be willing to talk with someone else, if Jenna thought it would be a good idea. There even came a moment when she took the role of therapist: "Are you going to tell your son the truth?"

It was Jenna's turn to be evasive. "I'm not sure the time is right. You know my story. Who I was. Who I'm still married to. I just don't think the time is right."

"You think Karim can't handle it? Or are you afraid that you can't handle the way he handles it?"

It was a good question. Too good. "I'm just not sure yet. Someday . . ."

"Tell him now. As soon as you can. There has to be a way. He's your son. You can't keep lying to him forever."

Jenna hadn't thought about forever; it was a luxury she had left behind long ago.

• • •

Hats. Dozens of hats, one more outrageous than the next. "Each of you pick one," Malik told Jenna and Laila, "and then you can find an outfit to go with it. We're going to the races—opening day at Del-Mar. Hats are *de rigueur.*"

It was a celebration, a kind of coming-out party for Laila, but also a big day for Malik, who had shipped a number of his top thoroughbreds to the California track for the racing season.

They helicoptered down with Farid as a fourth, and Jabr and one of Malik's regular bodyguards providing security. The scene at the racecourse was like a southern California version of Ascot. Women costumed as if for an Easter parade promenaded with men dressed in designer sportswear. Jenna recognized half a dozen movie stars, mostly of the older generation.

Malik's private box afforded some refuge from the crowd, but even there a number of men who looked as if they were not accustomed to being so deferential came up to shake his hand. An inordinate number of them seemed to be Texans who had horses at the meeting.

In the fifth race, Jenna and Malik sentimentally backed a desperate longshot named Desert Exile, and when the lightly regarded beast romped home ahead of the field, they jumped and hugged like children.

"Telephoto, boss," said the bodyguard.

Jenna saw the photographer aiming a long lens at them from twenty rows down in the stands.

"Don't worry about it," said Malik to the guard. "It's a free country, they tell me." But Jenna sat down and lowered the broad brim of her hat.

The next day at breakfast, a grinning Malik dropped a popular tabloid on the table. A front-page photo showed Jenna looking fearfully into the camera, her arm around Malik's neck. The headline read: "Mystery Woman Billionaire's Latest Flame?" Twenty-four hours later the mystery was solved: "Feminist Doc Is Megabucks Malik's Palm Springs Playmate" proclaimed bold type above a picture of Jenna tugging furtively at her hat brim.

She felt violated, yet at the same time had to laugh. After countless excuses for avoiding book-jacket photos and television interviews, this! And what did it really matter? If Malik was right, a picture or two wouldn't make much difference in whether or not Ali found her.

That night she made her habitual call to her answering machine, hoping for word from Karim. To her surprise, she heard Brad's voice. The message was brief: "I see that I've misjudged you. Good-bye, Jenna." At first she thought he was referring to the deadline for his marriage proposal. Then she realized that he must have seen the tabloid story.

Well, my God! She wanted to catch the first plane home, tear out the answering-machine tape, and throw it in the fireplace—and do the same to Brad, if she could find him. How dare he jump to conclusions like that! Pompous, self-righteous bastard!

It took hours for her anger to cool, but when it did, the chill went deep. She didn't want to lose him. It was that simple. She called his home number. A servant, after asking her name, informed her that Mr. Pierce was unavailable. His receptionist told her the same thing six times the next morning.

Jenna's anger reasserted itself. All right, if that was the way he wanted it, she could live without him. Couldn't she?

• • •

She needed to go home. Laila was in competent hands. There was little more Jenna could do except be a good aunt. Besides, she was weary of the lazy warmth of southern California. Only a few more weeks and the air would be turning crisp in Boston.

"For you, cousin," said Farid, bringing a phone.

It had to be Brad. "Hello?"

"Whoa, Mom! Way to go!"

"Karim! Where are you?"

"Athens. You're all over the papers here, Mom. Malik Badir is like some kind of local god. I think he owns about half of Piraeus."

"I'm not seeing him, Karim. I'm visiting him." That didn't sound right.

"Uh-*huh*. I thought you told me you didn't know him."

"It's . . . it's a long story. I knew him a long time ago but haven't seen him for years—since you were a baby." That didn't sound right either.

"Why didn't you tell me?"

"I . . . I just didn't think it was important at the time."

"So what's he like?"

"Karim, listen. Don't believe what you read in the papers. Things . . . aren't what they seem."

"Uh-huh." He sounded vaguely disappointed. "Well, he sounds like a pretty impressive guy. I'd like to meet him. Look, Mom, I gotta go. There are a bunch of people waiting for the phone."

"Karim! You're well? Everything's all right?"

"Sure. Why should anything be wrong?" The infinite optimism of the very young man. "Gotta bounce, Mom. Love you."

How ironic. Her son finally approved of a man in her life—and the man was her brother. It was like a French farce. She had to tell Malik.

He laughed uproariously. "My God! Can you imagine what the papers would be like if they knew the truth? 'Billionaire Badir in Love Nest with Long-Lost Sister.' They'd put Elvis in the story before they were through. A ménage à trois."

Jenna laughed too. But she went to sleep that night missing Brad.

• • •

It was hard to keep track of time in the eternal balm of southern California. Had another week gone by?

Jenna was edgy. Time to go home. She wasn't really needed here. Laila was doing well; although she still tended to avoid others and to sleep a great deal, she hadn't missed a single appointment with the psychiatrist in Los Angeles, Jabr driving her there and back. She had even asked Jenna's opinion about writing a letter of apology to the banished boyfriend.

"Don't apologize," said Jenna. "Explain. Tell him how you felt then and how you feel now. If he's the man you think he is, he'll understand."

The reunion with Malik was winding down, too. His business was reclaiming his attention—meetings, international phone calls and faxes, discussions with Farid late into the night. And there were his racehorses.

Soon, too, Karim would be home, a new school year beginning.

And there was Brad. Surely she could find a way to make him understand. Her words to Laila echoed in her thoughts.

• • •

Finally, on yet another hazy blue-and-gold desert afternoon, after discussing her plans with her brother and Laila, she booked a flight to Logan for the following day.

Malik was on his way to the track, where his favorite three-year-old was entered in a major stakes race. "Come with me," he invited. "We'll make a little good-bye party for your last day."

"No, thanks, brother. I don't want to end up on the front pages again. Go and enjoy yourself. I'll relax by the pool. Who knows when I'll get a chance like this back East?"

"You're sure?"

"Will you please go?"

He departed with Farid, both of them still inviting her even as the door closed.

She chose a bathing suit from among the dozen Malik had insisted on buying. Surely she'd have the best collection in Boston. A call to the kitchen brought a cooler of lemonade and snacks. As a finishing touch, she found a novel with absolutely no redeeming value. Thus armed, she stretched out in the sun.

For a while, it was exactly the pure, mindless luxury she needed. But then the heroine of the novel had a terrible falling-out with the man who was obviously destined to be the love of her life. It was all a misunderstanding—totally contrived, thought Jenna disgustedly. But was it really any crazier than what was going on with Brad?

Maybe she should write him, just as she had advised Laila to do with her friend. *Don't apologize. Explain. Tell him the truth.* The truth about Malik, at least. But of course that would raise more questions—and more, leading finally to questions she'd have to refuse to answer. Or to answer with lies. God, she was tired of lies.

It was quiet with Malik gone, Laila upstairs. The house staff wasn't in evidence. Some of the bodyguards would have gone with Malik and Farid, of course. Still, that left half a dozen others, and even though they weren't obtrusive men, she normally would have spotted one or more of them checking on her by now.

Ah, there was one of them now, at the sliding door. Squinting in the brilliant sun, she couldn't see just who it was. Coming towards her. A message? A call from Brad? Or Karim? Malik must pay his men very well—look at that suit. A new man? She still didn't recognize him. Smaller than the others. Older too, gray at the temples. Oh, no. It couldn't be. Please, God, no.

"Hello, Amira. Don't freeze like a rabbit before a snake. Say something."

"What do you want, Ali? You don't belong here. When Malik comes back—"

"I won't be here that long, my dove, my heart. And no one else will interrupt our little chat, either—I've seen to that. But don't look so frightened. I'm not going to hurt you. Not today, not here. But someday, Amira—bitch—maybe when you're just walking down the street. Think about it. Think about it often. Will you be able to run and hide again?"

"Just go away. Please."

"Ah, beg. I like that. And my son, he'll go with me."

"Don't you dare touch him!"

"I won't have to. Do you think he'll stay with you, whore, after he finds out how you've lied to him?"

"Yes." It was all she could say.

"Do you know how I found out about you? Your picture in that trash paper. You look different here. But brown hair is black in a black-and-white photo. And . . . green . . . eyes are just dark eyes. And of course you were with that thieving brother of yours. It all became clear to me in a flash."

Suddenly Malik's voice came from the house, calling to someone: "No, the horse had an inflammation of some kind. Had to scratch him. They got me on the car phone." In a moment, he was outside. "Who's this, little sister? You!" He strode straight to Ali and slapped him backhanded. "How dare you enter my house! Out!"

It happened so quickly. Ali reeled with the blow. Then, with a snarl, he was on Malik like an animal, like the time he beat and raped Amira. And suddenly Malik, with only one arm, was down, gasping for breath as Ali's hands clenched his throat.

Even at that moment, and always after, Jenna knew that she could have screamed for help. Someone would have been there in seconds—Farid, Jabr, someone. But pictures were flashing through her mind, the way people supposedly saw their whole lives when they were drowning: Alexandria, the hospital in al-Remal, Ali's sneer just now when he threatened her life.

She didn't scream. She dashed inside, took the heavy blue-black little revolver from the chess table, pressed the safety lever, walked back to where Ali was choking Malik, aimed at her husband's back, and fired three times.

After that everything was confusion. Malik was holding the gun, and people were swarming: Farid, bodyguards, the chef, and two strangers who turned out to be Ali's men and had to be disarmed themselves. And Laila.

Malik, his voice a hoarse croak, was telling everyone, "He tried to kill me. I had to shoot." Then, while someone called the police and a bodyguard hopelessly tried CPR on Ali, he took Jenna aside. "I'm going to handle this, do you understand? No, not a word. Do you remember how I swore to protect those I love? I've failed everyone but you. You owe me this chance."

She was too numb to answer. Two questions battled in her mind. What would this do to Laila? And what would she tell Karim?

RETRIBUTION

Arrest. Indictment. Sensation.

From the first, things went badly for Malik. At his arraignment, bail was denied on the ground that his resources would make it easy for him to leave the country. Meanwhile, the publicity was like a poisonous cloud. Almost daily, the media trumpeted some damaging aspect of Malik's past—the espionage case, the fate of Laila's true mother, even questions about the circumstances surrounding Genevieve's death. Every story mentioned his vast wealth; the message was that here was a man who considered himself above the law. Well-timed leaks from the office of the district attorney, who was in a close race for reelection, fed the fire.

By contrast, Ali was portrayed as a Remali national hero and a friend of America, a royal prince with progressive ideas who might one day have been king. Whereas the photographs that the networks and newspapers used of Malik seemed to have been culled from a file of the most unflattering images possible, those of Ali showed a handsome, dashing pilot in his air force uniform. His grieving widow and children were interviewed.

The story of Amira's disappearance and presumed death was retold with sympathy for Ali: he had known tragedy in his foreshortened life. The fact that the lost princess had been the killer's sister was treated as the kind of bizarre interrelationship that occurred often in the backward, byzantine Middle East.

Malik's defense was straightforward. He had come home unexpectedly and found his old business enemy Ali. They exchanged words, and Ali attacked him. Nearly strangled, Malik managed to fight his way free. Ali fell to his knees, his back to Malik, but his movements made Malik believe he was reaching for a weapon. Malik drew his gun and began pulling the trigger.

He could offer support for this version of events. First, Ali undeniably was in Malik's home, apparently uninvited. Second, medical evidence showed that Malik had indeed been badly choked. On the other hand, no weapon had been found on Ali. And more damning than anything else, three bullets in the back didn't look like self-defense, even for a one-armed man.

The district attorney, making a great show of fair-mindedness in a televised news conference, announced that he would not seek an indictment for first-degree homicide, only for second-degree.

That was the charge the grand jury brought.

Unlike some of the notorious trials in recent California history—the Menendez brothers, the Simpson case—*People v. Malik Badir* would not be a long, drawn-out proceeding. Malik not only admitted to the shooting but ordered his two celebrated and very expensive lawyers to use no delaying tactics. The questioning of witnesses would be brief. In fact, no one claimed to have seen the struggle or the killing.

True, one of Malik's bodyguards had vanished and was rumored to be in al-Remal, as were Ali's two men—who, it turned out, had diplomatic immunity anyway—but none of this was admissible as evidence.

All of Malik's other employees had been elsewhere than at the pool.

His daughter had been asleep.

His houseguest, Dr. Jenna Sorrel, had been in the library, searching for a book, when she heard the shots. She knew nothing else of the matter.

That was the story Malik had whispered to her in the minutes before the police arrived.

"Promise me you'll tell them that, sister. This can't hurt me. An inconvenience. But it could ruin your life—and Karim's."

It was so simple and easy, and she was terrified and in shock. Then, once she had told the lie for the first time, she felt as if there was no going back. Through hours of questioning by homicide detectives, she never wavered.

Now she was wavering.

She had killed Ali. And she was at last free of the fear that haunted her for so many years. Why should Malik risk ruin, no matter what obsessive ideas he had about protecting his loved ones? He was confident of acquittal, but what if he were wrong?

Just tell the truth—the whole truth. Let it all out. Get it over with—finally, finally over with.

But what about Karim? The truth would send him out into life branded, the man whose mother had killed his father in a case that would be remembered for decades.

So maybe Malik was right after all.

She was a wreck. She had never before taken a tranquilizer, but now she downed Valium more regularly than she ate food. Sleep was a stranger.

She couldn't go back to the Palm Springs house. She would see the bloodstains by the pool, even if they had disappeared. She took a hotel room for the duration of the legal proceedings. The staff were accustomed to celebrity patrons who expected privacy, and they kept reporters at a distance.

Outside the hotel, Jabr took over, his countenance and the set of his thick shoulders giving pause to even the most determined camera operator or microphone-waving broadcast journalist from Eyewitness News. Jackals. She had come to hate them all. Look at the way they had savaged Malik.

Her practice had all but disintegrated. Ironically, her remaining patients now sustained her more than she them. Colleen Dowd offered to fly out and help in whatever way she could; the offer was sincere and, for an agoraphobic, incredibly courageous. Toni Ferrante *did* fly out. She walked right over Jabr's initial distrust. Within twenty-four hours they were all but partners, an improbable but highly effective security team.

Jenna visited Malik daily—he was unfailingly cheerful and optimistic—and Laila, whom Malik had forbidden to come to the courtroom or the jail. She conveyed messages to Farid and the lawyers and did what she could to aid the defense. During the *voir dire*, she studied prospective jurors closely as they responded to questioning. Body language. Hesitations in speech. A blush. A blink. After each session she reported to the lawyers.

They were quite a team: one a tiny, tough Donna Karan-suited New Yorker named Rosalie Silber; the other a tall, tanned, white-maned Texan, J.T. Quarles, given to string ties and snakeskin cowboy boots. In their profession both were superstars. Cordially jealous of each other, they nevertheless worked together like a championship doubles team.

Toward Jenna, their attitude at first was one of amiable condescension. They had their own experts for juror analysis—and their own tried-and-proved intuition. But there came a moment when the Texan turned to the New Yorker and said, "You know, Rose, there's a lot in what Dr. Jenna here says. Maybe we should take another look at number fifty-four."

"I concur in both statements," Rosalie replied.

From then on, Jenna was an unofficial aide in the defense camp. It felt good to contribute. At the same time, she had never felt worse. What did it matter that she was helping to prepare for Malik's trial, when with a few words she could set him free? It was as if there were two Jennas, one a loving sister and dedicated professional, the other a hypocrite who lied with every breath.

"It's not too late," she told Malik in the jail's visiting room. "Why won't you let me . . ." She left the question hanging.

"Absolutely not. Listen. I'm going to win this thing, and then it will be over with."

No, it won't, she thought. *It will still be going on—forever.*

"Laila asked me again if she could visit."

"Tell her I'm sorry—but no. I don't want her to see me in this." He indicated the orange jumpsuit, then broadened his gesture to include the room, the jail, the courthouse. "I don't want her involved in any of this. Don't forget that her own experience with the law was . . . very hard on her."

Jenna went away feeling as if she were only treading water in an endless, empty sea of moral ambivalence.

The first days of the trial did nothing to ease her mind. The forensic evidence was literally sickening. Photos of Ali's body with blood everywhere. Close-ups of the wounds. The shocked looks on the jurors' faces told her how they saw it.

A string of police testified, from the Palm Springs officers who had answered the 911 call to a noted homicide detective brought in from Los Angeles.

The district attorney, Jordan Chiles, was trying the case himself. It was a risky tactic—he was far more of a politician than a trial lawyer—but it would bring priceless publicity for his reelection campaign. Tanned, athletically trim, he could easily have been one of those slightly over-the-hill actors who still turn up full of hope at every casting call.

"In your experience—your expert experience," he asked the Los Angeles detective, "how would you characterize the shooting?"

"We see a lot of this in drug situations," the man replied. After a rain of objections from the defense, the jury was instructed to disregard the reference to drugs, but the witness was allowed to continue. "I would characterize it as an execution-style shooting," he said.

No! Jenna wanted to shout. *You don't know what you're talking about!* Yet, in a way, hadn't it been an execution? She tried to make herself answer that question. She couldn't.

After a few pro forma witnesses, the prosecution rested. The point of the state's presentation was not that Malik had committed the killing—the defense had stipulated that from the first—but that he had done so in a way that precluded self-defense.

Three shots in the back. Sometimes Jenna could almost hear the jurors counting.

But now Rosalie Silber of Manhattan and J.T. Quarles of Houston had their turn. They called a few of Malik's employees—Farid, Jabr, a maid, a horse trainer, a pilot—to establish that Malik had not been expecting Ali, and indeed had not expected to be at home that fateful afternoon.

Jordan Chiles's cross-examination could have come from the daily papers. At every turn he pounded the theme that Malik was an obscenely rich international scoundrel who took what he wanted—including lives. Objection after objection from the defense was sustained, but the jury could not have missed the message.

Jenna was not brought to the stand, nor would she be. Malik had ordered Rosalie and J.T. not to call her for the defense, and the district attorney's office had decided that she was worse than useless: she had not seen the shooting and could only create sympathy for the defendant.

The key witness for the defense—the only witness who really mattered—was Malik himself. It was necessary for him to testify because no one else could put his version of events on the record.

He performed impressively. The empty sleeve was eloquent in itself, and when Malik explained the reason for it and why he carried a gun, two male jurors nodded in unconscious agreement. Later, under cross-examination, Malik never lost control or let himself be pulled into a discussion of his past: he simply waited for his attorneys' objections to be sustained.

Yet something was wrong. Jenna could feel it. In a business deal or a social situation, Malik could throw up a smoke screen of charm, jokes, mock anger, even tears—whatever was needed to carry him through. But this was a courtroom, and as good as Malik was at deception, he wasn't really good at plain lying. Jenna knew the signs. She could see them on his face, hear them in his voice. Could the jury recognize them, too?

In the postmortem that evening, J.T. and Rosalie seemed worried. Unspoken signals that Jenna couldn't decipher shot back and forth between them.

"They'll be done with our client tomorrow morning," J.T. told Jenna. "We'll have a little redirect, then rest. Judge'll probably adjourn for the day. Then summation shouldn't take more than another day, wouldn't you think, Rose?"

"Better make it two," said Rosalie. "Chiles is going to be on a soapbox."

"Yeah, make it two. Then it's in the hands of twelve ordinary citizens, good and true."

"What if—" said Jenna. She stopped.

"What if what?" asked Rosalie.

"What if I testified?"

The two lawyers glanced at each other.

"Testified to what?" said Rosalie.

"If I just testified for my—for Malik."

"Well, I don't see how that's gonna happen," J.T. finally drawled. "I told you we're not gonna call you. And the bad guys aren't gonna call you either."

"We couldn't call you regardless," said Rosalie. "You're practically a member of the team."

"I see."

Another look between the lawyers.

"Is there something we should know, Jenna?" asked Rosalie.

It was like standing on the edge of a cliff, wondering what it would be like to—

"No," she said. "Just a crazy idea."

Back at the hotel, she opened the vial of Valium, then closed it. She wanted the calm—wanted it badly—but she needed to think clearly. Once before, she had saved herself through a deception, and it had cost the life of someone she loved. Could she go through that again? There was still time. She could just stand up in court. But no, they would shut her up, and no one would believe whatever she managed to blurt out anyway. After all, the whole world thought she was Malik's lover. *God, Jenna, how did you end up in this three-ring circus?*

She could call a press conference. *They* wouldn't shut her up. No indeed.

The jackals would want their feast. She couldn't—just couldn't, that was all. Besides, Malik thought that he would be acquitted. So did J.T. and Rosalie—didn't they?

And there was Karim to think about.

Whatever she did or didn't do would be wrong—and she had done so much wrong already. She thought longingly of the Valium. Maybe even a drink. Sleep.

There was a tap at the door. Toni and Jabr.

"Someone wanting to see you, boss," said Jabr. Through hard effort, he had trained himself not to call her Highness. "Not a reporter, I think."

"From Boston," said Toni. "Says you know him. Here's his card."

But Brad was already standing behind her in the hall.

"Yes, it's okay," Jenna heard herself saying. "Yes, I know him. It's fine. Come in. Come in!"

Toni and Jabr hesitated for the briefest moment before standing aside and closing the door behind Brad, who had never taken his eyes off Jenna.

"I had to see you," he said. "I couldn't leave things the way they were. I had to tell you I was wrong to try to force you. I don't care what else has happened, Jenna."

"Shut up," she said. "Just hold me. God, just hold me!"

The world became his arms around her, what she had wanted, what she had needed through it all.

"I love you, Jenna. I'll always love you. Always."

"I love you, too."

• • •

She had dozed but now was wide awake. What time was it? It had to be long past midnight. She curled close to Brad's strength and warmth. She ran a finger lightly down his chest. He stirred, brushed her forehead with his lips.

"What is it, love?" he whispered.

"I have to tell you something."

"Tell me."

She told him everything.

Now and then he interjected a question, now and then a word of anger or astonishment. "My Christ," he said when she had finished. "What you've been through, my love! What you've been through!"

She fought down a quick little spasm of sobs. "It's not over. I've got to do something."

"Yes."

"I don't know what to do. What would you do?"

"What difference does it make what I'd do?"

"Don't tell me that! Tell me what you'd do."

He stroked her hair lightly, thoughtfully. "Who else knows about all this?"

"Nobody. Malik knows some of it. And his daughter. Jabr, a little. You're the only one who knows the whole story."

"What about Karim?"

"No. He doesn't know. Not anything."

"I don't know what I'd do," said Brad after a moment, "much less what you ought to do. I like to think that I'd tell him, then tell the world."

He got out of bed, went to the window, and cracked the curtain to peer out into the night. "But there are consequences to think of. Your life will change, and so will Karim's. In the short run at least, those changes won't be for the better. There's no getting around that." He closed the curtain. "I can't decide for you, you know that. All I can do is tell you that whatever you decide, I'm with you. If you want to keep the lid on forever, I'll help you hold it down. If you want to break it open, I'll be beside you all the way."

"You think I should tell, don't you?"

"Yes," he finally said. "For your brother and for yourself."

Again that feeling of standing on a cliff. Very clearly the thought came to her that it was now or never.

"What time is it in Boston?"

Brad squinted at his watch in the darkness. "A little after six."

She switched on a lamp and reached for the phone. Her hands, she thought distractedly, were freezing.

Karim answered on the seventh ring, his voice fuzzy with sleep.

"Mom? Where are you?"

"Still in California."

"It's the middle of the night there. Is something wrong?"

"No. Well, yes. Karim, sweetheart, can you come out here? Just for a day or two?"

"Well, gee, Mom, what for?"

"I . . . I need to tell you something. It's very important."

"So tell me."

"I'd rather say it in person, not on the phone."

"What, are you kidding, Mom? You mean they're tapping the line or something?"

"No, no. It's just—"

"So tell me. That's what phones are for."

"All right," she said. "But you'd better sit down. This isn't going to be easy for either of us."

"I can't sit down, Mom. I'm in bed."

"All right." She took a deep breath. "Karim, darling, I'm your mother, but I'm not who you think I am, who other people think I am. I didn't want it that way. I had to do it. But now it's time for the truth."

For the second time that night, she told the story.

As it slowly sank in, Karim began to interrupt. His pain and confusion were palpable—and infused with growing anger.

"You're telling me this guy, this prince, this creep that Malik killed—this guy was my father?"

"Yes, but—"

"Then what about Jacques? What about Jacques?"

"I made him up. Please believe me, I did it for you."

"Believe you? How can I believe you? None of this is real. It's just—it's crazy!"

"It's real, Karim, and there's more to it." She closed her eyes. "Please come out here, sweetheart. Or I'll come back there, forget about the trial."

"Mom, whatever it is, tell me now."

"I killed him, son. Not Malik. I did it."

In the next few minutes, she learned exactly how her brother had felt on that plane taking Laila out of al-Remal. She would never forget the words Karim used, the hatred he expressed. That she knew it was a defense reaction made it no easier to hear. And nothing she tried to say got through.

"How could you do this to me? You think about it! How could you do it? How?"

The phone clicked violently.

He was gone.

When the tears finally came, it seemed as if they would never stop. She felt Brad's arm across her shoulders, shrugged it off: no one could help her in this, no one could comfort her. Yet in all the agony, there was something else, a feeling long forgotten, a mingling of exhilaration and fear that approached pure joy.

She had stepped off the cliff. Was she falling or flying?

• • •

Morning spread colors slowly across the desert. Jenna ordered breakfast for two. Brad had fetched his one piece of luggage from his room two floors below.

Karim's phone was disconnected. Jenna, eyes still red and puffy from crying, wanted to go to Boston.

"Don't," advised Brad. "It won't do any good now. Let him cool down a little."

He didn't add that something remained to be done here, but it was on both their minds.

Jenna sipped coffee and nibbled a cinnamon roll. For the first time in weeks, food tasted good.

"The lawyers say that they'll rest the case today, and the judge will adjourn until tomorrow. I was thinking of calling a news conference after adjournment. But I don't want to." She shivered. "I don't want them all . . . screaming at me."

He looked at her quizzically, with a glint of amusement. "Are you joking, Jenna? Maybe you're too close to this thing. You don't realize how big it is. Not just here. Everywhere. If you don't want to deal with a crowd of reporters, if you'd rather have a quiet hour with Dan Rather or Diane Sawyer, all you've got to do is pick up the phone."

"I hadn't thought of that. You're sure?"

"I'm sure."

"Do you know either of those people?"

"Sawyer and Rather? I've met them both. I don't really know them."

"Never mind. I've got it. You'll think I'm crazy, but . . ." She went to the phone and called information. Then, taking a deep breath, she punched the number.

"Mr. Manning's in conference," said the voice in Boston. "May I take a message?"

"Tell him it's Jenna Sorrel."

Barry Manning was on the line in four seconds. "Doc! Great to hear from you! My, but you've been a busy little bee since the last time I saw you."

She told him what she wanted.

"An hour today, Doc? You got it." He shouted instructions to someone—"Bump Moynihan. That's right, I said bump him!"—then came back to Jenna. "Wait a minute, Doc. Aren't you in California?"

"Yes. I want to do it here. Today."

"Yikes! Doc, I gotta ask: This is big, right? I mean, you didn't just suddenly decide to push a book or something."

"It's big. I'm told it's very big."

"Then you got it." More shouts to the background: "Book the first flight to LAX. Scratch that. Charter one. Half an hour. Me and the whole crew." He sounded slightly winded when he came back on. "Don't move a muscle, Doc. I'll be there."

"I have to go to court. I won't be hard to find."

"I'll find you. Doc? Thanks."

She hung up and breathed a deep sigh. Then she was laughing.

"What?" said Brad.

"My deep, dark secrets!" she said, and laughed harder. "I've been hiding them my whole adult life, and now suddenly I'm babbling them over and over like a . . . a crazed parrot! Who says God doesn't have a sense of humor?"

• • •

The defense rested at five minutes to noon, and the court stood adjourned until the following morning.

Jenna had a brief moment to spend with Malik before he was escorted back to his cell. For the first time, he seemed deflated, his customary cheer nowhere in evidence.

"I didn't like the way they looked today," he told her, meaning the jury. "I may be in trouble."

"Don't worry, brother. It's going to come out fine."

He brightened. "You think so? Of course, you're right. I'm getting to be a worrier."

Three hours later, she went on the air with Barry Manning. He had brought video equipment as well as audio.

He introduced her without his accustomed brashness. Clearly, he saw this as his graduation to the big time. "Doctor Sorrel tells me that she has something important to talk about, but she hasn't said what. The sensible thing for me to do is get out of the way and let you listen. So here's Jenna Sorrel."

An hour later, she, Brad, Toni, and Jabr practically had to fight their way out of the rented studio. At the hotel, police ringed the entrance. Jenna looked at Brad.

"It's okay," he said. "They're here to protect you—for now."

REDEMPTION

That night the hotel was a castle under siege. Scores of reporters and hundreds of idly or malevolently curious citizens from all over southern California milled outside. At one point a helicopter hovered, roaring, a few yards from Jenna's window, a cameraman leaning from the door. His shot of Jabr closing the curtains went out live on CNN.

Jenna, completely drained, could barely focus on the TV, which was replaying the story in endless detail. From time to time, she tried to reach Karim, without success. Brad took charge with an air of quiet command. His first task was to find Jenna a lawyer.

"What about Rosalie and J.T.?" she wondered. She was comfortable with them.

"They're Malik's lawyers. I'm not sure it's ethical to work for us, too. But I'll try. You have an unlisted number for them?"

"That little lady's a pistol," J.T. laughed when Brad reached him. "Tell her we're holed up like in the Alamo over here, thanks to her. Tell her we love her anyway. Tell her we admire her. But doggone it, we just can't represent her. Y'all are from Boston. Ever hear of a Boston fella name of Sam Adams Boyle? Hell of a trial lawyer."

Half an hour later, Sam Adams Boyle was on retainer.

"He was watching your interview with Barry when I called," Brad told Jenna. "It was too late for the network news back East, but they were running excerpts on a special bulletin."

"God."

On the TV in front of her, Jordan Chiles was proclaiming the whole thing a desperate stunt and promising to carry forward the murder charge against Malik. Chiles looked a bit desperate himself. The election was barely a week away, and his showcase was blowing up in his face.

Moments later Malik called from jail. His name was on a very short list of acceptable callers that Brad had given the hotel.

"Amira, why did you do it? Another day or two and it would have been over. We were winning, I could feel it."

"I'm sorry, brother. I know you were doing it for me. But I just couldn't let you. And I had to stop lying sometime. For myself."

"Who answered the phone?" The protective big brother, even from behind bars.

"Brad Pierce. You'll meet him."

"Ah, baby sister, you've been holding out on me. Bring him to court tomorrow." Jenna could picture his mischievous smile. The man was irrepressible.

After Malik's call, Brad had a long talk with someone in Washington, D.C. "A friend of mine," he explained. "Known him since we were kids. He's pretty high up in the State Department these days. I'm worried about your immigration status—Karim's as well—so I thought I'd try to head off trouble before it starts."

In all the madness, Jenna had forgotten completely about the fact that she was in the United States on fraudulent terms. "You mean they could deport me?"

"They won't. If worse comes to worst, there are a couple of congressmen who'd be only too glad to do me a favor."

She let it go. It was all becoming very distant anyway. She was exhausted. She closed her eyes.

Someone was pulling at her. ". . . to bed," Brad was saying.

"What about you?"

"A few more calls. I want to get some security people down here from our California division. Toni and Jabr need rest, too."

She kissed him, bumbled off to bed without even washing her face, and fell into a dreamless sleep.

• • •

A cordon of police lined the courthouse steps. As Brad hurried Jenna to the building, she was astonished to hear cheers from the crowd. A group of women on the sidewalk lifted signs; some read WE'RE WITH JENNA, the rest, WE'RE WITH AMIRA.

Malik was seated with Rosalie and J.T. at the defense table. He turned to smile at Jenna, looked Brad over for a long moment, and nodded. After a long delay, the judge appeared and immediately summoned the defense lawyers and Jordan Chiles into his chambers. When they emerged a half hour later, J.T. was grinning broadly and Rosalie was looking as elated as she was ever likely to. Chiles, scowling, glanced at Jenna with daggers in his eyes.

The judge explained that unofficial developments outside the courtroom normally had no effect on a case in progress. However, he had learned that at least two jurors had become aware of Jenna's interview with Manning. In his judgment, their knowledge would have to be considered prejudicial.

Therefore, he was declaring a mistrial. He gave the prosecution seventy-two hours in which to decide whether to file new charges.

Malik wasn't free, but people were shaking his hand.

"He'll never file," J.T. was saying. "Not a chance."

"Reasonable doubt, what can you say?" Rosalie agreed.

Brad and Jenna left the courthouse by a side entrance. At a makeshift podium in the lobby, Jordan Chiles was holding a news conference.

They didn't go back to the hotel. Jabr, after first making sure no one was following, headed west on I–10, then south through a maze of freeways to the coast road. The house, in Laguna Beach, belonged to a friend of Brad's. Jenna was beginning to see that, for a quiet and very private man, he had a great many friends.

After the desert, the chill moisture of the sea air was as refreshing as a waterfall. The timeless crashing of the waves was better than any tranquilizer. Jenna could almost imagine that she and Brad were back at Marblehead, and that none of the rest of it had happened.

Almost. There were Toni and Jabr, and Brad's security men, mounting watch. There was the fact that her brother was still in jail. There was the possibility that within a day or two, she would be there herself. (Jordan Chiles had hedged in his press conference. He was confident, he said, that Malik Badir was the perpetrator in the shooting of Ali Rashad. But a wild card had been thrown on the table, and his office was actively investigating the claims made by Dr. Jenna Sorrel.)

And, of course, there was the constant worry over Karim. She called everyone she could think of who might know where he was. His closest companions, Josh and Jacqueline, she had called repeatedly. She was almost certain they were lying when they said they hadn't seen him, but there was little she could do about it. *Please, God, let this be over soon so that I can get back to Boston and find my son.*

Sam Adams Boyle arrived on their second day in Laguna Beach. He was a tough, red-faced, silver-haired, old-time southie with the sour expression of a Boston police captain hearing that his division's budget was being cut. He was in time to watch Chiles sing a new tune to the press. The DA conceded that because "new developments" made it unlikely that a prosecution of Malik Badir could succeed "regardless of its merits," the state would not refile. As for Jenna Sorrel, alias Amira Badir and Amira Rashad, the investigation was ongoing, and he would not comment on it.

"What does all that mean?" asked Jenna.

"It means your brother's free," said Boyle. "Or will be as soon as they run through the paperwork. No more than a few hours, I'd imagine."

"What about me?"

"Well, there it is. I met Mr. Chiles this morning—he was none too happy to see me, I assure you. He spent a good deal of time lying—the very same drivel you just heard about an 'ongoing investigation.' I'm certain he means to charge you."

Jenna gripped Brad's hand.

Boyle noticed the gesture. "No fear. He's got as much chance of a conviction as I've got of winning the marathon. But hc has to do something or lose his election. He's going to lose it anyway, in my opinion, but I think he'll take this last shot. Besides, he's a vindictive sonofabitch, pardon my French."

"Let's say he brings charges," said Brad. "What next?"

"We go in and surrender. I'll try to arrange for her immediate release, on recognizance or on bail." He frowned. "I have to tell you, though, that I'm a bit worried about that part. Our friend Mr. Chiles will ask that bail be denied on the grounds that Ms. Sorrel's brother's resources and her history of traveling on false documents make her a risk to flee to avoid prosecution. A judge might very well go along."

"That means I'd go to jail?" asked Jenna.

"For a time, at least. It would be an injustice, and I'll do all I can to prevent it, but it may happen."

"How long? Until the trial?"

"I sincerely doubt it. As I said, Mr. Chiles is going to lose his election. And I've taken the precaution of speaking with his opponent. In a general way, of course. But I have the strong impression that she'll be more reasonable than Chiles."

"How reasonable?" Brad wanted to know.

"Our discussion was very general. But I wouldn't be surprised to hear an offer of probation in exchange for a plea to, say, involuntary manslaughter."

"And what if it goes to trial?" asked Brad. "What's our defense?"

"I'll know more about that after I've had a long talk with my client. But based on what I've heard, we've got classic self-defense or defense of the life of another. There's also the battered-woman angle, which is very strong these days." He looked at Jenna. "I don't know if you're aware of it, Ms. Sorrel, but you're quite the heroine out there just now for a lot of people. Women especially, but men, too. And that's another thing: by the time I get through with Ali Rashad, he's going to look like Satan's signpost."

"I'd rather you didn't do that, Mr. Boyle. I have a son—wherever he is—and Ali was his father."

"Well, there's that. I see your point. No more than necessary, then. No more than the truth."

That evening at dusk, Jenna and Brad walked down to the ocean. What Boyle had said, the likelihood of separation, hung between them. There were so many things to say that they found it hard to speak. The first stars were coming out when Brad finally broke the silence.

"Jenna, this will be over soon—sooner than we think, thank God. When it is, let's go away somewhere. A month, maybe two. The islands. A cottage in Ireland. You tell me."

"That sounds nice. But it's not over. And I can't go anywhere until I know what's happened with Karim."

"Well, that will work itself out. He's upset now—it's only natural—but it won't last forever."

"It's more than that. You don't know Karim. And then, you know, sooner or later I need to get back to work. It's been so long. It'll be like starting over."

"It'll be like that whenever you go back. Take the time before you get caught up in it again." He looked up at the evening star, unbelievably brilliant in a western sky that had darkened to cobalt. "We could make it a honeymoon," he said. "No one could blame us for taking time off for that."

She wanted with all her heart to say yes. She traced a pattern in the sand with her toes and said nothing.

"It's not an ultimatum," Brad went on. "It's open-ended. It runs till that star burns out. I love you, Jenna. That's never going to change."

"I love you. It's just . . . it's just too much right now." How could she explain? It wasn't just Karim, or Malik, or Laila, or anyone else. It wasn't about going back to work. It wasn't about marriage. It was about shooting a man to death. Ever since Sam Adams Boyle had mentioned the possibility of a plea bargain, her thoughts had been in turmoil. She didn't feel guilty—yet she knew she was. She could have screamed, that day at the pool; she could have run for help. But she had done something else entirely. Much of her life's work was devoted to healing the effects of violence. Yet, when the choice had been hers, she had chosen violence.

"Whatever you decide," said Brad, hearing what had not been spoken, "just remember that Jordan Chiles isn't a man to make fine moral distinctions. Don't give him any more ammunition. He'll use it to make you look like a murderer."

It was dark now, and cold. They headed home.

• • •

At the house, lights were blazing. A Rolls-Royce and a Lincoln Town Car lounged smugly at the curb. On the deck looking out over the sea, Malik, Farid, J.T., and Rosalie were raising glasses.

"So much for a low profile," said Brad.

Jenna ran to embrace her brother. Farid joined in the hug. The two lawyers wore the easy smiles of warriors whose battle was won.

In a corner Laila stood quietly with a handsome, weather-burned young man.

"My friend David Christiansen," she said to Jenna. "We just stopped by to thank you."

"For what?"

"For telling the truth."

• • •

The next day at noon, Jordan Chiles went before the cameras to announce that a grand jury had indicted Amira Badir Rashad, alias Jenna Sorrel, on a charge of second-degree homicide, and that a judge had issued a warrant for her arrest.

Boyle called. "This is it. We're going in now. Otherwise Chiles is likely to show up with a television crew and handcuffs." He instructed them to meet him at a stop on the Interstate. He mentioned a few—very few—personal articles that Jenna should bring. "Wear layers," was his final piece of advice. "Jails are always too hot or too cold."

From the rest stop, they drove to the courthouse in Boyle's car. There was a crowd, police, trucks with satellite dishes, signs supporting Jenna. Chants. Cheers.

"I took the liberty of letting a few people know we were coming," explained Boyle. "It can't hurt for the voice of public opinion to be heard. All right, now: we march in like we own the place."

Someone, Jabr, opened the car door, and Jenna stepped out to a surge of cheering from the crowd. People were calling her names—both her names. Then she was racing for the door with her hand in Brad's, Sam Adams Boyle hustling blockily in front of them like the old fullback he undoubtedly was.

EPILOGUE

Aftermath

Jordan Chiles's last important public achievement was to convince a judge that no bail should be set for the defendant in the case of *People v. Rashad.* Two days later, he was overwhelmed at the polls by a thirty-three-year-old corporate lawyer and former public defender named Jennifer Faye Edmondson.

Sam Adams Boyle blasted Chiles in court and in the media for waging a vendetta against the Badirs, brother and sister. He appealed the denial of bail. With much less sound and fury, he opened negotiations with Jennifer Edmondson.

"It'll take a little time," he told Jenna, "but it's the only way—and the best way."

"How long?"

"Worst case, three months—that's when Edmondson officially takes office. Best case, if we can steamroll Chiles, three or four weeks. I know you don't like to hear that, stuck in this place, but there it is."

"What then?"

"I'm working on that. A plea of some kind, like we talked about. With luck, there won't be any more jail time. Even if there is, I can guarantee that it won't be much."

"That sounds good. Thanks, Sam."

"No thanks needed. I'm just doing my job. So how are you holding up, kid?"

Jenna had to smile at "kid." Boyle had become distinctly avuncular as they had come to know each other.

"I'm fine, Sam. Really—I'm okay."

The funny thing was that it was almost true. Unlike most new prisoners, Jenna needed to learn the trick of living one day at a time. She had lived that way before, in the women's quarters of the royal palace in al-Remal.

True, in the palace she and the other women had access to every physical luxury their whims might suggest, whereas here luxury was an extra slice of bologna in the lunchtime sandwich. But psychologically the similarity was remarkable: when it came right down to it, the women in the palace had been prisoners, too.

The jail, at least the women's wing, wasn't especially grim. Essentially a small dormitory, it wasn't even crowded; Palm Springs was hardly a high-crime area. Most of the handful of inmates were single mothers who worked in minimum-wage jobs or survived on public assistance, very much like women Jenna had known at the free clinic in Boston. Their typical offense was shoplifting or writing bad checks. At first, they treated Jenna like a celebrity, even a heroine. A housemaid named Latronia Parrish broke the ice.

"You that princess shot her husband?"

"Yes."

"What you shoot him for?"

"He was trying to kill my brother."

Latronia nodded as if this were nothing out of the ordinary. "What's it like bein' a princess?"

They all wanted to hear. After lights out, nudged along by a dozen questions, she began the story of her life. It went on for several bedtimes. She began to feel like the girl of *A Thousand and One Nights*. The others wept when she described the events in al-Masagin, gasped in disbelief about Alexandria, cursed the beating that had hospitalized Amira. By the time it had all been told, the others treated her less as a celebrity and more with the respect due a survivor.

For all that, the loss of freedom was hard, and hardest of all was Jenna's inability to go to her son. Every day he was slipping farther away from her—she could feel it—and there was nothing she could do. She didn't even know where he was. If only she could see him, talk with him, for just one moment. Wouldn't a word, a touch be enough to make him remember, to change his heart? Sleeping on the hard prison cot, she dreamed that the jail's steel bars were modeling clay, the kind she and Karim had played with when he was a little boy. She could bend them aside and slip through, back into the cozy apartment in Boston, back into the past. She hated waking to find that the dreams were only dreams.

It was during a visit from Toni that Jenna had an inspiration.

"You're gonna love this," Toni said chattily. "Would you say that Jabr and I work well together?"

"Very well." It was true.

"I'm glad you think so. Because we've got this idea. You know I've been looking for something to do with my life, some kind of career. And Jabr wants to go out on his own, too. So what we've come up with is a security service, investigations, stuff like that, the two of us as partners. What do you think?"

"I don't know. It's not exactly my field of expertise. Have you mentioned this to Malik?"

"He thinks it's a great idea. In fact, he's going to back us financially, help us get started."

"Toni, that's terrific!"

"Yeah, I'm happy with it."

It was then that Jenna had the idea. "What if I gave you your first job?"

Toni looked surprised. "Name it. We're yours."

"Find Karim. Find him and . . . talk with him. That's all. Just talk with him, find out what he's doing—*how* he's doing."

Toni nodded. "Okay. I'm sure my new partner will approve."

"Take him with you. Karim is so enamored of everything Middle Eastern, and Jabr is certainly that. Besides, he knew . . . Karim's father."

Toni pulled out a notebook and pencil. "Give me the names of his friends—girlfriends especially. Addresses and phone numbers if you can. Classes he was taking at school. Places he likes to hang out."

Jenna gave the best information she could.

"We'll go tomorrow," said Toni. She grinned. "By the way, it's on the house."

• • •

Malik was in his best mood of sunny optimism.

"Everything will work out, little sister, you'll see. With Karim, too." He approved of Toni and Jabr's mission. "When they've located him, maybe I'll fly him out. You said he likes me."

Jenna was less certain. "A lot has changed for Karim, brother. Invite him, if you like. But whatever you do, don't pull a stunt like you did with me. It'll just make things worse."

He smiled guiltily.

"How's Laila?" asked Jenna.

"Fine." But he was suddenly more somber. "She'd like to see you, you know, but I think she's . . . nervous. And to be honest, I've discouraged it. You know what a circus this thing has become. She doesn't need to be part of it."

"I agree. Please tell her it's okay."

"The truth is, I've suggested that she go back to France for a month or two, until this is over. I've talked with David about it. He'd go with her, at least for part of the time." He smiled again. "I hate to admit it, but I like that young man. I think he's good for Laila. No business sense, though. Do you know, the captain of my yacht will be retiring soon, and I mentioned the job to David. Offered him an absurd salary. Do you know what he said?"

"What?"

"He said, 'I've seen pictures of the *Jihan*, sir, and she doesn't appear to have sails.' " Malik laughed, then added, "He loves what he does. I respect that."

Jenna felt a little better. One thing, at least, was working out. And it was a hopeful sign, too, that Malik and Laila were acting like father and daughter again. Not so long ago Laila had hated Malik—as Karim now seemed to hate Jenna.

• • •

Brad was in for the weekend as always, flying from Boston late Friday, returning late Sunday. In his quiet way he had made acquaintances among the guards and police and did little things that made imprisonment a bit less onerous for Jenna and the others—for example, the chocolate cake that mysteriously materialized on Latronia's birthday.

Characteristically, he was more restrained than Malik in analyzing the Karim situation. "We knew it would be tough when we took this route. Karim was in a difficult, rebellious phase to begin with. It may get worse before it gets better—but it *will* get better. It's just going to take time. What we need to prepare ourselves for is the possibility that it may take a *lot* of time."

It was true, Jenna knew, but it wasn't enough. Even Brad's "I love you" as he rose to go wasn't enough—not here, not across a table in this harsh, sterile place, under cold fluorescent lights and the eyes of the guards. What she needed was his strong, gentle touch, his arms around her, his words whispered against her skin.

And she needed her son.

She was counting on Toni. Toni would know how to handle Karim. Hadn't she been through something equally tough, maybe even tougher, with her own sons? And Jabr. Jabr was like a force of nature. Together, they would bring Karim back to her.

• • •

One look at Toni's face told Jenna that she had been dreaming again, foolishly dreaming.

"What happened?"

"We found him. That's the good news. It wasn't hard. He was crashing at Josh Chandler's apartment, sleeping on the couch, that kind of thing. Strictly temporary."

Obviously Josh had moved out of the Chandler house, but Jenna couldn't think about that. "You saw him? You talked with him?"

"Oh, sure. That's kind of the bad news. He let us in, very polite, but he didn't want to hear anything we had to say. He told us he'd made his plans and didn't intend to change them."

"What plans?"

Toni looked straight at her breaking the news. "Jenna, he says he's going to al-Remal—permanently. He's just waiting for the paperwork to go through, some confusion over his legal identity. Supposedly some of his relatives—his father's people—are taking care of it. He said it wouldn't be more than a few days."

A few days. Her son would be lost to her in a few days.

"What was he like? What did he say?" What did he say about *me*, she meant.

"It's funny," said Toni. "Mainly he talked with Jabr. Lots of questions about al-Remal, the customs. Islam—very interested in Islam. Jabr got very serious then and quoted some verses from the Koran about honoring one's mother. But that may not have been the way to handle it."

"Why?"

"Because Karim clammed up. Not exactly clammed up, but he got stuffy."

"What do you mean?"

"I don't know if you want to hear this."

"Of course I do."

"Okay. I took notes as soon as we were out of there." She took out her notebook. "This may not be verbatim, but it's pretty close: 'My mother has lied to me all my life. She purposely hid my birthright from me. I never knew my father, and now I'll never know him, because she killed him. I have no desire to see her or speak with her. That's final.' "

All through Karim's childhood, his adolescence, his new young manhood, Jenna had used those very words in accusing herself, dreading the day that her son might use them. Now it had happened. "That's all?" she said. "Nothing more?"

Toni shook her head. "He showed us the door. Politely, but there was no question we were being given the boot. I asked him to give it some thought, just take some time to think it over. He didn't even answer. I'm sorry, Jenna. We blew it."

"No, you didn't. You did what I asked. You found him. You talked with him. You didn't blow it. I did."

"No. That's not right. Jenna, I know you. I know your story. You did the right thing, the only thing you could do. Don't blame yourself. It's . . . just a bad break, that's all. I know how you feel. I know exactly. But it's not the end. You should know that. You're the one who helped me learn it."

• • •

With Toni's report, Jenna's hope turned to desperation, and what had been worry over Karim turned to torture. He was about to vanish from her life, maybe forever. She cast about wildly for a solution, any solution. What if she changed her story, denied that she was Amira Badir? There had been impostors, more than one over the years, claiming to be the lost princess. If the Remalis thought that she was just another pretender, would they still take Karim in? Or maybe she should tell Malik to forget what she had said and send red-haired Ryan on another abduction, this time of Karim.

That was nonsense, of course. It was too late, too late for anything. And then one evening it really was too late: the little television in the women's section brought the news that Karim Rashad, son of the victim and the alleged killer in the Ali Rashad case, had returned to his native land as an honored member of its royal family.

It was almost as if he had died. Jenna knew that she could never go to al-Remal, never. The other women, sensing her torment, tried to console her, but the pain was too deep.

Even the promise of freedom barely lifted her spirits.

"I believe we'll have bail fixed for you by Monday or Tuesday," Boyle told her with gruff satisfaction. "Ms. Edmondson has agreed to file an amicus brief with our appeal of the bail hearing. She's going to tell the court that her office intends to drop the charge of second-degree homicide. She's willing to reduce the charge to involuntary manslaughter. If you agree to plead guilty, she'll recommend a sentence of time served, probation, and a couple of hundred hours of community service—free counseling or something of that sort. I recommend that you consider the offer very seriously. On the other hand, I happen to believe that you're innocent of any crime and that I can prove it in court. But it's a brutal process, and an expensive one. The decision is yours to make."

"I'll plead guilty," said Jenna. "I killed him. I didn't have to."

"Think about it for a day or two."

"No. I'm sure. Tell her today."

Boyle nodded and closed his briefcase. "You'll be out of here by this time Tuesday," he said.

The next few days were longer than all the others that had gone before. Jenna couldn't drive the past from her mind, couldn't separate it from the present. The run from Tabriz. Philippe dead. Years of hiding, lying, fear. All of it to keep her son, to protect him. And now she had lost him anyway, lost him to the place from which she had risked her life to take him.

Saturday. Visiting hours. A guard called Jenna's name. The visitor would be Brad. She almost didn't want to see him. He would be bubbling about her release and his plans for going away together, and she had no heart for it.

But the person in the visiting room was Laila.

"Hello, Aunt Jenna. I . . . I'm sorry I didn't come sooner."

"Please, there's nothing to be sorry about. My God, it's so good to see you!"

"I got to thinking . . . about my mother, you know—my real mother—and what you did for her. And for me. I wouldn't even be here without you. I had to come. Not that there's any comparison, of course. With what you did, I mean."

"I know it was hard for you to come here, Laila. And you did. That's all that matters. But Laila—wait. I thought you were supposed to be in France."

"I was going there. But I went somewhere else, Aunt Jenna. I went to see Karim."

"You did?" Jenna felt a surge of wild hope. "What happened? What did he say?"

Laila shook her head. "I can't tell you what you'd like to hear. He's gone. There's nothing you could have done to hold him. You probably know that, anyway. But maybe it's not quite as bad as it seems."

Jenna waited.

"It was David's idea," said Laila. "I was always talking about you and Karim, always saying, you know, *quel dommage*. And one night David said, 'Look, no one this kid meets for the rest of his life is going to understand his problem like you do. There's the phone. Why not give him a call?' And so I did. I got the number from Jabr."

Laila peered around the room with open curiosity, probably wondering, Jenna thought, what lay beyond the door that led to the cells.

"At first, he didn't want to talk. Then he did, but it was all . . . bitterness. Anger. I wasn't getting through to him. So the next day, I flew to Boston. David came with me. Karim was packing. His visa had just come through. The Remali consulate had sent him a ticket and some money. But I managed to talk with him some more. For hours, really." She shrugged helplessly. "I tried to show him what I had learned for myself, about my father. That it wasn't his fault—wasn't your fault. That both of you had done what you thought was best. Karim didn't want to hear that. I wouldn't have listened, either, at that stage. But at least I planted a seed. I think he'll remember. It's a start."

"Laila, whatever you did, I can't thank you enough."

"Don't thank me at all. I didn't accomplish much." She looked at Jenna with deep sadness, then suddenly brightened. "But do you know what, Aunt Jenna? I think it'll be all right. I think he'll be back someday. He won't hate al-Remal like I did—and even I could see that the place has a kind of . . . strength. And beauty. But he's no more a Remali than I am. The time will come when he'll long for home—his real home. And he'll be wiser then. He'll begin to understand why you did what you did. I'm sure of it. I *know* it. What I'm saying is, don't give up hope."

"Laila . . ." Jenna couldn't hold back tears. She couldn't help seeing, in her mind's eye, the other Laila, that night in al-Masagin. And now it had come full circle.

Laila smiled. "Don't cry, Aunt Jenna, or I'll have to send you to a shrink. Listen, here's the good news: I made Karim promise to stay in touch with me. I'll call him—I don't know, as often as he'll put up with it. That way, it won't be as if he's totally disappeared." She spread her hand on the glass partition for Jenna's hand to meet. "It'll work out—you'll see. But now I have to go."

"But you just got here!"

"Someone else waiting to see you. 'Bye. See you soon in better surroundings."

She hurried out, stopping just long enough to smile at Brad as he entered.

He sat at the partition and looked long and longingly at Jenna.

"I just talked with Boyle," he said. "It's done. You'll be out on Tuesday. Three more days."

"Good. Thank God."

"I talked with Laila, too. A remarkable young woman—no surprise, considering her family. Listen, we're going to have plenty of time for all those trips I've been talking about. I finally realized that they might not be what you want right now. Would you settle for a long weekend at Marblehead? We could take it from the top. Maybe I'll get it right this time."

"Yes," said Jenna. "Yes. That sounds good."

It did. It sounded very, very good.